I0579314

A ROGUE'S PASSION

❖ S. M. SAVOY ❖

بساله

Published by
Ace Lyon Books
March 2020

Copyright© S. M. Savoy, February 2020
All rights reserved. No part of this book may be used or reproduced in any form or by any means, electronic or mechanical, including photocopying, recording, or by any information storage and retrieval systems, without written permission of the Publisher or Author except where permitted by law.

Published by
Ace Lyon Books
Acelyonbooks.com
First Edition
Cover Design by S. M. Savoy
S. M. Savoy *A Rogue's Passion*
ISBN: 978-1-947122-35-2
eBook: 978-1-947122-34-5
Hardcover: 978-1-947122-36-9

This is a work of fiction. Names, characters, businesses, places and incidents or events either are products of the Author's imagination or are used fictitiously. Any resemblance to actual events or locales or persons, living or dead, is entirely coincidental.

DEDICATION

To the men and women who dedicate their lives to make us all safe.

This book is a work of fiction. The places portrayed in it have no basis in fact. The cadets taught at Annapolis were an inspiration for this story, their bravery, dedication and the sacrifices they make to serve their country, but the story itself is a complete fabrication, both the people and the place.

S. M. Savoy

CONTENTS

A ROGUE'S PASSION

Other Books By
S. M. Savoy

Valor
A Warrior's Fury
A Sun Priest's Magic
Beyond Valor
A Rogue's Passion

Related Series

Return of the Fae
Enter the Frey
Coming Soon
Danu's Children

Coming Soon
Essence of the Storm

- 1 -

REPORTERS

The nightclub was loud and jammed with kids all eager to party hard before school started in a week. Charlie signed to his brother to grab a table and waited by the door for Stasia, snickering to himself as the crowd made way for him.

Intimidating aura kept the people entering from pressing to close, *or maybe it was his guard Manny's glower*, Charlie mused as he held a hand to Sara.

She grinned when she took it and practically pulled him to the dance floor.

Charlie peered over his shoulder to ensure Stasia had made it inside. She'd stopped right inside the doorway to talk to their other guard, Tony, who looked uncomfortable out of his usual uniform.

As one of the only people over thirty in the large room, Tony stood out even without the Hawaiian shirt he'd left untucked to hide his gun. He wore a ballcap and sunglasses and waved Stasia away as Charlie watched.

Charlie nodded a greeting but followed Sara to the dance floor. He forgot about his bodyguards and just enjoyed himself as he and Sara danced. His aura kept a small space around them clear and he took full advantage of it. Sara practically bubbled with happiness. She loved to dance, and he promised himself to take her more often

"This is fun!" she yelled to be heard above the thumping bass. "We should come here again!"

Charlie nodded agreement. The dance hall was just a short sail away and not far by car either. He'd rented a boat and had taught Sara how to sail it. They hadn't returned to shore once in the week they'd been back from the *Truman*. A vacation she more than deserved. She and Oz had been working long hours getting Valor Industries up and running.

He glanced at his wristcomp to see if Oz was on his way yet.

Sara said, "He called while you were dressing. He'll be late. The new girl wanted to go eat first!"

Charlie grinned, shaking his head, amused by her amusement. Oz had a new girl practically every other day and Charlie wondered how he found the time to meet them all. So far none had gotten a second date, and for a moment he worried, but he forced his thoughts away, not wanting to worry Sara.

"He's fine," she said but Charlie knew she was a bit worried too.

She grimaced and stopped dancing to hug him.

He returned the hug, leaning down to kiss her temple. The brief caress filled her with lust, and he released her before the lust could build and echo between them.

She giggled and kissed his hand, her eyes dancing with mirth when he yanked his hand away.

"If you want to stay…" he said teasingly, and she winked as she began to dance again.

The magic inside of him stirred restlessly, a feeling of pressure beneath his skin. It wasn't unpleasant yet, and he tamped it down easily by concentrating on the dance. She was concentrating too; the familiar sensation was relaxing and within seconds the magic was quiescent again. They were getting much better at controlling it.

He scanned the room as he danced, more from habit than he was worried. Manny nodded at him when Charlie caught his eye and Charlie nodded back but Manny had already resumed scanning the crowd.

Sara's large purse bumped a girl dancing near them, and she called apologies as she tucked it over her other shoulder.

"Leave it at the table!" Charlie said.

"My mom's letters are inside," Sara said, shrugging at his surprise.

Before her death Sara's mother, Meredith Barlow, had written to her daughter about her dreams for her future and her hope that she'd find a man to make her as happy as she was with Sara's father. The letters were funny and sweet and full of advice.

Meredith had adored Sara from the moment of her conception and had left everything she owned to her only daughter. But the letters her mother had written to her on her birthdays were her prized possessions. As far as Charlie knew no one except him had seen them. Even her father had never read them. Mr. Martin, the lawyer in charge of Sara's mother estate and now Valor Industries, had delivered them to her on her sixteenth birthday along with the rest of Meredith's worldly possessions.

Charlie tucked Sara's free hand against his chest, hoping contact would ease her growing sadness.

She said, "I'm okay. I'll always miss her but I'm so grateful she left me these." Sara hugged the purse tighter. "She really did love me."

"She did," Charlie agreed then winced at his spike of anger. Without him saying a thing Sara knew he was angry over her father.

"He's an ass," she said lightly but he could feel her hurt.

"I love you," he said and smiled in relief over her surge of happiness. With effort, he pushed Tomas from his mind. His anger over her father's treatment would only upset her.

She said, "I meant to ask Brenda to take them back to the bank for me, but she left before I had the chance."

Charlie shook his head, his smile growing at her affronted expression. She could feel his amusement over her chagrin. Brenda had brought a bunch of Sara's mother's dresses with her, and Sara had been utterly distracted trying them on.

"You look beautiful," he said, his heart thumping hard at the wave of love that echoed between them.

He turned away and cleared his throat. The emotions he sensed from her faded and she passed him, headed to the table Rick had staked out, giving them both time to get their magic under control. Strong emotions agitated the magic and if both felt the same way it tended to make it want to appear.

He said, "Give the bag to Tony. He can watch it for us."

His brother had picked a table by the wall and it was a bit quieter. He didn't have to yell so loud to be heard.

"I should've left it on the boat with Rhea but…" she shrugged and trailed off.

"I'll ask Tony to keep an eye on it," Charlie said as he plucked the bag from her grasp.

She bit her lip, and he laughed lightly as he leaned down to kiss her. "Fine, I'll ask Manny to guard it with his life."

Her relief made him chuckle. Manny not only looked like a badass with his shaved head and bulging muscles, he was one. The patrons were giving him a wide berth unlike Tony who kept having to change position to keep a clear line of sight on them.

Manny headed to them when Charlie signaled.

Sara said, "Look at them." She nodded toward Stasia and Rick. Stasia clasped Rick's hand hard in hers but it was her envious expression as she gazed at Sara's hand clasped in his that made Charlie's pulse pound.

Sara said, "She needs him to have magic too."

Charlie frowned then forced a smile. "I know but we're not worrying about it right now."

Sara smiled brightly and turned back to the table. But the smile was a lie. She was as worried as he about Stasia.

Stasia had a quick temper. She was passionate and impulsive, and he wasn't sure what her magic would force her to do. As much as he didn't want to try to make another magic wielder, especially another warrior, he knew they had no choice, not if they wanted to keep Stasia calm and in control of her magic.

Stasia grinned and clapped her hands when Sara reached the table. "Oh, the dress looks amazing on you. You look just like your mother in *Summer Night*."

Charlie tried to banish his worries about his rogue and focused on Sara, letting lust sooth his magic.

"Her clothes were so beautiful." Sara glanced down at the dress, running a hand along the soft fabric, a sad smile on her face. "I'm glad my father saved them for me."

"Have you spoken to him lately?" Rick slid further back in the booth, pulling Stasia closer to make room for his brother.

"No, I send him updates on my whereabouts, but he never replies. I told him Charlie and I are engaged, but I didn't expect to hear from him."

"The dress does look beautiful on you." Rick leaned over the table and kissed her cheek.

Sara smiled softly and ran a hand over Charlie's cheek. "My mother would've loved you."

Charlie brought her hand to his lips and kissed her engagement ring.

The only jewelry Sara ever wore were the pieces he'd given her although she owned a heap of expensive jewelry her mother had left her.

"You do look beautiful" Charlie whispered, relieved her sadness from thinking of her mother's death had fled so quickly.

He turned to scan for Manny. Manny had circled and was halfway between them and the bar, but he was facing away. The set of his shoulders was tense and immediately tighten Charlie's. Charlie's tension ratcheted up when he spied what had captured Manny's attention.

"What?" Rick asked as Stasia stood, stepping in front of Sara and lowering a hand to her thigh were Charlie knew she carried a sheathed knife.

Charlie said, "That guy was at the docks earlier taking Sara's picture." Charlie reached into his pocket and pulled out a set of stickycoms that he placed as he waved Stasia back. "Stay here. It's probably nothing."

Sara gave him a small worried glance but sat and said to Stasia, "Sit and we can talk about Oz's idea to boost Carmichael's poll rating."

Rick followed him to the bar. Manny started forward but turned and headed to Sara and Stasia when Charlie nodded in their direction.

The crowd around he and Rick melted away and the man at the bar saw them coming. He smiled sardonically and lifted his camera to snap off a shot.

"What can I get you," the bartender asked, his nervous gaze fastening on Charlie.

Charlie ignored him, approaching the man with the camera. "What are you doing?"

"Taking pictures; it's a free country!" The man continued to stare at Sara, not even glancing at Charlie although he slid as far away as the crowd allowed. Other patrons stepped away until Charlie stood by himself before the bar. Most continued with their conversations or headed to the dance floor but some hurried for the door. The bartender called after the fleeing patrons.

Charlie ignored the crowd's reaction to his anger and narrowed his eyes at the man. "*Why* are you taking pictures of her?"

The man smirked and didn't answer.

Charlie lifted his wristcomp, snapped the man's photo, and tapped the icon to call Oz. "Run this guy for me. Find out everything."

The man glared at Charlie.

Charlie ignored him, stepping closer to run a laser from his wristcomp over the man's glass on the metal counter. Oz might be able to pull prints from the measurements. His aura made the man pale and jerk away, jostling the kids behind him. He snatched his glass.

"Hey!"

"Watch it!" the kid he bumped exclaimed then mumbled something to his companions and the entire group headed to the dance floor.

Charlie took a deep breath and tried to speak in an even tone to keep his anger in check. "Want to tell me who you are and why you're taking pictures of my fiancé?"

The man smirked at him again although sweat now beaded his brow. "Aren't you a little old for her? She's what, eighteen?"

Charlie frowned thoughtfully. No one looking at Sara would guess that was her age. He was only a year older than her and could pass as early twenties himself. Sophisticated clothes and hair, combined with her natural poise, made her appear older. This man knew who she was but didn't know who he was. He was tempted to step even closer and cast enrage to make the man bolt, but he'd likely cause a riot. He took a step back and consciously calmed his anger.

"Any hits, Oz?"

"Edward Fontair. He writes under the name Ned Font for Idol magazine," Oz replied a moment later.

"Send me everything you have; he's been following Sara." Charlie turned to the man at the bar. "So, Ned, you know she's a minor, so you can't print any of these pictures."

"Who's a minor? What pictures?" With another smirk, Ned tossed back his drink and headed to the door, darting glances back at Charlie.

Charlie's anger had fled. A reporter was no big deal although any publicity for Sara was dangerous. Taking the man's camera was sure to escalate into a fight, and the dance club was crowded. Protective Aura would force everyone to attack him, which could cause even worse publicity if the police were called and got caught in his aura. Besides, the Valkyrie operating system would be big news soon and he'd have to get to use to people staring.

He sighed and turned back to the table, absently taking the drinks Rick handed him. Sara smiled from across the room, and he brightened. The boys brought the drinks to the table.

"Just a reporter." Charlie kissed Sara's cheek. "Forget him. Stasia, you said you'd dance with me." He held out his hand to her. She took it to rise but dropped it before his magic became painful to touch.

Rick smiled at Sara, and she laughed as she stood to dance.

Charlie forgot all about the reporter.

- 2 -

HOUNDED FROM TOWN

Charlie's roommate Paul called on Monday. "Is Sara getting into acting now?"

"No," Charlie said in confusion. "Why do you ask? She's happy working for Valor Industries."

"Her picture was on the cover of Idol. I saw it in the checkout line."

"About the Valkyrie system?"

"No, it was, *um*…" Paul trailed off.

"Goddamn it! I knew I should've grabbed that bastard's camera! Thanks, I'll call you back." As soon as he hung up, he headed to the store.

A picture Ned had taken of Sara wearing a white bikini on the docks sat side-by-side on the cover with one of her mother in a similar bathing suit. The article showed both her and her mother in the same dress she'd worn dancing.

More pictures of Sara followed. All had been taken when she was unaware, and all were very revealing. A chart compared their measurements. A facial close-up on the next page contained a side-by-side comparison. Sara was an inch taller and her hair a bit lighter, but that was probably from all the sun. Both she and her mother had the same startlingly gorgeous eyes in a shade of purplish-blue he'd never seen on anyone else. Magical blue. The resemblance was unmistakable.

The pictures made his pulse pound. He placed a quick text to Sara saying his anger was nothing to worry about, followed by a call to Mr. Martin.

"Can he print that? Ned knows she's a minor."

"Eighteen is legally an adult." Mr. Martin sighed. "All the pictures were taken in public. I'll see if I can get an injunction to stop future ones, but I wouldn't count on it. The most I can do is limit the, *um*, provocative ones. Is she very upset?"

"As far as I know she hasn't seen it. When she does, she's sure to be embarrassed and worried. The danger to her from publicity…"

"This kind of thing blows over fast," Mr. Martin said. "She's beautiful, so she makes a good cover, but she isn't famous. Once the Idol trots out all her mother's films and recaps the gossip over her death, it'll die down."

"Should I tell her?"

"How likely is she to find out, and will she be mad if she realizes you knew and said nothing?"

Charlie grimaced. "Damn, I guess I should. Her mother is very important to her. I hate that she's being used against her like this."

"The pictures are vulgar, but they said nothing bad about either of them. Tell her. Don't let her be surprised in public."

Charlie thanked him, bought a magazine, and went home. The house was quiet when he arrived. Muffled dog barking quickly silenced lead him to Sara sunbathing with Hawk in the backyard. Rhea and Tank lay in the grass and both picked up their heads when he entered but neither dog rose. Scrap greeted him with a short bark and then raced away to circle the house and Charlie grinned in amusement at the dog's joy in his work. Scrap was compulsive about checking his perimeter. The slightest noise would have him racing to see if his territory was being invaded.

A stack of books lay beside Sara. The top one was labeled *Advanced Theory of Electricity: And Magnetism*. Every one of them had the words electricity or magnetism in their titles. Hawk was reading a book on veterinary medicine.

Her eyes wide in alarm, Sara sat, dropping the book in the grass.

Hawk glanced over, straightened and closed his book.

"No big deal." Charlie handed the magazine to Sara and sat beside her on the chaise. The expression on her face didn't change although she grew angrier by the second.

"I already spoke to Mr. Martin. He says there isn't much we can do, but it should die down soon." Charlie took the scrunched-up paper she handed him and threw it to Tank who happily shredded it.

"You saw this in the checkout line?" Her eyes narrowed as she waited for his response. The anger echoed now and built. Able to sense emotional response, the magic amplified ones they shared, making it difficult to remember who was angry about what and the emotions hard to control.

"Yes, but Paul called and told me it was there," he admitted.

A pink flush crept up her neck and settled onto her cheekbones.

"Don't worry about it. A week from now someone else will be the main news story." Charlie traced the pink with his thumb as he leaned over and kissed her brow.

The soft sound she made when he touched her cheek excited him. Lust competed with anger now, and she pulled him down for a deeper kiss.

"What the hell?" Hawk jumped up and ran to the wall that separated their backyard from academy grounds. Careful to keep his motions within a human range, Hawk leaped over the wall and ran.

Charlie stood and saw right away where he was going. "Stay here! Tank, Rhea, guard!"

The two dogs hunkered to either side of Sara, growling low in their throats. Their peaceful playfulness of just moments ago was replaced by savage snarls.

Someone stood on the roof of the stone building in front of them. Hawk had caught up with the man and was already arguing when Charlie arrived.

"This is private property! I know you don't have permission to be here, and I'm positive you don't have permission to take pictures of anyone in my backyard." Hawk grabbed the camera, smashed it on the ground and stamped on it. He grasped the man by the arm and called the police using his wristcomp.

Military police arrived within minutes followed by civilian police.

Hawk and Charlie explained they'd caught the man on the roof of the building taking pictures.

"My girlfriend was sunbathing in the garden; she's only eighteen!"

Charlie's heated glare stayed on the man making angry gestures and pointing at the smashed camera as he spoke to the military police by the back of the cruiser.

The civil officer stepped away from Charlie and laid his hand on his holstered gun as he took their statement. Charlie tried to reign in his anger before his aura caused the officer to do something unfortunate. Hawk motioned him away and spoke to the officer himself.

Charlie gave Hawk a rueful grimace and shrugged lightly. He didn't spend much time around normal humans and tended to forget how strong his aura could be. It rarely affected his classmates, the magic recognized them as teammates now. He made a mental note to work harder on controlling his anger.

The officer handed Hawk a yellow slip of paper. "Expect to be sued for the camera. I'm not saying I wouldn't have done the same thing, but in the future, let us handle it. We can charge him with trespassing and privacy infringement, but he'll be out in a few hours." The officer paled and flicked the snap of his holster open.

Charlie stalked back home, leaving Hawk to deal with it before the man shot or arrested him, and found Sara pacing in their room.

He said, "Another reporter. The police arrested him, but he'll be out in a few hours." He wanted to tell her to stay inside, but that was unfair, she needed the sunlight and had every right to go outside and enjoy the sun while she read.

He called Master Sergeant Guthrie. "We have a slight problem. A reporter is hounding Sara." With terse words he informed Guthrie on what had happened. "Can we get someone to patrol in the back so it doesn't happen again?"

"I'll see about getting permission to alarm the roofs there," Guthrie said. "Meanwhile, one of the Scouts will keep an eye out. Sara, make sure you're being careful. Don't assume it's just a reporter trying to take a picture. If anyone approaches you, or aims anything at you, hit the panic button. Get us linked up; we can always stand down if it's a false alarm."

"Sara and I had talked about going away this week anyway," Charlie said. "School restarts on the twenty-eighth, but I thought we could go to Maine with Rick and Stasia. I'll see if Joy and Drew want to go too."

"Did you have a place picked out already?"

"Yes, a campground. I'll send you the link. We'll be clamming and fishing and renting a boat to catch our own lobsters." Charlie smiled at Sara, knowing she liked the idea. "If Hawk and Oz will come too, we'll be perfectly safe and hard for the reporters to find."

"Sounds good but take a few more Scouts."

"Sure, whatever you say." His shoulders lowered and tension eased as Sara relaxed beside him. Charlie smiled at her before returning to his phone call. "Let me know how many campsites to reserve."

Guthrie said, "Send me the link for the camp and I'll handle everything and call you back with the details."

Team Valor headed to Maine and arrived as the sun set. They made camp right on the edge of the mud flats. Brenda and Tony already had the tents up and we're waiting for them.

"Joy and Drew are out clamming already," Brenda said as she helped them unload the cars. "Toric and Marcus went to see about renting the boat. Sam and Todd are getting firewood and something to cook in. Nobody remembered to bring pots or frying pans."

Charlie took a deep breath of sea air. Sara did too and winced then laughed.

"Doesn't smell a thing like home," she said.

"Nope. Let's go clamming." Charlie tweaked her ponytail and headed to the mudflats. Sara followed laughing.

Stasia, Toric and Tony were the favorite cooks, but everyone tried it. They only let Sara try once.

"How can you operate on yourself, but not be able to fry eggs?" Brenda poked the runny black eggs on her plate.

Sara pursed her lips and eyed the plate of eggs before her. "I could learn to fry them if I had more to practice on."

"There aren't enough eggs in the state," Hawk said in disgust as he fed his to Tank.

Charlie snickered, the snicker turning into a full-blown laugh at his wife's offended expression. "Give them to me. I'll cook them. My wife's so smart she figured out how to *not* have to make eggs."

Sara laughed and punched his arm, eyed the black frying pan in dismay, and then with a deep sigh, began scrubbing it.

"Go catch us lunch. I got this." Charlie took the pan from her. She grinned and headed off. Toric ran to catch up with her and Charlie was glad he always felt concerned when she left him because she didn't glance back. Tony, Brenda, Manny and Marcus rose to go with them. Charlie signed to Brenda to wait. Once Sara was out of earshot he spoke. "Have Toric assigned to Beta."

Brenda frowned. "Problems?"

"Yes, I don't want him near her. He tried to influence her magic once. She trusts him— I don't," Charlie said shortly.

"They like each other, but that's all it is." Brenda squeezed his arm.

"That's all it is on her part," Charlie agreed. "I appreciate that Alpha team is willing to be changed by her in an emergency. Now, while she's happy and unstressed, it isn't a problem, but he'd take advantage of any weakness on her part. He wants her for himself. Put him on Beta team. I thought I could live with him on Alpha team, but I see how he looks at her and I just can't take the chance."

"Whatever you say, but I think you're wrong, Chief." Brenda took the now clean pan from Charlie. They finished the dishes and began preparing a fish stew for lunch.

Tank ran back to camp caked in mud and reeking. From her spot by Charlie's feet, Rhea wrinkled her nose at him.

"Ask him— I'm not wrong." Charlie nodded toward Toric who walked beside Sara as the others returned, bringing more firewood and a bucket of clams.

Sara's glance flicked from him to Toric and she took a step away. Charli winced and shook his head, smiling a smile they both knew was a lie but her return smile was real and full of love and within moments love echoed between them.

He hugged her hard already forgetting he was angry at Toric

- 3 -

RUMORS

Team Valor returned home on time with coolers stuffed with seafood for their parents. Guthrie met them at the house and helped them unload the cars. Sara and Stasia hugged their guards goodbye. Charlie bumped fists with Manny and took Sara's bag from Toric. He debated warning him off but decided it wasn't worth the effort especially as Toric never did anything inappropriate. *Getting him reassigned was good enough,* he decided and waved a goodbye.

"Oh god, Mom made pasta." Stasia took a deep breath when she opened the door and went right to the kitchen and kissed her mother's cheek. "We brought back a ton of seafood. I hope you made a lot; I'm starving!"

Camila laughed and pointed to a big pot simmering on the stove. "Enough for everyone and then some."

A smile lit Camila's eyes as she served the food, cutting up the crusty bread and placing it on the table. Two large platters of meatballs and sausage followed, set beside two heaping bowls of pasta smothered in her homemade sauce.

Charlie kissed her cheek before taking a seat by his father.

"Before we eat, you should know there was another article in the Idol about Sara," Guthrie said as he sat at the table and eyed the food appreciatively.

Sara rolled her eyes. "Who cares. I'm sure this will blow over soon." She kissed Camila's cheek and sniffed the sauce before taking her seat. Contentment echoed between them. He liked to have his family all gathered too.

After dinner Charlie asked to see the paper while Sara tracked down her cat, Lucky. His eyes narrowed at the picture of Sara kissing Hawk on the cheek on the cover. They narrowed further on page two. She wore a blue bikini laughing with Hawk in their backyard. A photo of Oz and Sara smiling at each other with Oz's hands on her waist and hers on his shoulders had made the centerfold.

Charlie snorted and threw the paper to the tabletop. "Man, she's going to be pissed. Without saying it, they made it seem like she and Oz are a couple and she was cheating on him with Hawk. How can they print this crap? If they know Oz lives here with her, they must realize Hawk does too."

"Sensationalism sells papers." Guthrie leaned back in his chair and rubbed his stomach. "Lies are much more titillating than the truth."

"Don't show her unless she asks." Charlie pushed the paper back.

The next day Sara went to pick up their uniforms and shop with Stasia. Right before she called, Charlie felt her annoyed impatience. "Stasia needs a ride from the cleaners. Can you get her or send someone for her? I was afraid they'd ruin your uniforms."

"Who would ruin them?"

"A random group of girls followed us there from the mall. When we got the uniforms, they started grabbing at them and hollering at me, so I left. Stasia needs a ride. She stayed to make sure no one stole them."

"I'm sorry, yeah, I'll get her. It's not fair, but I think you should stay home a while," Charlie said reluctantly.

"I will."

Charlie picked up Stasia.

"They wanted to know who her boyfriends were," Stasia said as she got into the car with their dry cleaning. "Someone called her a slut for cheating on the blond. Two started fighting over that. What the hell were they talking about?"

Charlie told her about the pictures.

"That explains the huge argument over the blond or brunet guy. It was getting seriously heated. I was afraid they'd attack her or something. This can't be just from those two articles?"

Charlie shrugged. "Meredith was one of the most beautiful women on the big screen, known for her love affairs with famous men, until she married Sara's father anyway. They're trying to sell papers by implying Sara is following in her footsteps."

"If she sees that paper, she'll be pissed." Stasia glanced at him from the corner of her eye. "She'll hate they make Oz and Hawk look bad."

Charlie winced. It was clear Stasia hated it too.

He said, "Yeah, hopefully she doesn't see it."

When he got home, he searched the web for Sara, his shoulders tightening when he found three websites dedicated to her love life. All showed old pictures of her from their gaming days and new ones, some obviously edited. Not one mentioned the Valkyrie system or Valor Industries, which puzzled him.

Sara was growing more anxious by the minute and was really worried by the time he joined her in their room.

She had the report they'd been working on open before her. He'd hoped it would be years before they even tried to change anyone else, but she couldn't go on like this for years.

She said, "Stasia—"

"I know," he said, interrupting her with a hard hug. "We'll try to change Joy first."

Sara nodded and her grip on him tightened.

He said, "Nothing will come between us. I love Stasia but I won't let her come between us either."

"She needs Rick to have magic."

Charlie kissed the top of Sara's head. She needed Stasia happier with her and Sara's magic wanted another warrior. The two pressures were really weighing on her.

"We'll make Joy a warrior," he repeated and released her to send the report.

Charlie, Stasia and Hawk returned to school, and Sara and Oz returned to work. Charlie hoped the rumors in the Idol had all blown over. He was happy to get back into their normal routine and Sara was excited at work. Whatever she and Oz were working on consumed her.

The next week's cover was a picture of Sara hugging Toric goodbye after their vacation in Maine. Identified as one of her many boyfriends, his expression in the picture was slightly sad. Hers wasn't showing. Pictures of Toric lifting a suitcase out of the trunk and watching Sara enter the house gave the impression of lovers parting after a weekend away.

Brenda called Charlie. "Toric's been moved to Beta. Glenn has taken over Alpha and asked him to reroll his main."

"Thanks. I don't blame him for wanting her, but I don't want him near her either."

"He's aware it's a problem." Brenda heaved a troubled sigh. "I'm asking Major Harris to lift the ban on out of the Marine's sex. I doubt we can spread it. Not one of us has ever even a flicker of magic."

"I think it's harder to spread than we thought," Charlie agreed. "Stasia has been trying to give her magic to Rick and can't do it. Sara has spells to both take, remove and store magic. I think that's why she can do it."

"When will you try to give Joy magic?"

Charlie was surprised she'd already been informed, although he supposed he shouldn't have been. The Scouts would all be affected by this decision whether it worked or not and Sara's magic was unpredictable. It might try for them all and they deserved a warning about that. He made a mental note to be sure Toric was out of the zone when they made the attempt.

He said, "Soon, Sara is nervous about it. She doesn't want to share me either."

"How likely is that?"

"How could we know? We both like Joy, but neither of us want a connection, so I'm hoping our magic recognizes what we want, but it's just a hope. My magic doesn't seem to want another warrior. Sara's magic seems to be enough for it. Sara's might. She has no sexual desire for Joy, so even if she wants Joy's magic, it should stay platonic. It's a risk for us though."

"And Joy?"

"Yes, risk exists. Before Sara can heal her, we need to wait long enough to give the magic a chance to take hold. If we wait too long, we could kill her. If we don't wait long enough, she won't get the magic. Add to that we have no idea if it's even possible to give her magic or what the magic will do to her…. well, all Joy's suffering could be for nothing."

"It's a big risk for all of you."

"Sara is putting up magic. When she has a good reserve, she'll ask the lightning to change Joy. The plan is to wait six months then deliberately let her magic become desperate. If she can stay away from Joy, if my magic is still enough, we'll do Rick next. It's all subject to change though depending on how everyone feels."

"I hope I'm on the list somewhere,"

"Yes. I'll never change Toric though."

"Never is a long time. I understand your position, but things change."

"Thanks for getting him put on Beta."
Charlie ended the call.

- 4 -

I ALMOST UNDERSTAND IT

The next day Oz went looking for Sara and found her lying on the roof of the Valor building, clicking two flashlights on and off.

"What's up?" he asked.

"Thinking." She sat and put the flashlights down. "The magic appears as light, but it isn't. The blue cloud we see has mass and differing physical properties depending on where it manifests but it always remains the same color, even though it shouldn't. I've been studying it in different phases. It isn't anything we have words for, and for the life of me, I can't figure out why it appears blue."

When Oz shrugged, she answered her own question. "My theory is, it's pure matter, unformed, in a state of flux. When we cast, we form it somehow. Magic isn't really blue, that's just how our minds perceive it. The color is an illusion. The mind does amazing things. The first time this phenomenon manifested and someone 'saw' it, I think the magic made itself blue as a way of being a type of visible the human mind could comprehend, but I need to think about this a while. Did you read my paper on electricity as matter?"

"Yes." Oz sat beside her and picked up a flashlight.

"Everything is connected— everything is energy. The quantum connection… The terminology scientist use is too imprecise— matter- light- energy." Blond hair fell over her cheek as she shook her head and she impatiently brushed it back. "Humans are limited in our perceptions. Some things are just harder 'light-energy', so easier to see. Magic, our magic, is the ability to communicate and change the light-energy, tweak the connections." Sara paused a moment. "Not communicate; program or use..." Lines etched her brow as she trailed off.

"Light is energy." Oz flipped on the flashlight in his hand.

"Yes, light is energy, but what is that really?" Sara ran her hand through the dim light of the flashlight. "An entirely new vocabulary is necessary for what we do. So many questions remain, even about the things we can already make. I need time to understand."

They talked about the spell bracelets and how they worked.

Oz finally said, "Does it matter if we don't know as long as it works?"

"I want to know." Sara lay back down and flipped the flashlight back on. Oz handed her the other flashlight and left her there thinking.

Two days later he called Charlie. "Sara has been on the roof for a few days now."

"Yeah, I saw her there yesterday and the day before."

"She doesn't come down."

"At all?" Charlie straightened in surprise. Every day he visited her there, and she greeted him enthusiastically and then played with her flashlight. While she flicked the flashlight on and off, he studied or did homework.

"She stays there all day? Not just evenings?"

"She uses the bathroom and goes right back up. I haven't even seen her eat. Day and night, she's on the roof," Oz said.

"What's she doing?"

"Thinking." Oz sounded concerned.

Charlie was too. Usually, when one of them became distracted in thought the other not only knew what about, but it had never lasted days before. "That's what she told me too. We talked about her new theory that light is everything, but she won't talk now. She just says she needs to think and study the connections. Thanks for calling. I'll make sure she eats."

Charlie called Guthrie and asked him to get him a broccoli and mushroom pizza from Sara's favorite place after explaining why he wanted it.

"I was going to call you myself," Guthrie said. "I was getting concerned. Pizza will be here for twenty hundred hours tonight."

Charlie hung up and went to the cafeteria where he sat with Hawk as usual. Stasia joined them.

Hawk was telling his roommates about a girl he'd met before they went to Maine. Surprised, Charlie leaned forward to hear better, this was the first he'd heard of her.

"Have you met her yet?" Charlie whispered to Stasia.

Stasia nodded. "Once, for a few minutes." Stasia scowled and leaned closer. "Honestly, I didn't like her. She was too pushy."

Again, Charlie was surprised. Stasia got along with almost everyone. "How so?"

"To aggressive, hanging all over him when they just met. And she was rude. We've only been back in school a week and she's always calling and asking to see him. She just rubs me the wrong way." The scowl deepened, and she stabbed her food with the fork.

"Is Hawk as interested in her?"

Stasia shrugged. "Guess we'll find out, but I hope not."

Later that night Charlie picked up the pizza from Guthrie and delivered it to Sara on the roof.

As always, she was happy to see him, and for the millionth time he blessed his magic for letting him feel her emotions. He loved how she felt when she saw him.

"Still thinking?" he asked as he leaned down to kiss her cheek.

Someone had brought up lawn chairs, and he set the pizza on an empty chair and handed her a water bottle.

"Yes, there's so much to think about." She leaned over the pizza box and inhaled. "That smells great."

"When's the last time you ate?"

She shrugged. "Can't remember, I've been distracted. The sun is enough."

He frowned. "Make sure you eat every day."

She shrugged again.

"Sara, promise me you'll eat every day, or I'll worry."

"I promise," she said and kissed him. "No need to worry. The roof is safe. I'd rather be in our yard, but it's too distracting watching for reporters. I'll make sure I eat every day. You don't need to worry."

She finished her slice of pizza, leaned back in the chair, and casted a smite, canceling the cast before it went off. The flashlights were discarded under her seat. When she noticed him frowning at her, she took another slice of pizza.

"Please don't worry, Charlie. I'm so close, I almost understand it. Just a few more days."

"After we're done eating, we're going for a run. You need exercise too. Then you're taking a shower and going to bed at home. Tomorrow, get some exercise and food, and *then* come up here and meditate all you like." Charlie handed her another slice of pizza.

She laughed and placed the box of pizza on the floor and sat in his lap to kiss him. "We could skip the run and both go home and exercise there." Soft, and husky her breath caressed his neck. The pizza forgotten, she kissed his neck and then his mouth. Her intentions were clear without the magic.

He groaned. "I can't. I have to be back in an hour, and I can't leave the campus without permission."

"*Mmm.*" Not deterred, she began undoing the buttons of his shirt. "No one comes up here." Soft lips and warm hands trailed over his skin. Charlie groaned again and helped her with the buttons on his uniform.

Over the next week Sara took over the conference room, filling it with virtual whiteboards. Oz began sitting in the room with her, staring at the boards. Occasionally, one or the other of them made a change, but they rarely spoke.

Stasia, Charlie, and Hawk came daily. "Still at it?" Stasia asked at lunch as she checked her wristcomp for their whereabouts.

"They're getting over it." Charlie chuckled. "Both went jogging early this morning, and Oz isn't doing all the teaching himself anymore."

"Have they said what they're trying to do?" Hawk asked.

"Nope, I don't think they're trying to do anything. They're trying to understand."

Hawk handed his roommate the salt and turned back to Charlie. "Any progress on the game?"

"Not sure." Charlie admitted. "VI received another contract for five more installations. Sara and Oz are teaching installers that Pierce hired this month. My father has been working on production of wristcomps. We already have massive orders for them. Valor Industries security division will be in full swing in a year."

Hawk blushed and cleared his throat. "Susan asked me for a tour."

Stasia frowned at him. "You and she are, *um...*"

"Sort of, it's complicated. She isn't a Marine, but she really likes me, and I like her." Hawk grimaced at his sister and then grinned at Charlie. "I want to take it slow, but she's kind of in a hurry."

"In a hurry?" One dark eyebrow rose as Stasia pursed her lips.

Hawk flushed and nodded. "Susan's coming over this weekend, and you can meet her then, Chief."

"Will you be home this weekend?" Charlie asked Stasia.

"For a few hours Saturday," Stasia said. "Rick and I are going for breakfast before the game Sunday."

Charlie grimaced, making Stasia laugh. He'd almost caused a riot at the last game. His aura had forced a group of fighting spectators to attack him. He hadn't hit back but his classmates had jumped in to pull the mob off him and the fight had gotten serious.

"I hope Sara and Oz figure out how to convince the magic Army and Airforce are teammates," Charlie said as they headed to the conference room.

Sara and Oz glanced over but didn't rise when they entered.

"Is this area secure enough for all this?" Charlie gestured at the whiteboards projected in deep layers around the room and on the ceiling.

Oz laughed. "Guthrie is guarding it, but even if you saw it, would you know what it was?"

"We don't even know what it is," Sara said, her frown growing. "I'm trying as hard as I can, but I just don't get it."

Hawk wandered the room, pausing before each clump of boards and shaking his head. "Maybe you need a break."

Sara shrugged irritably. "I'm so close, every time I almost grasp it, it slips away."

"Hawk's right." Oz tapped on his holographic keyboard a moment and the whiteboards began to disappear. "Let's put them away and do something else."

Sara nodded unhappily. "Fine, let's go home."

Charlie took her hand, worried over how frustrated she was. She was uneasy enough to wake his magic, which pushed for release.

Afraid to get them caught in a loop, he pushed his own worry away by focusing on his anticipation.

He did his best to distract her with stories about his classes as they walked home and by the time they reached the yard she was laughing and anticipating their evening as much as he was.

He winked at her as he held the door and she giggled as she called greetings. His magic was happy again. He made a mental note to speak to Oz as he called greetings to Camila.

EVERYONE S CLOSE FRIEND

Saturday afternoon Sara greeted Susan at the front door with a friendly smile. "Hawk, your friend is here!" Sara called, gesturing for Susan to enter. "Come on in. He's putting the dogs downstairs. The dogs are well behaved though; maybe you'd like to meet them later?"

"I don't like dogs," Susan said absently as she glanced around the room. "Is Oz here?"

"In the garden out back." Sara closed the front door. By the time she turned back to Susan, she'd already reached the patio door in the living room. Sara shrugged and returned to the kitchen where she was helping Stasia and her mother make pickles.

"Hawk's friend is here." Sara nodded toward the window overlooking the garden. "She's, *um....*"

Stasia laughed. "Yes, she is. I don't like her either."

Camila frowned and went to the window, gazing out at Susan speaking with Oz.

Oz glanced at the backdoor surprised to see a stranger enter his backyard. Neither he nor Sara had ever invited anyone over before. He stood slowly, scanning the girl for weapons and then remembered Hawk had invited a date.

The girl eyed him like he was a steak and she a starving dog but with a certain smugness that made him mentally roll his eyes.

"Hi." Susan held out her hand to Oz.

He shook her hand.

A smile on her full red lips, Susan placed her other hand on their clasped ones, keeping Oz's hand in hers. "I'm Susan. Hawk has told me so much about you, and it's so nice to finally meet you."

"You too," Oz said insincerely as he tugged his hand away.

Susan stepped closer and licked her lips. "I know we'll be very close friends."

Oz frowned. "Aren't you Hawk's *close* friend?"

Susan laughed a low husky laugh and ran a finger across his cheek.

He batted her hand away.

She said, "I have a lot of close friends. Hawk doesn't mind."

"*Uh huh.*" Oz turned to go inside.

"Charlie was a very good friend of mine before I met Hawk. Now that I've met you, I know we're destined to be amazing friends." She trailed a hand across Oz's shoulder as he passed.

Oz stopped dead shocked by her lie and hit record on his wristcomp.

Susan's lips parted when Oz leaned close to whisper, "You're saying Charlie Hayes was your lover and Hawk didn't mind?"

"He knows it's over between Charlie and I, and we're all still friends." She winked at him, smiling like they had a secret. "If you were my lover, I wouldn't care what Hawk thought."

"Charlie Hayes was your lover?" Oz rose an eyebrow and held out a hand, stopping Susan from getting closer.

Susan laughed low and husky and took Oz's outstretched hand. Warm breath caressed his fingertips a moment before he could yank it back. For the first time he felt a distinct sensation from his magic. He'd felt the magic before, but it had always been Charlie's feelings. This time he felt his magic's unease when Susan had breathed on him. It surprised him so much it took him a moment to realize she'd continued speaking.

Susan stepped forward and slid her hands slowly down Oz's arm. "He was, but I like you better. Charlie wasn't... man enough for me. I bet you are."

Oz pushed her away. His face felt hot from a combination of anger and strain. His magic wanted to appear. As Charlie had described, he felt it like pressure beneath his skin. "You're a liar."

Susan threw her head back and laughed, running a hand down his arm again. She stepped even closer to brush her breasts against his chest. Her voice a soft sultry purr, she whispered in his ear, "You don't believe he wanted me? He did, and probably still does, but *I* want you."

Oz laughed and stepped back. His magic relaxed, the bloated sensation easing, he supposed because he felt no fear of her. *This desperate seduction was pathetic*, he thought as he stepped even farther back. "No way Chief would sleep with someone like you."

She laughed again and kissed his cheek. "All men would sleep with someone like me if given the chance. This is your chance."

"What about Hawk?" Oz rolled his eyes and pushed her away again, wiping his cheek then brushing his hands on his pants.

"He'll do for now. Call me when you're ready to be friends."

"Don't wait by the phone for that call. Let's see what Hawk and Charlie say about this."

She shrugged one shoulder as she took a lipstick from her purse and reapplied it. "Charlie will deny it. Boys like him always do, pretending to be so honorable and reliable when inside they're anything but. Confront him if you want to ruin Sara's image of him. Even if she says she believes him, she'll always doubt him afterward." Her smile widened. "Hawk wants me, and he'll believe everything I say, so tell him whatever you want."

"Get out of my house!" Oz turned to the door and yanked it open. "Now!" He was seriously angry now. This stranger was willing to drive a wedge between him and his best friends. She really thought she was in control, and she might've been if he didn't have the recordings or the magic to show the others the truth of her lies.

She trailed a red manicured fingernail over his chest as she went through the door. Oz slapped it away.

"You'll call me." After giving him a wink that didn't hide the anger in her eyes, she went inside. "Hawk?"

Hawk ran up the stairs from the cellar.

"Let's go for a walk." Susan grabbed Hawk's hand and kissed him.

When Hawk tried to speak, she kissed him again and giggled while tugging him to the door.

"Hawk, don't go with her." Oz pushed by and stood before the front door.

Still holding onto Susan's waist, Hawk rose an eyebrow and turned to Oz.

"She isn't who she's pretending to be," Oz continued as he opened his wristcomp and started a search program. "Get away from him." Eyes narrowed, and hands held apart ready to cast, Oz glared at Susan.

"He's just mad because I rejected the pass he made," Susan said as she pulled Hawk closer to the door. Hawk shook her hand off, an expression of hurt and betrayal crossing his face.

The look on Hawk's face made Oz angrier and his magic surged. "Get out!" Oz opened the door and pointed to the street.

Susan put her hands on her hips. "No need to be like that. So I turned you down. Don't try to ruin what Hawk and I have."

"Like you turned down Charlie? Oh right, I forgot, you slept with him, and I could have you too." Oz yanked her arm and pulled her through the door. "Just get out. You're obviously a liar, and I'll find out what else you are." He tapped his wristcomp, making the screen where the search program ran bigger.

Susan glared at Oz and denied making a pass again.

"This wristcomp is a security device, which means I have recordings." Oz rose his voice, talking over her heated protestations that Oz was lying.

Hawk turned to her. "Get out." He flushed and backed away from her reaching hand to open the cellar door. Tank bounded up the stairs and stood in front of him, hackles raised, growling at Susan.

Susan stopped on the bottom step and faced Hawk with tears in her eyes. "He could make the video show whatever he wanted. Don't let him ruin what we have. Maybe you should find out why he's lying. Call me!" She turned and ran down the street crying.

"What was that all about?" Stasia asked from where she, Sara and Camila had gathered in the kitchen doorway.

Charlie came out of his room shirtless in sweatpants. He'd been taking a nap. Sara's anxiety had woken him.

"What's going on?"

Sara was upset, but not afraid. Whatever worried her wasn't personal, but she was worried enough to agitate his magic. His gaze traveled the gathering and rested on Hawk who paced by the front door, running a hand through his hair.

"Hawk's new friend was anything but." Oz put a hand on Hawk's shoulder. "No way Susan is a high school student. I'm running her now. I'm so sorry, Hawk."

Hawk nodded jerkily, called Tank, and they headed out the door.

Stasia went after him. Sara started to follow when Oz grabbed her arm and stopped her. "Stasia can handle this. I'm sure he's embarrassed for falling for her lines. I wish I could get a fingerprint from her."

"You think she was up to something then?" Charlie asked.

"She's definitely up to something. I'd ask Hawk to trail her, but... I'll use locate instead. We need to know what she was up too."

"I just heard the last part of that, *um*, conversation," Sara said. "Did you record the entire thing?"

"Yeah, everything she said was a lie." Oz went to the top step and stared down the street at Stasia and Hawk. "As soon as Stasia comes back I'll disguise myself and track her down."

"Poor Hawk," Sara said softly.

"My son's no longer a boy," Camila said. "He has a man's problems now. His position in Valor Industries will bring women seeking to take advantage, and he needs to learn to recognize them. A woman who approaches out of the blue should set off warning bells."

"I never realized Valor Industries affects you guys." Sara gave Oz a sad smile.

Oz hugged her. "My search continues unhindered. In fact, I have a date tonight. Don't worry about us, Sara. Camila is right though. Hawk needs to be more suspicious and not just because of Valor Industries or the magic. He's young, handsome and a career officer. Some women will try to take advantage of that as well. Then there's you." He hugged her again. "It isn't your fault, but I get propositioned a lot because people think we're an item. They want to brag about scoring your boyfriend. I'm sure that happens to him as well. Susan was probably one of them."

"It doesn't happen to me," Charlie said in a disgruntled tone and then laughed at the flare of jealousy mixed with anger from Sara. "I just meant I *am* your boyfriend. How come everyone on Earth thinks it's anyone else except me?"

Sara leaned into his side and kissed him. "This is getting out of hand. I can't go anywhere without people hounding me about my love life. So many rumors and pictures are posted online, it's ridiculous. We're going to need to do something about this if it doesn't stop soon."

Charlie kissed her brow. "Like what?"

"Go public with our version. Post footage of the actual day I hugged Toric. We can show what really happened and expose how the Idol is fabricating the stories. We have security footage of Hawk and I, and of Oz and I. They used the pictures completely out of context, and we can prove it. And maybe proving it will make nuts like Susan leave Hawk alone."

Charlie nodded. "Okay, but let's see if it dies down first before adding fuel to the fire."

Hawk returned home with Stasia embarrassed and apologetic about bringing Susan into their lives. He asked Oz to see the recordings. "I don't doubt you told the truth. I just want to see what she said."

Oz showed him the recordings. "I'm sorry, Hawk. If it's any consolation, I'm sure it wasn't me personally that interested her. No one is that aggressive without an agenda. The search program got no hits on the name and age she gave you. A Susan Beck attends the local high school, but it isn't your girl. I did get a hit with an eighty-five-point-two probability from the DMV in Massachusetts that she's the same girl who applied for a license under the name Ingra Arnault two years ago. She has no record."

Hawk viewed the reports Oz already had. "These are the photos of the school she showed me. Damn, who the hell is she really?"

"Do you have anything that might carry a fingerprint?" Oz asked.

"Nothing I can think of. I can't believe I fell for that." Hawk paced the room with his fists clenched while Tank growled low in his throat.

Oz laughed. "A pretty girl like that shows interest, well, anyone would fall for it. It sucks, but we both need to run security checks on everyone."

Hawk sighed. "Doesn't matter, I have no time to date anyway. I should've known she was too good to be true."

Sara said, "As soon as she said she didn't like dogs, you should've had second thoughts. Jeez, what were you planning to do, keep Tank in the cellar his entire life?"

"No, I thought I'd introduce them eventually, and she'd grow to like him. Who wouldn't like him?"

"Someone who doesn't like dogs, knucklehead." Oz grabbed Hawk in a headlock and rubbed his crew cut.

Hawk laughed, and the tension eased.

Oz and Charlie went to find Stasia.

Charlie said, "We need to find out what she really wanted. Sorry to ruin your day off. Oz can locate her, but you'll have to do the spying."

"We better call Major Nelson," Stasia said.

"The major wants us to call Agent Lewis," Stasia said a few minutes later as she ended her call. She placed the call and again explained what was happening. "Agent Lewis will meet us here in thirty minutes. Oz, get some bugs ready. I won't be able to hang out there."

"I'll get them and meet you back here." Oz ran back to his lab for the bugs.

Charlie gave Sara an apologetic grimace and followed Oz.

Oz located Susan at a small house twenty miles away. Charlie waited impatiently as Stasia snuck in and planted the bugs. She returned to the car with a water glass that she handed to Agent Lewis.

Stasia said, "She's definitely not seventeen and hasn't been living here long either. I don't think this is a Barlow groupie. The house is mostly empty. One bedroom is done like a stage of a teenager's room, but the rest of the bedrooms are empty. The kitchen only has a few items. There's a couch, two chairs and a television in the living room, no other furniture. She seemed angry, pacing and slamming things around."

Agent Lewis said, "The bugs are in place?"

"Yes, and the receiver." Stasia bit her lip, looking anxious. "She's obviously up to no good. I'm worried about Hawk."

Charlie was too.

Agent Lewis said, "After viewing the recordings Oz took, I'm convinced she wasn't after Hawk but a way into the lab. No one tries that hard at a seduction unless time is limited. Let's run these prints and see who she really is."

"A corporate spy," Charlie mused and forced his shoulders to relax.

Oz ran a laser light from his wristcomp over the fingerprints on the glass. "I'll take better ones when I get to my lab. If she's in any database, I'll find her."

"Keep me informed on anything you learn. I'll be listening to the bugs." Agent Lewis opened the small laptop Oz handed him that connected wirelessly to the bugs Stasia had planted. "The warrant to plant them should be here any minute now. We've just jumped the gun a little. I'll let you know if I find out anything, and I'll keep Sergeant Guthrie informed."

"Wednesday night is going to be a long board meeting," Oz said as they entered the house again. "Sara and I have a bunch of stuff to show you guys and now this."

"One damn thing after another." Stasia put an arm around Oz and leaned into his side.

Charlie sighed hard and followed them.

- 6 -

HOME FIRES

Sara and Oz where just finishing giving their classes Monday morning when Sara's wristcomp notified her Scrap had set off an alarm, followed moments later by two more alarms that windows had broken and the temperature had changed in her in-law's and Hawk's room. She flicked her wrist and brought up the display.

"Shit, Oz, our house is on fire!" Not waiting for him, she raced out the door.

As she ran, she asked her Valory to show the whereabouts of everyone living there. No one was home except Lucky and Scrap.

She raced across the campus, ignoring surprised looks and hails, and hopped the wall by the house.

Scrap cowered by the garage. She grabbed him and set him on top of the wall, told him to stay, and then ran to the burning building.

Oz grabbed her arm. "Stop, that fire was set!"

"Sara?" Charlie asked over her wristcomp.

"Lucky is inside. Make sure everyone else is out!" Sara yelled over her shoulder as she ran to the back door.

"What's happening!" Charlie yelled.

"Lucky is trapped. Come on, come on," she muttered while stabbing her code into the security panel. The door unlocked, and she raced inside to her bedroom. Lucky wasn't there. Tears filled her eyes from a mix of grief and smoke. She placed an arm over her mouth as she ran upstairs and into Charlie's parents' bedroom.

Flames licked up the walls and across the floor, rippling over her shield. The bed had already been reduced to ash and charred wood, and fire had eaten through part of the floor. Heat beat at her face and glass bottles on the vanity exploded. On her knees, she peered under the remains of the metal bedframe, ignoring the flames that crawled over her shield.

"I can't find her, Oz," she said into her wristcomp. The crackling roar of the flames grew as the far wall caught. "Where is she?" She backed out of the room and shut the door.

Sara's fear and worry had hit Charlie like a punch, and he'd let out an oof of surprise and glanced at his wristcomp. Notifications scrawled across the small screen. His eyes widened, and he pressed his panic button, cursing himself for muting the alarms. Test or no test, he should've kept it on.

A combat HUD popped up by his right arm, showing location and status of every team member.

The teacher stopped speaking as Charlie jumped to his feet, held up his blinking wrist, and hurried for the door. As soon as Charlie was in the hallway, he ran. One quick tap on the stickycom behind his ear and he had audio.

His questions seemed to be heightening Sara's worry and he didn't want to distract her. He could feel her desperate concentration, so he tapped the icon for Oz. "What's happening?"

"The house is on fire. Sara is inside searching for Lucky. I'm going in too," Oz said in a rush.

Stasia and Hawk were already sprinting across the yard, heading home. He caught up with them at the back wall.

Inside the house Sara called for Lucky, her voice strident and scared.

Oz grabbed her arm, thick smoke obscuring sight, he pulled her with him. "Lucky is right above us!" he yelled to be heard above the roaring fire. A loud whoomph blew their hair back and a wave of fire coursed over the ceiling, making them both jumped. "Must be accelerants. Let's get her and get out!"

Flames curled from Hawk's room when Sara opened the door. Fire had eaten through most of the floor already. Only a small patch of flooring by the stairs remained, the reinforced posts holding the stairs taking longer to burn through. Sara shielded them both, and they ran up the attic stairs. Billowing flame coursed over the magic shields surrounding them.

Oz paused to put down freezing rain by the stairs as Sara ran down the small hallway in the converted attic space. Lucky cowered in a corner of the farthest bedroom.

"I got her!" Sara casted a Greater Shield and Soothe, which did nothing, on the terrified cat as she tucked her tightly against her chest and ran back to the stairs.

Outside of the house, sirens and lights announced the fire departments arrival. Fire trucks converged and men shouted as they unrolled hoses and sprayed the building with water. Three firefighters entered the backyard and told Charlie Stasia and Hawk to move back.

Charlie ran to the front of the house. Flame shot from the windows in Hawk's and Stasia's rooms and thick black smoke gusted out. Fire crawled over the front, grabbing hold and burning bright orange with a dark blue tint. Both sides of the house smoldered. Small flames licked across the siding that the firefighters extinguished with their hoses, trying to keep the blaze contained in their house.

The houses on either side were evacuating. Police and firefighters escorted the occupants out as they clutched treasured belongings and pets.

Partly ablaze, the back of the house, where Sara and Oz had entered, emitted thick smoke. Charlie realized the fire was spreading unnaturally fast. The magic within him surged as his rage grew. *Arson, not accident.*

At the back wall, Stasia and Hawk stared at the fire with grim faces. Hawk held Scrap, but his eyes were unfocused. Charlie assumed Hawk was using Lucky's eyes to see what was happening inside the house and by his relaxed posture Sara and Oz were fine.

The fire roared, competing with the firefighters yelling and approaching sirens. More firefighters entered the backyard and told them they had to leave.

One of the firemen removed his face mask and gestured to the house. "Is anyone inside?"

Charlie hesitated; Sara and Oz didn't need help; he was sure of that. He was also sure they'd be seen exiting. With all the smoke there was too much chance someone would notice people shapes passing through it even if Oz casted Invisible Duo on them. "I don't know," he finally said. He turned to Stasia. "Is your mother out?"

"Our parents are safe at work. Just Sara and Oz are missing, but they're probably at work too." Stasia bit her lip and shrugged.

The fireman reported the possibility of two people in the house. Charlie, Stasia and Hawk jumped up on their wall for a better view.

"She has her," Hawk muttered.

"I've got her," Sara said unnecessarily.

Charlie had felt her relief.

"Get out before the roof falls in," Charlie said.

"Working on it," Oz replied. "Jump down the hole by the stairs and we can exit through a window."

"Shit, Oz, wait. You need a new shield. Fifteen seconds until I can recast. Use your Ice-Shield when this shield expires. I'm following you, and I'll get the next shield. Shield three."

Stasia said, "I'll run to the lab and grab the white bracelet.

Oz said, "Don't bother. We're almost out."

Charlie winced at the loud crashes that accompanied Oz speaking. Oz must be blasting right through the wall. The roar of the fire and burning timbers tumbling from the roof muted the noises from inside. Thick gray smoke billowed from every window now.

"Sara!" he said warningly.

Hawk ran to the bottom bedroom window and Charlie followed.

The cat in Sara's arms panicked, snarling and clawing desperately to escape. Charlie reached to pull Sara out. Extreme heat battered against his face. Sara tightened her grasp on him and the cat, wincing as Lucky's claws scratched across her face and chest.

The ceiling on the second floor fell in with a thunderous crash, knocking a blazing timber from the ceiling that sent fire billowing from the bottom windows. Charlie pushed her to the ground and rolled them, smothering the flames that had just begun to catch on her shirt. She'd gone through all her shields.

Stasia had grabbed Oz's hand and hauled him from the building. She pulled him with her to intercept the firefighters who yelled and spoke on their headsets excitedly when they appeared.

Charlie pulled Sara to her feet, taking the struggling cat from her.

Covered in scratches from the panicked cat and black from soot, but unharmed, Sara held up a hand to stop him from hugging her and laughed when he ignored it.

"This is one uniform you'll never wear again," she murmured as she returned the hug.

Hawk took Lucky from Charlie, calming her in moments. They all returned to the back wall. Stasia and Oz returned, followed by paramedics carrying a stretcher. Everyone backed away as the house settled, sending embers into the air as flames shot through the roof.

Sara and Oz assured the medics they were fine and no one else was inside.

"Chief, hang back," Oz said.

Charlie grimaced ruefully and waved Oz away. His aura would freak the officers out. It was better for Oz to deal with everyone.

- 7 -

SALVAJE EL DIABLO

Oz went to speak with the fire chief. "Everyone is out. We received the first alarm from our security system fourteen minutes ago. This fire spread way too fast; it must've been set."

The fire chief nodded in agreement. "I'll have our team going over it. Our priority is stopping the spread. You're sure everyone is out?"

"Yes, everyone is out and accounted for," Oz said. "We have a good security system but haven't had a chance to check it yet."

"It wasn't destroyed in the fire?"

"The system itself will be, but not what it knew. I can check the data from work," Oz assured him.

The fire chief rubbed his chin, picked up his radio and made a call. Two police officers approached. He informed them of their conversation and introduced Oz as a resident of the house. "I'm Dr. Simmons." Oz shook their hands. "The fire appears to have been set, and I'll need access to your reports. My colleague and I live here and work with classified materials. The FBI will probably be taking over the case."

"Do you think this was an attempt on your life then?" an officer asked.

"No, they would've done this at night if it was. I don't know what this was," Oz said. "The house security system is top of the line, so we probably have pictures of the perpetrators. I don't know if the FBI will want us showing you though," he finished with an apologetic grimace.

The officer sighed heavily. "I appreciate the honesty. Until I'm officially relieved, I'm in charge here. Come in and make a statement and we'll proceed normally until then. You and your colleague should take extra safety precautions in case this *was* an attempt on one of you."

"We will."

Oz and the officer watched the firefighters for a few moments. Oz heaved a deep sigh and turned back to the officer. "I'll make my statement after I get cleaned up if that's okay?"

"That's fine." The officer handed him a business card. "Your insurance company will need reports, I'm sure."

Oz waved his hand, interrupting him. "We have lawyers to handle all that. I'll be in as soon as I can."

Guthrie approached, and Oz beckoned him over. "Master Sergeant Guthrie is the head of our security." Oz introduced him to the police officers. "Guthrie can answer any questions you have. I'm going to clean up and see what our security system has to say." He shook their hands again and left.

"That kid is a doctor?" The fire chief lifted an eyebrow as he watched Oz leave. Dressed in sneakers and jeans with a white button-down shirt, now black from soot, Oz wore his shoulder length hair caught in a ponytail. His blond hair was hidden under a layer of ash, and grime covered his face, making his blue eyes stand out. He looked like the teenager he was.

"That kid is a genius." Guthrie smiled and nodded toward Oz. "The President of Valor Industries— a private security company for the government." His smile turned to a grimace as he surveyed the smoldering wreckage. "This is going to be a long day. Special Agent in Charge Lewis from the FBI will be here soon and taking over the investigation. Do we know anything yet?" He gestured the officers to precede him to their car.

Oz found the rest of Team Valor in the backyard staring at the smoldering wreckage that was all that remained of their home. He glanced at his wristcomp. He'd received the first alarm twenty-seven minutes ago. Firemen still surrounded the house hosing it down.

"This is FUBAR." Hawk put his arm around his sister when she nodded.

Charlie put an arm around Sara, and she pulled Oz over to them and stood with her arm linked in his. Charlie pulled Stasia closer, putting an arm around her waist too.

Master Sergeant Guthrie found them there ten minutes later, still staring at their destroyed home. "Reporters are here. Clear out. I'll handle this."

They walked slowly to the new lab building. "You guys better get back." Oz said, scowling at their uniforms. "Those uniforms are ruined."

Charlie inspected himself and grimaced. His uniform was black where Sara had leaned against him and scratches from Lucky's panicked attempts to escape had left red blotches across his chest.

He said, "Heal yourself as soon as you get inside."

"No need. I'm healed already. Lucky and Scrap are too," she assured him. "I'll keep an eye on them in case they need more healing from smoke inhalation."

"Let us know what you find out, Oz." Charlie kissed Sara and slapped Oz's shoulder.

Oz tapped his wristcomp. "Already on it. Meet us tonight at the office to discuss what we're going to do now."

"I'll call your parents," Sara said to Charlie and Stasia. "We need to figure out where we're going to stay, and they'll need to get clothes and stuff."

Charlie hugged her again and gave her another light kiss. "We'll work it out. Don't leave the academy grounds alone. Stay together."

Sara nodded against his shoulder.

"You guys be careful too. We don't know what that was about." Sara stepped back from Charlie and smiled ruefully at Stasia and Hawk. "I would hug you too, but..." She gestured at the mark she'd left on Charlie.

Stasia laughed, then sobered. "You two be careful."

"We will be," Oz assured her.

Hawk handed Lucky back. The cat was filthy but calm. Oz and Sara watched them walk back to their dorm. When they were out of sight, Oz turned to Sara. "Get cleaned up and meet in my office."

Sara nodded and went to tell Camila about the fire. Camila had been watching the security footage and had already spoken to Hawk. She took Lucky and Scrap, promising to clean them up.

Sara used the small shower in her own office and put on her gym clothes, which were the only other ones she had. Then she called her father-in-law.

"I've been reading the alarms and I've already spoken with the sarge," John said. "You're okay?"

"Everyone's fine. Lucky and Scrap too. The house is a total loss. You'll have to stay at a hotel or something until we can figure out what we're doing. We're holding a meeting here tonight at eight."

"I'll be there. You guys be careful."

"We will." Sara flicked her wrist and the picture of John Hayes' worried face disappeared. She made another quick call to Oz's father to make sure he knew to take precautions and to be at the meeting that night. Rick, Brenda, Joy, Drew and Major Nelson were already in Oz's office when she got there. Oz also wore his gym clothes. They moved next door to the conference room. Oz sent the security feed to their wristcomps.

"Who the hell are *Salvaje El Diablo's*?" Major Nelson leaned forward, peering at the screen. Three men wearing black leather vests with *Salvaje El Diablo's* emblazoned across the back squirted liquid on the house, then threw glass bottles with burning rags.

"Obviously, retarded gang members," Oz said. "A sign hung right out in front of the house saying it was under surveillance. The real question is why did they do it." He flicked his wrist to open his flat screen and began typing. A few minutes later he sat back and groaned. "You've got to be kidding me." He flicked his wrist again, making the screen big enough they could all see it, and Sara made a small annoyed sound.

"Do you think they're done now?" she asked.

Angry blue eyes met.

Oz shrugged. "They're clearly really stupid, so hard to say. I'm guessing they blame us for their pal dying in prison."

Major Nelson rapped the table with his knuckles. "Fill me in. You know those guys?"

"No, we met two of their friends briefly last year." Oz brought up the relevant police report. "Sara and I bumped into them as they ran from a robbery; I'm sure you remember."

Major Nelson nodded.

"Well, one of the men died in prison, and I'm guessing they blame us for getting him sent there."

Busy at his flat screen Oz groaned again. "Holy crap, listen to this." A choppy audio played.

A man said, "Serve the bitches right, *Salvaje El Diablos* don't take no shit from anyone. Jack our hombre up and payback is tenfold."

While another said, "Should've done this shit at night and killed them all."

To which the other man replied. "No, I got some plans of my own for the girly."

Sara reached over and turned off the recording. "So, it has nothing to do with the magic or Valor Industries just revenge for imagined wrongs."

"I'll bring copies of this to the police." Oz took a USB from his pocket and attached it to his wristcomp. "We can handle them."

"Sergeant Guthrie ordered us here," Rick said, "and we're staying until this is straightened out. Where are you staying tonight?"

"Here, I guess." Sara frowned at the boardroom table and small couch. "At least until we talk to the sarge and work out a new place."

"I'll bring this to the police station." Oz rose and headed to the door.

"And I'm going shopping. Send me a list of what you want, and I'll pick it up," Sara said as she stood to go.

"Rick and I will stay with you," Brenda said. "I know you can handle these guys, but we aren't taking any chances. Besides, you can't get your car out of the garage today, maybe not for a few days."

Oz headed to the police station with Joy and Drew while Sara went shopping with Rick and Brenda.

At the precinct Oz asked for the detective who'd given him his card. He handed him the flash drive and explained what he thought had happened. Agent Lewis and the police chief joined them. Oz sent Agent Lewis a copy of the file with his wristcomp. "I don't think they knew who we are at all really. They probably recognized Sara from the tabloids and decided to get payback for their dead friend."

"Protective custody can be arranged until we apprehend the men involved," the police chief said.

"She has two guards with her. She'll be fine," Oz assured him. "We'll handle our own security. You can see from the recording that Scrap set the alarm off as soon as they arrived. If she'd been home and they'd tried to break in she would've had time to get to the safe room."

"That's the smallest guard dog I've ever seen," the detective said with a snort of laughter after watching Scrap hit the alarm on the tape.

"We have bigger ones, but they were with us. We went back to the house to get the cat," Oz said as the footage showed first Sara then him running into the burning building.

The detective rolled his eyes. "You could've been killed for a cat."

"She loves that cat. She went, so I followed." A light blush on his cheeks, Oz shrugged. "Agent Lewis, I assume you'll be in touch with the sarge and inform us about anything else you find out?"

"I will. We'll get this crew rounded up in no time, but stay alert, and don't let Charlie hear the audio."

"We won't," Oz assured him. "She's trying hard to stay out of the news."

"Not her fault." Agent Lewis tapped the printout of the men's faces. "We'll get them and keep her safe. You two don't have to worry about it, just remain cautious."

Oz thanked them and joined Drew and Joy who waited in the lobby, and they headed back to campus.

- 8 -

PRESSURE

Sara headed right to her and Stasia's favorite store in the mall and filled a few bags that Rick took to the car for her. The cashier recognized her but didn't make a big deal other than to say hello. By the time she'd bought everyone two changes of clothes, underwear, and sweat suits she'd filled four more bags.

The next stop was a bigger department store for shoes. A few patrons snapped her picture on cellphones and asked for autographs, so she left without buying anything. The shoppers followed her out, holding out cellphones, calling after her and filming as she hurried away. A crowd mobbed her at the mall entrance.

Girls wanting pictures and autographs crowded around her. Flashes dazzled, and gawkers shouted questions as more people gathered.

Rick got in front of her and started pushing people away. Mall security arrived and tried to get the people to move back. Sara kept a hold of Rick's shirt while Brenda stood close behind her, trying to keep the people from touching her. Someone grabbed her hair. Brenda hit the hand holding it with her taser light.

"Get her out of here, Rick!" Brenda yelled.

Rick turned and swung Sara up into his arms. Brenda got in front of them and pushed roughly through the crowd while Sara hid her face in Rick's chest. The mob followed them out the door.

Her phone rang. "I'm fine, Charlie," Sara said, having to yell to be heard over the crowd.

She winced as their HUDs formed, triggered remotely by Charlie.

The crowd exclaimed and surged closer, talking excitedly about the HUDs now.

Brenda waved Rick forward as she said, "Sara is fine. People at the mall mobbed her. As soon as we're clear, she'll call you."

Once past the door, Rick sprinted to the car.

Only a few people followed, and none approached the car.

"This is so stupid." In the backseat, Sara removed her gloves to run her hands over her face and straighten her ponytail. "Next time I leave the house, I'll use Oz's disguise."

"Even disguised don't go alone," Rick said as he eyed her in the rearview mirror smoothing her hair and fixing her clothes.

She nodded agreement and called Charlie back. "Sorry, I'm fine, just a bit overwhelmed. I won't go out again undisguised."

"You sure you're okay?" Her anxiety thrummed along his nerves.

"I am. Did you guys get in trouble for leaving?"

"No, I talked with the commandant. He needed to know there might be security issues on his campus."

"We know who did it, and it's nothing to worry about. We'll fill you in tonight. I love you."

"I love you too. Don't hesitate to call me."

"I'm good. You better get back to class." She flicked her wrist, ending the call, frowning at the long list of supplies she still needed. "I still need food for the dogs and cat. And Lucky needs a new litter box."

"Send me the list." Brenda tapped her wristcomp. "We'll bring you back to your lab and get the rest of what you need."

Sara nodded and forwarded the list to Brenda. "Thanks, sorry about all this."

"No problem. Marcus and Todd should be at your lab now. Don't go anywhere without at least two of us."

When she returned to the Valor building, Sara helped to carry in the packages and then called Mr. Martin and informed him on the day's events. He promised to handle the insurance agents and to get in touch with Master Sergeant Guthrie about the status of the case.

Sara took another shower and put on her new clothes. Unable to concentrate in her lab, she headed to the roof. The wind brought the scent of smoke, ruining the peace of her sunny hideaway.

That night they held an informal meeting to discuss what had happened and what their plans were.

With a flick of his fingers Oz turned on his holographic flat screen and made it large enough and two-sided so everyone could view it. He told them what they'd found out and that the police were handling it. "We need to be cautious while we investigate this, but that's standard for us anyway." A finger tap opened another screen. "Mr. Martin will handle our insurance claims and needs itemized lists from everybody."

"Oz and I will stay here in the lab tonight," Sara said. "We need to find a more permanent solution though."

Mr. Hayes cleared his throat. "This is a good time to bring up an idea I've been working on. I want to move Valor Industries to Texas."

"I can't leave here." Sara paled as she faced her father-in-law.

"You and Oz can stay here; I'll move the offices and fabrication to Texas. We can save a lot of money that way." Mr. Hayes turned to

Charlie. "Your mother and I will go there and get a house, one with enough rooms for everyone. I'm sure you'll have to come there occasionally over the next few years. When you graduate, and are assigned somewhere, you'll have a home there with us whenever you want one."

"Why Texas?" Charlie took Sara's hand, surprised by how upset this made her.

"A lot of reasons. A report I've been working up on the advantages of the move is in your inbox. I was thinking to do this in a year or so, but now, well, it seems like a good time. Your mother and I have enjoyed living with you, but the company would do better in Texas." Mr. Hayes turned to Oz's father. "We'll need you to go there too, Jer. Camila can stay here, but we want the factories and shops there."

"We've talked about this, I just thought I'd have more time with my boy." A scowl on his ruddy cheeks, Jerry gazed sadly at Oz. "I've really enjoyed working with you on the designs, Oz. I'm so proud of you, son."

"We can still do that." Oz rose and hugged his father. "Maybe not in person, but online. I'll miss you, Dad."

"How much will a move slow production?" Charlie asked.

"Not too bad," John said. "I'll keep these offices going here until I find us a spot. Figure a month or two while we make the move and shake out the kinks. It'll be easier to do it now before the company grows." John turned to

Hawk. "I want to take all the dogs with me except Rhea, Scrap and Tank. We'll use some at the offices, but I want them in the factory for security."

"I can go there and make sure the dogs know what you want," Hawk agreed.

"Pierce is still vetting all of our employees. He'll be sending us people to train to do the installations," Oz said. "Will we still make our deadlines?"

"Yes, I'm sure we will. I recommend you keep the best two or three guys and send them on to me in Texas to train future installers. The only thing holding us up would be programming. You and Sara will have to do that yourselves until you can train another programmer."

"Fifty programmers are training right now. All specialized programming will have to be done here though until I'm more confident in their abilities." Oz opened a screen and began taking notes.

"The parts manufactured for Sara's lab require secure shipping," Jerry said. "Now we use the Scouts to escort them to her to ensure no one else gets access."

Oz made a note and tapped his fingers on the table a moment. "I'll talk to Guthrie and see what we can work out to keep the things you're making for her secure."

"When will you go?" Sara's hand trembled in Charlie's.

"In the next day or so." John patted the hand that clutched his son's. "It'll take time to find what I'm looking for, and I'll need to work out security with Pierce before I do anything, but I'll aim to be in full production in Texas by January."

"Another year and another change." Tears filled her eyes, and she squeezed them shut a moment and then cleared her throat.

"Nothing will change with us," Charlie whispered as he kissed her cheek. He turned to his mother and asked, "Where will everyone be staying until we work out something more permanent?"

Mary said, "Master Sergeant Guthrie is already installing security at the Sheraton for us. What are we doing about this gang? You think the fire is because of what happened last year, but what if that's what they want you to believe?"

"Sara and I will plant bugs." Oz rose and gave Mary a quick hug. "I don't care that we don't have a warrant. We need to be sure; I agree."

Charlie frowned. "Just you two? Wait for the weekend and we can all go."

"Please— disguise and invisible, we'll be fine." Oz rolled his eyes at Charlie, and Sara giggled.

"Bring back up at least. Have a few Scouts listening in. Get in group six for an extraction if you need one." Charlie glanced at his brother.

"Yes, Dad, we'll wear our raincoats too." Oz laughed at the dirty look Charlie gave him. "Sara and I are both staying here in our offices for a few days, but we can't stay indefinitely. Guthrie needs to find us a place."

Sara sighed and rubbed her forehead with two fingers. "All this is taking time from our research. If John wasn't here to pick up the slack it could tank our fledgling company, we're spread so thin. I still want to go to Massachusetts and talk to those professors this week. I don't have time for all of this," she finished unhappily.

Camila patted her shoulder. "Send me the lists of everything that needs doing, and I'll see to it. The lab is slow at the moment. I'll meet with the insurance agents and whoever else we need to meet, and I'll see about replacing everyone's clothing. Everyone send sizes or requests to me and I'll handle it. Don't worry about this. I really don't mind. Anastasia got her shopaholic gene from me."

Sara brightened. "That would be a huge help. Can you make sure whatever spot Guthrie finds has a sunny area— a private sunny area?"

Camila laughed. "I'll see to it. Sebastian's dogs will need room as well. I'll get the cars moved out of the garage as soon as I can too."

"We can park them here for now, but this has to be temporary too," Oz said.

"When are you going to Massachusetts?" Charlie asked. "I don't want you out of the zone."

"Well, as soon as I can. I'll take Brenda, Manny, and Marcus with us in group six. We'll be fine, Charlie. I don't plan on being there long at all, just a day or two." She squeezed his hand. "The conclusion he postulates confuse me. I really need to talk to him."

Charlie just sighed well aware of her obsessive complusive need to understand. "And Joy?" Both of them were nervous about the upcoming event and being careful to not let their magic mingle to ensure Sara would have enough unadulterated magic to use on Joy.

"Sunday, if everything goes well, I guess." Sara kissed him and rested her cheek on his a moment.

The contact didn't ease him.

- 9 -

KEEPING SECRETS

The next day, after they'd taught their classes in the morning, Oz and Sara met Stasia to steal her invisible spell using the blue bracelets.

"Check in every thirty minutes. If you miss a check in, I'm summoning you back." Stasia tapped her white bracelet.

"Don't worry, we'll be fine." Oz gave her a quick hug. "We'll have backup with us if we need help. We won't need backup though. They won't even know we're there."

Marcus drove them to the known addresses of every gang member. Sara and Oz planted all thirty of his prototypes.

"Not enough receivers are ready, so we have to come here and download them once a day," Oz said as they returned to the car after placing the last one. "The computer program will scan everything, but we should listen until we get a better feel to tweak the programing so we don't miss anything. I need to make more bugs to set where they hang out."

"This is so frustrating. I hate having to spend time on this crap." Sara slumped into the backseat and closed her eyes, leaning her head back.

"Let us do it for you." Marcus glanced at Sara in the rearview mirror. "Might as well make use of us."

Sara smiled back. "You're still up for my experiment today?"

Marcus laughed. "Yes. I figure the worst that happens is I lose my big toe."

"What experiment?" Oz turned in the front seat to face her.

"I had an idea for replacement limbs, or I should say multiple ideas. I'm testing a new spell device on Marcus, replacing his big toe bone with a plastic magic ampule programmed for my summons. The idea is if he ever needs help, he can smash his toe and summon his group."

"You're going to try the metal bone as well, right?" Marcus glanced in the mirror again.

"Yes, your poor toe will be removed four times today, but I promise I'll put it back." Sara leaned forward and squeezed his shoulder. "You won't feel a thing and can watch if you want."

"Can I watch too?" Oz glanced back with an inquisitive lift to his brow. "Why are you removing it four times?"

"The first attempt will be to replace a missing limb with an artificial one, a small metal toe, and then a real toe from a cadaver. After that, I'll try the plastic spell toe and if that works, I'll replace his toe with another one."

"Why use a toe? Why not just in his side or something?" Oz asked.

"I need to be able to break it while tied. If it was in my side or leg, I thought it'd be harder to get to," Marcus said. "Sara will try the artificial toes first. If they work, then even if the spell toe doesn't work, she can replace mine with a new one." Marcus smiled at Sara again. "Even if she can't, it's just a big toe."

"When we figure out how to heal everyone, I'll be ready." Sara casted a heal and let it bounce around the car between them. "Right now, it's just the Marines and Navy, but I hope we figure out how to give everyone a heal someday."

"I don't think they'll let you reattach missing limbs, Sara. It's too much exposure for us," Oz said.

"I know." Sara grimaced. "Until we can give a heal to everyone, we need to be discreet, but if a Marine is injured and sent to me, I could do a reattachment if he or she hadn't had time to realize the extent of their injuries. I can't stand the thought of people suffering to preserve our secret."

"I don't like it either." Oz reached into the backseat and patted her knee. "But discretion is necessary. If we told the world what we could do, well, people would panic and riot. Other nations would attack us to get control of us or demand our deaths. The longer we stay under the radar, the more time we have to figure this out, the better."

Sara closed her eyes and rubbed them hard. "Meanwhile, people are dying and suffering."

"People died and suffered before you were born and will continue to after you die," Marcus said. "Do the best you can. It's neither your fault nor responsibility."

He pulled the car up in front of the Valor building and got out. Sara and Oz followed.

Sara hugged him a moment. "You're a good friend, Marcus."

Marcus kissed the top of her head and gave her a squeeze. "You are too, Sara."

- 10 -

BOARD MEETING

The next night at the monthly board meeting, Sara announced the results of the experiments on Marcus.

"Just a few quick slides to show everyone," she said as she started her presentation. "I removed Marcus's big toe and successfully transplanted both an artificial one, and one from a donor. The spell toe worked, but I need to monitor it for m-radiation leakage." Sara turned to Marcus as the pictures of the surgeries played on the large screen behind her. "Marcus?"

Marcus stood and faced the raid. "I feel the difference, but it doesn't hurt. I'm sure I'll get used to it in no time and forget it's even there. It doesn't set off metal detectors and looks normal. When I discharged the first one it hurt, but not unbearably. Equal to a stubbed toe. Both the artificial toe and the cadaver toe felt normal to me." He pointed to the picture of his big toe on the screen. "If it doesn't spread radiation around it'll be an amazing safety feature for us if we can keep it secret."

"It only holds one spell?" Major Nelson turned the small sample ampule in his hand.

Sara said, "Yes, it's as small as I can make it and still almost bigger than his toe was. I can't add any more programming or stored magic without adding to the size." She rolled another small ampule to Brenda.

Major Nelson handed the plastic device to Gina who sat beside him. "Could you replace a leg bone maybe?"

"In theory," Sara agreed hesitantly. "It would be much heavier than your real leg bone though, and I'd need to figure out a way to access the stored magic inside of it. It's not like you could or should just break your own leg."

"She picked the toe because it's both easy to use yourself in an emergency and relatively easy to place," Oz explained.

"And you think you can replace lost limbs on Marines now?" Major Nelson rewound the footage and scrutinized the reattachments.

"I believe I can." Sara turned to frown at the screen. "It's a wholly magical process though, impossible for any other doctor to duplicate, so it has to be done discreetly." She leaned forward and slid a folder to him. "I want you to bring me candidates for testing. Included in my report is a list of what I need, the time it would take per limb, and my ideas on how to fool the patient."

Major Nelson flipped through the file and grimaced. "I'll see what I can do, but no promises."

Sara nodded at him. "I'd like to recruit the more injured Marines to work at the lab. I know it will be a security nightmare but there are men and women out there I can help. They could lead productive happy lives and I'll need help in my lab, so why not offer them a cure and give them jobs? They can relocate. Is all they need do is join our version of witness protection— leave their old lives behind.

She slid a thick folder to Major Nelson. "I know it will be a lot of work to make sure they don't talk but I really want you to look into this."

Major Nelson took the file and Sara continued, "I'm working on making my heals available to anyone, but still no luck. It's my top priority. Well, that and understanding what the magic is. Oz made progress with our ray-gun and produced a prototype of a belt holding Charlie's magic. We're also working on new uses for the buoy, specifically adding a modified ray-gun to form a shield."

Oz put a picture of a belt on the big screen. "This is our idea for Chief's magic, to hold his rage potion. It has advantages and disadvantages. It's bulky but it can be pre-applied and engaged with just a push on the left-hand side of the buckle and disengaged with a push on the right-hand side." He flipped to a new picture.

"This one is much more streamlined. The buckle is placed on an existing belt and hooks to a container that resembles an ammunition cartridge. It takes a good thirty seconds to put the belt on and hook the buckle to the belt and the cartridge. The disadvantage here is anyone investigating the cartridge would release the magic and the cartridge would be empty, causing people to wonder what it was. If this method is chosen, everyone needs to carry patches in case the cartridge itself is shot to stop the release of magic as soon as possible."

"It holds enough of Charlie's magic for fifteen smaller spells or nine larger ones." Sara flipped the picture on the screen to show the interior of the belt and cartridge. "The belt has enough for approximately six larger spells, there's just no way to fit more magic in the belt without bulking it up even more."

Oz slid samples of both items onto the table. "They weigh about the same, but the fake cartridge is all on one side, which could be awkward. Let us know which you want or if you have a better idea."

"Can this store his rage potion as well?" Major Nelson asked as he hefted the fake cartridge.

"Yes, and Sara could recharge the cartridge if she had access to Chief or a potion," Oz said.

"Sara's magic could be placed in a cartridge holder and use the belt buckle delivery?" Major Nelson asked.

"Yes," Oz agreed.

"I think we should switch our taser light to the rage potion and use Sara's magic in the cartridge. That would give us about sixteen spells from her and she could refill it herself." Major Nelson tapped his chin with one finger. "Everyone could carry backup magic for Chief's bracelet in their light. Or— could you make another cartridge for Chief with one button to disengage Chief and engage Sara's and the other button on the belt buckle do the opposite?"

Oz opened a screen before him and examined the schematic of the belt. "Yes, we could do that but either the belt would need to be bigger or have a smaller magic reservoir to fit two lines. Sara's magic is more potent than Chief's so you'd get more of her spells from a cartridge. You could wear both cartridges and bracelets too. Keep at least one of each bracelet for everyone. They're much faster to apply than the belts are with less chance of an accidental breach. We had an idea to add piping to the sleeves to hold magic and we could make the spell bracelets much smaller but we're still working on the aramid material."

"Let everyone try both the belt and cartridges for a while." Major Nelson slid the samples to Guthrie to examine.

"We've decided to use packs conjured by Oz as standard gear, so we can each carry quite a few potions," Sara said.

Charlie frowned and leaned back in his seat. "Someone is bound to see the glowing V on the back."

Oz shrugged. "It shouldn't matter. We can claim it's experimental and classified. Since no one except the user can open them, there's no way anyone can know how much one bag can carry or how the V on the back is lit. We'll still need to be discreet when removing items, but I really can't see how using them will expose us now. The packs are completely bulletproof. Wearing one negates the need for back armor and as soon as we iron out the kinks on the aramid materials we're developing and patent it, we plan to design a magic receptacle to be worn beneath the packs."

"That's great news," Major Nelson said. "I really like this idea. Oz, can you make up a tag for them, a tracker to deter thieves? Make it really obvious looking but it doesn't matter if it works or not. I assume you can find them?"

"Sure, that shouldn't be a problem."

"Don't overload yourself," Charlie warned.

Major Nelson waved his hand dismissively. "We know how much we can carry."

"Hot food, clean clothes and ammunition. I've already bought an inflatable cabin. I wonder if I can squeeze in a motor for an inflatable boat?" Marcus said happily.

Sara laughed and patted Charlie's hand.

He frowned then sighed. *They'd just have to learn the hard way.* Just because you could carry hundreds of pounds didn't make it easy. A pack loaded to capacity was tiring to lug around, while one that was safely beneath your limits felt almost weightless.

Sara handed Major Nelson a small box. "Two more skin wristcomps. At two a month maximum, it'll be a year before the entire raid has one. I was debating letting Liz sedate me and having Charlie harvest all the material necessary in one shot, but Oz is really close to a breakthrough on the artificial power source."

"And I don't want to do it." Charlie's shudder made Brenda laugh but he wasn't faking. It horrified him to contemplate skinning Sara, sedated or not.

Oz tapped the box containing the wristcomp. "The wristcomps without skin have received some improvements, so bring yours in and I'll upgrade them. Energy gains and transfers has been taking up a lot of my time and I'm on the cusp of solving it. I've also been working on the ray-gun and have managed to get it to dissipate sooner, but danger remains of hitting our own aircraft or boats. If you aimed the gun into the ground the effects could be catastrophic. In theory, the light could continue to the Earth's core and while the holes would be small, too many could potentially weaken the Earth's crust. Unlike a smite, the light doesn't break up when it hits its target. It does grow weaker, but the unused energy remains and is dangerous. We know it's possible to make it softer, able to pass through targets while doing no damage because smite can do it, but we have no idea how the phase changes yet.

"The ray-gun isn't a viable weapon until I can regulate the energy output better and work out the programming needed to do a complete scan of the area the light travels through to determine if it's safe to shoot. I just hate to spend time doing that when I think Sara might be right and we're barking up the wrong tree with this."

"At least for now we are." Sara shrugged and tapped the screen in front of her, making it larger. "Once we figure out how the magic programs our spells, we can rethink it. Our time might be better spent on defensive weaponry, at least for now."

"You've had progress on the artificial shield?" Guthrie asked.

"Insights, but no tangible progress, but we've been working on the ray-gun and energy." Oz made a sound of annoyance. "We've been working on lots of things. I finished designing our game console, so we just need to do the exterior cosmetic design. The game itself is far from complete, but we can put out simpler games until it's ready and subcontract for games, or we can hold the release until our game is finished. I'm sending you the files on the different options. Send me back what one you like."

"How long until our game is ready?" Hawk asked.

"At least two years. None of us has that much time to work on it. Combined we spend less than five hours a week on it." Oz sent the estimates to Hawk with a tap of his finger.

Hawk eyed the estimated time needed to finish each project, his frown growing. "What if we dedicated more time to it? Say Thanksgiving break and one week of Christmas break?"

"If we could agree on specs and spells, the rest is just programming. The entire point of the game was supposed to be fun for us though. If we do that and hire more designers we could finish faster, but it'd be work, not fun," Sara said.

Stasia shrugged. "It'd still be fun, but I see your point. Let's compromise. Finish the basics and one zone. Release the zone super cheap and get people hooked while we iron out the wrinkles and kill the bugs."

"Okay, I'll move the game to the front of my list." Oz made a note on a screen in front of him. "I'll start hiring game programmers and teaching them. We can hold a private meeting and decide whose zone gets done first and get something ready for next Christmas. I'll need the console done and in production by spring of next year so we can advertise. That means a big chunk of our government loan taken out to hire all these people."

"Do it." Charlie slapped Hawk's shoulder and smiled when he grinned. "We need to make more money for magical research. I don't want

Sara spending any more of her own money on that."

"Our money," Sara corrected. "But I see your point. We need to save enough money to finance one of these projects if our government loan gets withdrawn. We're far from broke though. If I have to, I can sell my mother's clothes and jewelry."

"No, we aren't doing that." Charlie frowned at her. "As you said, we're far from broke. This fire didn't help, but we have more than enough to live on."

"About the fire." Major Nelson rapped the table to gather attention. "Is there any news yet?"

"Sara and I will go move bugs tomorrow." Oz laughed when Marcus snorted and said, "I mean, someone will go move the bugs around tomorrow." Oz changed the image on the big screen to a map of Annapolis. "We have good leads on where that gang hangs out and does business. We've heard zip about the fire so far except for one quick comment about someone named Diablo being seriously pissed. My database tags Diablo as an alias for Carmen Diego and marks him as one of the leaders. This gang has members here and Washington as well as in New Jersey and California. They mostly deal in stolen goods with arrests for drugs, both selling, buying and stealing cars, but the police don't consider them major players in anything. More middlemen with pawn shops and a few garages slash chop-shops. Every business of theirs in this area will be bugged this week."

"The main office and factories of Valor Industries will move to Texas as soon as possible." Charlie tapped his wristcomp. "I've forwarded everyone the complete report my father submitted, and I agree it makes sense to move there."

"Oz and I will live here in the lab until the sarge figures out where to move us," Sara said.

"Speaking of living arrangements." Liz cleared her throat. "The ban on fraternizing outside of the Marine Core has been lifted for raid members, but not for Team Valor. That being said, if you ever experience any magical manifestations, stop what you're doing and report right away."

Liz smiled at Joy's alarmed expression. "Fraternizing within the raid is still permitted, but anyone who has full magic must be careful." Liz cleared her throat again. "And speaking of full magic, would you consider changing Brenda, not Joy, first."

"No!" Sara snapped and then cleared her throat. "No," she said again in a calmer voice with an apologetic glance at Brenda. "I'm sorry, but Brenda is a priest, and I won't take the chance that Charlie will want her magic. We picked Joy because even if I want her magic, I won't want her sexually. She's the safest one for us. If I don't want her magic, and Charlie doesn't want her, then I'll consider Brenda, but not now. I know he likes priest's magic."

"We won't do it." Charlie ran a hand over Sara's cheek, surprised by how upset the thought of it made her. A cold hand grabbed his and squeezed. The coldness of her skin alarmed him. He rubbed her hands, trying to warm her.

"This entire process is scary for us," Sara continued. "If Stasia didn't need Rick, I wouldn't do it at all."

"So, Sunday you're going to try to change Joy?" Liz glanced at the notes before her.

"Yes, as long as everyone still agrees, we'll go out on a boat with Joy. We need a private spot and we figured that would be best. Hawk, Oz, Stasia, Guthrie and you will be on a nearby boat while we attempt to change her. Afterward, you can bring her to the lab and monitor her. Charlie and I plan on keeping our distance. A complete emergency set up will be on your boat if we need to be resuscitated. You can use a white bracelet on Charlie or I, but don't use any heals on Joy until she's either changed or dying."

Sara's hand tightened in Charlie's when she said that, and a black wave of guilt ran over her. She turned to Joy, her blue eyes shiny with unshed tears.

"Joy, Charlie and I will do our best to make sure you don't die, but it'll be painful, and you'll likely lose your hair and have the same patchy skin we did. We can resurrect you if you die, but you'd still be bald and patchy." Her guilt intensified as she said, "There's no guarantee you'll get magic or that a resurrection would work. I could kill you. I could change you in ways we can't imagine or predict."

"I understand," Joy said steadily. "Liz and Camila will monitor me every moment, and I'll be trying to cast. The entire raid will play online with me to duplicate the circumstances of your change as much as possible. In my head, I'll be being a warrior as hard as I can."

Joy rose and knelt before Sara, taking her hand and squeezing for a moment. "If it doesn't work, don't blame yourself. I certainly won't blame you. If it works, but something unforeseen happens to me, don't blame yourself for that either. I accept full responsibility for this."

Sara nodded. "Liz will be filming and running tests. Oz will check on you too. Charlie and I will be staying away; try not to think of us at all. As much as I love you, I don't want to form any sort of bond with you."

Joy nodded. "I understand. I don't want that kind of bond with anyone."

"Hey," Drew said in mock outrage.

Joy rolled her eyes. "I love you, Drew, but I don't want that sort of bond. I like my privacy way too much."

Drew laughed and winked at her.

"Okay, back to business." Stasia changed the picture on the big screen to show the financial report. "You've seen the financial reports. VI is officially making money, none of which we'll see a penny of, it's all going back into the business. If anyone has a problem with the budget, now would be a good time to bring it up." She glanced around the table. "Okay then, the official budget will be released in January. Everyone will receive copies. Please bring questions or problems to one of us right away."

"One more thing before we close this meeting," Hawk said. "We need to do more training, specifically with the bracelets and wristcomps. If we're called out, it's going to be a disorganized mess. I propose we find a secluded spot in this state. Someone summons us to the spot and Liz can stay here and summon us back. Oz was working on a program to show us the raid group composition to change it so we all know who is in what group."

"The program is ready." Oz tapped his screen, changing the picture on the big screen again, this time to a raid layout. "Just ask your wristcomp and you can see it."

Twenty-two flat screens appeared in front of them.

"As far as I know this is the current composition. Everyone now has raid assist, so if you move someone, make sure you say so aloud for the wristcomps to track." Oz tapped each segment as he named them. "It's a simple command. Raid group composition move Marcus to raid group one and Sara to raid group six. As you can see, they've been moved. Raid group composition, move Mark, Todd, and Brenda to raid group six." All showed as being in group six. "Sara, summon them, see if it worked."

Sara moved to the doorway and casted her Call-For-Help, summoning her group members. She got Major Nelson, Todd, Brenda, and Tony. "Whoops, someone left Tony in group six." Sara punched Tony in the shoulder, and he ruffled her hair.

"Okay, I'm resetting the raid composition." Oz named every member and their group position. "Charlie or the major will reset raid positions before engagements just like always, but meanwhile this will keep us organized."

Sara said, "Marcus, if you use my summons spell, I need to make sure it uses the bracelet's magic and not the magic in your toe. I think it can only do that if you smash your toe, causing it to engage, but it hasn't been tested."

"Yes, ma'am," Marcus said with a smile and saluted her.

"I'm working on some scenarios for my Valory to program into our version of the game so we can practice using both bracelets," Oz said. "It won't be as good as the real thing, but it should help us learn to make the best use of the magic."

"I'll find a practice area somewhere in the zone this week." Major Nelson tapped the file on the table in front of him to neaten the edges. "For now, practice will be held without you. School is your priority. When you graduate, we'll do the serious practice. You've only been back in school a few weeks. There's no rush, let Sara talk with professors. Oz can work on what interests him. I know you're both also teaching three hours a day, don't overbook yourselves. Leave time in your schedules for fun and relaxation. I love the new gadgets, but you don't have to change the world in a year."

"I'm patenting the new motor we use to power the buoys." Oz changed the screen again to show the new motor. "It will revolutionize boating. Right now, the skeins can't gather enough kinetic or thermal energy to power a cruise ship, but it's more than enough for smaller boats. Unlimited, clean, renewable energy. In time, I can do the same for wind and sun. The engines don't even cost that much to make."

"Who else knows about that?" Major Nelson sat back in his chair, both brows raised.

"Just us."

"Can you send me your report on it to show the president? I think he'll want a heads-up if the power industry will take a hit."

"Sure," Oz agreed. "That brings up another topic. This is the president's last year in office. Sara and I were discussing ideas we had to get him reelected. The incumbent is to anti-military for us never mind the danger that exposing our secret to others is. The problem is our government grant. Even if we spend our own money on our ideas, it'll look shady."

"I'll tell the president you want to help," Major Nelson said. "I'm sure he'll be glad to hear it. One of his campaign managers can meet with you or something. If your ideas are good, I'm sure his campaign can use them."

Oz cleared his throat, folded his hands, and stared at the ceiling. "If someone could, *um*, magically make the vote come out the way they wanted it to, I mean hypothetically, if you could rig the election without anyone knowing, would you do it?"

Major Nelson laughed. "No, he isn't a cheater." Then he frowned thoughtfully. "I don't know that I could say that about his competition. If he were cheating at the polls, it'd be good to expose him. I'm sure the president wouldn't condone cheating on his behalf though."

"Yeah, we didn't think so either." Oz heaved a heavy sigh. "We just need him to stay the president so much."

"Have his campaign manager call on us next week," Sara said. "We need to move on some of our ideas right away." Sara suddenly sat up straighter. "Oh yeah, I almost forgot. I have a list of names here for Pierce to check for me. I'm sure this list will grow. Potential students for next term for Oz and I not in the military. We plan on teaching them, then hiring from within them."

"I'll see that he gets it." Major Nelson placed the list in the folder before him.

"Does anyone have anything else they want to talk about?" Stasia asked after checking the time.

Charlie glanced around then rapped his knuckles on the table. "Meeting adjourned." Without fanfare, the meeting broke into small groups of people talking together and reviewing the recordings on their own screens. Charlie drew Sara aside into her office. "I love Stasia too, but we don't have to do this."

Sara hugged him tightly, shivering in his arms. "I don't want to do this. The thought of sharing you with Joy makes me sick, but we need to do it though."

Charlie sighed heavily. "I understand what you're saying, but I feel how it upsets you."

"Joy's the best choice for a first attempt." Sara kissed him, then snuggled her face into his neck. "I'm a crazy jealous person too," she said in a muffled voice. "I hate the thought that you might want her."

He slid his fingers through the thick weight of her hair and rested his palm on her skull, the heat from her body was reassuring as he pulled her closer and kissed her neck.

"I won't want her."

He wanted to say if he wanted Joy, it'd be for magic, but she knew that already, mentioning it wouldn't help.

Sara nodded against his shoulder.

"We can always put it off. There's no hurry after all," he said.

"Maybe," Sara agreed. "But there is sort of a hurry. Stasia really wants Rick's magic, and it will take at least six months before we even think about changing someone else after Joy, so the longer we wait, the longer she has too."

"Yeah, I understand that too, but..."

Sara interrupted. "I'm not being altruistic here, I'm being selfish. If her magic wants a warrior's magic, she could want you if she can't have Rick."

"*Hmm*, I never thought of that." Charlie's eyes narrowed. "She's shown no sign of wanting my magic."

"No, her magic hasn't mingled yet, but what if it does? We need to be ready. I'm hoping either Rick is changed or you're both out of school before it does. We can always move away from her. You'd be safe from her out of the zone." Sara shivered again. "I hate that I even think that, but I don't want to share you."

"Believe me, I understand." Charlie rubbed her back. "I don't want to share you either." Both were silent a few moments. "Stasia would be more dangerous to us than the raid is. You'd need to change one to share their magic, she could just do it. If she ever shows signs of taking mine, stop her. Don't let her touch me or me touch her."

Sara nodded again. Locked in an embrace worry echoed between them.

~ 11 ~

SUSPICIOUS INCOMPETENCE

The next afternoon Sara was again on the roof of her lab, but this time she was going over her notes on the classes she taught while eating her lunch. When the door to the roof opened, she glanced up in surprise. Charlie rarely got away from school until after six. Her eyes widened further at Susan Beck and she hit her alarm.

"How did you get in the building?" Sara asked in amazement.

"The dumb ass never took me off the visitor's list." Susan smirked and gestured to Sara's wristcomp. "Give it to me."

Sara laughed. "No."

Susan frowned. "Give me the wristcomp, bitch."

"No," Sara repeated. "Police are already on the way here."

"You'll be dead by the time they arrive!" Susan sneered and sauntered closer.

As soon as his alarm triggered Charlie ran from his classroom. Stasia and Hawk entered the hallway as he hit his audio. Linked with the other ones, his wristcomp let him hear what Susan said and Sara's reply. All three headed to the lab.

"What are you hoping to accomplish with all this?" Sara gestured around at the empty roof. "This is a securities firm and you've already been spotted by any number of cameras."

"I'm being paid a lot of money to use this." Susan held up what appeared to be a small hard drive. "If I'm caught here, I still get the money plus extra for every day I'm in jail, but I won't be caught. I couldn't care less who sees this face. This one job is enough to retire on."

"So, you're what, going to seduce me into installing it for you?" Sara asked sarcastically.

Susan stepped closer. "No, I'm going to make you do it. If you do it quickly, without causing me any trouble, you get to live. Keep giving me shit, and I'll kill you and do it myself."

"Did you ride the short bus to get here?" Sara asked snidely. "Obviously, if you could do it yourself, you would have. Therefore, you need me to do it, and I'm not going to. With no weapon— how will you force me to do it?"

"Who says I don't have a weapon?" Susan grinned, pulled out a switchblade, and flicked it open.

Sara rolled her eyes, took two steps forward, and kicked the knife from Susan's hand.

Susan gaped at her in amazement and reached for her other pocket.

"Don't." Sara sighed and rolled her eyes again, her hands on her hips. "Just don't. I don't want to hurt you, but if you pull another weapon on me, I will. Even if it's another lame-ass plastic one."

"I'll admit you surprised me." Susan cracked her knuckles and glared. "I thought you were the eye candy here. I guess it's time to get serious." Her hand darted into her coat pocket and emerged holding a small pistol.

"A plastic gun, really? It has what, one good shot in it before it blows off your hand? Your plan sucks. Who the hell would hire someone as incompetent as you?" Sara took a step closer.

"Stop where you are, or I'll shoot." Susan waved the gun and stepped back.

Sara halted and held out both hands, asking softly. "Will you shoot Tank and Rhea too?"

"And me?" Guthrie said from behind Susan.

Susan whipped around. Tank, Rhea and Guthrie stood behind her. As soon as she made eye contact both black shepherds began growling. Ruffs lifted and teeth showing, they separated and hunkered down, one going to each side. The dogs blue-eyed gazes were no longer friendly, but cold and feral.

Susan spun back to face Sara and found she'd retreated. One high-heeled foot stamped in frustration.

"Decide which one you're going to shoot while the other one attacks," Guthrie said as he stepped closer, pulling his own gun.

Susan spun again and backpedaled, trying to keep everyone in her sights. The gun in Susan's hand wavered as she shifted her aim on everyone before deciding and pointing at Guthrie. Both dogs snarled and lunged at her, and she screamed. Still shrieking, she changed her aim to Tank, Tank's magic forcing her to aim at him, but it was too late. Tank connected, hanging from her arm and shaking his head, biting down hard. Rhea snarled and bit Susan's other arm as she flailed, trying to get away from Tank.

Guthrie plucked the gun from her. "Stop moving and they'll let go."

Both dogs tugged, and Susan fell to her knees, screaming shrilly.

"Tank, Rhea, release." Guthrie snapped his fingers. The two dogs released Susan and crouched before the sergeant with their hackles raised and bloody teeth showing as they snarled. "You have ten seconds to get face down on the ground or they attack again, and this time I won't call them off."

Susan dropped to the ground, curled into a ball, and sobbed.

"I think we need some girl time here, Sarge." Sara poked Susan with one sneakered foot and gestured Guthrie to the door. "Okay, it's just you, me, Tank and Rhea," Sara said as soon as the sergeant left the roof. She pulled Susan up by her shirt front and grinned at her. "As you can guess, I really don't like you." Sara snapped her fingers, and the dogs rushed to her snapping and growling. "Who was paying you?" Sara's eyes narrowed as Susan glared. Sara nodded to the dogs. "Tank, attack!"

Tank snarled and lunged.

Susan screamed and cowered as Tank grabbed her arm again, this time by the sleeve and shook his head hard. "I don't know. It's a blind drop to protect client confidentiality. I'm being paid in installments," Susan gasped between sobs.

Charlie waited by the door, his confusion echoing with Sara's. If this was meant as a real attack it was wildly inept. One woman armed or not would pose no threat to any of them. He hung back hoping Sara had a plan.

Sara snapped her fingers and Tank dropped Susan's arm and returned to Sara where he hunkered down, growling low in his throat. "Rhea isn't as well trained as Tank, so I'm not sure I can call her off." Sara released Susan's shirt and sat back on her heels, tapping her bottom lip. "Tell me everything, email addresses, payment methods, your real name, and I won't tell her to attack."

"You really are a bitch." Susan sat up, cradling her bitten arm.

Sara nodded and smiled at Stasia who was invisible behind Susan. "I'm counting to three here." Sara began to count.

Susan shook her head. Blood dripped from her arm between the fingers clenching the wound. "My name is Ingra Hedberg, and I'm twenty-eight. Originally, I'm from Sweden, but I work internationally."

"As a spy?" One eyebrow rose, and Sara examined Susan with pursed lips. A glance at Stasia who appeared doubtful with her own lips pursed and eyebrows raised as she shook her head, and Sara snorted a laugh.

Ingra said, "Yes, this was supposed to be an easy gig. Seduce a nineteen-year-old boy, I mean, anyone could do it."

"Anyone except you, apparently," Sara agreed with a real smile.

"I could do it. I just rushed it, but that tactic almost always works. Boys and men always try to one up each other."

"So, you seduce Oz to what end?"

"To plant this here in a computer." Ingra held up the portable hard drive. "I looked around and didn't see any computers, but I figured you must know where they are." Ingra glared at Sara, glancing around as if she expected a computer to be on the roof.

"How did you know where I was?"

"Hawk told me you're alone up here all the time."

Stasia winced.

Sara grimaced. "And then?"

"I came here hoping he'd made arrangements for me to visit, which he had. So, I just came in."

A smug smile on her face, Susan grinned at Sara then winced and glanced away, the smile changing to a frown as she used her shirt tail to staunch the blood running down her arm. "The metal detectors missed my weapons. If you didn't have the damn watch—"

Sara stood and put her hands on her hips, her eyes narrowing. "You knew I had the wristcomp and how they work. You saw Oz use his."

Susan shrugged. "I thought you were the girlfriend and didn't realize you'd have access to the technology."

Sara sighed. "One more lie, and I let Rhea go."

"The police must be here now, you can't." A grin on the corner of her mouth, Susan glanced up.

"Rhea at—"

"Wait!" Susan yelled. "Yes, I realized you worked here, but thought I could intimidate you easily, and you'd give me your wristcomp. Then I'd make you put this on one of the computers."

"What would be the point? Or were you planning to kill me so no one would notice it was there?"

Susan smirked. "No, my orders are to just connect it; it didn't need to stay. I assume there's a virus on it or something."

"I doubt any of that is true." Sara petted Rhea's head and the dog's hackles lowered. "Give me every email address you own."

A flick of Sara's wrist opened a flat screen display. Another screen popped up beside the first. Oz already had a search program running, finding everything he could about the name Susan had given.

Sara entered Susan's email address and hacked her account, a garbage account with no useful information. "Sarge, we need a clear fingerprint. The police will believe the dogs protected me. Why save her if she won't answer the questions? Let the dogs kill her. Is all we need is one finger."

Susan stared at Sara and licked her lips. Her gaze darted over the dogs. Before she made up her mind to speak, Guthrie returned and took a fingerprint and then patted her down, removing a cell phone that he handed to Sara. In the doorway, he passed Charlie.

Charlie gave Sara a kiss then zip-tied Susan's hands and feet and slapped quick bandages on the dog bites while Sara plopped down in the lawn chair and went to work on the phone.

Once Charlie immobilized Susan to his satisfaction, he gave Sara a longer kiss and grinned at her.

"You're so bloodthirsty. I love that about you." His gaze swung to Susan who sniffled on the ground, rubbing her nose on her shoulder, her terrified gaze locked on Charlie. A thoughtful frown on his face, he sat in the other lawn chair and opened a flat screen on his wristcomp.

"Oz has her real name, Ingra Arnault, twenty-six from Massachusetts. Let's see— what else… high school records where she did poorly, and look, she attended community college for one year and studied acting before flunking out. No jobs since she was eighteen when she worked at McDonald's for four months and he's found three bank accounts so far, mostly empty."

Charlie snorted and glanced at Susan. "No account has anywhere near enough money to retire on. Aren't you the trusting fool? How did you plan on making them pay you when you're in jail?"

Ingra glared at them as a red flush climbed up her neck.

Sara winked at Charlie, her fingers flying over the keyboard. "Oh nice, she can go now. The cellphone gave me everything I need. You truly are an idiot, breaking in here with your cell phone on you. Enjoy Guantanamo." A satisfied smile on her face, Sara gave a little finger wave as Guthrie returned and pulled Susan to her feet.

"Guantanamo?" Susan squinted back over her shoulder as Guthrie pulled her from the roof.

"What you just did was an act of war against the United States. We work on government security's here, so they can hold you indefinitely."

Sara snickered as Susan protested at the top of her lungs.

"Can they really?" Charlie glanced at Sara in surprise.

"Don't know, don't care. Let her worry about it," Sara said absently as she entered data into her computer. A moment later she hit her panic button opening all wristcomps. "Two wildly incompetent attacks in one week can't be coincidence. Something larger must be at play here. To combat it, we should change our routine drastically. If these are staged attacks, they must be to get a reaction from us. The most likely response is what we've done already, gathered together. I think we need to separate. If enemy X knows about our raid composition, group three will be perceived as our weakest group because they spend the least amount of time with us. Manny, be especially alert. Every group sweep for bugs, bombs, and anything else you can think of. Contact your loved ones and make sure everyone is accounted for. Warn everybody something is going on and to stay alert."

"What do you think this is about?" Major Nelson asked.

"I have no idea."

She rubbed her eyes as she sighed, and Charlie winced in sympathy. She was annoyed, worried and afraid. She gave him a reassuring smile and her feelings dimmed as she straightened in her seat. He frowned, not knowing if she were blocking them from him or herself or if she felt better.

She shrugged lightly and said, "But, I'm sure it's something. Oz and I will search for a connection. No way are two such incompetent attacks unrelated, so we need to break our pattern."

Charlie frowned at Sara. "Maybe that's what enemy X wants us to do."

"It could be," Sara admitted. "We need more information. Both attacks had Oz, and I targeted, which makes me believe you, Stasia, and Hawk, are the real target. I think someone is watching to see if, how, and when you come to our defense."

"Could Ned Font be part of that?" Oz asked thoughtfully. "Ned came out of nowhere and hounded you into changing your pattern."

"Look him up; check his finances and bug his house and office." Sara opened another screen with her wristcomp and contemplated the raids' position. "Randomize the raid. Split yourselves up and stay somewhere else for at least one week. Stasia, you and Hawk need to change your pattern. Hawk, stop coming at the same time of day to see Tank."

Sara paused when Hawk didn't reply. Charlie leapt to his feet. The sudden surge of fear from Sara took him by surprise. The room gained clarity and he knew his eyes had flared blue. He wished he had his sword.

"Hawk?" Eyes huge in a suddenly pale face, Sara flipped her wrist, and another screen opened. A moment of typing and the screen showed the interior view of the room he and Stasia were in. "Damn, Hawk isn't there just his wristcomp is. Stasia, did you see him leaving?" Sara ran the security recording back, keying on

Hawk. Hawk had thrown his wristcomp down and stormed out after Susan had said he'd let her in.

"Oh, thank god. He left on his own. Should I summon him back here?"

"Yes," Major Nelson said. "That could be what enemy X was waiting for."

"Okay, I'll summon him in a minute. When he arrives, he'll be upset and need a few minutes to calm down. Get started checking everything, every single piece of gear, all vehicles, all apartments, everything. As soon as we find out anything more, I'll send a notice." Sara canceled her raid wide call and summoned Hawk.

Hawk appeared before her with the rest of Team Valor. Before he could say a word, Sara and Stasia hugged him. Charlie relaxed his tense shoulders and slapped Hawk's shoulder.

"Never do that again, I was so worried!" Muffled in his chest, Sara's voice was indistinct. "If you need alone time say so and keep your wristcomp on."

Hawk stood stiff and unresponsive in her embrace.

Sara released him and stepped back. "Are you mad at me? I'm sorry I was so mean to her. I was just trying to get some truth from her. I wouldn't really have killed her." Tears filled her eyes when Hawk continued to glare.

Charlie stepped forward again to comfort Sara who now felt guilty and nervous.

Hawk gave Sara a quick hug then turned away. "I'm not angry at you. This is all too much— girlfriends who are spies trying to kill you. I can't believe I forgot to take her off the damn list." Hawk spun away and paced, slamming his fist into his hand.

Stasia bit her lip, her troubled gaze following her brother's angry movements.

"We all forgot." Oz clapped Hawk on the shoulder and then embraced him. "It's been a hell of a week, I agree, but we've had worse."

The unhappy scowl on Hawk's face deepened. "That doesn't make this better, it makes it worse. I need a break from this. I need the forest and clean air and to be alone. Please, don't summon me again unless it's an emergency."

"Okay," Sara agreed instantly. "You should know what we've found out and what we think first though. Hawk, she was a bad person who took advantage of you. None of us blame you in any way. We love you. Go to the forest but please keep your wristcomp on."

For a moment Hawk covered his face with his hands before rubbing his cheeks hard. Then he heaved a heavy sigh, put his wristcomp on, and stalked from the room. Stasia followed him out while the rest of them exchanged uneasy glances.

"I'll disguise myself as him," Oz said. "If he isn't back by tomorrow, Sara can be him while I teach my class, then I'll be him again while she teaches hers."

Stasia returned and slouched in the seat beside Charlie.

"I'll be him until bedtime." Sara exchanged a determined glance with Oz. "You be him at night. Everyone has a weekend pass already, so we only have to do this for two days. Wear the voice modulator. Charlie and Stasia, keep the stickycoms on in case we need an answer we don't have."

"Won't you lose the disguise when you fall asleep?" Stasia asked.

"I don't think so, but if I do, I'll just recast it when I wake." Oz gave a small shrug. "I'll set my wristcomp to wake me thirty minutes before his roommates get up and I'll make sure they're sleeping before I sleep."

Stasia nodded. "We could ask the major to get him permission."

"We will if we don't think we can pull this off." Sara knelt beside Stasia and hugged her with one arm. "Let's try first. The major won't understand his need for the forest and will want him back here."

"I'll call the major now and tell him Hawk is here and fixed the wristcomps to show him as being here," Oz said. "I'll meet you downstairs after I get some stuff from my office." He left the room already calling Major Nelson.

Sara gave Stasia another hug. "Hawk will be back soon."

Stasia nodded and leaned forward, hiding her face in her knees. "I know how he feels. I want to get away from all this as well sometimes." Muffled and low her voice shook with distress.

Charlie put a hand on Sara's shoulder; her growing worry matched his. "This is overwhelming to all of us at times. Maybe we need more time apart. We spend all of our free time together." He tightened his grip on Sara as her anxiety spiked.

Stasia shrugged, straightening and wiping her eyes. "We have so much to do together and so little free time."

"After this crisis, we'll work out a schedule. All of this can wait." Charlie waved a hand indicating Valor Industries. "School is the priority. We need to pace ourselves better so these situations don't burn us out." He pulled Sara from Stasia and embraced her. Her worry was now fear. "Not us," he murmured as he kissed her temple.

Stasia smiled wanly at them. "I'll meet you downstairs. Just another damn bump in the road, and we'll work this out."

Charlie kept Sara in his arms. "Never us. I'll never tire of you or need a break. Never think that."

Relieved, she kissed him and rested her face against his. "It's still hard deciphering what you feel sometimes. I love you so much."

Charlie kissed her again. Sadness darkened her brightness. "What are you sad about?"

"Hawk, Stasia, this situation. I can't wait for Friday night. I want to be alone with you, just us with nowhere we need to be and feel you relaxed and comfortable beside me." Her breath hitched, and she held him tighter. "Now I'm sad because I miss you."

Charlie was torn, duty required him to return to his dorm, his heart wanted him to stay and comfort her. He stayed and held her.

A few minutes later she pulled away. "Come see me as soon as you can tomorrow, please."

"I will," he agreed huskily and needed to clear his throat. "You mean the world to me. I can quit if this is too much. The separation is almost too much for me."

Tears leaked from her eyes and she wiped them away with the back of her hand. "We can do this." Filled with determination, she stepped away from him. "Tomorrow."

Unhappy, he paused in the doorway and glanced back. "I love you."

After Charlie left, Sara went to her office and used the bed in her pullout couch and cried herself to sleep, trying not to worry about making Charlie miserable.

Charlie knew she was worried and crying, and it did make him miserable.

- 12 -

TIME SINK

Paul glanced up from the book in front of him as Charlie flopped into his desk chair and rubbed his face. "Rough night?"

"Someone tried to kill Sara, so yeah, it was rough." Unable to sit still he rose and began removing his uniform. "I hate leaving her alone."

"Jesus, for real? Right here on campus?" Book forgotten, Paul stood, laying a hand on Charlie's shoulder as Dave and Jeff turned to them in astonishment.

"Yeah, Tank was a hero. Sara could've handled it alone. I just hate that she has to."

"What the hell is going on?" Paul frowned and spun away, turning to the window and gazing out. "First your house burns to the ground and now someone what, sneaks into your lab and tries to kill Sara?"

"Sara doesn't think it's a coincidence either, but we don't know." Charlie hung his uniform up and donned his sweats. "I'm sure Guthrie is reporting to the commandant as we speak but keep this quiet until he makes an official statement."

The next morning at breakfast the commandant appeared. Everyone stood at attention when he entered the cafeteria.

He said, "A serious incident occurred on campus yesterday. The Valor building was entered by what is thought to be a corporate spy. A woman posing as a guest tried to force Doctor Mitchel to reveal classified work at gunpoint and was subdued by Doctor Mitchel's guard dog and her security team. We don't believe there's any danger to our student body, but everyone needs to stay alert. If you notice anything out of the ordinary, report it at once to your commanders.

"Those of you who take classes there remain vigilant. This is a naval base. Many situations like this will happen in your careers. Enemies will infiltrate using both covert and overt methods; use this as a learning opportunity.

"Doctor Mitchel is here as a civilian under our protection. Our duty is to protect her despite the risk to ourselves. Every one of you has sworn an oath to that effect. This is what we do as naval officers." The commandant surveyed the silent midshipmen and nodded in a satisfied way. "Carry on."

A babble of talk broke out as soon as the commandant left the room. Charlie's battalion commander sat by him. Charlie told him the same story he'd told Paul. "Sara is fine, completely unharmed, but a bit shaken. The woman is in custody with some nasty dog bites."

"How did she get a gun past the detectors?"

"A plastic gun. Oz is tracking the gun manufacture. The security system notified the guards as soon as she pulled the first weapon. She tried to scare Sara into cooperating with her." Anger cause his skin to flush and Charlie took a moment to breathe deeply before his eyes flared blue.

His commander looked angry too. "Doctor Mitchel is okay though, right?"

"Physically she's fine but emotionally..." Charlie trailed off. "I hate leaving her alone. Sara has no safe place now."

His commander nodded and slapped his back as he rose. "We'll do our best to see that she's safe here." After giving Charlie a tight smile, he left to speak with the commander of a different battalion.

Oz attended breakfast as Hawk then slipped away and traded places with Sara. She attended Hawk's morning classes. Before lunch she met Oz in the bathroom, and they switched places so she could go teach her classes.

Oz disguised himself as Hawk after casting invisible on Sara and she ran back to the lab. Two midshipmen sat on benches outside the building. Both rose and approached the door when it opened and no one emerged.

With a quick glance to make sure she wouldn't be seen, she knelt in the corner and broke her invisible with a cast. "I'm looking for my cat," she said as she opened the door again. "Have you seen her by any chance? A fluffy white cat with blue eyes." A flush heated her cheeks as she exited and called Lucky for a moment.

The two boys followed her. "No, ma'am, but we'll keep an eye out."

Sara thanked them and hurried to her classroom. Her students were extra polite and attentive. After the third yes ma'am, Sara sat in her chair with a thump and blew off the hair that fell across her brow. "So, you heard then? You're safe here." She hesitated and then approached Amy, Stasia's roommate. "Was Stasia very upset last night?"

Amy nodded. "She's worried. We're all worried. This is the second attempt in a week."

Sara considered her class. "From the evidence, they don't appear to be related. I admit it's one hell of a coincidence. Especially as both attempts were completely inept. I don't think any of you are in danger here."

"We aren't worried about ourselves. We're worried for you and Doctor Simmons," Amy said.

"Oz and I are being careful. Don't worry about us." A light blush on her cheekbones, Sara returned to the front of the class and turned on the big display with a voice command. "This test pattern identifies if all connections are done correctly. This is the first diagnostic."

She continued with her lesson and her students listened attentively. Most of them worked at Valor Industries in their free time. Forty-five minutes later she glanced at her wristcomp. "Okay, we're ending the lesson a few minutes early. I wanted to talk with everyone for a few minutes. This is about the game, not school related. You can go if you have no interest."

A tap on her screen opened a new picture on the monitor. "We've decided to move ahead and really push the game. These are the potential designs for the console. If you like one, vote on Oz's website for the final design."

"What I wanted to talk to everyone about is the programming." Sara perched on the edge of her desk. "We'll be hiring civilian programmers, but any of you who want to work on it in your free time contact either Oz or I and we can work something out. We want to make it clear we don't want you to resign from the service. The Navy will need good programmers who understand the new system. You know we design security. What you might not be aware of is we also design weaponry that uses the same system."

An excited babble erupted over that and she waited a moment for it to die down. "Our designs are still in research right now and won't be available for a while, but everything we work on uses this computer language and similar hardware. Everything we do here is classified. I wish I could tell you more, but I can't. What I can tell you is your country will need you in the future. Any experience you get with Oz's computers will be valuable. The VI website has information on the pay scale for programming work, and you can fill out applications there. The commandant has given us provisional permission to hire from the school as he believes the work experience will be good for you. Midshipman will be hired over civilians, but only on a part time basis, and your GPA must remain constant. This is unfair to you, but we'll never hire any of you fulltime. We in no way want to encourage you to leave the Navy."

Amy laughed. "Not even when we retire?"

"Okay, I'll add in a service clause. If you retire after your tours are up, you can work for us." Sara grinned at Amy, who was her artist. "Any original work will receive credit. If you have your own game idea and need help, just ask." Sara opened the door, signaling the end of her class.

"Did you find Lucky?" Amy asked as she waited for her classmates to leave.

Sara glanced away. "Not yet. I'm sure she's around here somewhere though."

"You should microchip her. If she was chipped, the sensors could locate her instantly inside this building."

"I'll have Oz make one for her." Sara cleared her throat and changed the subject. "We need to meet in person and talk about our zone, but my schedule is crazy right now. Email me some good times for you, and I'll see what I can work in."

"I got your email about the first zone being cheaper than the others, and I agree it's still a good one. Being the only level, it'll get a lot more promotion time. The first level will become the meeting place because most people will build there, so merchandising will remain strong for that level, which should make up for the initial lower cost."

"We have so much to talk about." Sara sighed, rubbing her temples. "I'm sure if the game is even a quarter as successful as I think it'll be, we'll do more zones, but it'll still be an initial financial loss for you." They both moved out of the way of Sara's incoming students.

"Sorry, Amy, I have no time to talk now. Email me and I'll get back to you as soon as I can." She gave Amy a quick hug and hurried to the front of her classroom. After the lesson, she repeated the speech about hiring.

At four p.m., her classes were over and she was starving. The small refrigerator in her office held a yogurt and an apple. Apple in hand, she ran to meet Oz, chewing as she ran.

He disguised her as Hawk and she attended the rest of his classes, then dinner where she sat beside Charlie and kept her eyes down, trying to be inconspicuous. Stasia sat on the other side of her, fielding all questions.

Charlie left with Paul after slapping her shoulder and saying, "Later, Hawk."

Sara stared after him, watching him stop and talk with a group of boys until Stasia poked her. Blushing, Sara hurriedly looked away and headed to the Valor building. Hawk had a free period and often came to the lab to see Tank during it.

Sara knocked on Oz's office door.

"Come on in. Hawk hasn't called," Oz said before she could ask.

Sara slumped into the chair in front of his desk and broke the disguise spell with a flick of her fingers. "I'm feeling a bit overwhelmed myself. So much is going on I don't know where to start."

"I think everybody is." Oz leaned back and put his feet on the desk. "Everyone should have replacement gear within a week; my dad is prioritizing it. The backup sets are in storage at the hanger. Marcus checked them and they're untouched. So far, everything the Scouts have checked is clear. Maybe it was a coincidence."

Sara blew a strand of hair from her face and leaned back in the chair.

"Yeah, I don't think it was either," Oz admitted. "I've spent all afternoon going through everything looking for a link and can't find one. There's so much information to go through, with so many leads, it will take us a few months at least."

"That's it!" Sara bolted upright. "That's the link. The attacks are time sinks. What would we be doing if we weren't doing this?"

Oz's expression lightened and he leaned forward. "Well, you would've gone to MIT to talk to those professors. I probably would've gone too. Let's see, I was working on the ray-gun. We were both working on the presidential campaign."

"The campaign." Eyes bright, Sara leaned forward in her chair. "It's the campaign. None of these attacks came close to harming us, ergo the attacker wants us unharmed. Who would want us unharmed? Someone who wants to use us. No one knows about the magical research I was doing. Even if they saw the white boards, I doubt anyone could make sense of it except us. So, it wasn't that. The ray-gun, well, maybe. Visits to other professors, highly unlikely. The campaign, yes."

Sara stood and paced. "If you were the president's opponent, you'd investigate everything he's done, looking for a weakness to exploit. So, you look and find us. Five kids he's gone out of his way to help. You realize we're smart. You learn about the security devices and find out everything you can about us, hoping there'll be something to leverage in the polls and then you realize you can't afford to alienate us. Our ideas are too new, too big. Mr. X doesn't know about the magic but realizes Alpha and Beta are our private guards."

"Yes," Oz dropped his feet to the floor and swung side-to-side in his swivel chair. "You then realize we like the president and you start to worry. What if these super smart people help him win?"

"No, it has to be more than that." Sara spun to face him. "What if these super smart people find out something I don't want them to? There must be something, and it must be big, and it must be something we might stumble on working on the campaign."

"How does Mr. X know we like the president?" Oz lifted an eyebrow.

"Someone told him, or he saw something that makes him believe it, or he doesn't know, but he assumes when we uncover what we shouldn't discover we'll tell the president." Sara sat again with a thump and leaned back in her chair. "The huge loan would be a big clue. I'm sure it can be traced to presidential influence."

"Someone told him, or he saw something, implies someone in the president's confidence, or at the very least, presence regularly."

Sara nodded.

"We could back track the connection through all of this information. Mr. X can't know how smart we are or all our resources."

Sara nodded again.

"The fact that he tried to distract us indicates we were close to discovery."

"If Ned Font is distraction number one, then the day we got home from the *Truman*. He was taking pictures five days later." Sara closed her eyes and leaned back in the chair, thinking hard.

"As a distraction it worked, we left town. What happened here that week?"

"Whatever it was, it occurred again last week." Oz turned his screen to flattop display and started typing.

"Leave no traces, Oz. Mr. X is throwing softballs now, and we don't want a hardball."

"Until we have proof, tell Team Valor only." Oz typed as he spoke, flicking through screens and taking notes. "The raid can follow these leads while we pretend distraction."

"We need to speak with the president privately," Sara said. "He could plant misinformation, and we could find Mr. X fast that way."

"We need misinformation to plant and a way to contact him."

Sara grimaced. "I'll go make another skin wristcomp. I can have it ready by Saturday night. We'll sneak into the White House and give it to him. Start thinking of a story."

"One problem," Oz said as Sara rose. "We already told Major Nelson to speak with the president about meeting a campaign manager. Mr. X is bound to hear that. I expect a hardball will be thrown."

"He'll try to kill us?" Sara asked in a shaky voice.

"It seems likely." Oz hesitated. "Or Charlie— if he killed Charlie..."

"God," Sara sank into her seat shaking. "Yes, it'd be as good as killing me, but it leaves the potential of using me in the future." She answered her wristcomp, "I'm fine. Come as soon as you can and stay alert. We need to talk. I love you."

Charlie hung up, tapped the stickycom behind his ear, turning it off, and glanced at the clock. Thirty minutes remained before he could go to her. She was scared; whatever she had to say wouldn't be good.

When the class ended, Charlie hurried from the room.

Paul followed. "Is everything okay?" Paul glanced at Charlie's white face and sweaty brow and tightened his lips.

"No, I'm worried about Sara. Sorry, Paul, I gotta run. We'll talk later." Charlie slapped Paul's back in farewell and ran across the Yard.

- 13 -

SNIPER

Charlie found Sara in her lab, harvesting her own skin. The process revolted him. She hated to do it too, and he was surprised she was doing it already. She'd just finished making a wristcomp right before the last meeting. When he entered, she flared up blue all over.

"Go see Oz. He can explain. I need a few minutes to get this under control." One hand waved around her, indicating both the skin sample and the magic. "I'm really worried, but I'll be fine," she added reassuringly as he hesitated.

He scowled and headed upstairs to Oz.

"Okay, I see the logic." Charlie leaned back in the chair and stretched, then shook his shoulders, trying to relieve the tension. "What do we do about it though?"

"The first thing we do is change all our plans for the weekend. The second thing we do is pretend great distraction."

"How exactly do we do that?"

Oz stood and grabbed a stack of folders from the table behind him then thumped down in his chair again. "Reports, lots of them. Enough reports that it seems like we're very busy writing them."

Despite himself a small snort of laughter escaped. "We would have to be to write them."

Oz rolled his eyes at him. "We won't write them, we ask our friends to, very quietly.

"The third thing we do is change your routine enough to protect you without looking like we are. Change where you sit in class. Walk with a different group to class. Go to class early or late or skip completely."

"I can't skip my physics class, there's a major test on Fridays."

"Sara will go to that class and shield you. If I was trying to kill you, that's when I'd do it, when I knew exactly where you'd be. What other classes would you never miss?"

"Well, all of them. I'm never late and never miss them, but that one is the only one with a regular test date. I have a test in history tomorrow too. It's posted on the teacher's website."

"She'll go to that one too." Oz tapped the air in front of him on his holographic keyboard and brought up a copy of Charlie's schedule. "She'll steal Stasia's invis towmorrow and follow you. Sara already has permission to attend any class she wishes and can sit in the back of the classroom out of sight of the two you have tests in. When you guys leave Friday, we're going to a random hotel. If anyone asks, the stress is too much so we're getting away for the weekend. If someone does plan a hit they'll have to strike before we go. Drew will be in a helicopter ready to go. Glen will have Alpha team on board suited up waiting."

"And Joy?"

"I don't know." Oz leaned back in his chair and flicked his fingers, closing the screens. "I think we need to put it off."

"What if that's the goal?"

"Then we have very serious problems. That means Mr. X knows everything about us."

"He might."

Oz looked extremely unhappy. "The evidence suggests he doesn't, but I admit the evidence is most likely planted for us to find."

"We change Joy, but not on the boat." Blue filled Charlie's eyes as his magic pushed. Anger at the thought of an unknown enemy and fear for Sara causing it to manifest. A moment of controlled breathing and decisive action soothed it. "Find a good spot, Oz. Get us the gear discreetly. We can summon Liz to us. And make sure our wristcomps are secure."

"I've checked and rechecked, and I'm certain no one is listening over the satellites. I can't guarantee one of the raid isn't copying our public transmissions on purpose. No one has sent anything using the wristcomps."

"I don't suspect them of transmitting data, but being bugged," Charlie said.

"We've swept for bugs, and I can see anything the wristcomps send or receive, it's all good." Oz paused thoughtfully. "A voice activated recording device left in a room then picked up later would work, but I doubt it would catch too much, and the Scouts searched. I find it hard to believe they could miss it."

"You wouldn't miss it. Run a locate for recorders. Stop once you leave the buildings." Charlie paced to the window and stared out over the peaceful grounds.

Sara came in as Oz left, following his locate spell.

"It's okay, a plan's in place already." Charlie hugged her, forcing his magic back from her, and told her the plan.

Sara nodded against his shoulder. "We'll cancel our classes. Oz can be Hawk all day. Who will we ask to write the bogus reports?"

"Paul and Amy. I'll call him now and ask him to come over." Charlie took a minute to rest his hand on her heart, letting the steady beat reassure the magic.

Sara did the same to him. Worried blue eyes met his. "Fine, I'll call Amy."

They met them downstairs at the entrance and took them to Sara's office where she told them her theory of distraction. Magic wasn't mentioned or alluded to.

Sara sat on the couch beside Amy. "We need help. If our guards are being watched, we need them kept busy too. We need you guys to write reports for us. The reports don't need to be brilliant, just time consuming so we appear busy and distracted."

Charlie sat on the arm of the couch beside his wife. "I'll give you all the data we have now, and I'll forward any new data we receive to you."

Amy's hazel eyes narrowed and lines formed on her brow as her knee jittered. "I can run the program myself if I had access to it."

"Use one of the prototype wristcomps. You know how they work. Oz will give you access." Sara placed her gloved hand on Amy's jittering knee. "If we're right, this could be dangerous for you. Don't get caught. No one can find out you're helping us."

Paul said, "If you're right, it's likely Chief is the next target, and someone will really try to kill him." He rose and stared out the windows with his hands clenched behind his back. "I don't like risking him this way."

"Me either." Sara hugged Charlie, resting her cheek on his chest. "One more day of classes. Oz and I will work on this all weekend. If we don't get a better idea or any leads, we'll do something else next week. If you guys send in reports as us, it'll give us time to track down Mr. X while he thinks we're busy elsewhere."

"How?" Amy asked

"I'm sorry, but I can't tell you because what I'm going to use to do so is classified." Sara sat beside Amy again, met her eyes, and folded her hands in her lap. "I trust you with my life, with Charlie's life, but I can't tell anyone about it."

Amy nodded as her knee stopped jittering and her face relaxed. "Fair enough, I trust you have a plan. I'll help. Give me the information, and I'll go write reports."

"I will too," Paul added hastily.

"Thanks, Amy." Sara hugged her and then went to her desk to retrieve the wristcomps. She removed two and spent a few minutes programming them and then introduced the wristcomps to Paul and Amy. "I'm sending you the files we have. Show Paul how to use the wristcomp. Send copies of the reports to Major Nelson, Master Sergeant Guthrie, and Agent Lewis. The contact information is in an email I'm sending you. If you happen across any real information, send it to Charlie, me or Oz."

Amy and Paul left together.

"The skin has to cure," Sara said.

His lip curled in disgust. Hers did too.

"I don't like it either," she assured him. "No luck yet on an artificial replacement but we're close. We've almost gotten the gains ironed out."

She waved a dismissive hand. "I'll need to make another extra one soon, and my regular two for the month so we have a backup one for emergencies like this."

Charlie hugged her tighter. "I'm sick of emergencies like this!" Without speaking they stood locked in an embrace. "We should call Hawk," Charlie finally said.

"He's fine and hidden. We need him, but he needs the forest. Let's give him until Friday night at least."

"Stasia is here."

"Oz will fill her in." Sara tightened her grip on him.

Charlie rubbed her back and kissed her neck in her favorite spot. It didn't get the usual reaction; it made her cry. Fear for him edged her brightness in black. A shiver went through her as she pressed harder against him.

"I'll be fine." He slipped his hands under her shirt and rubbed her bare back. She relaxed against him, but her fear for him didn't ebb. "Don't worry so much, I won't be easy to kill."

She nodded against his shoulder and kept a tight hold on him.

They stood together until he had to return to the dorm. Sara walked him out where Stasia and Oz waited. Sara hugged Stasia. "You're all in danger. I think the most likely target is Charlie. Oz is a possibility, but Mr. X appears to not want to harm us just slow us down, so it's not as likely. Stasia, you and Hawk are more likely targets if the goal is to disrupt Oz and I. Oz has warned his father to stay in a secure location. Your mother will be staying in our lab. You three are at serious risk. Mr. X could know the entire truth."

"We'll be careful." A blue glow lit Stasia's eyes. "Hawk is safer where he is."

At arm's length with both hands resting on Stasia's shoulders, Sara searched her face. "I agree. Let him stay in the forest until we go tomorrow night."

The glow receded, and a frown formed on Stasia's brow. "Hawk could stay in the woods until Sunday. We can infiltrate without him."

"Call him tomorrow night. Let him decide. He'll want to come." Charlie gave Stasia a quick one-armed hug.

Sara, Oz disguised as Hawk, Tank and Rhea walked to the dorm with them. Sara nodded a greeting to the two midshipmen sitting on the benches studying right outside the main entrance of the Valor building. The two midshipmen followed behind them, giving them space to talk privately.

"Different midshipmen sat by the door all day," Sara whispered as she glanced back at the trailing midshipmen.

"I think they're guarding us." Oz smiled at her and tweaked her ponytail.

Sara grimaced. "Is that safe for them?"

"I don't think they care." Oz shrugged. "They realize something's going on."

Oz handed Charlie a small sensor. "Stay away from windows. Eat nothing that could've been tampered with. Place the sensor on the door frame. If your door opens, your Valory will wake you. Tonight, search for anything we could be being distracted from with emphasis on the campaign."

"No one stay up too late. We need to be alert tomorrow," Stasia said as they reached the dorm entrance.

The two midshipmen joined them.

"Is everything okay?" one asked.

"Sara is worried about us. Could you see her back to the lab for me?" Charlie asked.

"Of course. Ma'am?" The other midshipman indicated he'd follow her.

"Just Sara is fine. Thanks for the escort. I'm sure I'm safe here though," Sara said as she walked away from her friends.

Charlie relaxed as he went to his room. His classmates liked her, and she liked them. Her tension had eased now that she knew his classmates were looking out for them too.

When he came in he found Paul working on a report, breaking down one of the many computer viruses the hard drive that Susan had brought to the lab contained. Jeff and Dave sat at their desks studying.

Charlie said, "I'm placing a sensor on the door. If it opens, my Valory will notify us. Sara is afraid for my safety, so I told her I'd use it to ease her mind. She could be right. There might be danger for you, sharing my room."

"We've known that since freshman year, and you're stuck with us." Paul slapped Charlie's back and hopped into his bed. He pulled up the flat screen feature and continued to work on his report.

Charlie changed and jumped into bed and used his wristcomp to check Sara's position and then the rest of the raid. Everyone was where they should be. He ran a web search for the local papers and started reading back issues and taking notes. At lights out, he put his screen away and lay in the slight glow of Paul's screen, thinking. When he woke in the morning, Paul was up typing on his computer.

"You haven't stayed up all night, I hope?"

"No, I slept, and studied for our physics test." Paul glanced up a moment. "Don't worry about me. You stay alert."

Sara was outside in gym clothes when he attended morning PE. She did the exercises with them and then left. For morning formation, she wore a normal outfit. A white button-down shirt, navy blue khakis, and black shoes with her hair in a bun on the nap of her neck, she stood beside him, invisible to everyone else. All day long she trailed behind him, her anxiety escalating his.

In his history class, she walked in visible and set a small round globe on the windowsill and sat in the back of the class visible to everyone. The professor teaching the class nodded to her and she shook his hand before returning to her chosen corner where she opened her flat screen display and viewed it during the class.

Charlie grinned when Paul sent in another report as Oz. Hopefully, Mr. X would think Oz was busy combing through the mountain of data and that's why he'd canceled his classes.

Sara left after the history class, found Stasia, and stole her invisible again. She followed Charlie everywhere staying invisible. After lunch, she broke the spell and went to his physics class visible. She placed the round glass globe on the windowsill and again sat in a corner after greeting his professor.

Fifteen minutes into the class Sara said loudly, "No one panics or looks at the window. You're naval officers and I expect professional behavior here. Charlie, put your screen against the far wall as far to the left as it will go."

"Hurry, Oz!" she said in aside. "When I say down, hit the deck. Be as fast as you can. You have less than two seconds to get out of the bullet's path."

She talked to Oz again as Charlie's screen showed a man on a rooftop assembling a gun with practiced movements. "Guthrie is bringing Rhea and the teams. Catch this guy, Oz."

Charlie couldn't hear Oz's reply, if any. His classmates fidgeted and stole glances at the window. As discreetly as he could he tapped the stickycom behind his right ear to activate it.

Sara turned to the professor. "Can you tell the teacher next door to get his class on the ground right now?"

The sniper on the screen adjusted his sights. "Not from here."

Sara glanced at Paul and then turned her attention to the screen before her, her fingers flying over the virtual keyboard. "Paul, raise your hand and ask to use the bathroom. Walk out calmly, tell the teacher next door his class needs to stay in the room, but get them low and out of the path of Charlie. If he's using a big caliber bullet it could travel through the wall. Come back in after two minutes or so."

Paul went through the motions of asking permission to leave the room as Sara spoke.

"Up to three minutes remain before he shoots." Sweat beaded on Sara's brow. "I'm running a program to show the bullet leave the barrel. If the screen flashes red, duck. Our security is on the way there now." Sara's hands shook and tears slid down her cheeks.

"Sara, it—"

"Don't talk, Charlie. The shooter's focused on you and will see. I'm fine." Her voice broke. She blew her nose, wiped her eyes and cleared her throat. "We need a few more minutes. If his trigger finger twitches, we'll see it."

Charlie's projected picture now showed a split screen. On the top, an image of a man wearing a blue baseball cap and black hoodie was lying across a cement wall on a roof with a .338

Lapua Mag. The gun specs scrolled beside the picture. Under that picture was an extreme close-up of his trigger finger.

"Charlie, lean forward like you're whispering to the guy in front of you to make him retarget. Oz needs more time to get there."

Charlie leaned way forward and pretended to whisper to the man in front of him. He turned his face away from the window to make it hard to read his lips and smiled slightly, trying to project innocent movement. "Stop crying or you'll miss his draw. I'll be fine." Fear jittered along his nerves, her fear. If the bullet connected, she could save him, but their secret would be out.

She gave a soft snort of laughter. "I won't miss it. I love you," she whispered.

Charlie sat back and then leaned down as if he was picking up his pencil. "I love you too. Where's Oz?"

"Almost there. Stasia is on the way there too. I'm going to them when they engage. I'm still scanning for other threats. Stay here and stay down."

Everyone stared at the screen on the wall.

"Come on, Oz," Sara mumbled as she watched his progress to the sniper on her HUD.

Paul opened the door to reenter the room, and Sara yelled down as the screen flashed red. Everyone dropped to the floor as the bullet smashed through the window, then the wall, leaving a gaping hole into the next room.

Sara jumped up and ran from the room.

Charlie said, "He knows he missed and that you're coming." Charlie stood with his class against the back wall of the classroom out of sight of the windows. The projected flat screen hovered in front of him. On the screen, the sniper had ducked down and was dissembling his gun, a furious scowl on his face.

"We'll get him. Stay there," Sara said from the screen.

Charlie hesitated, hating to let his team face even one armed man without him but he knew his aura would likely cause more problems than his presence would solve.

His Valory appeared. "Sir, I estimate Oz will reach the target location before backup can reach him. I'm using all resources to scan the area and have no reason to believe he is in any danger."

Charlie snorted a laugh despite himself.

"Did Sara tell you to reassure me?"

"No, sir. All team leaders are being informed."

"What resources—"

To Charlie's surprise Paul grabbed his arm and shook his head.

Paul said, "Valory, this is an unsecure location."

Charlie said, "Keep tracking. I'll want a full report to read."

"Yes, sir," Valory said, saluted and disappeared.

Charlie was tempted to ask Valory to show him Oz but doing so might reveal him using magic. Paull's expression warned it wouldn't be smart to ask for the footage Valory was using. Oz was likely hacking local security cameras. He gritted his teeth and forced himself to wait.

- 14 -

PEOPLE GET LUCKY

Oz entered the building the sniper was in and headed to the stairs, casting locate on the gun the sniper had used as he ran. If the sniper used the other stairs, he'd know if he got by him when his locate changed direction. He was halfway up when the locate moved. Oz ran through the door at the next landing. The sniper had picked a cooperate office building. One long hallway with closed doors spaced intermittently along it lay before Oz. "The target is moving down now and is ahead of me. What's your ETA?"

"Less than a minute," Stasia said.

"Five minutes." Guthrie said, sounding angry.

"At least four minutes," Sara said.

"We're here," Glen said, "and dropping on the roof."

Oz chased the man down another stairwell. Feet clattering on the metal stairs echoed in the enclosed space. "I'm directly over him." Oz casted Invisible Duo and jumped over the rail. The man in the black hoodie clutched a black case in one hand and was almost to the bottom of the stairs. He ran down fast, taking them two at a time. Sirens sounded in the distance.

As Oz fell past the assassin, he used Wink and teleported forward, breaking invisible and intercepting the man. He slammed the man's head into the wall, and then sheeped him. While the man wandered in small circles Oz pulled zip-ties from his pocket and then punched the man hard in the head, breaking the sheep.

The man shook his head, grabbed a knife from his belt, and flicked it open as he kicked out at Oz.

Oz leg swept him onto the ground and kicked him in the chest, knocking him back. His assailants head hit the ground with a dull thunk, and he laid still a moment. Without wasting time, Oz grabbed the knife and tossed it behind him and zip-tied the assassin's wrists together before hauling him up a foot off the floor by his tied arms and punching him in the head again. The landing vibrated with the struggle of the two men as Oz attempted to tie his feet while he bucked and thrashed.

Stasia arrived and grabbed his bound hands, twisted, and used her Knockout-Punch.

Oz nodded to her and got the man tied. Alpha team ran from the roof, their combat boots thunderously loud on the stairs. A tight grin on his face, Oz hauled the man to his feet and shook him before handing him to Marcus.

"Marcus has him in custody," Oz said. "Everyone is fine. Charlie, get to the lab. We can't assume this hitman is the only one."

"How did you happen to be so ready for this?" Guthrie's angry voice filled the line.

"Later," Oz said. "Find out whatever you can on the man. We have things to do right now."

Charlie picked up the round, glass ball, shut off the projection, and faced his classmates. "Thanks for helping to capture him. My, *um*, Sara will be relieved we caught him." Charlie turned to his professor and took advantage of Commanding Presence, his magic's ability to make others follow his advice, shamelessly. As a general rule, he tried to never tell his superiors what to do as they couldn't help but agree with him if he was angry and he was very angry now. "Security isn't sure he's the only one, so I'll need to stay away while we investigate this. I'll see the commandant before I go." He turned to Paul. "Can you forward us homework and lecture notes until we get back? It shouldn't be too long. I'll email you about the other project we were working on."

"I'll see to it." Paul clasped Charlie's shoulder. "You be careful. Find out what the hell is going on and keep Sara safe."

They shook hands. Charlie ran from the room and went directly to the commandant's office. He gave him the footage they had of both the sniper and his classroom. Sara had recorded everything.

"You expected a sniper?" The commandant frowned as he watched the footage.

"No— we didn't know what to expect or even if anything would happen. Sara was concerned though." He explained Sara's distraction theory.

"If she's right, Mr. X can't realize we're onto him, we have to seem distracted. She thinks this has to do with the election, but that's just a theory."

"So, what happens now that the sniper is caught and you're alive?" One elegant eyebrow arched over a hard, blue eye.

"We go away for a few days and pretend to be hiding while we track those convenient leads. It's too dangerous for the rest of the students for us to remain on campus until we figure out what's going on."

"I agree. Send me daily reports, and I'll send your classwork."

"Yes, Sir." Charlie straightened.

"You'll take your security?"

"Some of them. Oz and Sara need time to figure this out. I'm confident they can. Mr. X can't be smarter than they are."

"It seems unlikely, but people get lucky. Even a broken clock is right twice a day." The commandant stood and shook Charlie's hand. "Be careful, all of you."

"We'll be swift, silent and deadly." A blue glitter in his eyes, Charlie saluted his commandant and left the room, passing the police officers on the way in.

- 15 -

INFILTRATING THE WHITE HOUSE

After his meeting with the commandant Charlie ran to the Valor building where he found Sara waiting. His magic burst free at first sight of her, surrounding him in agitated swirls. He grimaced ruefully, closing his eyes and backing away, communing with his magic and forcing it back. To appease the magic, he removed his shirt and t-shirt and held her against his bare chest. Desire for her flared, and the magic stopped pushing, happy with the proximity and emotions they now shared.

"Guthrie is angry," she murmured as he stroked her back. "He realizes we know more than we're saying."

"He'll get over it." Charlie placed his palm on her heart to feel it beat, letting his magic be reassured without going to her. "Have I told you lately how glad I am you're so smart?"

A small snort changed to stifled laughter as she snuggled against him. A few moments later she stepped away from him.

He traced the outline of her brow before he turned aside to dress in the civilian clothes she'd brought him.

Blue eyes sparkled as he undressed, and she grinned and headed to the door, speaking over her shoulder. "I'll call the sarge while you call Hawk."

For the millionth-time Charlie mentally blessed his magic for letting him feel her passion for him. The magic loved how they felt now and it was hard to resist pulling her back into the room, but they had no time to make love.

In the hallway Sara leaned on the wall and called Guthrie. "Sorry, Sarge, we have a theory but nothing concrete. Tell the raid to behave as always. Do whatever you planned on doing and start sorting the mountain of data."

For a moment Guthrie didn't answer. When he spoke, he sounded sad. "You don't trust me?"

"I trust you with Charlie's life, and you can trust me too. When I get a minute, I'll fill you in, but it's about time and appearances right now. Talk to Paul or Amy meanwhile. I'll tell them to expect you. Make sure you still behave in your normal manner."

"Do you know who's behind this?"

"Not yet, but soon. Don't let on to anyone we're close." Sara hung up and went to pack a bag for Hawk.

Hawk answered Charlie's call on the first ring. "What's wrong?"

Charlie explained what was happening and what the plan was.

"I'm coming home."

Charlie didn't try to dissuade him. "Meet us at the lab. We'll bring your gear." Charlie dressed in jeans and a t-shirt, leaving his uniform hanging in the closet of Sara's office. Over a black t-shirt he wore a shoulder holster containing his SIG Sauer P229 and added a lightweight zippered sweatshirt. In a sheath on his ankle he carried a K-bar. Before he left the room, he grabbed the bag Sara had packed for them.

Oz waited in the hall, carrying one of his conjured packs.

"Where are the girls?" Charlie asked.

"Talking with Camila." Oz glanced at his wristcomp. "They'll be here in a minute."

The boys waited by the front door. Oz kept working on his wristcomp, screens flickering to life and closing as he typed on his virtual keyboard. A ghostly outline of another keyboard popped up, shimmering with pale yellow radiance, this one was covered with equation signs and mathematic symbols. Oz's fingers flew, tapping and merging screens as his eyes narrowed.

Charlie observed the sprouting of screens around Oz with a half-smile on his face.

Sara had another bag with her when she showed up and Stasia also carried two.

"Let's go," Sara said. "I've been thinking, and we need to see the president tonight."

Charlie tweaked her ponytail. "Tell us in the car, brainiac."

"Your mom's all set?" Oz asked Stasia as they walked to the car.

Stasia glanced back at the Valor building. "She's safe, but worried."

In the parking lot, Hawk arrived with Tank. Sara and Stasia took turns hugging him, then they both hugged him at the same time while he kissed their foreheads.

Charlie gave Hawk a quick hug too before getting into the driver seat.

Sara opened the recording of the shooting and scrutinized it as they drove to the hotel. "We need to speak with the president right away. As soon as Mr. X realizes distraction didn't work, he'll most likely try to kill his opponent. If I'm right, and this is about the campaign, the president is in danger right this second.

"Mr. X has to think we're hiding out here, so the reservation is under my name to be sure he knows where we are. I figure we have another two or three hours before he realizes his hitman wasn't incompetent, but foiled. Mr. X will have no way of knowing if we suspect or if that was regular security, either way will make him sweat. And scared people act rashly. We can't be seen leaving. Marcus is bringing us our gear and we'll meet him on Canal Street."

Sara checked them into the hotel, and they went up to the penthouse suite. Three small bedrooms attached to a living area, and a kitchenette adjoined to the dining room.

They dumped the bags by the door. Oz applied a blue spell-bracelet to his arm with a smack. "Steal Stasia's invisible to leave here," Oz said. "Once we're out, Spell-Steal my disguise and go in two groups to meet Marcus on Canal Street. Gear up and use new disguises and take separate taxis to Washington where we'll steal Stasia's invisible again and sneak inside."

Sara hefted the small black bag over her shoulder. "I need to bring this bag with me to finish the wristcomp and it has sensors in it."

"I'm starving. Let's eat first." Charlie rubbed his stomach.

Sara checked her wristcomp for Marcus's whereabouts. "He's almost there. We'll stop for fast food once we're disguised." Sara knelt and ruffled Tank's ears. "Sorry, boy, you have to stay here."

Blue bracelets engaged on their wrists, they stole Stasia's invisible and snuck out. Down the street from the hotel they found a busy bar and crowded into the bathroom where they Spell-Stole Oz's Disguise and strolled out one at a time.

Sara and Charlie caught a cab to the nearest McDonalds and paid the driver ten dollars to wait while they ordered food. The driver dropped them off two blocks from Canal Street and they walked the rest of the way there. Marcus was waiting, and Hawk was already there, suited up using his own invisible to stay hidden.

Charlie handed Hawk a paper sack from the restaurant and they sat in the back of Marcus's car eating under a No-See-Um while they waited for Stasia and Oz. A few minutes later they showed up. Stasia was invisible and Oz resembled an old man with gray hair wearing a threadbare suit.

Charlie grabbed the bags containing their armor from the trunk and handed them out. Everyone dressed quickly.

Marcus glanced from one to the other, a frown making deep lines in his forehead. "What's going on?"

"We have somewhere we need to be." Sara gave him a quick hug. "Tell no one we were here. No one at all. Find a new spot for us to change Joy and keep it secret. You and Joy summon us there, but don't switch the groups until the last second. I'm sure everyone is trustworthy," she continued when his frown deepened. "We know we're being watched, but not by who or how and everything needs to appear normal. Keep searching that information."

"I'm taking us off the grid for one day." Oz opened the raid positioning screen on his HUD and pointed to the small icons that showed Team Valor in the hotel. "You'll still see our vitals just not our actual position. This doesn't mean we don't trust the raid, it's because we don't know how they monitor us. Let everyone think we're at the hotel where the wristcomps say we are."

"Take care of Tank for me." Hawk handed Marcus a key to the hotel room.

Oz slapped Marcus's shoulder. "Keep vigilant. This is only a theory we're working on."

Marcus nodded. Stasia and Sara both hugged him goodbye.

They stole Oz's disguise again and left, going in separate directions, taking different cabs to their destination.

Outside the Washington monument they met up and stole Stasia's invisible and followed her into the Capitol building.

Inside the main entrance, they climbed over the desk by the metal detectors one at a time. Stasia waited, ready to cast Distract or Sap if needed, but everyone crossed without being noticed.

Hawk peppered the HUD with icons of guards in red, civilians in orange, and marked the president's location in green.

"He's in his private quarters."

Barely above a whisper, the stickycom magnified his voice inside the auditory canal. Oz had tweaked the programing making voices clearer, but they still had a robotic quality to them.

Stasia distract the guard in front of the hallway leading to the president's rooms, and they slipped by.

"Stasia, go get him and bring him to his office. We need a secure place to talk," Oz said.

Stasia glided away from them and distracted and then sapped the guard at the door and entered. The president sat beside his wife on the couch reading a newspaper. Stasia withdrew a small notebook and pen she carried from a side pocket, wrote a note and slipped it on the president's hand.

Eyes wide, he bolted upright, clutching the small paper in his fist, then leaned back in his chair as his wife glanced up from her book.

The president waved a hand at her. "Nothing, dear, I just forgot to do something. I'm sorry, but our evening will have to be put on hold." The president headed to the door.

Outside the door, the guard swayed. The president grabbed his arm, breaking the sap, and pulled him away from the doorway so Stasia could exit. Confused, the guard shook his head. The president pretended not to notice the guard's muddled state and placed a hand on his arm, leading him down the hallway while speaking.

"Sorry to disturb you. I forgot something in my office."

The guard at the end of the hall joined them and radioed in the change of position.

"I might be a while." At the doorway to the Oval Office, the president held the door open, standing to the side as he spoke then closed the door and leaned on it.

When he opened his mouth to speak, Oz appeared before him with a finger held to his lips. The president nodded, and Oz held up a finger and turned to face the room, casting Magical Locate for recording devices. In less than a minute, he'd found three. He placed all three on the president's desk.

The president watched this performance with narrowed eyes.

A minute later Oz said, "That's all the devices in this room, Mr. President."

The rest of Team Valor became visible beside the doorway. President Carmichael frowned deeply and approached the desk where the recorders lay. "The two recorders in my desk I was aware of. The one in my couch, I wasn't."

Oz nodded as Sara handed him the small black bag and he removed tools and took fingerprints on the black case.

"I'm sure you're aware of today's events," Charlie said as everyone watched Oz. "Sara thinks you might be the next target." He explained her theory.

"The fact they tried to kill Charlie is another indication I'm right." Sara glanced up from her position leaning over Oz's shoulder. "When did you hear we wanted to help with your campaign?"

"Four days ago. General Campbell called me," the president said.

"Did you hear it in this office?" Hawk nodded at the device.

"Yes. I received the regular written report through our secure channels, and then General Campbell called me. We talked a few minutes, just generalities, we never mention specifics on the phone. He wanted to be sure I took you up on the offer. I said something like, 'I'd be crazy not to take advice from the two smartest people on Earth. He said, 'I'd be bound to win with your help.' And I said something like, 'nothing is a sure thing, but with them in your corner, I'd take the bet. I feel better and better about this campaign all the time."

"If he can't stop us from helping you, the next logical step is to remove you." Sara handed Oz a small screwdriver, speaking absently, her attention on the device in Oz's hand.

"If someone on your opponent's team is willing to do this, murder a man for a distraction, he'll try to kill Oz and Sara if he's doing other illegal things and thinks they'll find out," Stasia said.

"Locate program is still running and every bit of data we have helps narrow the search." Oz placed the sticky tapes containing the fingerprints to the side and continued unscrewing the battery compartment. "Now we know it's someone who has access to this office. This device is passive; it needs to be picked up and replaced."

"This must be something Mr. X is doing as an ongoing thing, or why distract us in the first place?" Sara added.

The president sat at his desk and flipped the small light on, leaning forward to better observe Oz. "When did you first discuss helping with the campaign?"

Sara glanced up. "On the way home from the *Truman* aboard a military aircraft. Lots of people were on board. It was a full flight."

"My program is searching for the manifest," Oz held out his hand, and Sara placed a small paintbrush in it. "I remember we were batting around ideas. We talked about how to get out the vote in much bigger numbers using UBM."

"Yeah, we ran some quick numbers and figured our commercial idea would raise his poll rating by at least one percent with just that." Sara agreed. "Then we checked his approval ratings and what caused them to rise and drop." They both paused a moment as Oz took the prints on the batteries and then straightened. Oz hooked the recorder to his wristcomp and turned to Sara.

"I got sidetracked, remember? I started looking into his funding." Oz paused in thought. "We talked about how he should spend the money and how we should ask for records to see how he was spending it to better advise him."

"Yes!" Sara said in excitement. "The guy with the spilled drink! Who was it? I never really looked at him. We got distracted and when we spoke again, we talked about our game."

"If that guy spilled his drink on purpose to distract that line of thought, we need to know who it was." Oz flicked his fingers and another screen opened in front of him.

Stasia shrugged. "I don't remember anyone in particular."

"Me neither," Hawk said. "It didn't necessarily have to be the spiller who was distracting you either. I could easily jostle someone enough to spill."

"I was distracted myself, looking up vacation plans for Sara and me," Charlie said.

"There is no manifest." Oz groaned in annoyance and opened a new screen.

"Cross check who was away and who works here," Stasia suggested.

Hawk sighed and rubbed his brow with two fingers. "Mr. X is likely not working alone. Say a confederate on the plane heard us. He distracts you easily and isn't too worried, just some kids making big talk. Then he realizes who we are and reports, or he is Mr. X, whatever, but he decides distraction works so he sets up Ned Font and it works again. It works for a month."

Charlie said, "I'd wondered why all those news report and websites hadn't mentioned the Valkyrie system or Valor Industries. Maybe Mr. X was hoping publicity would shift Sara's focus to acting."

Hawk shrugged. "Whether he meant to annoy her or change her career goals doesn't matter. It worked as distraction, but he must have gotten nervous when he heard we still want to help. Maybe by now he's really nervous of us because he's had time to research us, so he gives us information overload. We still want to help. He hears it right here in the office, so he decides to kill Charlie, which would make you worthless for a long time."

"How does he know that?" Stasia asked.

"They're engaged, it isn't secret." Hawk shrugged and began to pace. "If Charlie was murdered, you could safely assume a young girl would take a long time to recover even without their connection."

"So, Mr. X plots the murder. He might have pre-plotted it as a backup plan and just put it in motion, ergo Mr. X doesn't want us examining the campaign funds." Oz slapped Hawk on the back and opened more screens.

"We keep extensive records of those funds, and it'd be a mammoth project to check them all." The president leaned back in his chair and rubbed his forehead.

"One more angle remains. If Major Nelson reporting our interest in helping almost gets Charlie killed, what conversation prompted the house burning and Susan?" Oz asked.

"The bar, the night Ned Font took that picture," Stasia said excitedly. "Sara and I talked about the campaign, both at the table and in the restroom. In fact, Sara mentioned getting the campaign fund records. She said she needed a month or so to go through them and we laughed about starting after our vacation. Sara complained about never having time to play our game and that we'd have to get moving to make a real difference on the campaign. I grumbled, and she said October was soon enough, she could get it sorted by Christmas, leaving plenty of time before the election to make a difference."

"I remember." Sara closed her eyes, a frown of concentration on her face. "That's the only conversation I ever had like that in public."

"I spoke with one of my dates, but just in generalities about ideas to help, nothing about campaign funds," Oz said.

"So, Sara's conversation probably triggered it." Charlie opened a screen before him and began typing. "Our house burns down on the twenty-eighth of September. Susan finds Hawk at the end of August but all of a sudden is in a rush the same week."

"She was put in play to do exactly what she did." Hawk flopped on the couch and put his face in his hands. "She probably doesn't even realize it. We were supposed to catch her and spend our time following those leads."

Oz glanced over at Hawk and nodded, a sympathetic expression in his eyes. "Yep, I'm sure that's why the hard drive she carried contained so many different and conflicting programs. None were meant to work, just waste our time figuring out what they do."

Stasia sat beside Hawk and put an arm around his shoulder. "We still don't know who," she reminded them.

Oz glanced up from the forest of screens surrounding him. "I'm sure the who will be made clear once we go over the records, but Sara wasn't exaggerating about the time needed."

"Pictures of the bar that night." Charlie pointed to his screen. "I recorded Ned Font. He wasn't close enough to hear Stasia and Sara though, but he took pictures too. We need his camera and the recordings he took that night. Oz, get clear shots of every face you can and use your locate program to see if we can ID anyone there who's connected to anybody here."

"Mr. President, if you recognize anyone..." Hawk trailed off.

"This will take me an hour or so." Oz began typing. "I'm setting my Valory to examine all phone records of every person inside the club. Some probably took pictures and recordings too. I also want to look through the entire building for recording devices sometime tonight."

The president said, "I'll call and arrange for you to come in as Dr. Simmons from Valor Industry. Pretend to use a new device to sweep for bugs tomorrow morning."

"I think I should stay with your wife." Stasia headed to the door. "Someone inside here is a very bad guy."

"Mr. President, I invite you to join our raid," Charlie said.

"I accept." The president had joined and left the raid before and reacted calmly when Stasia appeared misty to him when she turned herself invisible.

Hawk casted No-See-Um, and the president opened the door, holding it as open as he could, giving Stasia room to pass, and asked the guard to send for coffee.

Once the door closed again, Sara rummaged in her bag and removed a small case, which she opened and set on the coffee table. Next, she took out a Styrofoam box wrapped in brown paper and tied with string, handling it carefully, and knelt on the floor beside the table. A flashlight on a stand and a magnifying glass came from the case and she set them up in moments. Then she unrolled a length of black felt containing delicate tools and began working on the wristcomp.

"I'm making you a skin wristcomp. The skin won't be cured until tomorrow." She reached into the bag and took out a stack of sensors, the quarter size, gray opaque glass disks clinked onto the tabletop. Two bracelets and a regular wristcomp came from the bag next and she rose and handed them to the president. "Are you clear about the spell patterns you need to use to summon us?"

"I am," he assured her. "I don't know them all, but I can do that one and your heal."

"Okay, don't engage them, but watch my screen. Ascension pattern." A keyboard and screen appeared before Sara with highlighted keys. "Now do that with your fingers. If it turns green, you did it right. Your wristcomp does this too; you can ask to see any of our spell patterns."

The president hit the pattern.

Sara said, "Spell-Steal ally pattern." The screen showed another arrangement. "This is the hardest one. After you cast that pattern, chose who you're stealing from then hit that spell pattern. Pick Hawk, he's F-three. See his name above the key there? Now, pick his air-bubble. Pretend to tap the icon with the symbol on it. Now see how the spell pattern lights up?" She pointed to the lit keys. "Hit those. Good, it turned green, meaning you did it right. If it turns red, you have to redo it."

"I understand how it works, but I'm sure to be slow though," the president said.

"Learn shield by heart. No one will know you casted it unless they touch you. Engage the white bracelet and practice. I can refill it."

"Don't forget to disengage it to use the blue one," Charlie said.

Engaged simultaneously neither bracelet worked, instead heating. If left engaged and attempts to cast continued, the heat reached painful proportions until both bracelets burst into flame.

"The president's wife is safe and asleep," Stasia reported. "Send me the link and I'll look at the financials."

They spread out around the room, sitting cross-legged on the floor, Screens appeared in front of everyone as they settled down to work.

An hour later, Sara pointed to the picture on her screen. "I have a hit. Your secretary; it doesn't mean she's guilty," Sara said as the president rose and began to pace. "It just means she's linked to this guy here." Sara tapped the portrait of a young man in the video Charlie had taken of Ned Font in the club that night, "This man contacted her son. He might've said something to her someone else overheard."

Sara removed a small, blue, glassy ball from her bag. "Call her in here and hand her this in the morning. Ask her if her son told her what we said and if she mentioned anything to anyone else or if anybody else was present."

"What's the ball do?" The president hefted the ball in his hand.

"Monitors vitals. It's a crude lie detector," Oz said absently as he continued to scroll through the financials.

"The ball works pretty well. Not go to court well, but good enough for what we want," Sara assured the president. "Don't tell her what it is though."

Blue sparked in Charlie's eyes as his anger grew. "If she's guilty, our cover is blown."

"Yeah," Sara said worriedly. "If we approach her, it could escalate plans against him and us. It's a risk, but I'm checking her finances now and everything looks good."

"We could bug her instead," Hawk said.

"We could, but that'd most likely lead to nothing for a while at least." Sara sat back on her heels. "He should ask her. Then show her the recorder he found and ask her about that too. If she lies, we have a good strong lead. The president can ask her to keep quiet if she's telling the truth."

"If she's lying, I can keep her isolated," the president said.

"Does your wife know about us?" Charlie laughed when the president flushed and put the blue glass ball down. "We don't care; it just makes it easier for us to hide. Go back to bed, and we'll hang out in your rooms and keep working on this. It might take us a few days, maybe longer. Oz will have to come from the hotel and be seen returning from there for his security sweep. Do that first thing tomorrow."

Everyone stole Oz's invisible and followed the president to his rooms. He woke his wife and introduced them. "One of them will be with you, even if you can't see them," he said as Stasia faded from view. "Give her time to get through doorways. Don't be obvious but try to provide room." His wife appeared fluster, her gaze fliting over them as she bit her lip.

The president drew her aside and her face paled as he filled her in. "I have good security. This is a threat all presidents face. We can handle this."

For a moment his wife attempted small talk, but tears filled her eyes and she fled to the bedroom.

The president followed his wife into his bedroom and shut the door.

Team Valor continued to work in the living room. Sara fell asleep leaning on Charlie's arm.

"Everyone needs to rest." Charlie glanced at the time. "Get four hours of sleep now, Oz. Be at the hotel ready to go early." Sara woke when he picked her up. "Go back to sleep. I'm going to sleep a while too," he murmured as he carried her into the spare bedroom and grabbed a pillow and blanket and lay on the floor by the bed with her. In moments, they slept. It had been a long, stressful day for both of them. Hawk and Stasia followed them in and shared the bed. Oz snatched a couch pillow and curled up beside them.

Oz woke at four a.m., stole Stasia's invisible, and snuck out with the president's help. By five-thirty, the president was dressed for the day and working in his study. Team Valor still slept in the guest room. The president peeked in then closed the door, leaving them sleeping.

At seven, Oz openly arrived and began his search. Team Valor was awake and working again in the spare room. The president's wife was up, dressed and pacing, rubbing her hands together, unable to settle on anything.

Stasia pointed to her combat HUD, which showed the president's location and vitals. "We're keeping a close eye on him, Ma'am, and he has a white bracelet on, so he can Call-For-Help or we can summon him out."

A flush climbed across the first lady's cheekbones. "Please, call me Faith. I'm worried about what else they heard; we talk very candidly in here."

"Oz found no recording devices in here. I've searched for hidden and there is nothing."

"What you do, it's just so fantastical, it's hard to believe it works." The president's wife glanced at her, then away.

"We aren't relying solely on the magic, we're using tech, good tech. Sara and Oz will find whatever they don't want found." The low murmuring behind the door of the spare room grew louder. Stasia peeked in.

"We found something." Charlie grinned at her and slapped Hawk's shoulder. "It's small, but it's a start. Good work, Hawk. Keep checking. Only a billion companies to go."

- 16 -

A CIVILIZED DISCUSSION

They continued to work in the spare bedroom, laying on the plush blue carpeting. When Oz finished his search for recording devices, he snuck in food for everyone.

A bag of sandwiches was passed around and Oz sat beside Charlie while he ate. "I was there when the president questioned his secretary. He's pretty upset. Joyce knew about the recorder and lied about it. She told the truth about who heard her son, but it's a longish list. And she knows he realized she lied. Agent Lewis is on her like a tick."

After lunch, they spread out on the floor to make room for the flat screens around them.

Late in the afternoon Sara said, "I've been thinking, and I have an idea. If we took a month and went through these our next step would've been to go through the vice presidents. Let's go through his now. He's on our short list. If all of this was to slow us, let's skip ahead."

"I'll call my husband and ask him to come home so you can discuss it," Faith said.

"I can access those files," the president agreed when told what they wanted. "He'll realize I'm doing it though."

Charlie said, "Let's skip even farther ahead. Call Oz in again. Call in Vice President Danvers and give him the ball to hold. Show him what you're checking. Ask questions, make it clear we suspect him. Let's rattle him."

Oz stood and stretched. "Give me time to get back to the hotel and change back into my suit."

The president wrote a phone number on a piece of paper and handed it to Oz. "Call when you're ready. My driver will pick you up and escort you to my office."

Forty minutes later Oz was escorted into the president's office. President Carmichael introduced Oz to the vice president, and everyone exchanged pleasantries for a moment as tension filled the room. President Carmichael handed Vice President Danvers the blue glass ball.

Oz cleared his throat. "Excuse me a moment, Sir."

The president sat at his desk. Oz leaned over his shoulder and pointed at his screen. Two other screens sprang up. A combat HUD in front of his right arm and a larger screen in front of him.

The smaller screen he angled before the president showed a notification Stasia had just sent and video of the president's living room and his wife, Faith.

"How nice— your wife is visiting mine." The president tapped his fingers on the desk. "Oz is here going over your campaign contributions." He glanced at the screen Oz was displaying to him and his eyes hardened. "Come clean right now and maybe we can salvage this."

"You're caught," Oz said softly when Danvers licked his lips and hesitated.

"Why is your wife visiting mine?" The president asked in a voice silky with menace.

Faith waved her guest to a seat and offered refreshments then waited, frowning.

Anne Danvers sipped her tea, a smile at the edge of her lips and a glitter in her eye.

"Waiting for something?" Faith finally asked as her guest remained quiet.

"Just admiring the room." Anne gestured behind Faith. "Is that a real Monet?"

The first lady glanced behind her and her guest emptied a small vial of cloudy white liquid into Faith's tea.

Stasia frowned and cast a Distract behind Anne and switched the glasses when she peered behind her.

"They're all real, you know that." Faith turned back to her guest, the frown lines between her brow deepening.

"We're so lucky to be able to enjoy all of this." Anne nodded at the painting and trailed a manicured finger along the gilt of the antique table they sat at. When Faith said nothing, Anne smiled and sipped her tea, cradling the glass with both hands. "Our husbands work so hard to get here. As wives of famous men, we make so many sacrifices that no one sees." The glitter in her eyes deepened as she took another sip of tea.

Faith sighed and rubbed her brow, leaning back in her seat. "Get to the point. We both know my husband is investigating yours as we speak."

"And he'll find some minor discrepancies. Nothing he couldn't explain away if he chose to."

"My husband won't lie."

"I know," Anne agreed, her smile deepening. "Aren't you going to drink your tea? We're having a civilized discussion here." She sipped her own tea again. "Jeremy won't lie for himself, but for you I think he would." The smile faded, replaced with an aggravated frown. The teacup rattled as she placed it on the saucer and rummaged in her bag, pulling a small gun from her purse." Drink the tea." Cold and hard, her voice dripped venom. "No, don't move. I can kill you before help arrives. Drink it. It'll just make you sleepy."

Stasia removed her notepad, tore off a small piece and wrote in tiny script, *'I switched the teas, drink it.'* Distract caused both women to peer behind them, and Stasia placed the tiny note in the first lady's hand clenched in her lap. As Faith's worried gaze scanned the note, Stasia texted Oz.

Anne appeared angry and rattled. Stasia tensed behind Anne with her hand on her dagger

Faith licked her lips, picked up her teacup, drank the entire thing, and set the empty cup down.

A smug smile lit Anne's face, and she took out her phone and sent a text.

Danvers glanced at his phone as it vibrated. "My wife is poisoning yours. There's an antidote, but you won't get it until I get what I want."

"Which is?" The president lifted an enquiring eyebrow and leaned back in his seat, folding his hands on the desk.

"A few things. Some will take a while, so your wife has to go away where we can keep her alive while you do them."

Oz narrowed his eyes and laid a hand on the president's shoulder. "How long is a while?"

"Eight months."

"You want him to throw the election."

"Yes, he can choose how he does it. Scandalous affair, embezzlement, drunkenness, sickness whatever. Once he does, I'll release his wife."

"You expect to just walk out with her?"

"Exactly. Faith has fifteen minutes before the pain hits. If she doesn't get the antidote within fifteen more, she dies. Anne will escort her out and give her enough of the antidote to keep her alive. If you haven't thrown the election in eight months, well..."

The president picked up a pen and rolled it between his fingers. "Where would you say she was for eight months?"

"That she left you and is staying with friends, us," Danvers said, pointing to himself.

"And we go on our merry way when you let her go?"

"Well, first you're going to embezzle some funds, quite a lot of funds. No one will believe your story." Danvers smiled, then grimaced. "Your new friend should go with her." He nodded towards Oz. "Take the watch off." An age-spotted hand reached out for Oz's wristcomp.

"I will," Oz agreed, "but it'll alert my security when I do. The watch won't work for anyone except me. Let me notify them I'm removing it, or guards will automatically come."

"Fine, tell them something they'll believe."

Oz smiled and called Charlie. "I'm being kidnapped, and my kidnapper demands I remove my wristcomp. Don't send any guards."

Vice President Danvers lunged from his chair.

"You said say something they'd believe, and I'm sure they believe that. What did you expect me to say?" Oz asked in a self-righteous tone.

The president cracked a smile. "He's just a boy. What can he do?"

Oz said, "I'll go wait with your wife."

President Carmichael said, "Let him go. What harm could it do when his security already thinks he's being kidnapped. Let them see him walk out and they'll think he was joking. He can go with Anne. Who'd suspect her?"

Danvers said, "If he talks, your wife dies."

"I won't say a word." Oz made a zipping motion over his mouth and pretended to throw away the key.

Danvers hesitated then nodded briskly. "This is just politics. Say nothing. Jeremy will explain and no one will get hurt."

President Carmichael escorted Oz to the door. "Wait with Faith and say nothing. I'll handle this."

Oz nodded and the president opened the door. "Take him to the first lady," he said to the guard on the door.

The door closed behind Oz, leaving the two men alone in the room.

The president said, "It's just us here now. What's this really about?"

"My wife stole some money." Danvers sighed and rubbed his eyes a moment before straightening in his seat. "At first I didn't know. By the time I found out, it added up to quite a chunk. Both of us will go to jail for a long time if it's discovered." The vice president stood and walked to the window behind the desk and peered out. "We needed a lot of money. I thought we were replacing what we stole, but she had other plans. This wasn't my intent when I agreed to serve, and I'm sorry about this. I didn't plan it." He turned and faced the president. "We sold your reelection. I get enough money to pay her debts. You take the fall for the embezzlement if it's found out. I really hope you can keep it hidden."

"And the nation?"

"Goes on like always. It can take four years of a bad man."

"Who did you arrange this with?"

"You know I won't tell you that." Danvers sat on the small couch again and closed his eyes. "If you sacrifice your wife for the nation, I'll go to jail, but my wife will go free. There's no evidence against her, and I'll claim full responsibility. If I tell you, they'll kill her."

"Don't be a fool. To cover this up they'll kill her anyway along with me and my wife."

"Not if you do what I say. Throw the election. Pick any reason you want. Steal enough of the funds to be used as blackmail and retire peacefully with your wife."

"You know I won't do that." President Carmichael turned to stare out of the window behind him and engaged the white bracelet. He casted a shield on himself and turned back.

"I'd never leave the nation in the hands of people like you."

Danvers sighed hard, smiling crookedly. "I know, but I had to try. My wife's crazy idea. The nation was luckier than it deserved when you became president." He reached into his coat pocket and the president called for his guards.

The vice president made no attempt to shoot the president, he shot himself.

Horrified Secret Service agents hesitated in the doorway. "Close the door! Keep this quiet! His wife has kidnapped mine." The president picked up Oz's wristcomp. "Can you hear me?"

Sara answered instantly, "Yes, Sir, Mr. President. Stasia, Hawk, Charlie and Oz are with her, and she isn't dosed. I'm in your rooms. Let them go. Let's see where they bring her. I'm patching audio to you from Charlie's wristcomp."

"I'm coming to you." The president gestured to the Secret Service agent.

"Bring Oz's wristcomp please," Sara said.

"No one enters this room. Get Pierce Taylor and the head of my security detail," President Carmichael ordered his guard. The Secret Service agent ran from the room.

Two other guards ran up and the president ordered one to guard the door and the other to accompany him. His dark scowl caused the guards to nod nervously as he strode past on the way to his apartment.

Sara sat on the couch in his living room with a myriad of flat screens open around her. His guard followed him in.

She said, "Faith's security detail was called off. I'm checking now to see who did it. The car is bugged and both Alpha and Beta are on the way."

The president introduced her to his surprised agents. Eyes glued to the screen displaying the interior of the car, the president spoke to Sara. "You're sure my wife is safe?"

"Stasia is right there. They can't shoot her. I guess they could crash the car, but why would they?"

Anne sat in the passenger seat. Oz and Faith sat close together in the backseat. The talk between the driver and Anne revealed they were having an affair, but no details on the scheme or who was involved.

Stasia sat on the first lady's lap, using her invisible body as a shield. Oz crowded against her, ready to use his ice shield. The vice president's wife sat in the front seat laughing with the driver. Stasia recorded everything.

When the vice president's wife threw up, she was surprised, then furious, then hysterical.

Sara exchanged ironic glances with the president. "She knows she drank the wrong tea."

"You switched the tea, you goddamn bitch! How did you do that? I was watching the entire time!" A pained grimace on her face, Anne panted and stopped screaming to grab her stomach. "You've killed me, goddamn you!" The driver swerved wildly as she clawed at him. "Give me your gun. I want to kill her!"

"Stop it, before you kill me too." The driver knocked her grabbing hands away. "Take the antidote, stupid."

"There is no antidote! I used what I could get! You think it's easy getting poison? Bring me to a hospital. Oh god, I'm dying." Sweat streamed down her cheeks as she began to convulse.

The driver pulled the car over, opened her door, and dragged her out. Charlie slipped into the front seat from the roof.

Oz took the opportunity to whisper reassurance to the first lady. "My security team is surrounding this car and I'm armed. The driver can't hurt you. We could take him, but we want to see where he goes and who he calls. We won't let him hurt you."

The driver slammed the passenger door, got back in the driver's seat and glanced in the rearview mirror to check his passengers. "You're a tech at Valor Industries security? Aren't you a little young?"

Oz nodded but said nothing.

Stasia stifled a laugh.

"I'll let my boss decide what to do with you. The plan is shot now that the idiot killed herself. I wish I'd never gotten involved in this mess."

"Who's doing this?" Faith asked.

"Aren't you the cool cucumber?" The driver winked at her in the rearview mirror. "I guess we'll both find out. That was my boss. I'm just hired help." One thick thumb gestured back to the woman he'd left dying on the side of the road. "Stupid bitch. She made this plan and goes and kills herself."

Faith said, "If you turn yourself in now, and tell everything you know, I'll see that my husband pardons you. The rest of her plan is bound to be as bad."

"I'm truly tempted." The driver drummed his fingers on the steering wheel. "I believe you're a lady who keeps her word, but I don't think you could pull that off."

"Call him and see. Get a signed pardon. It wouldn't even be hard to do. So far, you haven't done much." Faith folded her hands in her lap, looking hopeful.

"The problem is, I know nothing except where I'm to take you."

"What could it hurt to call and see if that's enough?"

"Just giving back the first lady would be enough," Oz said. "You'll be a hero. Maybe you didn't even know the plan until Anne screamed about poison. Mrs. Carmichael isn't tied or anything. Maybe you thought she came willingly. There's time to do the right thing here."

"Joey Esposito doesn't do the right thing." The driver shook his head and the tempo of the drumming increased. "I'm cursed to always do the wrong thing. My mama says to me, Joey, why can't you ever do the right thing, then shakes her head and tells me I have my father's curse. Nicky Esposito had to do that one last job even though he was retired. My daddy's curse killed him, and it will surely kill me too."

"Break the curse," Oz pleaded. "Let her go and keep me. I know things about my company. Passwords and schedules, and I can get you access to the building. Those things are worth good money to the right people."

"I'll be sure to point that out," Joey said amiably. "You two are being right cooperative."

Oz exchanged a rueful grimace with Faith. "This would be so much easier on everyone if you gave yourself up."

"I never did nothing the easy way." Joey started on another story about his father and Oz sighed in disgust.

Sara was running the names Nicky and Joe Esposito through Oz's locate program. "Our link." She pointed at the screen in front of her. "His father was in *Salvaje El Diablos*."

The president watched her type, his frown growing.

"Don't worry, sir. The Scouts can extract her in seconds. The more we find out, the better off you are." Sara opened another screen while she spoke, and her fingers raced over her virtual keyboard. Quick taps on the screens and screens began to merge and enlarge. A group of ten small screens popped up and orbited the largest screen. "The threat to us is over. We found what we weren't supposed to. The threat to you and your wife remains and is worse. The more people we can find involved, the greater the chance someone tells all."

Secret Service agents spoke in low tones by the door. A moment later another agent escorted Pierce Taylor into the room.

Sara nodded in greeting but kept her gaze on the flat screens before her.

The president filled him in.

"What's the plan here, Sara?" Pierce squatted beside her and gestured at the array of screens.

"Two parts." Sara pointed to the different screens as she spoke. "I'll keep tracking these links of our known conspirators. The first lady is brought wherever they're going, and our security will be there in minutes and takes everyone they can alive. Every new piece of information narrows the search."

"While my wife is in danger." The president glared and crossed his arms.

"Some," Sara admitted, "but not much. This threat hanging over your head would be a greater danger. We're hot on the trail here. It's been only two days since we began searching and we have four people. Mr. X has to be sweating right now."

"You think it's the incumbent?"

"No." Sara glanced at him, smiling at his surprised expression. "Mr. X is trickier than that. If the vice president's plan had worked, and you went public and accused your immediate rival, it would ruin you both. We need to check out the next most likely candidates or even the ones after that."

Pierce frowned and rubbed his chin, then sat by Sara, reading her screens.

"He isn't my top suspect, but I haven't ruled him out," Sara clarified.

Sara tapped the icon opening the raid channel. "I'm rearranging the raid positions. Please check your new position." For a few moments, she whispered, reassigning groups. "Ready check?" All names turn green except Oz and the president.

"Valory, tell me if any of these screens flash." Sara rose and opened her bag, took out the Styrofoam box and the light and checked the skin. A magnifying glass on the stand already stood on the nearby coffee table with tools on black felt. With tweezers, Sara placed the skin under the glass. A few minutes of intense concentration followed as she leaned over the table putting the wristcomp together. The newest model was much smaller than the old, resembling an expensive wristwatch.

"Only my team members have used this particular model. We haven't tested it publicly yet only on my, *um,* friends. If it loses function, tell me, but I consider you a friend, so it should work regardless of whether you stay in the raid or not." Sara glanced at the president as she worked. "I'll apply it and introduce you. I've made a slight change in the programming. You won't automatically join the open channel. The tone will sound a double beep and a HUD will open exactly like ours, but with no audio. Hit the phone icon to receive audio or the X to close the screen or just tell it. Enter your five-digit PIN to remove the wristcomp or its memory will be wiped, and an alarm sent to us. Once it engages, it will ask for your PIN."

"I don't even know how to turn it on." The president leaned closer as she attached the strap to the wristcomp.

"Just tell it what you want it to do, or ask it how to do what you want," Sara said. "Ready? This might sting a second."

The president nodded, and Sara placed the wristcomp on his wrist and flicked a small heal on it, then walked him through the introduction. "You're good to go. Give it a try."

"*Um*, give me a flat screen."

A solid looking flat screen appeared before the president at eye height.

"How do I type on it?" he asked and white letters flowed across the screen, *'Would you like a visible keyboard yes/no.'* "Yes, please," he said, and Sara laughed.

"You don't need to be polite. Ask for tutorials or to see the starter guide, but it's incredibly easy to use. If you want audible answers instead of written on the screen tell it audio on. Stickycoms like we use are in the bag if you want to keep the audio private, but it will also work with any Bluetooth device."

"Can I change the screen size?" The president waved his hand through the screen and it flickered. Another message scrolled across the black screen asking what size he'd like. "How does it know I'm asking about it?"

'You're looking at me,' scrolled across the screen as Sara said, "It doesn't. It's tracking your eye movements. You looked at the screen or wristcomp when you asked, so it answered. If you were speaking to it and looked away it would still answer you. It's capable of computing who is likely being spoken to if you're in a group of people and it should learn your mannerisms and get better at anticipating you. For instance, if you were with your wife and asked it about a report and then ten minutes later asked a question about the report but your wife would not likely have seen that report or know the answer it would answer. If it didn't answer you just use its name to make it aware you were speaking to it. There's all kinds of setting for that so you can customize its responses to you."

"Jesus, it's smart." The president's eyes widened.

"No, Oz is smart." Sara grinned. "See, on the HUD here, it's showing us your vital signs. If you want to keep that private, you can limit who sees or tell it to turn off."

"I understand. I'll leave it on for now."

"You should also tell it who to call and how in different emergencies. Say someone comes into your dining room with a gun, you could preset alarms with keywords and motions. For instance, when I want to record where I am, I double tap the wristcomp face. I could change that to anything I wished, three blinks, a sneeze and a cough, a keyword, and if I'm wearing one of these small peripheral sensors, I can even use a foot stamp, or toe flex." She handed the president one of the health sensors. "Just remove the adhesive back and place it on your lower spine. It can map muscle movement for more accurate results of screen position and allows for limb interaction."

"How many commands can it follow?" An agent asked as he eyed the device.

"As many as he wanted. It could call unlimited people with prerecorded messages. He could order the building locked down, his security called, and notify his wife in one second. He could ask it to look up all information on something by just blinking twice while staring at it. So, if he was in a meeting and forgot someone's name he could set a nonverbal cue for Valory to retrieve it and he could have Valory display the information in varied ways depending on preset commands. For instance, if I've forgotten your name, I wouldn't want it to tell me or inform in a way that would be noticeable to the person so my screen would show up above their head if I wasn't wearing a stickycom. Or maybe the group I'm in would make that awkward so it would open a small screen and use one of my prechosen interrupts, a pretend call from home or whatever would be appropriate in the situation.

"Valory can walk you through of all those settings. It's limited to about five hundred thousand actions a second, and by that I mean preprogrammed responses, but that's a lot of actions in one minute."

"I want one," the man said enviously.

Sara laughed. "Tell your boss. Right now, the security program on the wristcomp is only available for government purchase. We're making a civilian model that will be able to display screens and run any program available now on the open market that will be integrated with Oz's voice activation program. The Valkyrie operating system practically makes typing obsolete. We expect them to replace desktops, laptops and tablets within a few years."

"You've fixed the battery life?" Pierce picked up the discarded regular wristcomp.

"We get ten hours of full use now with the regular version with a one hour forty-six-minute charge time." Sara tapped the watch in his hand. "We should have a handle on the, *err*, power issues we get with other model in no time."

"With hologram usage?" Pierce asked.

"Yes."

"It can do holograms too?" the Secret Service agent asked.

Sara flicked her wrist and a small hologram of a fairy holding a wand appeared before her. The fairy appeared solid and each flutter of her wings left a glittering of gold motes that trailed away.

"Show me outside the Oval Office." The fairy waved her wand and a new screen formed before Sara. She pinched the picture and pulled her fingers apart, making the picture much larger. Barbie-doll-sized people paced in front of the closed office door. "This is maximum size without a booster." Sara tapped the blue glass lens on the shoulder of her armor. Another motion of her fingers and the picture doubled in size. "With my booster, I can project up to life size." She tapped it again and a three-dimensional image replaced the screen.

"That's actual footage?" the agent asked.

"That's real time. Those people are there right now. We put sensors in last night in the Oval Office and in the kitchen." Sara turned the holographic image before her with a finger and zoomed in on one of the agents with a simple tap on his face. A small screen popped up and scrolled information about the agent until Sara flicked it closed. "Monitor that man," Sara said while looking at the fairy. The fairy appeared to sit, crossing her legs in mid-air and a tiny screen appeared before her.

"I can ask her to notify me about anything and program her to give me visual cues instead of speech so she doesn't interrupt my train of thought."

Sara reached over and tapped the tiny screen before the fairy and it immediately transformed into a standard size screen. The fairy fluttered to perch on Sara's shoulder. Sara flicked the screen with her finger and the fairy again sat before the tiny screen.

"Notify if he leaves that room."

The fairy saluted and leaned forward as if staring hard.

"Does it have to be a fairy?" one of the agents asked.

Sara laughed and made a shooing motion. The fairy disappeared in a colorful whirl of glitter. "Nope. The standard avatar it comes with is a Valkyrie, but you can use whatever you like.

"That is so cool," the man said as the fairy reappeared and pointed at the screen that formed before her. Soft yellow light ringing the screen grew brighter until Sara flicked it again, making the fairy and her screen disappear.

"You should do the entire place," Pierce said.

"I agree." Sara grinned at him. "Send us the contract and we'll get right on it. We did this to protect our friend. You want a full job, send us the contract."

"Can I see the kitchen?" The president reached out and touched the image, but nothing happened.

"Your wristcomp will do anything mine can, but to interact with images I'm projecting, I need to give permission. Same for you. If you open a screen, I can't close it, use it or move it unless you give permission. Tell your Valory what you want. If you want to set a shortcut tell it that too. For instance, Amy and I share screens a lot so if I double tap the left-hand corner, it unlocks it for her while Team Valor can use any of them any time."

The president asked for a list of sensors and examined each one. He left the kitchen hologram running when Sara received a notification from Stasia.

- 17 -

LOOSE ENDS REMAIN

"Okay, he's stopping. Drew land as soon as you can and get ready," Sara said as she pulled up an aerial view of the car and its environs.

"Our security team is there," Sara said for the benefit of the listening Secret Service who couldn't see them. They listened to the audio of Joey ordering Oz and the first lady from the vehicle.

"Stasia is inside the house. I'm checking the perimeter with Hawk," Charlie reported. "We're mapping now."

"Show me Charlie's map." A new hologram formed in front of her. The agents gathered around as she twisted the angle to give a bird's-eye view. "Remove the roof. Go down one floor. Okay. This is Stasia mapping now."

"Real time?"

"Yes, but not updated in real time, see the black border? It indicates a real picture, but not live. She has sensors and it will turn green when it's live. Ah, there we go." The border of the screen flashed and turned green.

The president inhaled sharply.

"We're live now. Maybe you'd prefer to view in private?" Her glance flicked to the Secret Service agents.

"Can you cut the feed instantly?"

"Yes."

"Let it run."

"Yes, sir."

"Agents are in the house?" a Secret Service agent asked.

"Yes, the first lady isn't in danger. He is." She nodded to the president. "Oh, here we go, Joey's making a call." Sara traced the number and then entered the name that came up in Oz's locate program. "I'm sorry, sir, your secretary again."

The president just nodded.

"I'm tracing the call your secretary's cousin is placing, right now." Two glowing keyboards popped up in front of Sara and she typed on each for a moment then flicked one, making it disappear. "Looks like we're playing phone tag." She repeated the numbers out loud as she typed them. "Split screen." Another screen opened in front of her and she entered the numbers into Oz's locate program as she traced them on the other screen.

"The calls are getting shorter and shorter. Damn that last one was fast, two seconds." Sara tapped keys rapidly then straightened and faced the president. "Senator Bishop is your man. I can't prove it in court, but the last call was to him. I'm sure henchman will show up soon. Valor can get your wife out now and leave our security there to pick them up."

"Do it!" President Carmichael clasped her shoulder a second.

"Take him, Stasia," Sara said. "We're all watching."

In the hologram, Stasia raced across the room and threw a punch at Joey who appeared distracted facing the other way.

Oz stood in front of the first lady using himself as a shield. In moments, Stasia had Joey on the ground in a headlock. She held up her wrist, turning the camera on herself, winked and waved, and Sara snorted with laughter. Charlie entered followed by Brenda, Tony, Sam and Todd.

"She really is a rogue," the president muttered and one of the agents laughed.

Sara pursed her lips as she examined the screens where Stasia was exchanging high-fives with Oz. Oz returned the gesture but was clearly distracted by the screens hanging before her. He was using Stasia's wristcomp.

Pierce said, "They are as their natures bide them, aren't they?"

Sara said, She's a rogue but not one of the backstabbing annoying kind. She's a prankster, a daredevil, a woman who acts quickly and decisively and doesn't take crap from anyone."

The president laid a hand on her arm and Sara flushed.

"We know. She doesn't worry us." He patted her shoulder and she cleared her throat to point to her screens.

"Drew will return your wife by helicopter in a few minutes." Sara patted the president's hand and opened the HUD showing the raids location. "Most of my security team is there now, and you know they can handle this."

"Thank you, Sara." The president sat on the couch and breathed a sigh of relief.

"Glad to help. You could still be in danger. Not to mention the leaks your secretary poses," Sara reminded him.

"Teams are already working on the leaks," Pierce assured her.

"Give Stasia the address of the secretary's house and let her and Oz search it."

Pierce snorted. "Like you need me to give you the address."

"I meant give her permission." Sara rolled her eyes at him.

Pierce laughed and tweaked her ponytail. "We will. You and Oz get back to making us cool gadgets while we'll track down the bad guys."

Sara turned to the president. "Did you get the report about my limb replacement ideas?

"No."

Sara frowned and said, "What about the new boat motor?"

"I did."

"The same day you heard about us helping your campaign?"

The president winced. "Yes."

"That explains why we weren't injured in the attempts." Sara sighed heavily. "We'll worry about that later. I'm just glad no one was hurt, well, on our side anyway. Oz recorded everything in your office earlier. Ask your Valory to see it. You can make copies on a micro SD card or send it in regular email."

She looked at her wristcomp and said, "Valory, write up a report listing my actions here, include all information you have on the phone numbers traced, prepare a graph showing all calls sent from those numbers and note all congruencies. Pierce, I can have Valory check to see if any of those numbers make new calls and follow those chains if you want."

Pierce said, "I'll need to get warrants."

She gave him a rueful grimace. "Will you need us now?"

"No, go eat and get some rest. You have a big day tomorrow." Pierce shook her hand as she rose. A simple voice command closed her screens, and she gathered up her tools and stuffed them into her bag.

Sara shut her eyes and rubbed them. The unused regular wristcomp sat in her palm. "Take this. I'll program it for you. If you get the warrants and want your Valory to map the calls just give me a call and I'll link the program to you." As she spoke, she opened the wristcomp and made the necessary adjustments.

"You'll send me a copy of the report?"

Sara's Valory materialized and said, "A report is already waiting in your inbox, Mr. Taylor. Sara has ordered copies of all information pertaining to this situation be sent to you and the president. I've included all recordings, and copies of the campaign funds that Valor had access to. I've noted the discrepancies they saw and their suppositions. If there's anything else I can do for you, you can email me directly. I can also be reached by text or phone. My contact information is in your contacts under Sara's Valory.

The secret service agent said, "It sounds like a person."

Sara said, "In lots of ways it faster than a person but it can misunderstand directions. We're still working on the programing. Its version of autocorrect can lead to spectacular mistakes."

Pierce said, "Can we set up a meeting to talk over the security protocols?"

"Take a few days to familiarize yourself with your Valory's capabilities and maybe have your legal team look over our security protocols. I can reprogram your Valory to your specific specifications with your clearances, but I'll need legal guidance on that as I have no idea what your position entails."

One of the secret service agents said, "Can it hear the actual phone calls?"

"In theory. It would require a new program. Valory understands the command words to listen but it also knows about privacy laws and right now it would warn you if you were asking for an illegal action. If you persisted or tried to get around its programing it would tell you that you were in violation and might shut down or even call authorities. We're still working on that with our legal team."

She held out her wrist and frowned down at the small computer. "It's a fine line between helpful and intrusive. We're constantly refining Valory's responses. All of these prototypes are running a program to help with that." She turned back to Pierce.

"If the requests for feedback get annoying, come over and I'll turn it off, but all of these prototypes have that program to help us make the Valkyrie operating system better. It won't send anything to us you don't okay first, so you don't need to worry about that, but it will be monitoring your heartbeat and sending us reports on your level of frustration when using the device and if it senses you're having issues it might offer to connect to one of us so we can talk about the cause and find solutions."

Peirce nodded his understanding. "Can I ask it to wait until after meetings or turn it off during them?"

"You can turn it off whenever you want and it has varied levels of reactivation from a simple on command or requiring a passcode spoken to wake it, or a hard reset by pushing the button there on the side, depending on how concerned you are about accidently turning it on. If you don't want your Valory to interrupt you just tell it not to. Its smart enough to understand phrases like don't interrupt me during calls or don't speak during meetings. And you could add exceptions like don't ever interrupt me unless it's my wife, or the hospital, or any designation you like. So you could make your own list of reasons, put people or situations into lists and tell it. That program is still being tweaked and you'll be asked for feedback on it."

A few minutes later she handed the wristcomp to Pierce.

"It has the security program in it and access to the raid programing. So make sure you're somewhere private when you learn those programs."

"Thanks, Sara, I look forward to working with it. I've read the reports before, of course, but I must say I'm excited to see it and learn what it can do in person."

She turned to the president.

"Every idea we had for your campaign is already in a report in your inbox."

The president said, "When I give my televised speech about the vice president's death, I'll make it clear you've informed my campaign managers about your ideas. Hopefully, that will stop the attacks on you."

Sara pinched the bridge of her nose and sighed. "So many loose ends remain to unravel."

"None are urgent." Pierce guided her to the door. "Go home and rest."

"Could I get a ride to the hotel? I have no home to go to."

- 18 -

SURPRISE VISITS

Marcus had taken Tank and left the lights on. After taking a shower, Sara put on one of Charlie's t-shirts and ordered room service.

Amy answered her call on the first ring.

"Everything is fine," Sara said before Amy could ask. "We caught our bad guy, or at least we know who he is. Pierce Taylor is handling it. Don't miss the news tonight, it's going to be a major story. Tell Paul you guys can stop writing reports, and thanks; you were a huge help." The girls spoke a few more minutes. After promising to call when she had more time, Sara hung up and started working on her report.

A knock on the door interrupted her. After putting on the complimentary robe she checked the peep hole.

Outside the door, her stepmother tapped her foot and glanced at her watch, then knocked again, a deep scowl on her face.

Shocked, Sara opened the door. "Are you okay?"

Tara slapped her, a sharp crack of flesh on flesh.

Sara glared and rubbed her stinging cheek, taking a step back. "If you touch me again, you'll regret it." She scowled and answered her ringing phone. "Tara's here."

* * *

Charlie straighten in surprise and his eyes flickered blue. Tara had hurt and surprised her, and she was angry now. He keyed into her wristcomp right as Sara double tapped it to start a recording.

"What do you want?" Sara asked shortly.

"You to disappear off the face of the Earth!" Tara snapped. "But I'll settle for you to stop being a complete slut and ending up in the tabloids every week." She whipped a wadded paper at Sara's head and looked surprised when Sara yanked it from her hand.

Charlie watched through her wristcomp with narrowed eyes, his anger growing with every word Tara spoke.

"You came here for that?" Sara sounded disbelieving. Charlie didn't believe it either.

"No, I came here to warn you. I'm getting tired of hearing from friends about you and who you're sleeping with this week. It's making me look bad, and I'm not going to take it. You might think this is a good way to get into the business, but I'll make sure it doesn't work!"

Sara laughed. "What are you going to do, slap me again? I wouldn't advise it. I'm stronger than you, and I bet I hit harder."

"Not only will I disown you and ruin your reputation, what little you have left, but I'll make sure you never work in Hollywood!"

"Go ahead. I don't want to work there. I have a job I like."

Tara ignored her. "And not only you. Keep trying to get in the papers and I'll ruin your father and drag your precious mother's name through the mud. Ask him, he knows I can. One more picture, Sara, and I'll make you sorry." A furious glower on her face, Tara stalked away.

Sara slammed the door and whirled away, magic surrounding her in a turbulent storm.

Charlie overrode her phone controls and unmuted himself. "What the hell is going on? Are you okay?" he sighed and smacked himself in the head over the stupidity of that question. Furious anger mixed with embarrassment and worry, she wasn't okay.

"I'm fine, just mad. I'm not taking the Idol's harassment anymore."

"Okay, but don't do anything until I get there."

"What could I do?" Sara shouted and threw the paper into the trash.

"I don't know, but whatever you think of wait, please." Charlie bit his lip, cringing as her anger spiked.

"Ned Font is not getting away with hurting my friends!"

"He won't." Charlie winced as her embarrassment and worry mounted. Whatever Ned had printed she was worried about him seeing it. "We'll be back soon. Order us food. We'll talk when I get there."

Food was waiting when he arrived, and Sara was calm and to Charlie's surprise nostalgic. He glanced at her screens as he kissed her cheek and smiled himself at the sight of their young faces.

Stasia had taken a great picture their first Christmas Eve together when Sara was fifteen. A soft smile on her lips, Sara traced the shape of his young face. Charlie flicked through the pictures, pausing on one of them in St. Vincent's and another of them with his parents celebrating his last birthday.

It was clear she was working on showing the truth of the pictures with short video clips showing how the pictures had been presented to mislead.

He paused again, nodding thoughtfully at the picture of Rick in Maine covered in mud from clamming, sharing a kiss with Stasia while Marcus stood in the background facing the other way dressed in a uniform, guarding them.

Next, she'd added a picture of Toric talking with Oz dressed the same way right inside the doorway of the lab where they worked. Brenda could be seen in the background guarding them in a great photo of Oz, Charlie and Hawk, laughing by the campfire in Maine and the same shot an hour later with Sara sleeping on his shoulder while he and Oz talked. On the other side of the fire, Stasia and Rick shared s'mores. Marcus was sitting by them wearing shorts, holding a soda can, clearly off duty and a friend.

Her choices did give a true representation.

"Put in the tourney shots and the ones with you and Stasia and Camila when you were younger before we played together."

He smiled softly and kissed her cheek. He felt exactly the same, so grateful to have met her.

Anyone who saw these pictures would see the truth, a group of close friends with him being her only boyfriend. All that remained was to figure out the best way to get these seen and her story told.

Marcus and Rick entered with Hawk and Tank.

Marcus said, "Brenda is getting rooms; I just wanted to see for myself you were okay." He turned to Charlie. "Don't leave alone. I've got it worked out for tomorrow." He paused at the door with one hand on the handle. "You know the drill, written reports ASAP. Stay alert." He nodded at everyone and left.

Sara turned off her screens, gesturing to the food laden table. "Foods here and getting cold. How did it go?"

"Easy," Hawk said as everybody crowded around the table.

Sara cast purify food and drink before they ate.

"We didn't even use magic," Hawk continued as he helped himself to a burger. "Two men arrived; we took them and searched them, then passed them on to waiting agents. Agent Lewis and his friends will be extremely busy."

"We stopped at the secretary's house, and I found a large stash of cash and recorders in her yard." Stasia reached for a soda. "I'm hoping she kept all of them. She had them buried in the vegetable garden."

"Did she say who she sold the information to?" Sara asked.

"No. I'm sure they'll check the money for prints," Stasia said.

Sara turned to Oz. "We need the list of all prints that show up for your locate program."

Oz paused with a French fry halfway to his mouth. "There's still a ton of information to go through. We found Senator Bishop, but how we found him won't be admissible in court. I'm hoping they keep us out of it. Our use of cell towers and satellites wasn't legal."

"I was thinking the same thing, and I have a solution." Sara leaned forward, her eyes sparkling. "Let's launch our own satellites and offer phone service."

"Can we afford to do that?" Charlie asked.

Sara nodded, grinning widely. "With Oz's computer system they'd be small, and we've already been working on the programing. We pay access fees now to use existing ones, but those fees don't give us the right to search like we just did. As to getting them out there, I was thinking we could use the ray-gun."

Oz dropped the French-fry and opened a screen. "Yeah, let's do it. We'll need to readjust the—"

Hawk cut him off. "The cost?"

"Off the top of my head, I'd say about twenty to fifty thousand dollars apiece. And we'll need time to design it and test it," Sara said.

Oz flipped his screen to show Sara. "We could add video and try to make a solar powered engine like the boat engine and be able to move them." His voice rose in excitement. "We could build a bigger one with a ray-gun on it and shoot down, not up."

Charlie laughed. "See what you did? You know you can't rile him up like that at bedtime, we'll never get him to sleep now."

Sara grinned, turning to Oz. "It's an interesting idea. We'll need to run simulations and design a delivery system. I'm thinking I can shield the small phone satellites and we just use the ray-gun to push them out, but bigger ones, I don't know."

"Okay, both of you…." Stasia reached over and flicked the screen closed. "Chill, we have enough going on right now. I'm not saying don't do it, but not right this minute, okay?" She turned to Sara. "Charlie recorded Tara. If she does try to make you look bad, we can use that."

"I don't care if my reputation is ruined." A frown erased her grin, and she stared at her fingers twining in her lap. "I'm so sorry, guys, but the Idol is making you look bad. It won't be hard to prove they're intentionally slandering us though." Sara turned to Charlie. "I want to do an interview with you on a respectable television show with a real reporter. Then I'm going to sue the Idol. We could lose, well, we probably will lose money even if we win the suit, but I can't let it stand."

"A TV show, you sure?" Charlie leaned back in his chair and rose an eyebrow.

"Yes, with a respected reporter. I can leave you out of it if you want. Being linked to me won't be pleasant for you."

"We share everything, the good and the bad." He frowned at her. "Do you still have the article? I didn't see it this week."

"In the garbage." Sara pointed to the garbage can as a red flush climbed over her cheeks.

Anger, embarrassment, and worry again buffeted him from her as he smoothed the wrinkles and flipped the pages until he found the pictures and winced.

"Yeah, I see your point." The pictures angered him, not for their content but because of how embarrassed she was for him to see them. The red on her cheeks grew darker as he flipped slowly through the pages." He laughed at the picture of her and Stasia hugging and glanced at her in consternation when she felt more worried. He followed her gaze to Stasia, and his laughter fled. *Stasia might be angry that the Idol insinuated she and Sara were having an affair.* He tried to project confidence but knew he wasn't managing it by her response. She worried more now about keeping Stasia happy and this wouldn't help.

He said, "The commandant knows the truth. Stasia and Hawk won't be in trouble for hugging. I find it interesting Ned got this picture, not only published so fast, but was there to take it that day as well. If we can prove Ned knew there'd be something worth seeing, he could be in real trouble."

With another wince, he handed the paper to Stasia. *It was better to get it over with.*

Stasia examined the pictures with a deep scowl on her brow and then handed it to Hawk who laughed and passed it to Rick.

Stasia shrugged and said, "We shouldn't have hugged in uniform, but Susan had just threatened you, so I think we can be excused. The last one when Hawk came back and we hugged him, Charlie had nearly been assassinated. I'm the only one in uniform and might get in trouble for it, but if so, it's my worry, not yours. The commandant knows he's my brother. Hawk might get in trouble for being out of uniform, but that could be explained by saying he just changed quickly after the chase. Everyone thinks Oz was Hawk when he started the chase."

Stasia studied the pictures again. "Either way it won't be bad trouble. For the school's sake, we should clear up the misinformation though. The Idol makes it seem like the school lets Sara rampage through the student body as her personal sex toys." She winced and glanced at Sara. "Sorry, Sara, but that's the impression."

"I know," Sara agreed angrily. "The whole potato chip analogy, no two are ever enough, gets me so angry...."

"Make it clear we're engaged and in love." Charlie kissed her brow, smoothing back her hair. Static crackled when he touched her. Small sparks flicked about them. Her magic was also upset, and his frown deepened. "Sue them. If we lose a million dollars, so be it."

"It won't be a million, I promise. More like a hundred thousand." Sara snatched the paper from Rick and crumpled it up again.

Oz cleared his throat. "Sara, Hawk and I get propositioned all the time because of you and that will happen to Charlie if you announce you're a couple."

"We *are* a couple." Charlie snorted and rolled his eyes. "Sooner or later someone is bound to notice."

Sara rubbed her face with her hands, muffling her voice. "I'm sorry you guys get bothered."

"Oh, it's no bother. I don't mind at all," Oz assured her with a wink. "Those girls never make me glow blue."

Sara blushed, and Hawk looked thoughtful.

Stasia laughed and then rolled her eyes at her brother. "Don't even think about it!"

Hawk laughed and blushed, and they all knew he was thinking about it.

"Easy for you to say." Hawk nodded at Rick. "Every girl around is too old for me."

"Don't drag me into this." Rick waved his hands and stood. "I'm an innocent bystander. What room is yours?" Stasia pointed, and he headed for it. "I'm going to go shower. Thanks for dinner."

Sara gazed hopefully at Charlie.

"Yeah, me too." Charlie grabbed Sara's hand, pulled her after him, and swung her into his arms. He was kissing her as he kicked the bedroom door closed behind them.

Hawk stared after them. "I envy him. Not for Sara," he added hastily when Stasia looked surprised. "For having someone he loves that much who loves him back."

"You'll find her." Stasia hugged her brother. "Right now, she's out there growing up. I admit, you probably won't find her for a few more years and waiting sucks, but I promise, you *will* find her." She headed to her bedroom as Oz and Hawk laugh over Sara's groupies, rolling her eyes again as she smothered a small laugh of her own.

Rick was just coming out of the shower. She grinned, pushed him back in, and closed the door behind them.

- 19 -

JOY

Sara woke before Charlie and snuggled against his back. Her body still and tense, she wiped a tear from her cheek and closed her eyes, rising a hand to rub her brow.

"I would put them in another electronic device that was allowed and take it out," she said softly.

"Take what out?" Charlie asked as he rolled over to face her.

"Sorry, didn't mean to wake you. Just wondering aloud how Joyce removed the recordings." Sara kissed him and rubbed her cheek on his morning stubble.

"I was awake a few minutes. You were worrying loudly." Her nightmares always woke him, but he didn't think she was aware of it.

Sara sighed. "Sorry, thinking how close you came to being killed."

"Not close at all." He traced the curve of her brow, then her bottom lip. "You were right there as always."

Anxiety mounting, her blue eyes searched his. "If I hadn't been there? What if I'd gone to Massachusetts? What if that shot had hit you?"

"One shot couldn't kill me, even a head shot." He shrugged and settled her more comfortably on his shoulder. "What if a meteorite hits, or aliens invade, or I get hit by a bus?" Charlie kissed her lightly. "Don't worry about what ifs. The life we live is dangerous. That will never change. Even if we lost the magic forever, we know too much. We can never go back to who we were when we were kids."

She shivered and pressed closer. "I could disguise everyone permanently with surgery—your entire family. We could escape, disappear and lead normal lives."

"No, we couldn't. I'm sorry, sweetheart, but you couldn't stop searching for a way to make your heals work on everyone. Oz could never stop thinking of new and better ways to do things. Can you really see Oz as a bartender or banker or whatever?"

"No, you're right." Tears filled her eyes. "I hate that by being me, I can get you killed."

Charlie laughed lightly and settled her head on his shoulder. "I love that you want to help those children, that giving your heal to everybody is so important to you. Your compassion is one of my favorite things about you. If I get killed, you can rest easy knowing I died doing what I love. I always wanted to be in the military. Our life is a dream come true for me, being a part of something this important."

Muffled in his shoulder, her voice cracked. "I can't help worrying about it."

He stroked her bright hair. "I know. I trust you to heal me. To stand behind me with your protection. Believe me, I'm happier taking the hits. I hate when you're the target."

"My warrior," she murmured, and kissed him, anxiety transforming to lust.

Filled with heat, he returned the kiss. Passion echoed between them. The magic's happiness pulsed, filling him with its pleasure.

Dressed for the day in jeans and t-shirts, they met the others in the dining room. "So, what's the plan for today?" Stasia excited gaze traveled them.

"Joy," Sara said unhappily.

"When?" Rick exchanged worried glances with Stasia and his brother.

Sara said, "As soon as possible, I guess. I want to get it over with."

"We'll try our best." Charlie squeezed Sara's hand. "We should meet with the commandant first and fill him in, and we have reports to write, and we should get started on sorting all of that information. Plus, we have bugs to pick up and place."

"You guys do Joy. I'll handle the commandant and the bugs. Oz can handle the reports. Attempt to change Joy and take the rest of the day to recover and relax," Stasia said.

"I'll call Marcus," Hawk offered.

Sara nodded. They were all quiet, listening to his conversation. Everyone was nervous about today's events.

"Okay, Marcus will summon us. Drew is already there with Joy. He'll summon Guthrie and Brenda, and they have the medical equipment. Lee is on her way here and will summon us back once we're done."

"Rick, you and Stasia stay away from us for a day or so," Charlie said. "Making one warrior might make her want more, so she'll be staying away from everyone for a few days."

Stasia nodded. "Rick and I will be at the lab with Joy until I return to school tomorrow. The female Scouts will be your guards for a few days as a precaution."

Sara frowned. "Not necessary. I won't need guards inside the hotel."

"You'll always have at least one from now on. Sorry, Guthrie's orders," Stasia said. "We count as guards, but Charlie doesn't. He's too distracted with you."

"Don't worry about it. Guards can wait in the hallway." Hawk laughed when her frown deepened. "They'll be working, not there to socialize. If you want to hang out with them, invite them in when a new guard shows up."

Sara nodded again, clearly not happy with the arrangements. "Let's get this over with."

Marcus summoned them and Hawk.

Before he could blink Charlie stood in ankle high grass on the side of a mountain. *Marcus had picked a nice spot,*" Charlie thought approvingly as he inhaled the clean mountain air. Warm sun shone down on him and thick pines ringed the small clearing.

Drew summoned Brenda and Guthrie. The sergeant arrived with a hand-held video camera. Joy was there already, wearing a gray sweat suit. Brenda took a blood sample from her, labeled it, and put it in a small cooler.

"We're ready here whenever you are. The Geiger counter is set up, the medical equipment is ready if we need it, and we have our white bracelets," Marcus said and tapped his.

"Don't use one on Joy. Use standard revival techniques, no magic," Sara reminded him.

"We won't use magic unless we have to," Marcus assured her. "We'll take good care of her."

Charlie pulled Drew aside. "You're okay with all this?"

"It's her choice, and I respect that. I'm worried, but I trust Sara's heals."

Joy kissed Drew's cheek. "I'll be fine. A few days of being sick than a lifetime of kicking your ass."

Drew laughed and pulled her into a hug.

"If it doesn't work, or ends badly, don't blame yourselves, okay? It's my choice." Joy gave Sara a hug.

"I know. I also know I'm doing this for selfish reasons." Sara rubbed her hands together, then clenched them into fists at her side. "Try your hardest to not want our magic. Don't think of us at all. We believe we got the magic by thinking of it. Try to envision not needing to share it, please." Sara let out a deep sigh. "My head wants you to be a warrior, but I'm worried I'll make you a rogue to keep you from Charlie."

"Either way I'm okay with," Joy assured her. "Drew and I are happy. I'll think of that and him."

"It isn't selfish to not want to share what we have," Charlie whispered. "Joy knows we're doing this for Stasia, and she's smart enough to know why. Everyone realizes we want to only share magic between us. That isn't selfish, Sara."

Sara hid her face in his neck, clutching his shirt with both hands. "I'm afraid."

"I am too, and you know exactly how much. Whatever happens, I'll always love you."

Sara took a deep breath and backed away from him. "Everyone better back far away. It's been very hard holding my magic back from Charlie the last few days."

"The area is warded. No one is near us," Hawk said.

Sara let her magic loose. Dark-blue and dense, already lit by sparks of static electricity, her magic swirled around her. Charlie's magic rushed eagerly to her. A warm wind gusted when the magic collided and thunder sounded. They both grabbed one of Joy's hands and she screamed as the magic, a two-toned cloud of blue twirling in shimmering arcs lit by static and small flickers of electricity, engulfed them. An electric hum filled the air that suddenly smelled of ozone. "I want Joy to be a warrior!" Sara yelled.

"I want Joy to be a warrior," Charlie repeated and reached out and took Sara's hand. The lightning struck Sara with a sizzling crash.

Sara screamed as Joy collapsed, their grip keeping her from falling to the ground. The lightning pulsed as it traveled through them. The blue of the magic coated them and glowed white at the edges, outlining them brightly. Hair lifted in the warm breeze as Saint Elmo's fire delineated each strand.

Drew glanced at his wristcomp. "Three minutes."

Sara collapsed, and the lightning still traveled through them in pulses. Charlie knelt slowly, keeping a grip on both Sara and Joy.

"Four minutes." Drew frowned at the HUD displaying their vitals. Joy was flatlined. She needed CPR and soon. Sara's vitals were low, her pulse intermittent. Charlie's heartbeat was irregular, his pulse fast. Sara's was too slow and getting slower.

"Five minutes." Drew clenched his hands. "We need to stop this soon or we'll kill them all."

"Stop it how?" Brenda asked dryly. Not waiting for an answer, she charged the defibrillator.

Drew bit his lip until it bled.

Brenda handed him the oxygen canister and breath mask and engaged her white bracelet. Thirty seconds later, the lightning disappeared with another whoosh of air and rumble of thunder. Charlie fell over.

Drew raced to Joy and pulled her away. Sweat trickled down his cheek as he placed the oxygen on her and started chest compressions. Brenda knelt beside him ready with the defibrillator, a needle of adrenaline in her hand.

Hawk crouched beside Charlie and Sara, engaged his white bracelet and healed them both. Sara sat and healed them both again and crawled into Charlie's lap crying. She placed her magic coated hands on his face. He leaned his forehead on hers and lifted his glowing hands to her cheeks.

"Are we clear of radiation?" Charlie's voice cracked, and he cleared his throat. Fire traversed his bones in painful waves that were slowly subsiding. Nausea roiled his stomach; Sara's misery was intensifying his.

"I'll check." Hawk brought them water bottles and ran a Geiger counter over them. "No, you're hot."

"Get Joy to the lab, and I'll dispel the area," Sara said shakily.

"As soon as she's breathing." Brenda didn't look up from Joy.

Charlie took his shirt off and Sara rested her face on him. He ran his hands under her T-shirt and rubbed her bare back. Contact with her bare skin eased the humming in his bones.

He said, "Sara and I need to be alone."

Neither asked about Joy's condition, they saw it wasn't good.

"Okay, I have a pulse. Let her breath on her own, Drew." Brenda flipped the defibrillator off and called Liz. "Summon her, Liz. Joy's alone with you in group six, emitting radiation and still unconscious."

"I'm ready here," Liz said, "summon three."

Joy disappeared. Sara rose and casted Dispel over everyone and the entire area. As soon as she was done, she put her face against Charlie's chest again.

"Are we clear?" Charlie asked impatiently. In the seconds they weren't touching, the hum had increased until it felt like fire ants beneath his skin.

Brenda nodded at the Geiger counter. "It's clear of radiation. Are you two okay? Did it work?"

"I'll report later. We need to be alone now." Anger edged his voice and magic filled his eyes. "Lee, can you summon us, please?"

"Summon three," Lee replied.

"Thanks." Charlie nodded at Lee when they appeared in the hotel room. His magic swirled about them growing denser as the hum beneath his skin increased.

Skin contact soothed the magic and he sighed with relief when he ripped her shirt off to hug her.

Sara started crying again. "That was horrible."

Charlie wrapped her in a tight embrace and carried her to the bed. "Don't stop touching me." The hum eased with contact, from a shout to a whisper, and he wondered if it was their magic communicating. For over an hour Sara lay across his chest. Their magic had disappeared, reabsorbed by their skin. Charlie went to the bathroom and vomited. A yellow heal hit him as he washed his face. Both removed their clothing and lay back down together.

Nausea burned in his gut and his bones ached, a deep burning sensation that Sara shared. The magic flickered over them, a new sensation, humming distantly as if it communicated on a level he couldn't perceive. Eventually, the humming desisted and his grip on her lightened.

His magic had dissipated but hers surrounded him. This sensation he recognized from last summer. The craving to touch him that wasn't her, but the magic. They'd woken it from its usual passive state.

He tangled his fingers in her hair and his kiss became passionate and she returned it, the craving becoming his, not just his magic's.

Afterwards, they fell asleep curled together. Charlie woke before her and left her sleeping as he showered.

Terrified fear slammed into him, making him grunt. He raced into the bedroom, dripping wet and sliding on the slick tiles, his summoned sword in hand. "What!"

In bed, clutching the sheet to her chest, Sara stared at him, her eyes wide in her pale face. "Nothing. Sorry; it scared me when you weren't here. I'm fine, finish your shower." The pounding of her heart and panting breaths alarmed him.

"I'm okay." She laid back down and waved him back to the bathroom. Her fear had been replaced by embarrassment.

He hesitated, adrenaline making his hands shake, and then returned to the shower. A few minutes later he returned to her, toweling himself off.

"What were you afraid of?"

"You were gone, and it scared me."

"Just in the shower. Need me to stay here tonight?"

"Yes, but you have school. I'm okay alone. You'll see me tomorrow, right?"

"Yeah, but where? I don't want to go near the lab."

"I need to see you." Sara sat up and grabbed him. A tinge of panic laced her voice and brightness.

"I will, I promise, just thinking of where we could go."

"I'll summon you here. Hawk can summon you back."

"Okay, kick everyone else out of group six. Are you sure you're okay here alone tonight?"

"Yeah," she assured him. "If I need you, I'll call."

A glance at the time showed they still had a few hours before he needed to report back. "I have a few more hours. Let's eat."

Anxiety tinged with fear met that request.

She said, "Let's eat here. I don't want to see anyone, just you."

He called room service and then held her close until it arrived. The nausea and burning had passed. The desperate need to touch had eased for him, but her magic was pushing her for contact with his. Relief when he touched her and anxiety when he wasn't touching her decide him. "I'm staying tonight. One night away won't matter."

Sara didn't protest.

He was surprised, then worried, then relieved he'd decided to stay. He called Major Nelson and told him he was staying with her.

"Are you both okay?"

"Getting there. It was horrible. We'll report, but not today."

"I'll clear it with the school. Stay with her as long as she needs."

"I planned to," Charlie said and hung up.

- 20 -

I CAN T DO THIS AGAIN

Dawn hadn't yet broken over the horizon when Charlie woke Sara. "Are you okay if I go to class?"

"Yes, thanks for staying." Soft, sleep-warmed skin snuggled against him as she stretched. Content and happy, she pulled him closer for a kiss then pushed him away. "Go get smarter. I'll summon you later." He rose, and she glanced at the clock. "Jeez, it's four-thirty in the morning." An offended expression on her face, she rolled over and pulled the blanket over her head.

Charlie laughed and pulled the blanket down to kiss her again.

"Hawk will summon me there. I love you."

"I love you, too."

Love echoing between them, he tucked the blanket around her and left.

Two hours later her fear surprised a grunt from him. He ran from the classroom while tapping the icon to connect them.

"Sorry, I'm fine. I forgot you left, and it scared me when I woke and you weren't there. You're okay, right?"

"I'm fine, just worried about you. Joy's doing fine."

"Don't say her name!" Sara yelled, instantly enraged and inflamed with jealousy. "Did you go see her?" she asked pitifully, her anger turning to fear, and she started to cry. "Don't go see her again."

"I didn't see her. Stasia told me. Are you okay?"

"I'm okay, but don't go to her."

"You're not okay." Charlie sighed and glanced at the time, he needed to get back to class, but her emotions were all over and a frisson of fear ran down his spine." I don't want her at all. Not in any way. You don't want her either, do you?" he asked in sudden alarm.

"No, I don't even want to hear her name. I'm calling Brenda. Liz needs to check my hormone levels. I'm a bit out of control here."

"I feel it," Charlie admitted. "Do you need me?"

"I think I'm okay, and I'll call if I get worse. I'll let you know as soon as I find out anything."

Another wave of panicked fear brought Charlie to his feet three hours later. He hit his panic button and ran from his classroom, holding his beeping wrist to show the professor. Scared and needing him desperately, Sara's anxiety agitated his magic, making his eyes glow. Unable to contain it, he ran into the nearest restroom and into a stall where he leaned against the door waiting for her summons.

"Summon me," he said as a greeting when he answered her call. "No one will see."

Sara summoned him to her.

"What happened?" he asked as Sara clutched him and burst into tears.

"I can't do that again, I can't!" Her grip was hard enough to bruise. "Don't let me go! I don't want anyone except you. God, I hate this, I hate this!" Magic rushed from her and engulfed Charlie. Sara screamed and recoiled, falling to her knees, trying to force the magic back.

"Calm down and let the magic go. Brenda, get out!" Charlie removed his clothes as fast he could down to his boxer shorts to give her as much skin contact as possible. He yanked her shirt off again and pulled her against his chest. "You don't need another warrior. I'm here. Let the magic go!"

The magic fluctuated wildly as she drew it back and it escaped her again.

Continuously moaning, "No, no, no" she fell to the floor again. Her hair hung in a curtain around her face as she sobbed and struggled to force the magic back.

"I won't, I won't, stop, stop!" Her breath came in panicked gulps as her muscles strained.

"Let it go!" Charlie yelled and shook her lightly.

A wild look in her eye, she let it go and collapsed against his chest sobbing, "I only want you, only you, I only want you!"

Sparks zapped his skin as her magic churned around them. Charlie grasped her by the arms and shook her a moment then pressed her face against his chest. "I only want you too. We're together and safe. Just us with our magic." He spoke to her in a soft, calm voice while rubbing her back, surrounding her in his magic as her magic receded. Shaken by the emotional storm, he sat with a thump in the nearest chair with her in his lap.

Sara rubbed her eyes with both hands and covered her face. "I'm so scared. I can't do this again."

"And we don't have to. Now we know what will happen, and we'll be together, and it won't be as bad."

Muffled in her hands, her voice shook. "I need the medicine Brenda has."

A headache throbbed behind his right eye and his shoulders felt tight from tension. Brenda answered on the first ring. "Leave her medicine outside the door. Don't come in." He held Sara tightly against his chest. Her desperate need to touch him was a thrumming under his skin, a need so strong it physically hurt her. He was afraid to set her down for the trip to the door. Magic escaped her and sought him randomly.

The package Brenda left contained a shot and a white pill. He gave her the shot and handed her the pill and a water bottle. "What's going on?"

"My hormone levels are higher. The shot should help, but if I can't control the magic it might not. That pill was to prevent conception from last night, but again, it might not work for me." Tears trailed across her face. "I'm so scared."

"I know, but this isn't the same, Sara. None of this is the same. The levels aren't as high, right?"

No, but it's only been a day. It took two weeks last time. Oh god, I can't do that again.

He shook her lightly to stop her hyperventilating. "It won't happen. Let your magic loose, don't hold it in. It's learning too. Don't be afraid, I'm here."

Her fear didn't lessen.

"You don't need to get away, right?"

"No."

"See, it's different. This is your fear. If you can relax, your magic will too. What are you afraid of?"

"That I'll go out of control and try to take the raid. I'm afraid you'll leave me for Joy. Oh god, Charlie, what if I'm pregnant?" Crying and shaking in his arms, she continued to babble. "I'm afraid you'll want Joy, want her more than me, and I'll be alone. I'm afraid I'm scaring you away with these hormone problems. God, Charlie, I'm so afraid."

Angry now, she dashed the tears from her eyes. "I'm afraid you'll get in trouble for being here. I know I'm not supposed to be afraid of that, but I am. Please don't go to Joy. This is so melodramatic, but I really do think I'll die without you."

"Joy means nothing to me. I don't want her in any way. Don't be afraid of losing me. We'll handle the hormones. We did before, and we can again." Charlie pulled her close and rubbed her back as she calmed. "Your magic wants to touch me, so let it out. If you need to leave here, we will. The Scouts can summon us away. I'll keep you from the raid. Do you need to change any of them?"

He was relieved when she shook her head no. "As to being pregnant, we take precautions, but nothing is foolproof except abstinence. No sex for us until your hormones are better. It won't matter; I could wait forever for you. If you're pregnant, we'll be a family sooner than we planned. I'll love any child we have. I love you so much; we're going to have an amazing life together. There are still so many things we never did together. I want to get a bigger sailboat, one we can live on, and we can sail away just the two of us." He continued to tell her his dreams for them as he held her close.

The fear receded replaced by a low-level anxiety. The steadiness of her emotions relieved him. Anxiety wasn't good, but it was better than the crazy highs and lows of last summer.

To soothe her magic, he concentrated on his love for her. The way he felt when her hair brushed his shoulder in the mornings when she snuggled against him all soft and warm. Pride when she learned something new. How lucky he felt that she loved him so intensely.

The magic might prove to be a deadly addiction for both of them, he thought ruefully, wincing at her spike of alarm. To survive her death, he'd need a priest's magic, but he'd rather die than live without her. She'd say the same, but the world needed her heals and incredible mind. Someday, when things were calmer, they needed to talk about that. If he were to die, she'd need another warrior's magic to survive, but this was definitely not the day to bring it up.

There was time to worry about that later, he decided when she stirred uneasily. She jumped from his lap and ran to the bathroom where she was sick. A few minutes later she returned to him and rested her damp face against his chest.

"It's normal from the shot and that pill, don't worry about it." She rested one hand on his heart, the other on the pulse in his neck. "This fear isn't for being sick, it's for loosing another baby. If my magic makes me pregnant again... well, it doesn't know how to." Her fear receded buried beneath intense concentration. "The magic does it wrong, it rushes the process too much. A pregnancy implanted in the wrong spot will kill the baby. But maybe I could use my magic to transplant it to the right spot. A transplant would be bad for the baby though and hard on the doctor doing it." Concentration turned to guilt, and hot tears trailed across his chest. "I really don't want to kill another baby."

"The first pregnancy wasn't viable. Trying could've killed you, and it wouldn't have worked anyway, just made you sick. You didn't kill our baby. If you're pregnant and it's in the wrong spot, we'll have to remove it. I'm so sorry, Sara, I don't think any doctor could do that operation on you." Every word he spoke filled her with despair. "I could try, but... I'm so sorry, Sara."

"Please, Charlie, I have to try!"

"What would we need?"

"A specialist in transplanting embryos. The surgery would be impossible for me to do on myself. I don't know how we would explain the pain of touching me."

"Could Doctor Elliot do it?"

"I don't know. Embryotic transplant is a specialized procedure."

"We can ask him. How long until you know if you're pregnant?"

"A week or so if things go normally." A violent tremor wracked her.

"We'll try to save the baby if it's not dangerous for you."

Her relief at his decision was overwhelming. "Sweetheart, I want you to have my children. I admit not like this, the regular way with no magical pressure. I wanted more time alone with you first, but I'll always want our children.

"We can find a specialist, get them clearance, and pay them tons of money, but we can do it." He kissed her temple and brushed her hair back from her face. "Let's not worry about that right now. That's weeks away. Now, we can just be happy to be together." He glanced at his wristcomp, checking her vital signs which were all nice and steady in normal ranges.

"Are you hungry?" he asked a while later.

"No, I'm kind of queasy still. In another hour or so I'll recheck the levels. Order room service if you want."

Before ordering food, he called Brenda and asked her to get supplies so Sara could check her blood.

"I have them now. Liz wants new blood work every twelve hours. Can we get you anything else?"

"Lucky and some food. Sara is doing better, but I need to be with her. Have someone go to a secluded spot with a tent or something in case she needs to get away. There's no sign of that, I just want to be prepared. Keep the raid away from us too. She doesn't feel any need to change anyone, but she's worried about it." Worried was such an understatement, he almost laughed. He wanted to know how Joy was but didn't want to ask. "Thanks, Brenda, we appreciate all the help."

"If you need anything, call. I'll be nearby. When Lucky and the food get here, I'll knock and leave them at the door. Everyone is fine. Don't worry about us."

"You're worried about Joy," Sara said and narrowed her eyes.

"A little, aren't you?"

"Yes, she's my friend. Drew's my friend, but I'm trying not to think of her. I really don't want to share you."

"We're going about this the wrong way. Instead of trying to ignore her, let's accept the fact we care about her and think of her as our child. It's okay to love her and want her to be strong and happy. The magic is probably confused as hell from us trying to push her away like this."

"Our child? Joy is sort of our child, I guess, we did create her together." Suddenly happy, she laughed. "Congratulations, it's a twenty-six-year-old girl."

Charlie laughed too. "Our first daughter. What should her curfew be? Maybe I better have a talk with Drew." Tension eased as they admitted to each other they cared about Joy.

Sara used her wristcomp to call Liz. "How's Joy?"

"Headache, diarrhea, not vomiting yet. She's playing the game. No sign of being able to cast herself. She's emitting m-radiation and her spirits are good. She reported feeling like her bones were on fire when the lightning hit. The signs are good, Sara."

"Text me updates on her condition please. Send her my love. I don't want to talk with her myself. Wait!" Sara squeezed her eyes closed and bit her lip. "Don't send her my love. Don't mention me. God, this really sucks."

"Sara, Joy knows you love her. She also knows why you aren't talking to her right now. How are you doing?"

"Better, I'm worried, but better with Charlie. I'll send more blood in for you to check. I'm still a little queasy, and I threw up once."

"Not surprising. Use your heals. Heals probably won't help if your magic is raising your hormone levels, but they won't hurt either."

"If I'm pregnant, I want to try to save this baby."

"I'm already searching for good doctors. I'll send you links to ones I think could help, and I'm sending links to Pierce. As soon as we know for sure, we can pick one and get them here."

"Thank you," Sara said, her voice ringing with sincerity. "I wasn't sure you'd help me. Well, not you, the government."

"I'd help you even if they order me not to," Liz assured her. "I'm studying up on the procedure just in case."

"Thank you, Liz."

"Let me know if you develop any other symptoms."

"I will." A relieved smile on her face, she straddled Charlie's lap and pressed against him, then blushed and started to stand.

He held her against him, keeping her in place. "It's okay," he murmured. "I'll live. I can't help responding to you, but I can ignore it. This is nice too." He rubbed her back, debating taking her pants off to give her more skin contact, but it was probably better for their self-control if her pants stayed on. In jeans and a bra, she tempted him enough. The uniform he'd worn here lay in a heap by the doorway, leaving him in his boxers. It was more than enough skin contact for the magic to be happy.

"What should we name our boat?" He asked as he stroked her hair, gently separating the strands with his fingers.

"Can we bring Lucky and Rhea?"

"Sure, Hawk can teach them how to be safe on board."

"*Rheal Lucky?*" Sara suggested.

Charlie laughed. "Perfect, we're going to have so much fun." He leaned down and kissed her temple. "No buying me a boat for Christmas. I want to buy it."

Sara laughed, "What difference does it make who buys it?"

"I want to pick it out, my gift to you."

"Okay." She sat up more to stare into his eyes. "I love you so much. I'd be happy with you anywhere."

Tears came to his eyes at the intensity of her feelings for him. He pulled her down and kissed her gently. "God, Sara, words can't express what I feel for you. You mean everything to me. I'd be happy anywhere with you too." He pulled her down on his chest again. "This is nice right here. I could live here."

"It's nice, but not sunny enough to live here. Our house was nicer."

"When we rebuild, we can put a deck off our bedroom."

"*Mm*, that would be nice," she agreed.

Charlie laid down on the couch, taking Sara with him, making sure she remained in contact with him. "Do we still need all of those bedrooms?"

"Might as well. It will help with resale. Why, did you want something else instead?"

"No, just asking. Maybe we should move up to the attic room and put stairs up to the roof so you could sunbath up there in privacy?"

Sara pulled away. "The yard is private if no one climbs on roofs for photographs."

"We'll handle that," Charlie said quickly, sorry he'd mentioned it. "Let's not worry about that today either."

Sara nodded and laid back down.

Charlie talked about the house more and she agreed to everything he suggested. "We need to replace our clothing."

"And my books." Her fingertips glided across his bicep as she spoke. "Camila will pick up anything you want. Stasia and I will go shopping when we get free time together, but who knows when that will be, and we'll have to take Oz too to use his disguise."

"Can't you just use it before you go?"

"Well, yes, but how can you tell what the clothes look like when you try them on if you don't look like yourself?"

"Good point," he said and laughed. Calm and content, she laid against him as they talked. The magic had settled, no longer showing itself or pushing for contact. *They really could do this*, he thought in relief. They were talking about other things they needed to replace when Brenda knocked.

Charlie opened the door and groaned. It wasn't Brenda leaving Lucky, it was Sara's father.

- 21 -

AGITATED MAGIC

"How did you get past our security? Never mind, one second." The mix of shock and anger made him laugh as he closed the door and turned to Sara.

"Your father is here." Charlie snickered over Sara's shocked expression. "I know. I can't believe it myself."

Her gaze flitted across Charlie's mostly naked body, and she giggled and slapped a hand over her mouth. A half-hysterical laugh bubbled from her, increasing as she glanced down at her undressed state.

"I better get clothes on and let him in." Still giggling, she ran to the bedroom and grabbed a shirt.

Charlie passed her, carrying his uniform, and closed the door.

At the front door, she paused a moment, smoothed her hair, and took a deep breath before pasting a fake smile on her face.

Sara's anxiety made Charlie dress as fast as he could. He opened the door as Tomas said, "Thank you for seeing me." Stiff and formal, Tomas greeted her. A single tear trailed from the corner of his left eye. "I'm so sorry. I've been an awful parent. Are you living with him now?"

"Yes, but not just him." Sara's eyes narrowed as her father curled a lip. "No, not what you're thinking. His parents, Oz, Stasia, Hawk, and their mother live with us. Didn't you get the letter announcing our engagement?"

A beringed hand lifted and waved acknowledgment. "Just yesterday I heard your house burned down. No one was hurt, I hope."

"Everyone is fine. What are you doing here?" Sara burst out.

"I came to apologize. Now that I'm here, I don't know what to say."

Awkward silence fell. Charlie hesitated and remained where he was, neatening his clothing. Her father wouldn't appreciate his appearance, and while he didn't give a damn what Tomas wanted, Sara's feelings mattered to him and he wasn't sure what she thought. She was still shocked with no strong emotion he could pin down except amazement and doubt.

Sara stepped away from the door and motioned Tomas inside.

Tomas entered and paced the room, rolling a diamond ring between manicured fingers. "Let me start by saying I loved your mother. I was obsessed with Meredith, and I believed she felt the same until—"

"She did," Sara interrupted.

"You have this fantasy image of your mother—"

"No," Sara interrupted again. "Well, maybe, but I know she adored you. Mr. Martin gave me letters Mom wrote. She wrote me the last one a week before she died and in it, she wished me to have a husband to love as much as she loved you. In every letter, she wrote of her love for you." Sara put a hand on her father's arm, snatching it back when he flinched.

He paled and his eyes brimmed with tears. "Can I see them?"

"Yes, but I keep them in a safety deposit box. I can email you copies, or we can go to the bank, but not today. Not for a few days. I'm sick. A flu, no big deal."

Tomas stilled and held a hand out to her for a second before he resumed rolling the ring on his fingers. "After your mother died, I couldn't face you. The older you grew, the stronger the resemblance, the harder it was. To see your mother's eyes… It's not that I don't love you. I just can't bear it."

"Tara called you?"

"No, she called you?" He frowned and paced again.

For answer, she played the recording of the encounter with Tara.

He said, "The tabloid stories only recently came to my attention. I didn't believe them," he added hurriedly.

Sara pursed her lips a moment and then showed him the footage she'd put together.

Charlie came from the bedroom and put an arm around her. Her doubt was as clear as his.

"I see," her father said after he'd watched the full video. He rose a hand to pinch the bridge of his nose as he turned back to the window. "This attack on your character is deliberate then, and Tara is threatening to make it worse."

"Yes." Sara paused and glanced at Charlie. "Can she hurt you?"

Tomas spun to face them, waving his hand airily but glowering. "Tara threatens as much as she breathes, ignore her."

Sara pursed her lips, glancing at Charlie again.

He shrugged, leaving it up to her what she told Tomas.

"I plan on going public with the real pictures, telling my story and making it clear I never intend to become an actress. That should appease Tara."

"Perhaps... I need to think about this." A suave smile replaced the glower as he halted his restless movement before her. "Tara won't harm you. I'll see to that. The harm I caused is more than you should have to bear. I'm truly sorry for my actions. Or rather, inactions. I tried to raise you the best I knew how to, and facing you now is harder than you can imagine."

Three fingers spun the rings on his finger as he resumed pacing. "You're happy with him?" A quick glance at Charlie was followed by a longer one at Sara, before he turned aside and gazed out the window.

"He's my world," Sara said softly.

A sob from her father made Sara and Charlie start in surprise.

Everyone remained quiet until Tomas cleared his throat and faced them again. "Your mother used to say that to me in that exact tone." A cold glitter in his eye, he glared at Charlie. "I'm a very rich man with contacts and connections all over the world. No place on Earth will be safe if you harm her."

"Sara will be my wife. I'll love and take care of her until the day I die."

"Don't ever threaten him again." Sara clasped her clenched fists to her side as her voice rose shrilly. She gasped in what appeared to be rage, but Charlie knew it was from keeping her magic back. He placed a hand on her neck where her pulse beat wildly.

"That wasn't a threat. Go to the bedroom. I'll be right there."

Without glancing at Tomas, she ran into the bedroom and slammed the door.

Once the door closed, Charlie turned to her father. "You're worried I'm taking advantage of her, or I'm after her money. And while I can't blame you for worrying about those things, nothing could be further from the truth. Time will show how much I love her. You're welcome to visit her, but give her a few days, please. She's been sick and needs to rest, not be upset."

Charlie strode forward and leaned over Tomas, letting his aura intimidate him. Sweat appeared on her father's brow, but he didn't step back. Charlie was impressed despite himself. Fearful Presence made it hard to stand up to him, especially when he was angry, and he was angry now. "I too, have money and connections. If you hurt her, you'll be very sorry."

Shoulders rigid, her father nodded and headed to the door

Charlie opened the door and found Brenda and Lee, with Lucky, Rhea, and a bunch of bags. "No more unannounced visitors, please. Sara's in the bedroom. Release Lucky, put the stuff anywhere, and see him out." Charlie left them and hurried to Sara, already removing his shirt. Her father had agitated her, and his threat had agitated her magic. Sara would need to share hers again.

Why the hell had the guards let him by with no warning? All her earlier relaxation had disappeared into anxiety.

"That was surprising," Charlie said as he hugged her, letting her take his magic and give him hers.

"Call Mr. Martin. I need to be sure he can't take me away from you."

Charlie laughed. "He couldn't take you with an army." He kissed her gently. "Nothing and no one will separate us." The occasional shiver wracked her as she clutched him. Her desperation worried him.

"Nothing will take you from me. It's just us." Encased in his magic the shivers ceased, but her magic wasn't appeased. "Please, Sara, believe that."

He wanted to beg her to calm down before her magic made her do something drastic, but she was already anxious about that.

Lucky rubbed around their feet. Sara leaned down and petted her, making Lucky purr and arch her back. Tension eased in Sara's shoulders.

Charlie carried Sara to the bed and sat with her against his chest, smoothing her hair and rubbing her arms, letting her magic feel his presence as he told her the ideas he had for the boat.

Rhea jumped up and settled on the foot of the bed while Lucky climbed into Sara's lap, purring, butting her head into Sara's hand, demanding to be pet. The cat's happy purrs and affectionate head rubs soon had Sara more relaxed.

Charlie kept talking. "What do you think about letting Tank breed Rhea again? Pups would be fun for the summer. Lucky and Rhea and a herd of puppies on the boat?"

Sara laughed and agreed.

Charlie kept the talk light, discussing what they would get everyone for Christmas and describing his zone in the game. He spoke about whatever he thought of that didn't have upsetting connotations until her fear eased.

Her fear was legitimate. The idea of her repeating her behavior of last summer scared him to the core. Hormones and how they affected her were totally out of her control. More than anything now, she and her magic needed to feel safe. Making a warrior had stirred it up. They should've expected that. He gritted his teeth as he realized they'd be doing this again for Rick.

Sara turned until she was lying with her head on his shoulder. Lucky laid on his chest, purring softly. Charlie was silent now, holding her close as both petted the cat. Calm and unafraid in his arms, he relaxed too.

When his stomach rumbled, she laughed and sat. "Go eat. I'm okay for a few minutes." She headed to the bathroom while he went to eat. A few minutes later she entered the main room, wearing the robe, and helped go through the bags.

The sight of the medical supplies alarmed her for an instant.

"Want something to eat?" He smiled hopefully and offered her a fruit cup, which she accepted.

As he ate, she leaned into his side and picked at the fruit halfheartedly. As soon as he finished eating, she hugged him. He undid the tie of her robe and tugged it open so their bare skin touched, and she sighed and relaxed against him

"See, we can do this. We're both feeling better and can take whatever time we need. I'm going to use the bathroom."

The untied robe gave enticing glimpses of tanned skin, and she laughed when he tied it. Charlie was both glad and disappointed she didn't share his desire.

While he was in the bathroom, she took new blood samples and laid in the bed with Lucky. Her relief when he appeared was enormous.

"Wait here. I'll give them to Brenda." The brief separation while he'd used the bathroom had strained her magic. It followed him into the other room even though he knew she was trying to contain it.

Since her father's unexpected arrival her magic seemed more insistent than ever to be with him, and it angered Charlie to think she was so afraid of her own father. Anger she felt, and he hurriedly pushed the thoughts from his mind and gave her a smile and shrug. She smiled back but remained anxious.

Charlie hurried to the door, gave Brenda the samples, and ran back to her.

Normally, he slept naked with her, but this time he wore his boxers. "Get some sleep. I'll be here when you wake up, and we're doing fine. I love you."

She fell asleep quickly, and he relaxed as the pressure of her need ceased. He woke when she slid on top of him.

She sat and tumbled over, then sat up again.

"What are you doing? Is something wrong?" Confused, he put his hands on her waist, holding her up. "Sara? Are you sleeping?" he asked and laughed lightly when she still didn't respond to him. *This was a first, she'd never sleepwalked before.*

Still not responding to him, she slid down on his legs and fell over again, then knelt and used her hands to push herself back up and tugged on his boxer shorts.

"Sara?" In growing alarm, he shook her, still sensing nothing from her. A frisson of fear ran up his spine. "Sara!" This time, he shook her hard. Intent on removing his underwear, she ignored him completely.

His eyes widened, and he jerked away. It wasn't Sara, but her magic.

"Stop!" Horrified, he pushed her away.

Clumsy in her attempts to hold onto him, she fell to the bed. He held her down on the bed with one hand as she attempted to sit. The clumsy effort to sit turned to uncoordinated thrashing, and he used two hands to hold her down.

"Jesus, stop it! Let her go right now!"

Seriously angry now, his magic appeared around him so abruptly it almost hurt. Her blue eyes were open and empty, and it was freaking him out. He shook her hard. "Let her go right now!" He knew the second the magic released her. Her confusion made him sob in relief. "Oh, god," Unshed tears blurred his vision as he grabbed her in a hug.

"Did you have a bad dream?" She rubbed his back, confusion changing to worry.

"I wish it was a dream," he mumbled into her neck.

Sara shivered as he breathed on her neck. "*Mmm.*" She made a small sound of contentment and arousal, then what he said penetrated and she pulled back to see him better. "What's wrong?"

Magic oozed from her skin, and her eyes widened in shock when he pushed her away.

Sara clutched the sheet to her chest as he ran to the door and flipped the light on.

"Stay there." He rose his hand in a stop gesture and pointed at the bed. "Do you remember what just happened?"

"I was sleeping, and you woke me when you hugged me. Were you dreaming?"

"Oh, god, Sara." His fear heightened, transmitting to her. "The magic was moving you, and I couldn't wake you."

Her eyes widened, then narrowed as she cocked her head, a curtain of golden hair falling over her naked breasts. "Moving me? Maybe I was asleep?"

"No, you fought me. That wasn't you."

"I tried to get away in my sleep?" Her voice rose. Magic flowed over her skin as she reached for him.

With a grimace, he approached and touched her hand. To his relief, it was the usual contact. Not knowing what else to do, he got back into bed and hugged her.

"You weren't trying to get away. I think you were trying to have sex with me."

She was quiet as she thought about that. "I really do want you," she said slowly, "my magic is trying to give me what I want even though it wants you too for its own reasons."

To his surprise that relieved her.

"I'm probably not pregnant if it's trying to use you." She was quiet again, and her fear escalated. "It can make me do things, things I don't want to do!" Horror filled her voice and dampened her brightness.

"Yes," he agreed equally horrified. "You were clumsy and slow and didn't speak," he said trying to reassure them both.

"This time. What about the next time?"

"No next time. If this happens again, I'll hold you down immediately. I'll recognize it instantly now."

"Charlie, my magic could do this anytime. Make me do anything it wanted me to when I was alone. It could practice using me and get better at it." A quiver rippled her skin, turning to continuous shivers as she huddled against him very afraid.

Before panic could overwhelm her, he needed to calm her despite his own fear. "We'll monitor you and train Rhea. It hasn't happened before, and we'll stop it from happening again."

Deep concentration followed his statement. A state familiar to him, so he left her alone to think.

"I couldn't stop you, Charlie," she whispered.

He was horrified when he realized what she meant. If his magic took him over, she wouldn't be able to physically stop him.

"What do we do?" His voice cracked when he spoke. "We need each other."

"I don't know," she admitted and pulled herself closer. Naked and warm against him, it was hard to ignore. The magic echoed her desire back to him. Worried the lust they shared was magically influenced, he tried to think of something else, and almost laughed aloud when he thought of running spell timers in his head.

He closed his eyes and rubbed her back as he ran the timers. His hand inadvertently brushed across her naked breast and she moaned. The small sound made him groan. He framed her face with his hands, her desire was fierce and her skin hot.

"We're not having sex," he murmured as she kissed his neck then his chest. "You know I want you, but it's the wrong thing to do." Warm lips on his skin filled him with heat, matching the heat of her skin.

"Yeah, sex is out," she agreed and kept kissing him.

Before he knew it, he was kissing her passionately.

"Oh god," Deep and low his voice caught as her hands trailed over him.

Sara's body heated until her skin felt feverish under his hands. Every touch made her moan or writhe.

"Oh god," he said again in an even deeper voice and pushed her down on the bed.

Hours later Sara drifted to sleep in a relaxed sprawl across his chest, her hair a wild tangle. They hadn't made love for hours, and he was exhausted now. The magic was sated, and he was hoping she'd wake as happy as she'd fallen asleep. He kissed her temple and drifted to sleep with a smile on his face.

- 22 -

DON T JINX US

In the morning, Sara woke happy and took the blood sample in a much more relaxed state of mind. The magic behaved in a normal way, making no demands and remaining unseen.

Charlie handed the vial to Brenda in the hallway outside the door. "The last sample?"

"Higher," Brenda whispered. "Liz will run this sample and get her more medicine after she sees the results. Don't count on the medicine working though. Liz doesn't think the medicine will do more than slow it and might make her magic produce more hormone in response."

Charlie nodded grimly and returned to Sara.

"I'm worse?" Calm acceptance to his verifying nod relieved him. "I feel better. Maybe this test will be better."

"We need to talk to Oz." Charlie eyed her uneasily, afraid to trigger a hormone induced panic. "He needs to make a special program for your wristcomp."

"For all our wristcomps." Sara remained calm, and Charlie breathed a sigh of relief. She smiled ruefully at him. "We need to warn them."

He traced the edge of her cheek with a finger. "We should report it," Charlie said softly.

"No!"

Her sharp spike of fear alarmed him.

"Not yet. I need to think about this. Charlie, if you report this, they might decide to kill me."

He frowned. "They? You mean the government? They won't kill you."

"Think about it. Oz and I figured out they had a plan in place to kill us months ago. It makes sense, they need to have one. We even found the gas canisters they plan to use to sedate us."

"Why didn't you say anything?" Charlie jumped up and began to pace. The room gained the clarity that warned his eyes had begun to glow.

"If we go crazy, they need to be able to stop us. I *want* them to be able to stop us. That's why I built them the stasis jar. The canisters are still in place. Preparation hurts no one and lets them sleep better at night. I'm sure they have other plans as well that we don't know about."

"I trusted them." Somewhere between shock and betrayal his emotion turned to anger.

"You *can* trust them. What would you do if you were the president?" Sara rose and held him.

"The same thing," he reluctantly admitted as his shoulders relaxed.

"What we just found out is dangerous for us. They could panic and kill me. No one can know except Team Valor."

"What do we do?" His hands took her magic and gave her his.

"Nothing for now. I need to think about it. Tell the team, that's all."

Charlie called them on a video chat. "You're all in a secure location where you're sure you won't be overheard by anyone?"

Stasia jerked backward, her eyes widening. "Rick can hear this."

Charlie glanced at Sara, who shrugged.

"Rick, I need a promise from you that my wife's safety supersedes your duty."

Rick entered the picture, standing behind Stasia.

"You have it." Rick frowned and took Stasia's hand in his. Stasia's hand tightened.

Rick said, "Whatever this is you better calm the hell down though, sport." He flicked the wristcomp he wore, reversing the picture and Charlie grimaced at the image.

His eyes blazed blue, shinning so brightly they cast a shadow on his cheeks, while magic eddied around him in dark-blue gusts.

He impatiently reversed the feed again. "The magic tried to make Sara do something she didn't want to. Oz, we need a program for all of us that can sense clumsy, slow behavior and report it to us only. Hawk, if you can train Rhea to see it, that would help. Rhea needs an alarm she can trigger to call us if she spots that."

"I don't know" – Hawk rubbed his chin— "Rhea would trigger it a lot."

"She won't be able to wake me," Sara said. "If she sees the behavior, she can nudge me or something. If I don't pet her, she can trigger the alarm."

"Are you okay? You didn't hurt yourself, did you?" Stasia leaned forward, her worried gaze scanning them.

Sara blushed crimson. "I'm fine. We're both fine."

"Sara, they need to know." Charlie placed a hand on his wife's flushed cheek. "This could happen to them, and they need to be prepared."

Sara nodded and hugged him, putting her face in the crook of his neck, the heat from her blush warming his skin. He took a moment to savor her closeness, hoping his love would soothe her embarrassment. He hated these revelations too and for the millionth time wished their relationship could be private.

"The last time Sara's magic tried to turn Rick and we stopped it, it tried to make her pregnant. It's trying again."

"So... She tried to, *um*." Rick flushed and looked away.

"Yes," Charlie interrupted. "She tried to force me, clumsy, slow and unaware, both during and after the attempt that she'd tried. When I held her off, she fought me. Slow and clumsy, but strong. If my magic tried that, she wouldn't be able to stop me."

He let that sink in a moment.

"Jesus," Rick whispered in horror.

"Maybe you should give it what it wants and get her pregnant," Stasia said hesitantly.

"It isn't that simple. Her magic can't do that right; we'd just lose another baby." Charlie rubbed Sara's back at the sadness and guilt that generated.

"Jesus," Rick repeated. "What can we do to help?"

"First, tell no one." Charlie told them what Sara had told him about the gas canisters.

"She's run amok before, and they didn't kill her," Rick said reassuringly.

"This wasn't me wanting to go to Charlie. This time the magic took me with no warning and kept complete control with an agenda of its own."

Charlie's fear echoed with Sara's as she spoke the words. He kissed her brow and tried to project love, but the idea terrified him, and he couldn't hide it from her.

Stasia lifted a shaking hand to rub her brow. "This is bad."

"Very bad." Oz took Stasia's hand in his. "How did you stop it?"

"Anger, I think. It's seriously uncomfortable when Sara is angry at me. The magic doesn't like it either," Charlie said.

"Well, that's good." Hawk heaved a sigh of relief.

"Keep tranquilizer guns handy." Stasia turned to Hawk, then Oz, her face paling as she glanced between them. "You're right, that could happen to any of us."

"I think you'll have warning, but I can't promise you will," Sara said. "We knew what my magic wanted and were thwarting it. It tried to get what it wanted without my cooperation, but it also knew how much I wanted him. We need more information, more tests, more time before we tell anyone."

"No one say anything." The blue of Oz's eyes brightened. "Sara is right, this could cause them to kill her."

"I can't believe they'd do that." Hawk frowned at him. "President Carmichael likes her."

"I'm sure he wouldn't be happy giving the order." Sara faced Hawk, smiling sadly. "But he would if he thought I was a threat to this country."

"You aren't a threat." Hawk reached out as if he could touch her through the picture, then dropped his hand.

"Not at this second I'm not, but I could be becoming one, we all could be. They might decide to do it now before we are. We can't take that chance. We need time to study this. If we're becoming threats, I'll make more jars."

"You're talking about killing us all." Stasia leaned forward and her eyes flared from brown to blue.

"No, she's talking about saving the United States and maybe the world." Rick pulled Stasia away from Oz and hugged her, running his hands through her hair. "And, we're far from needing to do it. She's right though, we need a plan."

Stasia nodded unhappily.

"A lot can change if Joy is successfully changed." Oz laid a hand on Stasia's shoulder as his eyes faded to their normal blue. "Your magic should be happy if it reproduces."

"It should, but now I'm worried it will demand more and just take me and do it," Sara said.

"Oh, god, I didn't consider that." Magic swirled faster around Charlie.

"Calm down guys," Oz said as he glanced at his wristcomp. "Your pulses are way up. Take some slow breaths and try to relax before the magic responds to your fear. Nothing has changed except our perceptions. Let's not worry about what ifs. Let's deal with what we have right now. It'll take me a day or so to make the program. Don't leave her alone until it's finished. How are you otherwise? We haven't heard much."

Sara said, "We're fine now. The first few hours sucked big time."

Sara's calm acceptance let the magic fade from Charlie as she spoke, leaving the room almost its normal vividness.

"The magic is playing with my hormones again, but I feel better today, so maybe it's giving up." Sara shrugged, and Charlie felt her frustrated annoyance.

Charlie said, "Neither of us desires Joy. Instead of trying to ignore her, we decided to adopt her." Charlie kissed Sara's brow. "Sara has no urge to change anyone, but she'll stay away for a few days just to be sure."

"The actual change was horrible." Sara shuddered. "The same burning sensation, but this time it took a few minutes before I passed out."

"Your magic is fine though?" Oz asked.

"We haven't tested, but it seems to be the same as ever."

Oz opened a screen and made a note. "Both of you need to run full tests to make sure you didn't injure it."

"Charlie was sick afterwards. In the future, I'll call the lightning by myself. No point in Charlie being hurt when I can do that alone."

Charlie released her and stepped back, placing his hands on his hips. "Doesn't matter if you can! I'm doing it with you."

A smile lifted the corner of her mouth, and she grabbed his hands and kissed them before setting them on her waist. "Next time we need a spot to be alone together immediately."

Hawk frowned. "You were together right afterward."

Charlie shrugged. "We need to touch more skin together. It was hurting both of us not to touch. Not sex just contact. The magic hummed. A real unpleasant sensation and proximity helped. I think it was trying to communicate but whatever was causing it, it really sucked."

"The need to touch him that way is very intimate, and I don't like doing it publicly," Sara added.

Oz said, "We're all learning still. Maybe if she did it herself the hum wouldn't happen?"

Charlie scowled and rubbed his temples. "I can't— she can't— No. You have no idea how hard it is to feel her pain, Oz. I just can't let her do that alone."

Oz made another note on the screen and Charlie bit back a laugh.

"Next time we'll have a tent right there you can exchange magic in," Oz said.

Stasia glanced at Rick and bit her lip. "Wear bathing suits. Wait to dispel the area until you've touched awhile."

"The entire process was truly horrible." Charlie placed a glowing hand on Sara's cheek. "Let's talk later. Just thinking about it is distressing, and Sara needs to be calm now. Her father came here yesterday and upset her."

He laughed at their shocked expressions. "Yeah, he surprised us too. I'll send you the video. See what you think. Send nothing upsetting to Sara for a few days. The hormones get her upset easily. The calmer she can remain, the better it is for her magic."

"I'm better," Sara said and kissed his cheek.

"Good, I want you to stay that way. It won't kill you to be out of the loop a day or so. They can send me all the emails, and if there's something you need to know, I'll tell you."

"The raid moved all the bugs around," Stasia said. "Oz has been making receivers nonstop. Waiting to gear up the factories for committee approval is such a pain in the ass." Stasia shrugged irritably. "There's no new news yet. Joyce had a system for placing the recorder in the office. She would bring it in with the mid-morning tea after the secret service swept for bugs and retrieve it at lunch and replace it again if she served him again in the evening and get it in the morning before the sweep. Which is good news for us as the president always met after hours to speak about us and she seldom served him anything after lunch. Joyce did get him talking about Valor Industries but so far nothing that hints at magic."

Hawk said, "I spoke to the commandant. Charlie is excused for the rest of the week. School is handled. Paul is getting your assignments and class notes."

"The midshipmen sit by the door of the lab. Someone is there until curfew every day," Oz added.

Stasia said, "Your classmates are dropping off notes from the lectures you're missing. School really is handled. The commandant gave us permission to keep the sensors on our doors, and Oz has his sensor balls in the windows of all our classes and our rooms. We're safe here."

The color and clarity of the room receded until it took on its normal hues and Charlie knew his eyes had stopped glowing.

Stasia smiled a hard, satisfied smile. "The brigade has also decided to stop anyone from filming either Hawk, I, or the Valor building. A four-person squad patrols the Yard looking for tourists with cameras pointed in any of our directions and stands in front of them. The brigade really is trying to help us, and no one believes a word of that rag."

Oz caught his eye and tapped his wristcomp, giving him the signal for a private text or call.

Charlie opened his messages to see a note that read, *'Don't watch the news with her.'* He erased it and inclined his head to Oz who nodded slightly in response.

"Why aren't you in class?" Sara asked Stasia.

"I am. Well, sort of anyway. This is a free period for me, so I'm working in the lab. Rick is here as a guard today helping Oz assemble receivers and bugs. Most of the raid is here working."

"I'm sure the commandant is counting the days until we graduate," Hawk said with a snort of laughter. "My class is doing calisthenics by the lab's back door. Don't worry, they won't miss me, but I should get back. I love you guys. Stay safe." He turned his wristcomp off and returned to class.

"How is he?" Sara asked when Hawk left the call.

Stasia shrugged. "Quiet, sad— he needs the forest and soon. Major Nelson got him another weekend pass. He can go right after his last class and remain until Sunday night. A little time in the forest and he'll be okay."

Rick grinned crookedly. "I think he's a bit upset that Tank misses you. That dog runs to your office every day and when you aren't there, he hangs his head, sighs, and mopes out."

"Maybe it's Rhea he misses." Sara patted her dog's head.

"Maybe." Rick smiled and shrugged.

Charlie leaned down and patted Rhea a moment as he said, "You've been checking on Mom and Dad?"

"I have, and they send their love to both of you. Harrison and Toric are with them. I'll tell them Sara is feeling better. They'll be relieved."

"We'll be in touch soon." Charlie disconnected the call.

Stasia turned to Rick. "This is really bad news."

"It is, but it's nothing we can't handle." Rick pulled her closer and kissed the top of her head. "Charlie and Sara learn more all the time about the magic, what it wants and how to handle it. We'll have a much easier time."

"I feel bad about that. They're suffering to make me happy." Stasia rested her face against Rick's chest.

Rick ran his fingers through her hair. "Yes, but they're doing it for themselves as well."

"I know, it's just... I wish this wasn't so hard on them. God, Sara must've freaked when she found her hormone levels were up again."

"Speaking of that, we need to be alert for you. You want magic from me, which I don't have. Your magic might try to solve the problem the same way."

Stasia tensed. "I never thought of that."

"I just thought of it," Rick admitted.

"Man, poor Sara. It does suck to worry about that, but I don't feel any different. No urge to take any of the boy's magic or try to give mine to anyone except you."

"All good signs." Rick stroked her hair. "If you do feel different, or want any of those things, go to Liz immediately."

Stasia sighed heavily, drew back and stood on tiptoe to kiss his cheek. "This must suck for you. I'm a horrible girlfriend."

"You're the best girlfriend." He lifted her so he could kiss her easily and kissed her a long time before setting her on her feet. "I have no complaints," he assured her and patted the engagement ring hidden in his pocket.

Stasia glanced at her wristcomp and winced. "I have to go. I'll be back after my last class. Will you be here?"

"Yeah, and off duty. Go. I love you." She kissed him quickly and ran from the room.

Rick returned to making receivers.

- 23 -

MAGIC S CHILD

Sara called Liz to check on Joy.

"Joy's progressing normally. Nothing to worry about," Liz assured her. "Your last blood test was better. The levels are dropping. Keep taking the blood samples for at least this next week."

"I feel better already," Sara said. "Thanks, Liz."

Sara smiled at Charlie as she hung up the phone. "The medicine is working. I think the magic is giving up."

"See, this isn't like last time. This isn't too bad. I don't mind keeping the magic happy at all," he said huskily as he kissed her neck in her favorite spot.

She laughed, then moaned as he lightly bit her neck, then licked the spot.

An hour later Sara was dozing on the couch with her head in his lap. Charlie checked his email and then after a glance to be sure Sara was still sleeping, he turned on the news. The vice president's suicide was the leading story everywhere.

The story was mostly accurate. A clip from Oz's recording replayed over and over of the president saying he wouldn't let a bad man take the office even to save himself or his wife. The actual suicide was blacked out, but it was clear what had happened. Valor Industries Securities division was credited with finding and stopping the plot.

Pictures of President Carmichael's secretary and Senator Bishop were shown, but no mention was made of the recorders. Joyce and Senator Bishop had both been arrested and charged with involvement in the first lady's kidnapping and the death of the vice president's wife on testimony of the men arrested at the house where Joey had taken Oz and Mrs. Carmichael.

Charlie winced when the reporters asked questions about Valor Industries and all the Idol's pictures were displayed and commented on. The commentators weren't being flattering about Sara or her mother. Oz was right, this would upset her.

Oz had given an interview denying the pictures accuracy.

The president made positive comments about Doctor Mitchel's professionalism and competence. When asked point blank about her promiscuity, the president answered that he knew she was engaged, but couldn't speak for her actions. He went on to say that Ned Font was being investigated as a likely conspirator, adding it might have been unwittingly on his part.

Sara was right; they needed to set the record straight.

He checked Sara's email to make sure there was nothing in it to upset her. The email from her father said he'd called in favors and got her an interview with Bill Jenson. Charlie called the number provided, introduced himself, and was put on hold. To his surprise Bill himself took the call.

"Mr. Hayes, thank you for returning my call so promptly. Is Doctor Mitchel not available?"

"She's been ill and is sleeping now. I'm sure she'd be interested in doing an interview with you, with conditions."

"Such as?"

"Sara prepared video clips from our security cameras of the actual times and places those photos of her were taken. The video clearly shows how out of context they were presented. Intentionally misleading to a ridiculous degree. If you agree to play them unedited, I'm sure she'd talk about them."

"I'd need to view them myself first."

"Our lawyer can bring you a copy, and of course you'll have to agree to not use or mention them without her written permission."

"That can be arranged. Any other conditions?"

"I'll accompany her for moral support. No one needs to speak to me."

"Would you be willing to answer questions as well?"

"Sure, we have nothing to hide," he said, lying through his teeth. "I'm not certain how much you know about her, Valor Industries, or their involvement with the recent happenings at the White House."

"Only what's been on the news," Bill said.

"I'm not sure what's been on the news. Sara has been sick, and I've been sitting with her. This is what happened from our perspective." Charlie told the story almost exactly as they'd told the president. The part where Team Valor snuck into the White House he left out and let it be assumed Oz had called and met alone with the president. During his recital, Sara woke with no sign of magical upset, to Charlie's relief.

"This is a much bigger story than I'd thought," Bill admitted. "I'd heard about the shooting on campus but had no idea the events were related."

"We can't prove it was yet, but that's why Sara contacted the president and why they searched the files. Ned Font hasn't admitted contact with Senator Bishop, but I'm certain, given time, evidence will be found, and he'll be convicted. The stories he told about Sara were completely fabricated and he did it to fix an election. The fact that Ned was on the Yard the day the shooting took place tends to implicate him. I'm not saying he knew what would happen just that something would."

Bill made a small sound of interest. "Originally, I was going to do a minor segment on her as a favor. Now, I want to do an entire show. Let me view the video she made and do my own research, and I'll get back to you."

"That's fine," Charlie agreed. "Total strangers are harassing her and her friends and she wants to set the record straight. If we don't hear back, we'll assume you aren't interested and find another news outlet. Sara considers the president a personal friend, and I'm sure he'd help her."

"You'll hear from me soon," Bill promised.

"Mr. Martin, our lawyer, will drop off the video today."

Sara sat and gave him a crooked smile after he hung up. "I can't wait to get that over with. I'm so sick of strangers hounding me."

"We're fixing our problems slowly but surely." Charlie kissed her cheek and stretched, the joints popping in his arms. Sara lifted Lucky off the arm of the couch and placed her in her lap. The cat obligingly began to purr. "I'm going shopping." A flat screen opened before her and she started browsing.

Charlie smiled in relief over how calm her magic was and opened his own emails and then worked on his homework.

Sara asked his opinion a few times before she ordered, tapping on the virtual keyboard and opening and closing screens. The quiet of the room was filled with Lucky purring.

"What do you think of renting a trailer and living on our lot while the house is rebuilt?" She tapped the ad on her screen from a local rental company.

"I guess… I mean it will be you and Oz there most of the time. Will it be big enough and safe?"

"We don't need a lot of room. Privacy is another issue. As to being safe, I don't see why it wouldn't be. The perimeter can be alarmed just like a house."

"What about Stasia, Hawk, and their mother?"

"Guthrie already found them a condo nearby. The same security building they wanted us to use at first. Camila will live there until the house is rebuilt. Stasia and Hawk will stay there on overnight passes."

"Poor Rick," Charlie said sympathetically.

Sara laughed. "Are you kidding? Stasia will see him way more now. Rick will be working at the lab for a while, going over all this stuff, and she has her own office there. She can see him every day the same as I see you."

"Things are working out for all of us, aren't they?" He smiled at her emotional response and kissed her neck.

"Don't jinx us," Sara said quickly.

- 24 -

SETTING THE RECORD STRAIGHT

The radiation suit Stasia wore hampered movement and limited vision. She leaned over to see Joy clearer.

"Feeling pretty bad?" she asked sympathetically as she ran a gentle hand over Joy's dark hair.

"This is awful." Joy admitted weakly. "You guys thought you were dying; I know I won't and it still sucks."

"We were dying. It's a miracle we didn't." She lightly stroked Joy's hair again. "You aren't Joy who wants to be sick. You're a mighty warrior who wants to defend the defenseless and protect the weak. You're strong, and brave, and fierce."

Joy nodded. "I'm swift, silent, and deadly," she whispered and started mumbling spell timers.

Stasia left the room and joined Liz and Drew who were watching Joy's monitors.

Liz said, "She's as sick as you were when you were brought in. I expect she'll go downhill just as quickly. We aren't treating her though, so I expect the transformation to happen sooner." Liz gave Stasia a quick hug. "No need to worry. We also don't need to pass through any quarantine procedures and can be with her in seconds if the change progresses faster than expected. Sara's spell bracelets will dispel the radiation from us. We're monitoring around the clock. She isn't left alone for even a minute."

"I hate seeing her suffer like that."

"She's refusing all pain medication at the moment. Fifty more hours and we should know," Liz said encouragingly.

Stasia hugged Drew. "I feel horrible about this," she whispered. "She's suffering and it's my fault."

"Her choice," Drew said then kissed Stasia's cheek. "This is no one's fault. I love her, and I don't blame any of you. She was determined to do this. She wanted to jump in the lightning the night Sara and Charlie got married. I stopped her. I knew she would try eventually— with or without permission."

To Stasia's surprise, he laughed. "She won't be a warrior; she's a rogue at heart."

"She's trying to be a warrior."

"Yes, for Sara's sake, and yours, to put your minds at ease, but she isn't one, not really."

"God, what if it doesn't take because she's a rogue?" Stasia said in dismay

"Then she'll try again as a rogue, I know her," Drew said.

"I don't know, Drew, if this doesn't work, to get them to try again…"

"I didn't realize they'd had such a hard time." He pushed Stasia away to see her face, then turned to Liz accusingly. "You said they were fine!"

"They are. It hurt them and made them sick. Sara's magic freaked out, but they're recovering." Stasia assured him. "They both said it was horrible though. I know they won't be eager to do it again."

"Her magic freaked out?" Drew asked.

"It's a private matter," Liz said when Stasia hesitated. "They'll tell you if they want you to know. It's getting better. I'm monitoring it, but no, it wasn't easy for them. They won't want to repeat that soon."

"Did she hurt anyone?" Drew asked grimly. He knew what Sara's magic wanted and what she'd done before.

"Only herself, and she's getting better," Liz said. "It scared her, but she'll be fine."

Joy began vomiting, and Drew hurried to her. Liz handed Stasia a stack of white bracelets. "Have Sara refill these, please, as soon as she can. We're using a lot of dispels here."

"I'll see that they get to her," Stasia agreed. She left to find Rick and gave him the bracelets. "Don't go near her. Give them to Brenda," she reminded him.

"I'll drop them off on my way home," he said. "We need to do something about Oz. He's working too hard."

"I'll speak with him." Stasia kissed Rick goodnight and went to find Oz.

"You're starting to worry everyone; you can't absorb energy from the sun like Sara can. Go eat and get some sleep and take a shower," Stasia said.

"I'm in the zone here." Oz didn't even look up from his display.

"You can stay in the zone for two more hours, then I'm having Marcus and Todd forcibly remove you. You're starting to smell bad. You really need a shower."

"You better send more men."

"They'll sheep your sorry ass and haul you into the shower, I mean it, Oz, I'm worried. You're killing me here. Just eat, shower, and sleep a few hours. Is that so much to ask?"

Oz glanced up and his expression softened. "Okay, let me finish this up. You don't have to send anyone. I'll eat something and get some rest." He peered around his lab as if expecting to see a sandwich materialize.

Hey, it was Oz's lab who knew, maybe he could do that, Stasia thought and snickered to herself.

"I don't know what I'll eat, but I'll find something. Then I'll shower and sleep. I promise, you don't have to worry about me," Oz said reassuringly.

"I'll get you food. Any requests?"

"No, I don't care. I'll eat whatever you bring." He returned to his display screen and continued working. She left to find him some food. He needed a keeper. Without Sara here, he got too involved. She was just realizing how much they took care of each other and kept each other grounded. She promised herself she'd look out for him more while Sara was away.

She cornered Paul in the morning and told him to bring Oz breakfast when he went to his class. Amy would bring him lunch and she would make sure he ate dinner. "Just until Sara is back. She usually makes sure he doesn't miss too many meals and gets enough rest. She's feeling better and will be back soon."

"She's sick?" Amy asked in dismay.

Stasia slapped herself in the head. "It's not common knowledge. Keep it to yourself, but yes, stress makes her physically ill, and as you can imagine, she was pretty sick over this last week. Don't mention that to anyone."

Three nights later Stasia's entire battalion was watching the Jenson show. Oz was already seated by Bill Jensen and it was clear the two had been speaking. Oz wore blue suit pants and a striped oxford with the sleeves rolled up, exposing his wristcomp. *One of the new models,* Stasia noted. His blond hair was pulled back with an elastic and he carried a peripheral projector.

Sara walked into the interview room holding Charlie's hand. He wore his dress uniform. She wore a simple dress. A thin, black belt separated a dark blue skirt from a white top with short, tight sleeves and a modest neckline. Stasia recognized it as one of her mother's dresses but doubted many would. White kid gloves covered her engagement ring and protected from her magical shocks

They suited each other perfectly, Stasia thought as she watched Charlie seat her then sit himself.

"Thank you for agreeing to this interview Doctor Simmons, Doctor Mitchel, Mr. Hayes," Bill said.

"Please, call me Sara," Sara said with a charming smile and smoothed a loose strand of blond hair back into the fancy bun on the nape of her neck.

Bill turned to the camera. "For those of you who don't know, Sara Mitchel holds two doctorates, one in medicine and one in languages. She graduated *summa cum laude* with both degrees from Johns Hopkins University when she was eighteen and she speaks fifteen languages fluently." He turned back to Sara. "You're still eighteen, aren't you?"

"Yes, I'll be nineteen in December," She agreed.

"And Mr. Hayes, your nineteen now?"

"Please, call me Charlie. Yes, I'm nineteen," Charlie agreed.

"You attend the Naval Academy in Annapolis, and you're in your second year there?"

"I've just started my third year," Charlie corrected.

"You're also on the board of Valor Industries?"

"Yes, I'm the chairman of the board. Oz— Oliver Simmons—" Charlie nodded toward Oz— "is the president. Sara is the vice president of the company.

"Valor Industries is a security firm with exclusive contracts with our government?"

"Among other things, yes," Sara agreed. "The security division works exclusively on government contracts. We also have a gaming division as well as a general division."

"And you and Mr. Hayes are engaged to be married?"

"Yes, after Charlie graduates, we'll marry. I've been in love with him since I was twelve," Sara said, smiling at Charlie.

He smiled back and lightly touched her gloved hand.

"You live together?"

"Yes, I live with the entire Team Valor and their parents. All of our names are on the deed to our house."

"Why don't you live with your father or stepmother?"

"My father travels extensively for work. I was legally emancipated from him when I was fifteen. I lived with a friend for a year in Florida, Major Elizabeth Harris; she's in the Air Force. My father wanted me to travel with him. I wanted to stay near Charlie. My father agreed to let me live with Liz, and we decided being emancipated was best for both of us. I wanted to be able to choose my own schools and teachers without needing him to sign things all the time. He agreed it was easier for us both that way. Liz was reassigned to California; Charlie, Stasia, and Hawk got accepted to the Naval Academy in Maryland, so we all moved there. We bought a big house and live together. Oz and I attended Johns Hopkins. The midshipmen don't get a lot of time off, but when they do, they stay with us."

"I see. Let's clear up who Team Valor is."

Charlie laughed. "It's what we used to call ourselves when we played video games and the name stuck."

Pictures showed up on the screen behind them. A picture of Stasia in her uniform with a big caption underneath it saying Anastasia Morales with Stasia in parentheses, then a picture of Hawk with a caption that read Sebastian Morales with Hawk in parentheses, then a picture of Oz labeled Doctor Oliver Simmons with Oz in parentheses.

"We've been friends since we were eleven," Sara said and the picture behind them changed to a photo of their first picture in Video Gamers magazine when they'd won second place.

Bill straightened and his expression turned serious as he turned to Charlie. "You were recently the victim of an attack at your school, a serious attack. Your house was burned down, and Sara was attacked at work. Can you explain what happened?"

Charlie nodded. "I can explain what I think happened, but we're still working on getting the proof. We know who burned down our house. The gang members were caught in the act by our security cameras. We caught the woman who broke into our lab and tried to force Sara at gunpoint to give her security secrets, and we caught the sniper who almost killed me."

Sara clutched his hand in both of her hers, the expression on her face revealing her fright over the incident he spoke of.

She said, "You didn't mention the attack on my character and the character of my friends. We haven't found out who instigated that, but Ned Font and the Idol knowingly tried to make me look bad."

"And all of these events were linked to Vice President Danvers' suicide?"

"I believe so." Sara told the story they'd told the president.

"You think you can help his campaign?"

"He's a great man, honest, hardworking, intelligent, strong, and decisive. I think people can see that themselves in the clip from that day.

Oz and I do have some good campaign ideas, which we've already shared with him."

Bill said, "You've given me a video that proves your version and shows the truth of the pictures printed in the Idol. I'd like to play that now."

Stasia watched the reaction of her classmates as the pictures rolled by. Most of them seemed interested and looked as if they believed it. Bill stopped the tape occasionally and asked who people were.

"This was clearly an attempt to make you look bad, I agree. Will you sue?"

"Yes, our lawyer will file tomorrow," Sara said, giving Charlie a rueful smile.

Bill said, "You do look like your mother; will you attempt to get into acting?"

"No, I'm a scientist like my father. I look like my mother, but I'm not her. I only have vague memories of her. I love her dearly, and I wish I had more, clearer memories. She left me everything she had; this was once her dress." Sara released Charlie's hand to smooth her dress. He kissed the back of her gloved hand when she took his hand again.

"These things and some letters are all I have left of her. I love watching her movies, but I never wanted that for myself. I want what I have, Charlie, my friends, and my job at Valor Industries."

"And your father?"

"We aren't close; he was away most of my childhood. I barely know him."

"And your stepmother?"

"We aren't close anymore either," Sara said and Stasia snickered at the understatement.

Bill faced the camera and said, "Dr. Simmons also graduated *summa cum laude* with a double doctorate in mathematics and computer engineering."

He turned to Oz. "Dr. Simmons, thank you for taking the time to meet with us."

"You can call me Oz. I'm grateful to get a chance to speak publicly. There's a lot of money invested in old technology. Sara and I will have powerful enemies. The American people have a right to know what technological advances are available and decide for themselves if the changes, hard as they may be, are worth it. We're lucky this attempt to stop us was so mild."

"You don't believe the attempt on Charlie's life was connected with the vice president's suicide?"

"It was absolutely connected but it wasn't about campaign funds, or at least not directly. The men behind this, the ones who tried to buy the election, those are the people the American public needs to be weary of. Those men see the danger to their personal wealth in Sara's and my work. President Carmichael is a very dangerous man. He sees what the future could be and is willing to disrupt the power structures in place to achieve better lives for everyone, not just Americans."

Bill said, "Most have heard rumors of the Valkyrie operating system, how crystalis will replace the systems we use now, but I'll admit I was shocked when you showed me what the machine is capable of. I'd never imagined such huge advances in my lifetime. But I, like most, think the new power source is the more important invention with such far reaching consequences it's hard to envision how the world will change.

Bill turned to speak directly into the camera. "The wristcomps Valor Industries have devised use a new type of power source they call skeins. These skeins gather heat caused from friction—" he laughed lightly and shrugged. "I'll let the doctor explain."

Oz placed the projector he carried on the desk and removed a small box that housed a computer from his pocket. He handed it to Bill as he said, "Crystalis alone, while faster and smaller than the usual computers, wouldn't be a big enough change to disrupt the current infrastructure to the degree a new power source will. The wristcomp wouldn't be able to replace laptops and desktop machines without a power source that could supply it." Oz tapped the top of his wristcomp and a Valory appeared. He gestured and the Valory grew to life-size and waved its glowing sword. A line of blackboards appeared behind Oz.

He said, "Processing power and projections like this takes much more power than a small battery can provide." As Oz spoke equations and graphs appeared on the blackboards behind him. He said, "The technology we've invented can be applied elsewhere. We've mastered this smaller delivery method of power and are working on ways to power bigger things."

Bill said, "A new fuel source."

Oz nodded agreement. "Exactly. Clean renewable energy. As you can see, this will put us in direct opposition to a very entrenched, lucrative system. People will lose their jobs, their wealth, their businesses. The transition won't be easy for most people, but progress is hard. I'm sure all the horse and buggy owners hated the new cars at first too."

"And you're certain this new system is safe and stable?"

"The skeins that run the wristcomps have been extensively tested and work flawlessly. We're still improving them. Our goal is to use the skeins to supply all the power necessary to run the Valkyrie system, and we're close now but we aren't yet using that system to its full potential."

Bill quirked a brow.

Sara said, "The programing is ongoing, and we expect to make significant improvements in what your Valory will be able to do for you. Our problem is the skeins work almost too well. We gather more power than we can use now." She lifted her hand and pulled back her glove to display her wristcomp. "Our bodies supply the power we need to run this. Skeins harvest body heat and the heat generated by the processor. Power usage can vary as can energy gains and with no way to store the energy we just turn off the collector once the onboard battery is charged. The battery is continuously being recharged by the skeins. Heavy processor usage produces more heat, which produces more power. Unlike traditional appliances, which lose power as they run, ours gain it. It's the downtime when the device is used very lightly where we run into issues. Which is why we need to master power storage. I'm simplifying of course, but that's the general gist of it.

Oz gestured to the small box Bill was fiddling with. "The black leather-like material on the bottom is a skein. Place it on anything that gives off heat or flip it over and place it in a sunny window and it will run indefinitely."

Bill laughed and stood to grab one of the spotlights. He angled it to shine on a corner of his desk and placed the computer in the light. A Valory appeared a moment later. This one was a woman with flowing blue hair and Stasia knew Oz had helped Bill pick the avatar and showed him how to use it by the ease with which he interacted with it repositioning the new screens that appeared behind his desk. Oz's screens faded away and his Valory shrank to perch on his shoulder.

Oz said, "Once we master a way to store the energy and regulate input from stronger heat sources, we can gather other types of energy, kinetic, chemical, thermal— almost every form of movement and every source of heat generates energy. Energy we can learn to harvest."

Bill nodded along as Oz explained how the skeins worked. The screens behind Bill's desk transformed into one bigger screen that displayed greatly simplified pictures of Oz's work as he spoke while Bill's Valory used its glowing sword as a pointer.

Bill shook Oz's hand "It was a real pleasure meeting you. Your work is fascinating. Thank you for the advance copy of the Valkyrie operating system. I can't wait to get a wrist model." He released Oz's hand to shake hands with Sara and then Charlie. "Doctor Mitchel, Mr. Hayes, thank you for coming. I hope we meet again under pleasanter circumstances."

Oz, Sara and Charlie left together, and Bill finished his commentary going over all of the facts again and making the links clear. He sat on the edge of his desk and tapped the small blue box that housed the new computer.

"This thing is amazing. Doctor Simmons showed me how to use it in under five minutes and I plan to do an entire segment on the Valkyrie operating system next week, so mark your calendars. For you gamers out there, I've also received permission to show a sneak peek at the future of gaming." As he spoke pictures of

Valorian flickered across the screen behind him. He grinned and stood and the space around him transformed to the same forest lane showing on the screen.

"It looks great," Amy said proudly.

Stasia punched her shoulder and exchanged high-fives with her as the show wrapped up and the cadets around them spoke in excited tones.

Stasia said, "Hopefully, that clears it all up and we can stop worrying about reporters trying to get pictures that make us look bad."

"I'm sure there'll be even more around now," Amy disagreed. "But they'll probably be more honest in the pictures they take. It's shitty that they tried to make it look the way they did. It's stupid too. Hawk hugging you guys after an attempt on Charlie's life is a way better story."

Paul joined them. "Sara looked good. She didn't look sick at all."

"She's all better," Stasia said. "I expect Charlie to be back to school soon. We'll keep tight security on them both, but it should get back to normal around here."

She glanced at her watch, made her excuses, and hurried away. She needed to be somewhere private for her summons.

- 25 -

NO GRIZZLY BEARS

Charlie and Sara waited to meet Joy on the mountainside where they'd called the lightning that transformed her. A tent was set up nearby in case the magic awoke and needed contact. Chilly, late November breezes rustled the dried leaves in the clearing and disarranged Sara's hair.

Dressed in jeans and sweatshirts, she and Charlie hugged, not for warmth, but for comfort. The magic had stopped making demands for contact, and Sara's hormones had returned to normal, but both were anxious over this meeting.

"Don't be so nervous. If either of us wants her, she'll be out of the zone in seconds," Charlie said as reassuringly as he could.

Scouts were positioned on the state lines ready to summon any of them at a moment's notice. Within two minutes Joy could be three states away.

Sara dropped her hand from her mouth and rubbed the jagged thumbnail she'd been biting. "I'm afraid of what my magic will do to me."

"We'll handle it together." Charlie kissed her brow and rubbed her cold hands between his. "You're better now. Except for that one incident, it wasn't so bad."

Sara snorted and he winced.

That one incident still terrified him. He glanced at her fingers rubbing her wristcomp, compulsively checking the notifications, afraid her magic would take her and she wouldn't notice.

"Ready?" Charlie covered the small screen on her wrist with his hand.

"I guess." Sara took out her tranquilizer gun and held it loosely by her side.

Charlie took a deep breath, slapped the white bracelet down on his wrist to engage it, and summoned his party. Joy arrived with Drew and Hawk. Sara's eyes filled with tears and she stepped forward, then halted.

"Oh, Joy," she said in a soft sorry voice.

Now completely bald, patchy skin shiny with cream showed where deep sores had been. Dark circles ringed her eyes but they glinted mischievously.

Joy smiled. "I'm fine, and my hair will grow back." She slid into her invisible stance. A misty shadow of her former self, she smiled wider. "Thank you, Sara." The smile lit her eyes as she turned to Charlie. "Thank you both. Stasia and

I've been practicing. I'm a full rogue and can do everything she can. I'm sorry I'm not a warrior for you."

"Do you feel any need for us?" Charlie asked.

"I feel grateful, but no, I don't want you, either of you." Anxious brown eyes gazed at them. "Are you okay?"

"I don't know," Charlie admitted. "I don't want your magic, and I don't want to kiss you or anything, but I do want to touch you."

"I do too." Sara's worry echoed with his. "I want to feel your heartbeat. This isn't normal, Charlie. I never wanted that before with her."

"I feel it too." He stepped closer to Joy and held out his hand. "Please, Joy? I just want to know you're okay."

Joy stepped back uncertainly; her smile fled.

"Let one of them touch you," Hawk said softly, "We need to find out what's happening here. If it gets out of hand, we'll stop it."

Joy hesitantly reached her hand to Charlie. He lightly touched her wrist. Sara sighed and smiled at him.

He rested his fingertips on the pulse in Joy's wrist for a few seconds, then smiled and hugged Sara, his eyes bright with unshed tears. "You felt it?" he whispered.

Sara nodded against his shoulder.

"Our magic loves her." Foreheads resting together, they released their magic. The magic swirled about them in lazy arcs and dips for a moment before dissipating.

"I love her too," Sara said.

Charlie nodded agreement and wiped the tears from the corner of her eye before turning back to the watching group.

"We're okay. Congratulate us; we just had a baby girl. We do love you, Joy. Differently than before. Not in a sexual way, a protective way. It isn't about your magic, but yourself. Can Sara touch you now?"

Joy absently rubbed the cream on her high cheekbones as her worried gaze flitted over them. "Do you need to?"

"No, I'd like to give you a hug and feel you breathe. I don't need to though if it makes you uncomfortable."

Joy stepped forward and Sara hugged her. A fierce protectiveness, a strong love, and no desire whatsoever echoed between Charlie and Sara. Sara ran her hand over Joy's bald head and stepped back.

"You're okay? No new feelings for anyone?"

"I'm good. The same as ever." Joy grinned and gestured at her body. "Want to see what I can do now?"

Charlie nodded, and Joy leaped forward, landing gracefully thirty feet away and sprinting away inhumanly fast. Halfway across the field she disappeared and reappeared behind Hawk and a second later appeared behind Sara. She gave

Charlie a quick hug and handed him his tranquilizer gun.

Charlie laughed and took it back. "You're happy to be a rogue?"

"Yes. I love what I can do now."

"We're happy for you," he said, knowing it was true for both of them.

Drew put an arm around her. "Joy was meant to be a rogue. Will you try again for a warrior?"

Charlie glanced at Sara and grimaced ruefully. Neither of them were looking forward to the next attempt. "Eventually, let's make sure nothing develops with Joy first. Neither of us has any desire for her, but we want to wait a while and make sure none develops."

"And the process totally sucks," Sara added.

"Will you go back to school this week?" Hawk asked.

"Yes, Sara is fine now." Charlie ruffled Sara's hair and kissed her cheek.

"The entire raid will be practicing with Joy." Drew pulled her closer.

Sara sighed in disappointment. "So much remains to clear up. Practice will need to wait for me."

"Before Sara meets with the raid, we'll meet with the warriors one at a time to make sure, but she thinks she'll be fine," Charlie said.

"You guys need to stay in shape, to make time to practice," Drew said.

Joy bumped her hip into Drew's. "You need practice if you're going to keep up with me now."

Drew laughed, grabbed her in a headlock, and rubbed her bald head.

Charlie yelled his attack cry, intercepted Drew, and yanked his hand off Joy.

Sara pulled herself to Joy and healed her. A silvery shield appeared around Joy as Sara turned to Drew who was fighting for his life.

Charlie had thrown him as far as he could, then charged and swung his fist. If he'd been carrying his sword, Drew would've died. Instead, he just got some broken ribs.

"Stop!" Joy grabbed at Sara's arm, disrupting the orange smite growing in her hands.

"Jesus Christ!" Hawk fumbled for his tranquilizer gun and shot Charlie. "Chief, get a grip. Sara, stop him!"

Charlie bellowed berserk and leapt at Hawk. A shocked expression on his face, Hawk leapt away and ran. Moments later, the tranquilizer took effect. Charlie stumbled to his knees, calling Joy's name as he crashed to the ground.

Hawk stopped running and turned back to them, raising his empty hands as he approached.

Sara spun to face Hawk and crouched, her glowing eyes darting between him and Joy. Joy's stricken gaze traveled Hawk and Drew as she reached for the tranquilizer gun on her hip.

"If you touch her, I'll kill you." Blue eyes flared inhumanly bright as she shielded Joy again. Hawk shot her as a shield formed around Charlie.

Magic brightly lit with arcs of electricity swirled from Sara. As she fell to her knees, it sucked back into her as if fighting a vacuums suction. Less than a minute had passed.

Joy ran to Drew.

Hawk followed, engaging his white bracelet, a yellow heal flowing from Hawk's fingertips as he ran.

Drew laid on his right side on the ground, bleeding from the nose and coughing up blood. His left arm dangled, cradled by his right as he attempted to stand. Hawk healed him again. Drew's arm straightened, and the bloody wounds closed.

"Holy Christ, he almost killed me. What the hell was that?" Drew's voice and hands shook as he stood and leaned on Joy.

"Did anyone see that coming?" Hawk glanced from one to the other.

"I thought they were okay, talking normally." Drew stretched and wind-milled his arms a moment. He felt his jaw and rubbed his arm.

"They were okay— until you touched her." Hawk cast another heal on Drew. The small ball of yellow light faded into Drew's skin.

"I was standing there touching her for five minutes before they attacked," Drew said disbelievingly.

"He was protecting me," Joy said softly. "Damn it! We're in trouble here. If that's an instinct, I'll need to stay away from them."

Drew rose an eyebrow and rubbed his arm. "Protecting you— from me? He knows I'd never hurt you."

"Charlie knows. Does his magic? It was instinct. They didn't even hesitate. They both attacked instantly," Joy said.

Drew glanced at Sara's crumpled form on the ground. "Sara didn't."

Joy crouched over Sara and felt her pulse a moment before straightening and speaking. "Sara was using heals on me. I'm sure she would've in a second. She threatened to kill Hawk."

Drew's eyes widened, and he took a step back. "Oh, this is so not good."

"I agree. The two of you better leave." Joy headed to Charlie.

"Leave you alone with them? No way!" Drew yanked her back.

"I'll be fine. When they wake and I'm not here, what do you think they'll do?" Joy sighed in aggravation. "If they wake and you *are* here, what do you think they'll do? No, you have to go. They need to wake and see me. We can talk, work something out, but no one else better be around until they calm down. Put me in group six. If my vitals fluctuate, pull me out."

"Keep an open line." Hawk straightened Charlie and checked his pulse. After placing Sara beside Charlie with their hands touching, he called Stasia for a port out.

Drew and Hawk appeared in Stasia's office at the lab.

"That bad?" she asked in consternation, eyeing the dried blood on Drew. She went into her small bathroom and wet a cloth that she handed to him. "What happened?"

"We need Liz," Stasia said when they'd told her. "She can give them something to keep them calm. She really threatened to kill you?" Stasia bit her bottom lip as she turned to her brother.

"She warned me, not threatened. She was more worried about Joy than Charlie."

"Yikes." Stasia reluctantly called Major Nelson and informed him on what was going on. He was staying by the stasis jar ready to summon in case one of them ran amok.

"Joy?" Major Nelson said on the open line.

"They're still out." Joy opened her video feed and scanned the mountainside.

"You felt nothing?"

"No, they reported loving me, but no desire. Charlie touched me, and it made them both happy. He felt my pulse a minute and made a joke about having a baby girl. They seemed fine."

"I recorded the entire thing," Hawk said, and every raid member clicked the link.

"Man, he wasn't kidding. He wanted to kill Drew," Major Nelson said after he'd watched it.

"No," Liz disagreed. "He wanted him off Joy. Charlie could've killed him instantly. Pulled his head off or broken him in half. Instead, he threw him. Sara didn't attack either. She might have if Hawk came closer, I'm not denying that, but she went right to Joy and healed her. I agree with Joy, it's an instinct. Look, you can see on the recording, she looks at Charlie and starts to go to him and then Hawk moves and she's instantly at Joy's side, casting another unnecessary heal and shielding her. We can help them control an instinct."

Liz put a report up on the screen. "They say right here they decided to not fight how they feel for her and instead to think of her as their child. Joy is their child. They protected her. Granted, she didn't need protection, so we teach them not to overreact."

Major Nelson groaned. "How do we do that?"

The report Liz had placed on the screen was replaced by a live picture. She sat behind her desk in her office at the Valor building. Hands clasped in front of her, she leaned forward into the camera. "Let them observe her fight everyone and see that she's fine with it. How we keep them from killing you while we do it, I have no idea."

"We need a cage. A big strong cage. Neither could get out of a cage," Oz said.

"Sara can cast through bars."

"Stand out of range." Oz shrugged. "We don't have to all fight Joy at once and make them panic. Go slowly with Joy coming to them and letting them check her pulse between matches. Start with simple moves, no punches or kicks. Work up to that."

"I'll sit with them in the cage. My aura should help." Hawk glanced anxiously at Oz.

Toric said, "Sara's magic has blown through walls. It better be a damn strong cage."

"I know a place we could use." Guthrie sent a link to a topographical map. "There's a cave not far from the mountain top where we could put two or three rows of new bars in. It used to be a mine and there are old bars already in place to block access. They couldn't break out anywhere, except from the bars."

Oz enlarged the picture and frowned. "Crap, Sara will hate being confined. Make sure it's well lighted with no tables anywhere."

"I'll get right on this, but it'll be a day at least."

"Go get started." Major Nelson pinched the bridge of his nose, then massaged his shoulder as if he was tense. "Joy, when they wake, calm them down before telling them the plan. Summon Brenda, Hawk, and let me see— Marcus, to you now. You guys hang out of sight until Joy calls or needs you. We need people there to catch them if they quit the raid and run. If they do try to run, tranq them immediately, Charlie first."

- 26 -

INSTINCTS

Charlie woke three hours later and for a moment couldn't remember where he was. When he did remember, he sat and looked around for Joy and saw Sara. A glance at his wristcomp reassured him she was fine just knocked out. He pulled her into his lap and rubbed his aching head. Joy sat twenty feet away.

"Better now?"

"I'm sorry, Joy. We didn't mean to hurt Drew. Is he okay?"

"He's fine. You remember what happened then?"

"Yes, he attacked you and I went crazy. I realize he didn't really attack you, but I thought he did. I'm so confused." He smoothed his hair back then rested his hands in Sara's hair, combing his fingers through it, removing the small leaves and twigs.

Joy crouched beside Charlie, plating the long grasses at her feet as she spoke. Late afternoon sunlight cast long shadows and the air had cooled.

"You knew— your magic didn't. Does it know now?"

"I don't know. That was bizarre. I felt exactly what Sara did at the same moment, as if I was both of us."

"What did you feel?"

"I needed to protect you. Drew could hurt you. He didn't hurt you, did he?" Charlie asked suddenly anxious. "I didn't hurt you, did I?"

"I'm not hurt. I'm worried about this, but not hurt."

Charlie bit his lip and looked pitiful.

Joy laughed. "You want to touch me to be sure?"

"I really do," he admitted. "I'm not sure I should give in to that though."

"What happens when you fight your magic?"

Charlie sighed. "Can I please touch your wrist for a few seconds?"

Joy nodded and leaned forward, holding her hand out.

Charlie rested two fingers on the pulse of her wrist.

"See, I'm fine."

"Yes, thank you," Charlie said in relief and cleared his throat uncomfortably. "This is awkward."

"It is, but it's nothing we can't work out. Needing to feel my pulse is better than a lot of things that might've happened. Would you be okay if I left here?"

"Yes," Charlie said without hesitation.

"No urge to follow me or make me stay with you?"

"No, try it and see. But, Joy, please come back if I call you, okay?"

She nodded and walked away. The trees surrounding the clearing swallowed her from sight in moments.

"That went well," she said to Brenda when she reached them in the woods.

"Yes, his pulse stayed nice and regular when you left." Brenda tapped the HUD showing their vitals.

Hawk smiled and tension eased in his shoulders. "That's good. It means he doesn't want you. His magic saw a threat and acted. We can show it Drew isn't a threat."

"We can try." Brenda rubbed her brow. "If it can't learn, then Joy needs to stay away from them. Sara's awake. Go back and talk to her."

Joy walked back and sat beside them on the trampled grasses. "How's everyone doing here?"

"Good, embarrassed, sorry, a bit worried about overreacting again." Sara glanced away, tension in every line of her body.

"That about sums it up." A slight red flush on his cheeks, Charlie glanced at Joy, then leaned down and kissed Sara's brow. "Can we get another Scout here to see if we can control this?" Charlie paused. "A fast one."

Joy laughed. "None of us can beat your charge. I'll call two in. That way one can shoot you while you charge the other one."

Charlie agreed and remained seated on the ground with Sara in his lap while Hawk and Brenda slowly approached. "It's fine. We don't feel any need to protect her from you. I'm sorry about earlier, Hawk."

"God, Hawk, I feel terrible about what I said." Sara lifted both hands and dropped them. "The need to protect her is just so strong. I love you too, as much as her, but my magic loves her more."

"Forgiven and forgotten," Hawk said breezily. "You know how when you and Oz make a new prototype of a device and make a ton of mistakes and have to redo it, but the next one goes much easier and it's better and cheaper to make?"

Sara nodded. "Our learning curve."

"Yes." Hawk patted her hand. "You and Charlie are our prototype. You're making mistakes and learning and correcting them and redoing things. It's hard on you guys, but the rest of us will have an easier time because of it. I'm sorry this is all on you two, that we can't help with this. I thank you for telling us what to expect even though it's private and personal and you'd rather not share it. Someday, when I marry, my wife and I'll have a much easier time of it because of that."

Brenda sat cross-legged on the ground and nodded at Hawk. "We all feel like that. You make a mistake and we learn. Not that this was a mistake exactly. It's just all new. It's hard on you guys; we keep breaking and fixing you. Someday, we'll look back on this and think, god we were so stupid. If we'd just done this or that it would've been so much better. We'll have it figured out and can criticize our past selves. But right now, we're in this together, working to make our prototype better."

Joy patted Sara's hand. "This outcome is workable. A few experiments to find out what upsets you and what doesn't."

"Yeah, we should do that." Charlie laughed suddenly. "I bet you thought you were done with the overprotective father stage of your life."

Joy laughed too and took his hand a moment. "My father *was* overprotective, and I'm grateful for that, for how much he loved me. My mother would argue with him when I wanted something he was afraid would hurt me in some way and she could usually talk him round. I miss them. They were good people."

Brenda gently patted her hand, then stared in alarm at Charlie and snatched her hand away.

"Gentle touches don't do a thing. I wouldn't recommend hitting her or anything though." Charlie took Sara's hand in his. To his relief, her skin was warm again.

"So... What are we stalling for?" Sara narrowed her eyes and pursed her lips.

"Not stalling, taking our time," Hawk said. "We have a plan that needs some set up, but we thought meeting a few of us at time would be best."

"You need to immobilize us somehow and let us watch Joy with the others. Doctor Gotlieb could probably help us too. Our magic needs to learn to take Joy's word when she's says she's okay," Sara said.

Brenda sent a text asking Liz to contact Doctor Gotlieb. "We'll get the doctor and we're working on a way to immobilize you now. Any ideas?"

"None that I want you to do." A shiver shook her, and Charlie tightened his grip. "Don't tie me up. I really couldn't stand that. Maybe you could tie me to Charlie? He couldn't move if I was tied to him.

Charlie bit his lip. "I don't know, Sara. I'm afraid I'd hurt you to help her."

"No you wouldn't."

Hawk rubbed his chin. "We could surround them with barbed wire and tie them together. He wouldn't pull her through it."

"That's cruel." Brenda glared at him. "We can't do that."

"It wouldn't hurt them at all. They would be forced to be still."

"What if it didn't work and he dragged her through the wire?" Joy rose an eyebrow and cocked her head. "No, we can't take the chance. You saw how fast they reacted. They might not care if they got hurt. Besides, Sara could shield them, and he could just leap out."

"A pool of sharks?" Hawk grinned and glanced between them. "I always wanted to dangle someone over a pool of sharks."

Sara laughed. "No sharks, no wire, no grizzly bears. Just a cage. A strong one, well lighted. We'll go quietly. Doctor Gotlieb can help us. Maybe Liz can sedate us a bit. We'll try to teach the magic the difference between good and bad touching."

Liz turned to Guthrie. "Sara and Oz are very in tune with each other. That's almost exactly what he said."

"Is Doctor Gotlieb on his way?"

"He is. The cage will be ready, and he'll be here tomorrow."

"Let them go home and rest. Tomorrow is bound to suck for them. Charlie might need to stay out of school longer."

"We'll cross that bridge when we come to it." Liz rose and escorted the sergeant out.

- 27 -

FIGHTING INSTINCT

Charlie and Sara willingly entered the cage and sat holding hands. Dressed in tank tops and shorts in case they needed skin contact, they sat on two wooden chairs before the bars. A tent was set up behind them with sleeping bags and a small portable toilet sat behind a shower curtain in the corner.

Hawk wore his combat gear and sat behind them, holding a tranquilizer gun. Outside the cage, Guthrie leaned against the bars holding another tranquilizer gun. Blue exercise mats covered the ground in front of the bars.

Battery powered lamps brightened the dim sunshine that filtered in. Rhea and Tank laid outside the cage bars, ears cocked and noses sniffing.

Hawk pointed to a small canister. "That's sleepy gas they can set off remotely in case you turn on Guthrie and me. If you need us to stop, say so. Doctor Gotlieb can see and hear everything here. We decided it was too dangerous for him to be near you until we have a better idea of what you're going to do, but you can talk to him whenever you want. Are you guys ready?"

"I guess." Charlie rubbed his sweating palms on his shorts and took Sara's hand.

"Come on in, Joy!" Hawk called.

Joy entered holding Drew's hand. Rhea and Tank greeted her. After getting their ears scratched for a moment they returned to the bars and laid down.

"Good so far?" Guthrie asked.

"Yes." Charlie tried to keep his breaths nice and even, knowing he was making Sara nervous but unable to stop himself from worrying. He had new sympathy for her. He hated being so out of control that he'd attack a friend. For those moments, he'd ceased to exist, and it terrified him.

"Okay, let's do the easy stuff. Drew, give her a kiss." Hawk motioned Drew and Joy forward.

Drew kissed Joy's cheek, then her lips. He pulled Joy tightly against him and really kissed her. "Her pulse is racing now, want to feel it?" Drew winked at Charlie., smiling smugly.

Charlie rolled his eyes, but his shoulders relaxed as his magic stayed passive.

Drew laughed, picked Joy up, and swung her around, then kissed her again. Nothing he did got any reaction except a blush from Sara.

"We're going to spar now, just small stuff. If you need us to stop, we will."

Joy took a defensive stance, and Sara and Charlie yelled stop at the same time.

"Wait, we need a second." Charlie turned to Sara. "As soon as she did that I felt like we should go to her. How do we tell the magic she doesn't need protection?"

"Maybe we can't," Sara said unhappily. "Joy, come closer and let me feel your pulse while you do that."

Sara rested her fingertips against Joy's wrist as Joy took a defensive stance. "That's not working."

From the projected flat screen beside them Doctor Gotlieb said, "Try just telling it." Think really hard at it. Tell it that she's just practicing."

"Joy, do some solo moves." Charlie frowned and turned to Sara. "That seemed a bit better, but I still want to help her."

Sara took his hand and raised her magic. "Do it again, Joy."

Joy shadow-boxed for a moment before them. "Better, but I'm still uneasy."

Joy and Drew took defensive stances. Arms outstretched they circled, looking for an opening. As soon as Drew touched Joy, Sara and Charlie rushed the bars. Charlie clenched his hands on the bars, panting as he forced his magic back, trying to reassure it and himself that Joy didn't need help.

"Let us feel your pulse." He took deep breaths, trying to calm the adrenaline surge.

Joy let them both touch her wrist. "I'm fine. You don't need to help me. If I need help, I'll call you."

"Release your magic and let ours feel you fight." Sara nodded at Drew.

Drew boldly stepped into the magic swirling around Joy. Sparks trailed over his skin, slowing as he kissed her. For a moment, they sped up as he threw her to the mat but slowed again when she laughed and appeared behind him and threw him. Before long, the magic swirled in lazy arcs and dissipated, leaving Sara and Charlie calm as they watched Joy spar with Drew.

Joy spent the day fighting the raid one at a time in their magic.

To everyone's surprise, Sara had a hard time letting Stasia fight her. "I'm sorry, I just know how dangerous you are. I keep expecting you to really use magic on her."

By the end of the night they could accept everyone touching her, except Stasia.

Outside of the cave Sara and Joy wandered away from the others. "I'm trying, but please don't go near her for a while."

Joy placed a hand on Sara's shoulder. "Until you're comfortable with me going near her, I'll be careful and won't let your magic see her near me. Don't worry about this so much. Tomorrow, we can see how you do with strangers. The magic is learning. If it takes a few weeks to teach it, that's okay. And even if we can't, that's okay too. While I'd miss you guys, becoming a rogue is worth having to stay out of the zone and only meeting you privately."

Later that night Doctor Gotlieb and Liz conferred in a video conference.

"Sara is afraid of Stasia," Doctor Gotlieb said. "Watch the clips where Joy fights Rick. Sara watches Stasia. She's afraid of what Stasia will do for Rick."

"She has a legitimate reason. Stasia would kill for Rick; she's seen her do it." Liz bit her lip, her expression troubled.

"Keep Joy away from Rick and Stasia if Sara or Charlie are around. Time will probably help. It's good they can handle the Scouts near her now, but what about regular people?"

"That's a different story and will be hard to test. We'll bring them all to Andrews and let Joy mingle with the soldiers there. We'll have a guard with a tranq gun on Sara and Charlie. If they twitch, they'll be shot. Major Nelson is lining up people to bump into Joy and trip her, be rude to her, that sort of thing. Most people she meets in the real world won't be touching her at all."

Doctor Gotlieb rubbed his chin. "I recommend staging a road rage incident with Charlie and Sara in the car with her. It would be tragic if they killed someone for cutting her off or cursing her."

"I'll make sure we test that." Liz made a note. "How are they otherwise?"

"I dislike talking about them behind their backs. Therapy would work better if they knew what they told me would remain private."

Liz straightened and nodded, leaning forward across her desk. "I agree, but we can't afford to give them privacy, they know that."

"For what they're going through I'd say they're doing very well. That being said, Sara is very fragile emotionally. She could use a nice calm stretch of time to get more balanced. She's been going from crisis to crisis, big life changing ones, and needs a break."

"I wish I could give her one. Her life is dangerous; we need to make her stronger, better able to deal with these things," Liz said.

"She deals with them well, but the amount is daunting. Heighten her security. Put an armed guard at her home. She needs to feel secure and have a safe place. Her house was destroyed, her lab invaded, and she's terrified Stasia will try to take Charlie from her. Nothing in her world is stable. She needs something to stay the same."

"I can do all of those things," Liz agreed. "Would it help if I resigned and she thought I wasn't going to get posted far away from her?"

"No, she would blame herself for ruining your career. If you quit for a different reason, yes, it would help, but she's too smart to fool. I wish

Mr. Hayes had spoken to me first before telling them he wanted to move. She felt the loss of her family deeply. Coming home and finding them there every day was an important part of her life. Her home was totally destroyed by that fire, rebuilding the house won't fix it."

"How worried should I be?"

"If she gets some time to get herself on her feet, she'll be okay. If she suffers another big hit... I don't know. If that happens, don't leave her alone and call me right away."

"She's still suicidal?"

"No, that was the hormones. I'm worried that if she becomes too depressed, she'll subsume her own personality and let her magic take over."

"You think that could happen?"

"Yes, she controls the magic. If she gave up control, let the magic do what it wanted, that would be bad. It's like having a split personality except she does have a completely different person inside of her. Occasionally, she loses control when the magic has needs she ignores or denies, but she gets it back quickly and compromises with it a lot. If she gets so depressed that she doesn't care anymore, she'll let it out."

Liz leaned back in her chair, pursing her lips. "Charlie would never let her."

"Charlie keeps her stable, her one thing. He's her rock. If you remove that rock, well..."

"The school is too much for her?"

"You all know it is. She's trying her hardest to let him live his own life and still cling to him at the same time. It's impossible. One or the other has to give."

"Yes, I see she's balanced precariously. One hard nudge and she's going to fall off. If Charlie chooses the school, she'll let go is what you're saying?"

"Yes, you realize that too. Charlie is aware as well. You want me to magically, pardon the pun, make her stronger, to not need him. I can't do that. No one can do that. She needs him on so many levels that it would be impossible to free her of him. A million years of therapy can't change the fact she needs him to remain functioning and sane. Maybe if she had no magic pushing her to him, her need for him would lessen."

They were both quiet a minute.

"Do everything you can to minimize her stress and stabilize her situation," Doctor Gotlieb said. "Every time Charlie leaves her for the school it chips another block out from under her. If she had another safe and secure spot, she could withstand that better."

"She needs a home." Liz tapped the desk before her in emphasis.

"She does; we all do," Doctor Gotlieb agreed.

"He can't leave her homeless."

"I wouldn't recommend it."

"She needs him to finish school."

"It's a quandary, I agree with you."
"I don't know how to help her."
"Me either."

- 28 -

GETTING THINGS WORKING

Stasia and Rick were in her office running diagnostics on some newly programmed computers.

"What? You've been moping around here all day." Rick glanced at her as he connected a cable to the small black box that was the computer.

Stasia placed the computer she'd just finished on her desk and sat on the edge. "Sara doesn't trust me. She'll let everyone near Joy, except me."

Rick laid the cable aside and ran a palm over Stasia's cheek before resuming work. "She loves you, you know that. She can't help being worried you'll want Charlie's magic, and she knows how you feel about me. The fear is unconscious on her part. Her head knows you wouldn't do that, but her heart knows if you thought Joy was a danger to us, you'd kill her."

"I wouldn't kill her!" Stasia said indignantly. "Joy's my friend too."

Rick put down his tools and faced her. "Really? If Joy tried to take me, to use her rogue's magic on me, you wouldn't hurt her?" He laughed sadly as Stasia's hands flared up blue. "Can you really blame Sara for being worried?"

"I was her friend first. Sara should like me better," Stasia said sulkily. She picked up a screwdriver and absently twirled it between her fingers.

"*Ahh.*" Rick paused a minute. "This isn't about liking Joy more. This is a protective instinct. Joy is their magic's child now. Not their literal child, but they feel protective of her. Their magic demands it. You're not just a woman in love but a rogue. A rogue's passion is a scary thing. Sara knows what you're capable of, what your rogue's passion could force you too. You know they're working on it. Look what they were willing to do to soothe you. Stay away from Joy for everyone's sake. Sara and Charlie would be horrified if they hurt you, and they can't control their instincts yet."

Stasia set the screwdriver down and hopped off her desk. At the window, she gazed over the academy grounds as she spoke. "They let complete strangers near her with no problem. That really hurts, Rick. When they have a real baby, they won't let me see it or be near it."

"I guarantee they will. A real baby wouldn't be a threat to you at all. In fact, Sara will probably want you around to protect a real baby. She isn't wrong, you are the most dangerous person she knows." Rick put his arms around her and rested his chin on her head as he too stared out the window. "They know you would never hurt a child, any child. It'll be all right, honey." Rick held her a moment, then kissed her cheek. "Joy is a threat, not a real baby. Promise me, you'll stay away from her."

Stasia sighed. "I promise I won't go near her while they're around. I won't give up practicing with her though."

"Be careful they aren't anywhere nearby."

"Oz made us a program." She held up her wrist and showed him the screen. "It lights up and beeps if Sara or Charlie get within six hundred yards of me if I'm within thirty feet of Joy."

"P.O.S.?" Rick rose an eyebrow as he read the small screen on her wrist.

Stasia giggled. "Parents over shoulder."

Rick laughed. "Holy crap, Oz'll make a fortune with that one app."

"His father is already busy in preproduction of the wristcomps. Oz has almost licked the power problems. Valor Industries will start advertising and offer presales within months."

"How's the game coming?"

Stasia grinned and broke away from him. "We worked a lot out over Thanksgiving break. I have a prototype. Want to see?"

"Sure." Rick followed her into an adjoining room and examined the metal cage that sat in the center.

"Keep in mind this isn't the final design." Stasia handed him two, wide, wrist cuffs, a pair of gloves covered with bumpy protuberances, and a pair of glasses. She put the cuffs on her wrist and the gloves on her hands and attached the dangling leads to the gloves, so he did too.

"You don't need the holo console to play." Stasia rapped her knuckles against the metal brace. "This console is reinforced so Charlie can play it. The one offered to the public won't be as strong and we'll offer varying sizes at differing prices. Children wouldn't need a full-size one."

Rick stepped onto the padded surface. "Cushy." He bounced on his toes and stretched to touch the sides but couldn't quite reach them. "How's it work?"

"Voice activation. V I on," she said, and small blue lights along the outer frame lit. A mesh harness lowered with a gentle whir of machinery.

"We made this as easy to use as we could. Just step into it and follow the directions."

Rick nodded his understanding and followed the machine's directions to don the harness. Within seconds the machine warned him the floor would activate. He could barely feel it rise.

"If you want to play in privacy, tell the computer private mode and anyone looking at you will just see the VI logo projected onto a black background, although Oz is making a program that will give you choices on what is displayed."

She held up a black, triangular box with a gold VI on the top. From a felt lined box she removed four, dark blue, glass balls the size of a child's bowling ball. "This is the game without the holo console. You just place the balls around you and sit and they'll project so it feels like you're there. The necklace thing with the cloudy blue glass links is sending your movement to the box. I'll use this and meet you in the game. She donned a necklace and sat on the floor.

"Ready?" she asked.

"Yep."

"V I, Game consoles designs."

The room they stood in faded until they stood in an off-white box without furniture. An assortment of different color, size, and shape boxes appeared in front of them. Stasia put her hand out and slid the pictures to the side as if using a touch screen. New items appeared. "Pick one up."

Rick reached out his gloved hand and picked up a pair of gloves that hung in the air. "I can feel them," he said in delight.

"Smell them." Stasia waved a pair of virtual gloves under her nose.

He reached to his nose and sniffed. "Holy cow, I can smell them too. A plastic leather smell." He lifted his glasses and stared at his empty hand. "That's amazing, Stasia. They felt and looked real." He lowered the glasses over his eyes again, put the gloves down, and picked up a pair of glasses, opening and shutting them and then made the motions as if he put them on. He removed them and sniffed them too and laughed. "They smell like plastic."

"Try the glasses with red tint." Stasia handed him a pair.

He put them on and took them off a few times. "This is amazing programming. It really feels like I just took off red tinted sunglasses."

He stepped forward and reached out to touch the metal struts of the holo console floating before him. Again, he removed his glasses. "Holy crap, I forgot I was even on the platform. It feels real and the floor moves very naturally."

"Yeah, Oz worked hard on it. You can run, jump, climb, and he's working on floating but we can't get it really weightless yet. I can move too fast, but the program can almost keep up with me. I bet Oz gets it so even I can't move faster than the unit. It's mostly the climbing struts that slow it. Reach up for the top of the console your looking at, and you'll see how the bars react to your hand."

Rick spent a few minutes crouching and reaching while Stasia laughed at his awed exclamations.

"Those are the design options so far for what we're using right now. This is the game so far. Play Valorian, level one, load Stasis."

Thick, rough-hewn wooden plank walls formed around them in moments. An ornate floor-length mirror formed on the wall before them. Instead of reflecting them as they were, it showed Stasia as a copy of her UBM character, wearing a short leather skirt with a matching leather vest and a blue cloak. A large knife with a gemmed handle protruded from a holster tied to her waist. Long brown hair partially braided in thin strands hung over her shoulder.

Rick appeared as himself, except he wore plain brown linen trousers and an off-white shirt that tied in front. The brown sandals on his feet fastened with leather ties. Clothing peaked from a half opened closet door behind them.

A mostly empty weapon rack on another wall held a small sword, a rusty gun, and a dented shield. A bed with a feather mattress was pushed against the wall and covered with a worn, pink quilt with a brown chest at the foot.

In the corner opposite them, a round table held a glass hurricane lamp, lighting the room with a soft flickering glow. Glass bottles of various sizes, shapes, and hues rested on the table beside a brown leather-covered book with thick vellum pages. A hunk of cheese and half a loaf of bread sat beside a dried sausage and a knife beneath a glass dome on a shelf above the table.

A chair with a red velvet cushion and wide arms carved in intricate designs was pulled out from the table as if someone had just risen and walked away. Behind him, a large door with gold numbers and ornate hinges shimmered slightly.

Stasia gestured around. "This is my house. When you first start to play, your house is empty except for the mirror, table, book and the door behind us. You can buy a bigger home and make it as fancy as you want. Part of the fun will be decorating, finding rare plants for your garden or animals and birds. You're in guest mode now so you can use anything in my home. Pick what you want to look like by telling the mirror or using the pre-made images from the photo album on the table. Right now, we have three races, elves, dwarves, and humans, but we plan to add more."

Rick picked up the book, and after hefting it in his hand a moment, leafed through it with interest. Sections labeled with ornate tabs— Beginners Tips, First Day Journal, Spells, Photos, Maps, and Notes— flipped with a slight whir and breeze that smelled of old books. He opened it to First Day and picked an avatar at random.

"How do I do it?"

"Pick it up and put it on the mirror." Stasia tapped the picture he'd selected and pointed at the mirror on her wall.

"She said, "Valory, game design mode. Put instructions for use, place on mirror, beneath the premade avatars. Try a version with the warning in bright letters at the top of the page and remind me to check them tonight when I'm in my room."

Before Stasia had finished speaking the directions had appeared, written in ornate script beneath the small pictures in the book.

Rick placed his photo on the mirror. The mirror swirled, reforming into the image he'd chosen and moved when he did. Now his hair was long and blonde, held back by a leather headband revealing the tips of pointed ears. Shorter and slimmer than he was, his green eyes tilted and when he smiled pointed teeth gleamed. In the mirror, he wore no gloves. When he glanced down at his hands and feet they appeared as they did in the mirror.

"You can be taller or shorter, fatter or skinner just by asking the mirror to adjust it."

"How do I change my clothes?"

"You can use my closet, but if you were just starting out, you'd have to go buy some. I have gold in my chest. Take some and we can go to the store."

Rick opened the chest and took out a handful of gold pieces while Stasia entered the code on her door to leave. The gold had weight in his hand and clinked as he moved it. He followed her outside and stopped and stared in amazement.

"Wow, seriously this is amazing."

A narrow, winding cobbled street lay outside Stasia's door lay. Rough wooden and stone buildings hemmed them in, leaving glimpses of a purplish-blue sky. Two houses up, anther road intersected the one they walked on. No one was in sight. A flutter of paper on the wall proved to be a wanted sign. Soft breezes smelling of rain and warm stone wafted to him.

"It feels and looks so real."

Side-by-side, they headed down the narrow street. Once, they both stopped to let a cat race by chased by a dog. And once, Stasia pulled him back as a woman tossed dirty water from a window above them. The water splattered into the roadway and ran into a gutter, disappearing down a grate.

"You can only see water and feel it as sluggish movement if your swimming, it still needs lots of work. We don't really have weather yet. The sound of water is realistic though and we had to dial back on the smells. We got them a bit to realistic and it grossed out our testers.

Rick laughed and took exaggeratedly careful steps around the dirty water. Stasia snickered and punched his shoulder. Rick removed his glasses to see if she'd moved from the floor.

"That's so cool. I felt you touch me."

"Yep, we're keeping it light contact and only on limbs. I'm guessing there will be aftermarket harnesses offered for a full body experience, but we won't offer that.

"*Eww*," Rick said and Stasia snickered again.

A rat ran along the side of the street. Stasia threw her knife at it. The rat's legs kicked a moment before it died. She picked up the knife, wiped the blood off with a handkerchief she took from a pocket, and handed the knife to Rick.

"Level one critter. Worthless except as practice. Just like in traditional games the more you practice, the better your aim will get even if your hopeless in real life. The computer will adjust your aim using an algorithm based on time played, skills bought, and character attributes, including making your character tire the longer you play. We're still debating if there should be blood or wounds at all."

They proceeded to the store, following the twisting path.

The store was full of items. Magic potions, weapons, clothing, lamps, rope, rugs, food and packs lay in a wild jumble on the crammed wooden shelving. The storekeeper, a short fat man with a long, white beard wore simple brown pants, a white linen shirt and a blue apron. "Can I help you?" he asked in an accent somewhere between helium and New York.

"I need a small pack and some clothing," Rick said.

The man pointed to the packs and asked him where his adventures were taking him.

"Just around town at the moment." Rick picked up and replaced items from the shelves as he spoke.

"I have just the thing." The shopkeeper rubbed his hands together and pulled a box out from under the counter. He withdrew a leather vest and then a light green shirt that laced in the front from the box and sang its praises.

"How much?" Rick fingered the leather vest.

"Five gold pieces." The shopkeeper smiled and leaned forward, his eyes sparkling inhumanly bright.

"Ridiculous, we'll pay two." Stasia picked up the shirt and examined it. They haggled a moment and settled on three. "You can use his changing room to place the shirt on the mirror there or go home to change."

Rick took his glasses off. The room around him lost its brightness, becoming dim and indistinct. The shopkeeper and his shop were still visible. "Holy crap, you could spend hours just in the store."

Stasia removed her glasses as well. "You could, or you could change the setting to no haggling best prices. You can also always have a store with no other customers if you don't want to wait. Keep in mind what you buy you need to carry. You can buy a magical pack to carry more, but it costs more. The shopkeepers and towns people will pay you for working for them and you can sell them stuff you find. This town has a serious bandit problem, and you can make gold by catching them. If you can find a hideout, you could really clean up, but it would be wise to bring friends or have potions."

"How many smells can it do?"

"The gloves can hold twelve base odors, but the mixtures are still being worked on, and if you want smells you need to refill the cartridges periodically. Without gloves, you can't feel or smell things, it's more of a traditional gaming experience. We only have this one town done and some surrounding countryside right now, and we're still ironing out specs and talents."

"If you play for a while, do you start where you logged off?"

"Yes, you can teleport home and there are portal spells available. Once you buy the spell, you use the map section in your big book at your house, and we plan to add small maps that you can take with you to use to travel quicker once we have more zones finished."

"How are you handling talking to friends?"

"We're working on that. I think we're going to use a small floating cloud or an ornate wrist band where you would see scrolling text and there will be a voice option so you could just hear it. For raid communication, you would use a headset just like we did in UBM.

"Everything is so detailed it really feels like you're there." Rick ran his hands over the holographic shirt.

"Oz's computer language is easy to use. The programmers are outdoing themselves. We have a sound team now working with them. The floors will creak, doors will slam, guns will fire. The area we just walked through will have background noise, music, and more computer-generated people. We're debating putting real audio of crowds in. Like if you're in the town square you could hear what other players were saying regardless of whether they were on your friends list or not. Audio is a complicated project that Oz has brought experts in on as we don't want to overload people or inadvertently make private conversations audible to everyone, but we do want the sounds realistic.

"We thought it would be fun if you were inside a dungeon and had to really be quiet to sneak past things or if you could yell to frighten lower level pests away. But sometimes our ideas don't pan out in our test groups."

"How much is it going to cost to buy one of these?" Rick examined the console designs again.

"We're debating that too. I think they'll end up being a few thousand dollars. A holo deck will include everything one player would need to start playing. Additional gloves and glasses and stuff will cost more. The holo console could support multiple players but they'd need their own glasses, and gloves if they wanted to feel things and would have to play sitting like I was. This level will be included. The next level will cost more. The simpler game boxes will be much cheaper."

"How much does it cost to make a console?"

"Not that much actually, but the price isn't final until we pick a finished design."

"That's a lot of money for just one game," Rick said doubtfully.

"Oh, there are more games already being made by some of our programmers. We have a really cool sparing program already and a simple hunting game. Oz made a hide-and-seek game for kids and blind man' s bluff and pin the tail on the donkey. I love that one. The donkey is so cute. One of our designers is making a game for horseback riding in his free time. Oz is making one for sailing and surfing and another for climbing and he has an entire team working on a set of games for learning to dance, exercises of all types, and a rock band one.

"That last one is costing us a fortune. We have an entire legal team on it. We'll be using real live concerts and backstage footage. The idea is it will feel like you're part of the band. It will have its own website where the players can vote each other up or down the ranks. Sara wants to have a yearly finale with the winner doing an actual live show and all of those derails are time-consuming and expensive to work out.

"There will be games for every age and taste. The holo console itself can be disguised as almost anything and Oz predicts he'll be selling designer apps for it so people can leave it in the corner of their living room and it'll look like a tree or sculpture."

"You're going to make a fortune!" Rick said seriously.

"I know. Oz is going to make us all rich." Stasia flipped through the designs for the glasses as she spoke. "I feel bad about that sometimes. This game is all his brainchild. He doesn't need us to do this, he's letting us."

"Like you're letting the raid?" Rick snorted with laughter.

Stasia laughed. "You're right, we all help each other. Is the raid happy with how things are going?"

"They want to be in the field more, but we're needed here now, and they realize that. Everyone's excited about Joy. Thrilled it's going so well."

Stasia said, "It *is* going well. Sara and Charlie should really wait a year or two to be sure though."

"You know they won't. They're too worried about you."

"I know, and I'm worried about that too. I'm also worried Joy will develop a dependency, or they will. There's wasn't instant, it took a while."

Rick hugged her. "This is odd. I feel you and your holographic self." He stepped away and ran his gloved hands over Stasia's computer generated image. "Almost the same shape, but the depth isn't there." He shrugged and continued the conversation. "Charlie and Sara wanted to be together before the magic joined them. They don't want that with Joy.

"Do you want that?"

Rick stepped from the harness so he could trace her face with his fingers. "I want you. I don't know if I want your magic. To be a magical warrior like Charlie would be amazing, but I don't desire magic except to ease you."

"And their connection, do you want that?"

"Not particularly. I see how hard that is for them. It must be terribly confusing having someone else's feelings in your head all the time."

"Charlie told me it was the best thing that ever happened to him, and he pities other people for being so alone. I wouldn't mind knowing your feelings or sharing mine with you."

"I'll talk with my brother. You speak with Sara. They didn't know if their connection would've happened eventually or not, but we should decide if we both want that, you're right about that." He picked her up to kiss her, and she put her legs around his waist. "I love you. If that connection is inevitable, so be it, but if we can decide we should before it happens."

Arms around his neck, supported by his hands, she leaned her forehead on his. "I love you too, and we have time to decide."

- 29 -

MOVING FORWARD

The reporters seemed to have lost interest in them. None had been seen on campus in a week, and John reported calls to VI asking for interviews had almost stopped.

Construction had started on their house. Mr. Martin was still dealing with the insurance company, but Sara didn't want to wait until they received that money. She was hoping they could move back into their house by fall of next year. Camila was handling all of that. They'd made a few changes in the house but had left the majority alone.

Sara and Oz were now living in two small trailers parked in their garage. Almost every day they walked to work together. Sometimes one or the other of them would sleep at the lab. Both were working long hours.

Every weekend, Charlie came home and went with them as they visited people who she and Oz wanted to speak with. Sara wanted to go to Europe and speak with people there, but that needed to wait for a school break. Every day she spoke with someone on the phone or online. Some days that's all she and Oz did, answered calls or emails with requests for their insights.

The first week of December arrived and life had again settled into a routine. Before work, Sara went for a run as usual. On her return, she halted, and her eyes widened. Then she ran to Joy while tapping the automatic notification that alerted Charlie she was fine, and he wasn't to worry. Joy was never one of their guards and rarely at the Valor building.

"Is everything okay?"

Joy smiled and gave Sara a quick hug, letting her feel the pulse in her wrist a moment. "All good, just seeing Drew to work. I'm your gopher today. Camila gave me a long list of things you need and showed me your new artificial skin. Still no luck, *huh*?"

"No, I'm missing something. I need more time to think about it. We've had progress with our satellite design though. Oz went hog wild on that. We're going to try to launch one this weekend."

"The ray-gun will work to launch it?"

Oz has fourteen pages of equations that say it will." Sara held the door and gestured Joy to enter after nodding hello to the midshipmen sitting on the bench outside. "Getting it into position is the tricky part." Sara led the way to her office as they talked. "Brenda will have to position us exactly. We'll be outside on top of a harrier using the ray-gun and my shield."

"How the hell will you pull that off?"

Oz made a new cover for the back cockpit. We'll change it out with the existing one. Our gun and hand holds will be built right in. The satellites can only be moved a small amount, so we need to be as exact as we can."

Sara laughed at Joy's expression. "It's not like it will matter if we fall off."

"What's in the cases?" Joy gestured to the black cases with the red crosses on them standing by the door.

"My artificial limbs. A wide assortment is in them to replace almost anything at a moment's notice. I just finished packing them up. They'll go down in storage for now. Ideally, I could use donor parts, but in a time crunch, I could use those, then bring my patient here and remove that and put on a donor limb. They'd never know I did it," Sara said reassuringly to Joy's horrified look. "Marcus walked around for a week with a fake leg. The size wasn't exact, so he limped, but he couldn't tell the difference when I put his leg back on."

"Stop, you're grossing me out." Joy waved her hands and turned away. "I can't believe he let you do that."

Sara laughed. "I can't either, but he did. He's perfectly fine now. Not even a scar." Sara pointed to the case beside the door. "Marcus made it possible for Marines to walk again or have both hands. Without him trying, I couldn't do it. Major Nelson has arranged for critically injured Marines to be rushed to me. They'll be sedated and hopefully unaware of the extent of their injuries. I'll fix them up. Then Liz or Camila will apply camouflage injuries to them, so they have scars and whatnot. Doctor Elliot will be the doctor on record. They go home and no one except us knows the real story, and that's all thanks to Marcus letting me experiment on him."

"He's a real hero. I love you, Sara, but I wouldn't let you do that to me."

"I don't think I could do that to you." Sara smiled ruefully at her.

"You're still okay, about me, I mean?" Joy asked anxiously.

"I'm fine. The thought of you being near Stasia makes me sick to my stomach with worry, but everyone else I'm okay with. I'm sure I'll be worried when you go on missions, but they promised they wouldn't send you on one for at least six months. And if I can't handle my magic, they'll send you home."

"It's weird how regular people don't bother you at all, just the raid and people in uniform."

"Regular people aren't a threat to you. You could take a regular person with your eyes closed and no hands. I'm sure if I saw one pull a gun on you or something it would be a problem, but no, Charlie and I don't worry about regular people." Sara bit her lip then burst out. "Don't trust Stasia,

I mean, be wary of her. She could hurt you or kill you. She'd be sorry afterward, but you'd still be dead. And if you were too far away from us, you'd stay dead."

"I'm careful, but we don't really know how long that timer is. We're just guessing by game data."

"I mean it, Joy. You're a rogue like her, so you're a threat to Rick. Be very careful. If she even thought you were giving him your magic, I don't think she could control herself."

"I have no interest in Rick. Well, he is nice to look at, I'll admit that, but I love Drew."

Sara giggled, and Joy laughed.

Sara perched on the edge of her desk and swung one leg. "Are you going away for Christmas break?"

"We're going to his parent's house. We'll be back by the twenty-eighth though. If it bothers you, I can stay nearby. Are you going to Texas?"

"No, they're coming here. We rented the top floor of the hotel for the entire Christmas break. Thirty rooms, so there's plenty. More than we need even if the entire raid showed up. If you and Drew want one, tell the sarge. The idea of you leaving the zone doesn't bother me or Charlie but stay in touch in case it does once you leave."

Joy nodded and sat on the other corner of Sara's desk. "What did you get Charlie for Christmas?"

Sara frowned. "Nothing and it's been really hard to do that, but that's what he wanted, to let him get both of our presents this year."

Joy laughed and jumped up. "Well, I'm off to get this stuff. If you think of anything else you need, text me."

From the window of her office Sara watched Joy leave the building. Joy stopped and spoke with the midshipmen sitting by the entrance studying and then headed to the small parking lot. Sara didn't return to her desk until Joy was out of sight. With a small sigh, she got back to work.

- 30 -

SIMPLE PLEASURES

Charlie showed Paul a picture of Sara's Christmas present.

Paul's eyes widened. "Holy cow, you can afford that?"

"Pretty nice, isn't it?" Charlie ran a finger over the picture of the forty-foot sloop. White, with dark blue trim and shiny teak, it floated with one white sail raised. Sunlight glinted off the bright brass fittings in the next picture. The interior photos displayed navy blue cushions on the built-in furniture. A large bathroom with a normal sized shower and built in washer and dryer lay off the galley.

The galley contained all the comforts of home on a small scale, including a dishwasher. The wooden counters shone and matched the built-in banquette table. One stateroom held a king size bed with built in cabinetry surrounding it. The other was smaller. A full-size bed hugged one wall and built in cabinets lined a narrow aisle.

"I'll say. Am I invited?" Paul asked.

"Absolutely, we'll be on it every weekend." Charlie thumped into his chair and put his feet on his desk. "The table in the galley folds into a bed and the couches pull out. Eight can sleep comfortably."

"Damn, you sure are Rheal Lucky," Paul said as he admired the pictures.

"You'll be able to buy one soon. The games you designed are super fun." Charlie tipped back in his chair, balancing on two legs. "I especially liked Monster Maze."

"When will you shoot the first commercial for Virtual Imagery?" Paul sat at his desk, still flipping through the pictures of the boat.

"Well, we want to have it advertised by next August at least, but we still haven't selected the final designs. We plan to do that over Christmas break. Talk to Hawk about advertising your games at the same time; he's in charge of advertising."

"I'll do that," Paul agreed. "You guys are still coming skiing one of these weekends, I hope."

"We are. Sara's never been skiing. It should be fun. She loves to learn new things."

Paul laughed. "Learning is definitely her favorite thing."

"Well, maybe not her favorite thing." Charlie winked as he stood, then slapped Paul on the back and headed home to his wife.

He hated the trailers. Well, not the trailers so much, he'd like them if they were in a forest somewhere or an open field, but in his stuffy garage they sucked. At the house, he paused to examine the progress, which as far as he could tell was nothing, then went into their trailer.

He kissed Sara and changed into jeans and a sweatshirt. "I saw Joy going to the parking lot today and immediately scanned the grounds for Stasia like a lunatic," Charlie said as he sat at their small kitchen table.

"I did the same thing," Sara admitted as she placed a plate of pasta in front of him. "Eat!"

He glanced at it doubtfully, then shrugged and ate it. "Camila made us dinner?" He glanced up from his food in delighted surprise.

Sara beamed. "I made it. Camila's been giving me lessons. When I get a chance, I want to go to culinary school. I really like cooking."

"This is really good. You're the best wife ever."

A pleased smile on her face, she began to clean up the tiny kitchen.

"Not eating?"

"I ate while I made it."

Charlie snorted.

"I had to try it to make sure it was good," she said defensively.

The cake she proudly set before him was only a bit lopsided but otherwise looked and smelled great. "And, I made a cake."

Charlie closed his eyes to better see her brightness. The sparkle of her happiness as he enjoyed the food made him laugh. It never ceased to amaze him how much she appreciated the simple things with him. Sometimes, the complicated life they lead made him sad for her. Moments like this gave him hope that she could be truly happy despite the craziness of their lives.

"Want to go out tonight?"

"I have to be up at four in the morning. I was thinking we could stay in." She glanced at their small bedroom. Lust and embarrassment changed to anticipation as his lust echoed back to her.

"Yeah, we can do that," he agreed, enjoying the building echo. One of his favorite things was knowing how much she looked forward to touching him, when it wasn't influenced by her magic. "I'm going to shower first. I'll be right back."

He headed to the crude shower they'd hooked up in the corner of the garage. The shower in the trailer had limited hot water. When he was there, he used the cold water, saving the hot water for Sara. He grabbed the garbage on his way out and brought it to the cans behind the garage and laughed when he saw the mangled cakes and spaghetti sauce already there. A towel around his hips and his clothes over one arm, he returned to the trailer where he found her reading, her flat screen poised, taking notes.

"First satellite goes up tomorrow?" Charlie asked as he read over her shoulder.

"Yep, just rechecking the math for the hundredth time. I'm sure the satellite itself will work; it's getting it there that will be tricky. In theory, we can do it. Tomorrow will be interesting."

She flicked off her screen and pulled his towel off. He laughed.

Sara left with Oz at four in the morning to meet Brenda at a remote spot outside of Harrisburg Virginia. Brenda would bring the modified Harrier and they'd attach the satellite. The satellite had a six-foot circumference and weighed almost two hundred pounds. Sara planned to levitate it, but it'd still have mass and the bulk would be hard to manage as it was outside to the right of the jet.

Oz used a small crane to set the satellite in place. "Man, this would be easier if we owned the jet," Oz complained as they adjusted the metal straps around the front of the Harrier. "I'll release the front hooks. You operate the ray-gun. If I fall off, I can maybe Wink back on, so you don't have to come pick me up."

I can try to pull you back if you notify me quick enough," Sara said. "Check the quick release while I balance it." Sara cast Ascension on the satellite again and held it steady as Oz hit the front release. "Okay, Brenda we're all set back here, fire her up. If one of us falls off, come pick us up and we'll try again."

Another Harrier approached them as they reached the launch spot. "Damn it, we have to abort. We can never explain this," Sara said in aggravation.

"It's Drew. Carry on." Brenda waggled her wings. The other Harrier waved back.

Sara checked her wristcomp and sure enough, Drew and Marcus where inside the other jet. She shrugged and got back to work. "Brenda, keep as close as you can to our mark."

Oz turned to Sara. "Ready?"

"Program one is loaded in the gun, and my staff is primed. Ready when you are."

Marcus filmed them on the back of the jet, sending the footage live over the raid channel. Charlie sat on the small, brown couch in the trailer with his feet up, a flat screen opened before him. The coffee table held the remains of his breakfast and a fresh cup of coffee.

Oz slowly climbed to the front of the jet to release the straps holding the satellite in place. Sara would be checking her timers.

"Releasing now," Oz said as he hit the quick release." Damn!" he yelled as the hook whipped out and smacked into his leg.

Charlie winced in sympathy. Oz engaged his white bracelet and healed himself, but it still hurt.

"As soon as I'm in the green, I'm firing." She held a strap with a hand hovering over a large red button. Her hand hit the button. The hook released and smashed into her arm. She screamed and let go, falling backward and smacking her head hard on the side of the jet. She fell limply off into space.

"Jesus Christ!" Charlie leaped off the couch as Oz dove after her. The painful echo of her injuries tingled his skin.

"Sara, Sara! Charlie yelled into his wristcomp. "Tell me we have someone on the ground there to summon them." He glanced at his combat HUD and turned white. The only ones there were in the air and unable to summon in such an enclosed space.

Drew turned the jet and followed Oz. "Oz has her, and she's fine. Give him a second to heal her. I'm picking them up." Drew eased the jet under them as they floated earthward. Both were already levitated.

Sara said, "Don't bother, we can float down. I'll spell steal indivisible. No one will see us. We're both fine, Charlie. Marcus will stay on the ground this time."

"Did it work?" Drew asked.

Oz held Sara's gloved hand in his, already running diagnostics on a screen hovering before him as they floated to earth. "The satellite is up and in one piece. We just need to move it to the right spot. Before we place the next two, I'll redesign the release mechanism. I have to run diagnostics to make sure the ray-gun didn't damage it, but it looks good." Oz glanced at his HUD. "Jeez, Chief, you're going to stroke out. Calm down. She's fine."

Charlie watched anxiously as they landed and climbed back onto Brenda's jet. This time they tied on.

"You might not want to watch this part. We aren't sure it will work," Oz said cheerfully as he handed Sara a helmet. "But, I sure as hell hope it does, these things aren't cheap to rent."

"What are you doing?" Charlie asked with dread when they both put helmets on.

"Going really, really fast," Oz said happily. "Let her rip, Brenda. We're ready back here."

The jet lifted, then went forward. Drew followed to the side at a slightly higher altitude. Crouched on the back of the speeding jet, Oz and Sara were laughing as the jet went faster and faster.

"First stop coming up," Brenda warned.

The jet slowed, and Sara and Oz used the ray-gun again. This time they sent up an object about the size of a baseball. They opened the hatch and Sara climbed into the back seat. The hatch closed, and they took off again.

"Jesus, why didn't you do that to begin with?" Charlie yelled.

"And miss the fun? You should try it," Sara said. "It's very cool."

"You're killing me," Charlie said.

"That's why I'm inside now. All cozy in this dark, scary, tight space," Sara said agreeably.

Charlie laughed. "I'm sorry, I know you hate where you are right now, but please stay there."

"I will until we get to our next stop."

"What are you doing? I thought you were just launching the satellite."

"We're launching some A.C.D.'s as well."

"Auxiliary connection devices," Oz clarified. "So we don't lose the signal in the cities. We should have great reception with these as well as improved clarity in map apps."

"How many are you launching?"

"Sixty-seven today," Oz said.

"*Umm*, isn't that a lot of space litter?" Stasia asked.

"Meh, they're rigged to blow themselves if they get too close to anything. They'll fly apart in little pieces unlikely to harm anything. If someone launches a rocket into space, they won't hit one. Besides, they're mostly over populated areas. No one is launching anything there."

"You are," Hawk said dryly.

Oz laughed. "They'll burn up on reentry. It's fine."

They stopped in Texas for fuel and then headed to California making stops along the way to release more A.C.D.s. By the time she got home, Sara was exhausted and magically depleted from casting shields and dispelling to make the shields strong enough to pass through the atmosphere. She and Oz had run the diagnostics, and everything looked fine.

Marcus drove them back home while they slept. He called Charlie when he got near their house. "She's sound asleep. Want me to bring her in?"

"I'll get her. How's Oz?"

"Fine, not as tired as she is. Sit in the sun tomorrow." Marcus pulled into their driveway and Charlie came out and got Sara. She woke when he picked her up. He grinned, loving how content she felt when she put her head on his shoulder and went back to sleep.

Marcus called Major Nelson. "Oz is too tired to count as a guard. I'm staying until they're more alert."

"We'll be posting a full-time guard on the house using hired guards. You'll be back in the field as soon as the legalities are finalized to allow private armed guards on base. Work out a guard rotation from among the Scouts until they move into the hotel next week," Major Nelson ordered. "Don't use Joy."

Marcus snorted. "*Duh.*"

"You mean, *duh*, sir," Major Nelson said and hung up.

Marcus laughed and put his feet on Oz's coffee table. A holographic flat screen opened before him, and he began typing on an invisible keyboard.

Sara woke up at one o'clock the next afternoon. A rainy, dark afternoon. "Boo," she said when she walked out of the garage.

"I agree it's pretty dismal." Charlie tweaked her ponytail. "I have a few hours until I have to go back, and I'll be home again Thursday."

"The hotel will be way nicer than this," Sara said as they returned to the small trailer. "I'm sorry I'm too tired to go do anything."

"Let's go find a tanning salon. It's gotta be better than nothing." Charlie didn't like how dull her brightness appeared.

Sara loved the tanning bed. The girl at the desk wouldn't let her do it twice in a row so they went to another one. She paid for the longest time allowed and stayed in until they kicked her out. When she got to the car where Charlie was waiting, she was giggling.

He laughed at how happy she was and took her to another one. This time the girl just shrugged and let her buy two sessions. Charlie waited in the car.

When she wasn't back in an hour, he went to get her. The girl at the desk pointed to the room she was using but didn't get up. Charlie knocked. When he got no response, he knocked louder.

"She probably fell asleep; they do that all the time." The girl at the counter handed him a key. The tanning bed was off, and at first he thought she was sleeping, but he couldn't wake her. Cursing himself for bringing her here, he Spell-Stole her heal and healed her. Bleary blue eyes opened, and she smiled at him.

"I wuv you. You the bestest husband ever." She sat and banged her head on the top of the tanning bed. "Ow." While she rubbed her head, she peered around the room. "Where are we?"

She glanced back at Charlie and smiled the smile that said she had plans for him and made his pulse race. It took her two tries to get to her feet and pull him down for a kiss. "I'm naked; you should be too." Ignoring his demurs, she began to undress him. Magic showed, first on her hands, then her entire body.

Her skin felt hot as if she had a fever and heated more as he touched her.

"I think you're a little drunk. We might have overdone the sunlight a little bit." He choked back a laugh as he helped her stand.

She fell over, but caught herself. "I fine," she assured him in a slurred voice. "I feel great; feel me." She grabbed his hand and placed it on her breast.

He stifled a laugh and tried to get her dressed, but she didn't want to dress, she wanted his clothes off.

"Sweetheart, we need to go home now," Charlie said in a cajoling voice.

"Don't want to. I want you." Clumsily, she tried to push him against the wall.

"Is everything okay in there?" The girl at the counter called.

"Fine, she was asleep," Charlie called back.

"We have to go now." Charlie handed Sara her clothes. "Get dressed, please."

"No. I'll make her go away, and we can stay right here. I like it here." A dark-yellow ball of light began to form between her hands.

"No!" He grabbed Sara's hands and held them. When she started to pull away frowning, he kissed her. She stopped pulling away immediately and leaned against him, putting her legs around his waist.

"Oh god," he laughed. "Sara, we need to go home. We aren't doing this here."

"Here's good," she murmured and tried to kiss him again. The blue coating her body began swirling.

He debated a second, and then opened the raid channel. "Sara's drunk, and we need a port to a private spot right now."

"She's drunk?" Liz said in disbelief.

"Let's not worry about that. I need her out of the public right now."

"I'm in Oz's trailer," Marcus said.

"That will do. Summon us, please." Charlie scooped up Sara's clothes while she giggled and kissed him. He dropped the key on the chair and waited for the summon, trying to wrap her cloths around her, but she wouldn't cooperate.

"Oh, good we're home, take me to bed, Charlie," Sara said as she tried and failed to unbutton his shirt, giggling the entire time. Marcus headed to the door, a fiery red blush climbing his face. Sara didn't even see him. Charlie blushed himself, and then laughed as Sara tried to pull his buttoned shirt over his head.

"Let me go for one minute." Charlie tried to untangle his clothes from her grip.

"Turn off your phone call," Stasia said sweetly.

Charlie blushed again and turned it off. "Stop, Sara. I need one minute to get these off."

"One minute," she agreed and started counting, messing up the numbers completely.

She was noisy and bossy while they made love, not like herself at all, and he hoped she wouldn't remember any of it. Then he hoped Marcus had gone away, far away, as she screamed his name with a lot of oh gods thrown in. He tried to keep her quiet, but she wouldn't cooperate. Finally, he gave up and just did what she wanted. She fell asleep sprawled across Oz's bed. "You are going to be so embarrassed in the morning," he whispered as he smoothed her hair from her face.

Without waking her, he carried her to their trailer and tucked her in. She didn't stir when he kissed her goodbye after dressing in his uniform to return to school.

His face flamed red when he ran into Marcus out by the construction site. "Not one word!" he said fiercely as he handed Marcus the keys to the car. "It's at the tanning salon in tripoint plaza. Apparently, tanning beds get her drunk. Never mention this again."

Marcus snickered then coughed, then burst into loud guffaws. "She might think your god, but I don't."

Charlie's blush felt like fire on his cheeks. "She's going to be mortified."

"I was never here." Marcus snickered again as he crossed his heart.

"She's passed out. Keep an eye on her, please. I have to be back in five minutes."

"I will." Marcus slapped his shoulder. "Call Liz and explain."

Charlie ran to the dorm and was just in time for evening formation. Paul glanced at him, did a double take, then smirked. As soon as formation ended, Charlie headed to their room, followed by a still smirking Paul.

"What?" Charlie asked, and Paul grinned wider.

Charlie put his sweatpants on and hung his uniform up.

"Had a great weekend then?" Paul cracked up and turned away.

"What?" Charlie asked again in confusion.

"Dude, you're covered in scratches and hickeys."

Charlie lifted a hand to his neck, and then went to the small mirror over the sink. "Holy crap!" he exclaimed in disbelief. He'd forgotten to heal himself. When he saw Marcus, he was going to kill him. A peek under his shirt revealed his chest and back were liberally covered with scratches. A line of hickeys trailed from behind his ear down his chest. A blush rising to his cheeks, he hastily dropped his shirt. He healed fast. The marks would be gone in an hour.

"It isn't funny," he said when Paul laughed again at his expression.

"Sara has a feisty side." Paul laughed harder.

"I got her drunk. Not on purpose, but... tell no one. She'd be mortified."

"Cross my heart." Paul turned away still snickering

"I'm hoping she doesn't remember a thing." Charlie gave Paul a rueful grimace.

Paul laughed again.

"So, you remember then," Charlie said cheerfully. Her embarrassment had notified him she was awake. "Don't be embarrassed. I didn't mind, at least not once we left the salon," he assured her. "In fact, I'm thinking of getting you another Christmas present. How about a tanning bed of your own?" He laughed when she hung up on him.

Charlie grinned as he felt her emotions, tracking her progress from home to her office by her embarrassment spikes.

Her birthday was Wednesday, and Christmas break started the same day. He'd bought her small diamond earrings and debated really buying her a tanning bed. *Probably wasn't a good idea,* he finally decided.

- 31 -

HIJACKING

On the twenty-third, while they were at a restaurant celebrating Sara's birthday with Charlie's parents, Camila, Liz, and Oz's father, all of their HUDs activated.

Charlie glanced back to his mother staring after them, a worried expression on her face. John kissed her cheek.

"Don't worry. They'll be fine. What could happen to them with Sara there?"

Charlie tweaked Sara's ponytail, smiling smugly.

Major Nelson's image appeared on their HUD's as they jumped into Oz's car. "President Carmichael and his wife were on their way to his parents for Christmas. The plane is being rerouted to Libya. The hijackers are demanding we do a midair refuel. Oz will use his Wink and get on board to summon us. Do you still have the canopy you made for the Harrier?"

"Yes, sir," Oz said. "It'll need tightening."

"Sara, can you oversee the installation?"

"Yes, sir," Sara said.

"Get to Andrews ASAP. I want Oz in the air as soon as possible. Brenda, you'll fly him. I'm sending everyone the schematic of the plane."

A plane schematic replaced Major Nelson's image. The major highlighted the areas as he named them. "Oz, your safe spot to enter is marked in green. I doubt anyone will be inside that small meeting room but be prepared. We picked it because it not only has a good chance of being empty but there's also a low chance that you'll wink into anything or anyone except the chairs bolted to the floor there. There's a projector and screen at the front of the room so try to enter from the back. We estimate you'll need to wink about four feet to be sure to clear the hull but not land inside the seating. The room only seats twelve. If anyone is inside it, try to keep them there and quiet while you summon us but use whatever force necessary to preserve your life.

"Brenda, let him drop on top of the plane as close as you can to that spot. Then get out of there. Toric and Harrison are headed to Libya now. Meet them after the drop. I'm moving you all to group six. Oz will summon group one. They'll immediately switch groups and summon groups two, three, and five."

"Joy?" Sara's voice shook.

Charlie laid his glowing hand on her cheek, not liking how worried she was.

"Won't be on the plane," Major Nelson assured them. He didn't mention that she was already on her way to Libya. "Get suited up. We need to get in the air yesterday."

Sara, Manny and Brenda headed to the hanger where their rented planes where while the rest of them suited up. Charlie and Oz suited up and met them at the Harrier. Brenda and Oz took off moments later.

The helicopter the Scouts rode in followed slowly. They just needed to get to international waters while the plane was over them. They didn't need to be anywhere near it.

"Give her some privacy to change." The stickycom transmitted Charlie's voice clearly over the deep thwap of the helicopter lifting off. The Scouts obediently closed their eyes as Charlie held Sara steady while she removed her clothes and put her gear on.

"Is everyone's white bracelet full?" Without waiting for an answer, she began to fill the spell-bracelets. Oz hadn't gotten around to making the magic meter yet. Only two bracelets required a top off.

"Drop me as far to the front as you can," Oz said to Brenda on the raid channel. "Wink will get me onto the hull of the plane, but the airstream will send me down the plane at the rate of five feet per second and it'll take me about three seconds to deploy the magnets. Leave as soon as

I get on the hull. Don't give the pilot reason to be suspicious. I'm using duct tape to tie the magnet to my hand. Momentum will probably break my arm. My white bracelet is engaged. I'll be fine. I'm using a HOT and a shield. If I fall, I'll cast Ascension, and you can pick me up and we'll try again."

Major Nelson grabbed a hand strap and rose. "Stasia, when we get on board, after Hawk locates the president and first lady, you stay with the president. If the president doesn't have a white bracelet, give him one. You have the extra wristcomp. Give him that too if you can do so and remain unseen. President Carmichael is our priority. Lee and Todd will remain on the helicopter. If we can summon him off, we'll do so. I'll oversee rearranging raid group composition. We'll reassess the situation once we're on board and have more intel."

Sara said, "I see his wristcomp as in front of us. I think he's wearing it." Different size screens floated in front of Sara. "I'll send him a text on how to let us remote access it. I'll be discreet.

She thought a moment and then sent him a text. *If you can read this unobserved, what's my cat's name?* She gave him three choices and a ticking timer. *Hit the buttons as I type them.* She sent him the sequence to give her remote access. "I'm in. I'm turning on his health monitor and audio and routing it to my stickycom. Three people are within three feet of him. His vitals are fine. They're speaking Arabic, nothing important. I'm recording it all. I'm asking him to use his wristcomp to scan the room to give us a picture. His wife is in a different room. When we get on board, I'll let him know you're coming, Stasia. He can keep his wristcomp on the door for you."

Sara pointed to the combat HUD. "The blue dot is the president, the purple Oz. I'm the white dot. Oz is catching up fast."

Major Nelson peered over Sara's shoulder. He said, "When we engage, stun our own people. Then blindfold them and tie them if they can't be contained in a room unaware. We want no witnesses to what we do."

Everyone watched anxiously as Brenda caught up to Air Force One.

"I'm slowing to let Oz get in position," Brenda said.

"Good to go." Oz sounded excited.

"Moving up. We're in position, Oz. Good luck." Brenda hovered over the front of Air Force One.

"I'm going." Oz released and winked to the hull, crashing hard and bouncing. Wind seized him and tumbled him down the planes hull until the magnet grabbed, snapping his arm like a twig. "Shit, goddamn, that hurts!" Strained breathing and panting filled the line for a moment as the heals took effect.

Charlie forcefully held his magic back. Sara's worry echoed with his, making his magic hum uncomfortably beneath his skin. He repeatedly told himself Oz was fine, but the magic knew he lied. He switched to telling himself he was on the way to Oz and his magic stopped pressing so hard. The humming beneath his skin lessened and he was able to observe Oz crawl along the back of the plane to reach the green zone with some semblance of calm.

Oz winked through the wall of the plane and fell into a row of chairs. Mumbled swears made Charlie chuckle, and Sara gave him a dirty look. Charlie shrugged an apology. It was pointless to deny he found it funny when she could feel his mirth.

"Summon three," Oz said and started the cast.

Sara healed Oz as soon as she arrived and gave him a quick hug.

"We're in," Charlie said, and Sara rolled her eyes at him when he hugged Oz too. He laughed and lightly cuffed her shoulder.

"He'd laugh too," he whispered and kissed her cheek despite the face mask she wore. He wasn't worried, Sara was amused now too. Now that he was with Oz, the magical pressure ceased and all he felt was his own anticipation. Sara was calm with no strong emotions at all or maybe his were just so much stronger they masked hers. He shrugged lightly, mot caring at all just happy she was so calm.

Major Nelson rearranged the groups. "Summon when ready."

"Summon three." Everyone began their casts. Hawk started marking positions of people on the plane as summoned Scouts appeared. "The first lady is the light blue icon."

'Valor is on the plane and Stasia is on the way.' Sara texted the president. "Hawk, can Stasia exit this room unseen?"

"Two are right outside this door. No ID." A gesture made Hawk's HUD larger, and he tapped a yellow icon.

Major Nelson said, "Everyone except Hawk and Charlie Spell-Steal Stasia's invisible. I'll open the door on three. Stasia, T-one, Hawk, T-two. Keep it quiet."

Major Nelson counted down and opened the door. Stasia leaped through the open door invisible. One man was seated. The other held a gun on him. She sapped the seated man even though he was Hawk's target. Hawk instantly switched targets and shot the man with the gun.

Stasia blindfolded the seated man, gagged him, and led him to the room they came from. Major Nelson nodded approval and zip-tied the man to the seat.

Hawk and Charlie tied the man with the gun, breaking the stun. Wild brown eyes blinked at Charlie as he held the man on the floor, one leg kneeling on the man's chest while he pushed his shoulders down. The man didn't struggle or try to make a noise while Hawk gagged and blindfolded him. Charlie's Protective Aura kept the man too busy cowering to make a fuss. In moments, they had him trussed and tied to a seat.

Hawk updated his HUD as some men that had shown as yellow now glowed a malevolent red to him.

Major Nelson said, "Hawk, Charlie, steal Stasia's invisible and move up. Go to the president's room with Stasia. Oz, stay with us. Rick, Sam, Marcus, steal Oz's invisible and clear the first room on the right on my mark. Glenn, Tony, Drew, you're doing the same thing in the right-hand room. Sara is with me. The rest of you keep a sharp eye out. Be quick, silent, and deadly."

Major Nelson nodded and pointed at the door before him. "Go!"

Everyone went through the doorway.

"US Marines. Lay down your weapons!" Marcus yelled and immediately guns were fired.

Sara whispered, "Marcus," in a warning tone. Before Charlie could check his own HUD a yellow ball of light flashed past his face.

"Thanks," Marcus said, his whisper transmitting clearly through Charlie's stickycom.

"Stay behind the major," Charlie said to Sara and leapt forward without waiting for her reply.

"Our room is clear," Sam reported.

"Clear," Drew reported. "U.S. Marines, everyone stays here with this door closed," he said to the people inside the room.

Sam was saying the same thing in the other room.

Major Nelson said, "Four good guys, and the president and his wife are unaccounted for. Two of the good guys are the pilot and copilot. Hawk 'sees' four yellow in with the president. Yellow doesn't mean friendly. It means they had no relationship with the men he sees as red, but they could be hired hands!"

Marcus said, "Our shooter was dressed like wait staff."

"Be alert, Scouts. Stasia is in position outside the room where the president is being held." Major Nelson tapped his HUD. "Beta, get to the stairs, and clear the bottom floor."

"Oz, you're going to Wink through the door our first lady is behind and immediately go invisible. Get between her and the bad guy in the room. Kill him if you can do so without destroying the plane. Rick will be entering through the door and will get him if you can't. Go!"

They moved up and Oz winked through the door. Rick opened it with a hard kick and ran through. A muffled crack of gunfire sounded, and Rick reported tango down.

'Wife is clear.' Sara texted.

"Hawk, when you signal, we enter. Make sure the president will be safe.

Charlie and Hawk stood beside Stasia at the door and waited for the green flash. When his wristcomp flashed Charlie kicked the door so hard it broke into two pieces. He rushed through, taking gunfire, but no damage. Immune from harm for thirty seconds, he leapt to the first man he saw holding a gun and killed him with his sword. The dead body grasped in one hand, he spun to face the next man who gibbered in Arabic as his bullets thudded into Charlie with no effect. One quick thrust killed that man too. Stasia and Hawk had killed the other two men, leaving only the president alive.

"There's one with the pilot," the president said as he shook Major Nelson's hand. "My wife is safe?"

"Mrs. Carmichael is with the rest of the passengers. Mr. President, I invite you to join our raid."

"I accept," the president said.

Major Nelson added President Carmichael to group six. "Marcus, escort him to the rest of the passengers. Mr. President, I suggest you wait somewhere alone after you reassure your staff as we might need to summon you off the plane."

He turned to Stasia, "The pilot will be behind a secure door. You'll have to open it."

Sara winked at Hawk. "I'll disguise myself like the dead woman and knock. They can see me on the monitor, and I can talk to them."

"Can't hurt." Hawk snickered.

Major Nelson glanced from Sara to Hawk, a puzzled frown on his face. Charlie chuckled and cuffed Hawk's shoulder.

Oz disguised Sara as the dead woman and she knocked on the door. A man opened it. Stasia yanked him out and had him flat on the ground in three seconds. Sara gave her a high five, frisked the man and took his phone, and returned to the raid. Major Nelson entered the cockpit.

"U.S. Marines— the president is safe. Continue on the heading they gave you. We're going to clean this mess up."

The pilot turned to him in amazement. "How the hell did you get on the plane?"

"Classified." He beckoned to Sara. "I'm leaving her in here to listen for radio transmissions. Give her a headset and she'll let you know what they want.

Sara sat in the small fold down seat behind the pilot, removed her headgear and put the headset on. Major Nelson slapped her lightly on the back and left the room.

The pilot viewed Sara doubtfully. "You're special forces? Wait, I know who you are," he said in astonishment.

Sara smiled. "No, you don't. I was never here." She continued to hack the cell phone she'd taken.

The pilot nodded and turned back to his controls. Every few moments he snuck a glance at her from the corner of his eye.

Major Nelson spoke with the hostages while Rick released the man they'd gagged and blindfolded when they'd boarded. Glenn oversaw the prisoners.

Major Nelson gathered the rest of the raid with the passengers and said, "This plane is headed to Libya and will land as previously ordered by the terrorists. My team will disembark and take out whoever is waiting there. You'll fly back. Reinforcements are on the way there now. This plan is subject to change. It's going to be a long flight, so I suggest you get some sleep. Contact whoever you wish, but we want the bad guys to think their plan is working, so make sure whoever you talk with is aware of that and will keep your talks confidential."

"How did you get on the plane?" one of the suited men asked.

"Classified." Major Nelson said.

"Sir, we have a slight situation." Drew gestured for Major Nelson to leave the room. "Beta Team has found explosives."

"Of course they have," Major Nelson said sarcastically. "What plane hijacking is complete without blowing up the plane?" He sighed. "Can they defuse them?"

"Gina says eighty percent chance of successful diffusion. She recommends we jettison them instead."

"Steal Oz's Locate spell and comb every inch of this plane. Make sure we have them all." He gestured to Oz. "Wink outside with them, drop them, and I'll summon you back here."

"Yes, sir." Oz saluted and ran to find Gina. "Bring all the cell phones and electronic devices to Sara," Major Nelson ordered Drew.

Charlie followed Oz.

"These three cases, Oz." Gina gingerly handed Oz the cases, then slapped her blue bracelet down and spell-stole his Locate spell. An Ice-Shield shimmered around Oz.

Major Nelson joined them and handed Oz another case.

Cases clutched in his arms, Oz winked through the wall of the plane and dropped them. Charlie watched on his HUD as Oz cast wink again, getting farther away. The cases tumbled over his head.

"Summon," Oz said, and the bombs exploded. He landed at the major's feet laughing.

"Oh my god, that was so cool, like riding the biggest fireball ever."

"Loon," Stasia dusted him off, and then hugged him tightly. "You could've been blown to bits. Impossible to find over the ocean or resurrected. You're all singed."

Oz gave her a hug and winked at the major over his shoulder.

Charlie laughed as the major snorted and turned away.

The major said, "Everyone get some rest. Sara, how's the hacking coming?

"I've gotten into voice mail and am running the modulator program as we speak. We should be able to mimic any of their voices accurately within fifteen more minutes."

Then you get some rest too. Send notifications to me, and I'll wake you if we get a call. Tell the pilots to wake you if they hear anything on their radio."

"You heard my boss." Sara turned to the pilots and nodded toward the passageway. "Can I go stretch out in the corridor or something?"

"Yes, we'll come get you if we hear anything."

Sara stepped out of the cockpit and laid down on the floor and was asleep in minutes.

Charlie covered her with a blanket he took from his pack as the copilot asked, "So, who is she?"

The pilot said, "Doctor Sara Mitchel, Meredith Barlow's daughter."

"You're shiting me!"

Charlie stepped away from the door, staying within hearing range.

"Nope, that was her. She's some kind of super language genius. Guess they thought they might need one. How they talked her into coming and got on board I have no idea."

"Are you sure? I thought Meredith Barlow's daughter was a delinquent."

"Nope a genius. The whole bad girl thing was some sort of weird plot. Don't you watch television? It's been all over the news. She helped stop the last assignation attempt."

"That little girl?"

"This is the second time she's helped save the president."

"*Huh*," the copilot said thoughtfully.

Charlie grinned and headed back to the major as the pilot began talking enthusiastically about the Valkyrie operating system.

- 32 -

A SMALL DUST UP

Charlie tensed, laying a hand on his sword as the plane rumbled to a stop.

Oz flicked a glance at Sara as she said something in French into her mic, but he immediately turned his attention back to the screens floating before him.

The raid milled impatiently, everyone's gazes locking on the text floating across their HUDs.

Charlie read the notifications himself, translations of the conversation Sara was having with the hijacker's confederates who were giving her directions from the ground.

Oz was frowning hard, his fingers flying over the keyboard, searching for information on every name and location the men uttered.

As far as Charlie could make out, Sara was winging her replies. So far, the voice modulator program seemed to be doing its job, but she wouldn't be able to fool the men on the other end of the line if they thought to ask a personal question.

The longer she spoke, the more likely it was someone would twig to the fact that she was an imposter.

He grinned a feral grin. *It wouldn't matter a lick.* No one in range of his ranger would be able to get away.

Major Nelson said, "Andre, Todd, accompany Hawk. I want you three opposite us on this building here." Major Nelson tapped his HUD, highlighting one of the buildings on the map hovering before him. The 3D image of the airport flickered, a circled numbered one appearing over the building he'd tapped.

"Chief, you're on the biggest concentrations as Hawk points them out. Glen, you and Toric are taking teams here and here. Hold them until support gets there. Keep the showy stuff to a minimum. This area is likely under surveillance and there might even be official Libyan troops arriving or on scene already."

"Got it, Sara," Oz said suddenly in an excited tone, pulling Charlie's attention from the major.

The major stopped speaking and leaned forward to peer at Oz's screen.

Sara nudged Charlie's arm and flicked her screen closer to him.

"A connection to Joyce. I'm hacking the phone records here," Sara said. "Val, give me a three-dimensional map, highlighting calls place congruent to contact one. Cross reference and display all instances of congruency, filtering on sliding scale two."

Oz said, "Major, I estimate a force of one hundred with a small probability of an additional four hundred, but I really think they're unlikely to have deployed their full forces here."

"Roger that," Major Nelson said.

Oz said, "I'm intercepting chatter by their national guard who's just become aware of the seizure of this airport. Local law enforcement is asking for support."

Another grouping of screens sprang up around Oz, two of which showed local news stations.

"Civilian casualties, Sir, and they still have hostages. Police chatter has the hostages sequestered in the main terminal. Two planes have taken off without clearance and I'm tracking them now, but I have no idea if it was just pilots who realized shit was going down and got out or our bad guys taking this opportunity to steal planes. There could be more men on board planes in the vicinity."

Major Nelson said, "Stasia, I want your priority to be stopping the departure of any other planes or any types of vehicles unless you're certain said vehicle contains civilian personal."

"Yes, Sir," Stasia said.

She lifted her sunglasses to wink at Charlie. He bit back his laugh. He was sure his own eyes were glowing as brightly as hers. He couldn't wait to engage.

"We have movement on the left," Manny warned, his voice transmitting through the stickycom Charlie wore.

Hawk said, "I see twenty-six tangos and am marking them now."

The screens in front of Sara disappeared as she began to cast shields.

She said, "We've been ordered to open the door."

"Well, let's open it then," Major Nelson said, laughing as he slapped Charlie's shoulder.

Charlie stood in the open doorway of the plane, enjoying the expressions of confusion on the faces of the armed men who waited to board. He laughed as he pulled his swords.

A confusing mixture of English and French followed as the men shouted to each other and at him. The smell of gunfire coincided with the sound of the shots that hit his chest.

Bullets tumbled from the shield surrounding him, and he ran forward, yelling his attack cry as he swung.

The man firing at him dropped soundlessly. His companion shrieked, firing wildly as he backpedaled away.

Charlie swung again. A round of bullets tore along his right side, feeling like light taps and he turned to see the shooter. But the man was already dying, shot by Manny.

Charlie's magic surged as he spied Hawk racing away, trailed by Andre and Todd. His flicker of annoyance seemed to pacify the magic or maybe it was trusting in his sense of surety that Hawk was perfectly safe, but whatever the reason, it ceased to press him about it within seconds.

He and Manny circled left while Oz went right with Sara and Major Nelson. They met back at the open plane door within minutes.

Charlie flicked a glance at his HUD. Only three enemies were left forty feet from the plane. He couldn't see them, but thanks to Hawk, he knew they were hiding behind the white van.

"We got this," Major Nelson said, waving Charlie forward.

Charlie headed at a run to the biggest concentration of red dots on his HUD.

Gunfire continued to sound behind him, and he smiled grimly as it petered off into silence.

The men saw him coming and Charlie wondered if anyone had time to report or if they thought the gunfire was their men killing the civilians from the plane because they looked shocked to see him.

"U.S. Marines! Throw down your weapons!" he yelled happily, certain they wouldn't comply.

They didn't disappoint. Sara swore softly, and he glanced back but she waved him forward, swinging the folds of her cape forward and hunkering to let it cover her completely.

"Bastards!" he snarled and dropped one sword to pull his shield. Bullets curved in the air, being pulled by his magic to impact his shield. Somewhere in the distance a woman screamed.

His Valory said, "Warning, incoming aircraft. Probability eight-nine point seven-six of attack equipped jet. A split second later it said, "Pilot is Corporal Hess. Runway approach. Estimated landing grid four as potential destination.

Charlie could hear the jet now. It rumbled above him coming in low and fast.

"Three more air contacts. Presumed friendly," his Valory said

Sara said, "Oz, that recognition program needs work," and Charlie snorted with laughter.

Three more jets passed overhead.

Oz said, "Clear me to that terminal." and Charlie glanced at his HUD to see where Oz wanted to go.

"Roger that," he said and began to run to the building, leaving six more dead men behind.

Major Nelson began repositioning the teams. The small pockets of resistance wouldn't take the four-man teams long at all to mop up. Neither Charlie nor his magic was worried at all about it.

Two armed men guarded the door to the terminal, and both dropped their weapons, placing their hands in the air when Charlie approached. He ran by them, leaving the others to tie or question them. He had no idea if they were Libyan nationals doing their duty or terrorists, but they were no threat, so he continued forward to the next grouping of red dots.

The corridor was empty of people. Scattered files and overturned chairs marked where civilians had fled in haste. He kicked in the door of the control room.

He was certain the three men inside the control room were terrorists. Mindful, that Oz and Sara wanted the terminal intact and would likely prefer it not splattered with blood, he dropped his sword and shield to grab two of the men by the arms and yanked them from the room as they swore and struggled. Their swears became high pitched screams, whether from Charlie's aura or their own man shooting at him and not caring if the bullets hit them, Charlie didn't know.

He dropped the cowering men outside the doorway and ran back in to grab the last man, laughing as it transformed into a sheep.

The hall was silent, and he glanced over his shoulder to see Sara had hypnotized one of the men and was making him tie the other.

"Thanks," Oz said absently as he sat at the computer terminal and began punching keys.

"Stay here with Oz," Charlie said to Sara. "There's only a few more in that hanger right across from here. Brenda, get to Sara's position. I don't like you off on your own."

"Jeez, I just landed," she said laughingly.

Charlie continued to check for his teammates' whereabouts and conditions. All of them were with their assigned teams except for Joy who was at the lab and Brenda who was headed toward them. Two more Marine forces had arrived and were moving forward slowly on the west side of the airport. A large block of people Hawk had designated as yellow, status unknown, but likely civilians were in the buildings to his right.

The only large group of red was inside a hanger about six hundred yards away, but thirty men wouldn't take him and Manny more than a few minutes to clean up.

"Let's go," he said, clapping Manny on the shoulder as he passed him.

Sara and Oz were already siting in a forest of screens, talking excitedly as they hacked into a police database.

Sara said," Glen, send someone back to frisk the dead men by the plane. We want any electronics and IDs you can get."

"Yes, Ma'am," Glenn said.

She waved Charlie away when he hesitated. "Go. We'll be fine. We only have a few minutes before they notice the intrusion."

Oz snorted softly. "They already know but They should blame our friends here." He gestured vaguely to the doorway and the trussed men.

Charlie left them to it and led Manny to the hanger.

- 33 -

THE DEATH OF JOY

Charlie stretched and rotated his arms, trying to ease the soreness caused by holding back his swings. The magic wanted the enemy dead. It saw even the local police as the enemy, and it had taken real work to disengage and retreat to let the police do their jobs.

The fighting was over now but the magic knew the trussed terrorists waiting for pickup were the Enemy.

Charlie exited the hanger, leaving the men behind with Beta to check on the rest of the Scouts.

Sara stood outside the hanger with Brenda and Marcus, talking quietly. Charlie glanced at his HUD as Hawk reported one small group of people heading west on the edge of his range. Hawk couldn't tell if they were enemies or innocent bystanders.

Harrison had a group of men face down and tied by the building Charlie had just finished clearing. *He's got this*, Charlie told himself forcefully. The magic didn't agree. It wanted him to attack. Charlie snorted and turned his back, busying himself with checking his readouts. The magic settled but he was still uneasy. He finally gave in and headed to Harrison, reaching him just as Recon Team One did. Charlie helped tie the cowering men while Harrison snickered.

One of the Marines stepped forward, offering his hand. "I never got a chance to thank you. Mike Wallace. We met in Mexico."

"I remember," Charlie said, laughing lightly.

He shook Mike's hand. "Charlie Hayes and this is Harrison and that's my brother Rick."

Rick nodded acknowledgment but continued to pull his prisoners away.

"You'd think we were going to torture the fuckers or something," Mike said.

Harrison laughed again and helped herd the cowering prisoners away.

Charlie was growing annoyed at his magic's instance that he follow.

Mike stayed behind. "Your brother is on the same squad? That's odd."

"My future wife is too." He gestured to Sara. I'm sure Sara and Brenda will be happy to see you. Although I think Brenda might be happier…"

Mike snorted with laughter. "You guys get all the action— What is that?" Mike asked in perplexity as a blue cloud traveled over the building to the east of them. The cloud hugged the contour of the building until it reached the ground, then boiled in a roiling mass and raced for Sara.

Charlie turned to look right as Sara screamed. Charlie's knees hit the ground.

"Joy," he gasped, knowing she was dead. Sara's grief was overwhelming. *How did Joy's magic even get here?* He groaned and tried to stand against the weight of his grief. *She wasn't even in the zone.*

Sara screamed Joy's name as the magic engulfed her. She screamed again, this time in agony. Charlie echoed her scream, shocked at the feiry pain that engulfed her.

"Jesus!" Mike grasped Charlie's arm to pull him up.

Charlie moaned and staggered to his feet. The sword in his hand fell to the ground as he lifted his hands to cradle his head. Mike dropped his gun and used both hands to support Charlie, half dragging him toward Sara.

"What's happening?" Mike's confused gaze darted from Charlie to Sara. A blue cloud of magic swirled madly about Sara Brenda and Marcus. A bolt of lightning tracked down from the clear sky and struck Sara. She screamed again. The lightning didn't disappear. It stayed on her and jumped to Brenda and then Marcus.

Mike dropped Charlie's arm and ran toward them and tried to push Brenda out of the lightning with his shoulder. The lightning engulfed him.

Lost in grief for Joy, Sara continued to scream until she fell over unconscious. Joy's magic whirled around her, a blue cloud lit with static.

Charlie pushed himself up as men and women began to gather and call questions. The pain had ceased with a suddenness that made him feel sick and he staggered as he stepped forward, reaching for the icon that would connect him with the major.

"Joy is dead," he said tersely. Saying the words made his magic burst from his body and he staggered forward again, the magic's pain bringing him to his knees. "There's a lightning field on Brenda, Marcus, and Mike Wallace from Recon Team One."

"As soon as the lightning passes, dispel them and heal everyone," Major Nelson said. "Oz, Hawk, Stasia, go find Joy and rez her. She was to the east of us. Be cautious, obviously, there were enemies near her. Manny and Andre go with them."

Joy was here? How could she be here? Charlie thought dully as he struggled to his feet again. Color, sounds, smells were all so preternaturally sharp they were dizzying, and it took him a minute to sort out what he was seeing verses what he was sensing.

Major Nelson ran in from behind the building to the north followed by Drew, Todd, Sam and Tony.

"Spread out and keep civilians away!" the major ordered

Brenda had collapsed beside Sara. Marcus and Mike were sprawled face down on the ground half on top of them. Rick squatted beside him and he hadn't seen him arrive. Tears had tracked through the dirt on Rick's face, but he was grim now.

It took five minutes for the lightning to dissipate. Rick and Charlie raced in. Charlie healed everyone while Rick dispelled them. Sara sat up and screamed. Panic filled her, her desperation a physical pain so strong it brought Charlie to his knees again. Wild with grief and rage, she screamed again, and the lightning struck them all.

"Jesus Christ!" Major Nelson gestured everyone away as thunder boomed in continuous peels and the lightning field grew, encompassing everyone near Sara. Tendrils of lightning slithered along the ground as if searching. Magic boiled in sharp gusts, darting from one person to another in quick bursts. It careened between the present Scouts so violently it fluttered their clothing and lifted their hair. "Back away!" the major ordered as he ran farther away. "No one goes near them! Heal everyone except her. We can heal her when they're safely away from her. Harrison, once we're clear, you dispel this area. Oz, report!"

Saint Elmo's fire appeared. The blue-violet flames that didn't burn coated everything, spreading in waves and dissipating only to reappear and do it again.

"We can't rez her." Tears choked Oz's throat, making his voice thick. "It's been too long. Joy's truly dead."

Charlie gritted his teeth hard to stifle the scream that wanted to burst free. The magic cloud surrounding him wanted with a need past desperate.

"Retrieve her body. Don't bring it here until we get Sara and Charlie out of here."

Liz said, "If you dispel them again, the magic will search for her. Who knows what it will do if it can't find her? Let them come home first, then do it." Liz sounded as if she was crying.

Major Nelson ran a gloved hand over his head. "Right, get everyone affected on the plane. Harrison, fly them home. I'm leaving you in charge here, Glen. Clean this mess up and get us the intel."

The voices faded oddly, and Charlie welcomed the dark as relief from the pain of Joy's death.

On the plane headed home, Charlie woke and vomited. He'd barely gathered his wits when Sara woke. She began sobbing hysterically, begging for Joy. Tears slid unheeded down Charlie's cheek. Her magic surrounded him, seeking comfort from his magic. The blue cloud swirled in a growing frenzy.

A wild desperation filled her, growing over her grief and sadness. Charlie took off his shirt and hers, leaving her in her bra, hoping the contact would soothe her magic. Both still wore their armored pants and boots. The skin contact didn't help. Her body hummed against his, growing louder by the moment. He stole her Soothe and used it. It worked momentarily, but she was truly desperate.

"Joy," she moaned, and her magic flared. Panic, fear, pain, desperate need, loneliness, sorrow, washed over Charlie from her in growing strength. He was sad. The loss of Joy hurt. Sara was more than sad. Grief overwhelmed her. Her magic was desperate.

The rest of the Scouts were white-faced and silent. "What's going on?" Mike asked, frowning as Charlie removed their shirts. "Jesus, that's a headache."

Charlie didn't have the energy to spare to worry over him or anyone else. The rising hysteria in Sara's voice and on her aura yanked his magic from him. He closed his eyes and pressed her as close as he could, trying his hardest to convince the magic to calm down.

Quiet tears slid down Brenda's cheeks. Mike turned from Sara and Charlie and hugged her. "What's going on? What's the blue stuff?"

"Joy died." Brenda's voice hitched, and she wiped her eyes. "How did she even get there? How come she didn't show up on our HUDs?" Her glance slid to the man who sat unmoving with his head in his hands beside the major and her tears fell faster.

Major Nelson's lips tightened. "We'll talk about that later. Status checks now."

Everyone reported headaches. Major Nelson nodded. Sara and Charlie were still crying in the back of the plane. He glanced at Mike. "We're going to a secret facility. You were never there. Understand me?"

Brenda's eyes widened and she bit her lip. "We're not telling him?"

"No need." Major Nelson glared at her pointedly. "We'll clear everyone when we get home."

Brenda crossed her arms and turned her face away.

"What's the blue stuff?" Mike asked again, nodding to the blue glow surrounding Charlie and Sara that now gave off sparks and smelled of ozone.

"Classified," Major Nelson snapped. "You don't see it."

Mike shut his eyes and leaned his head back on the seat-rest.

"Oh god, Joy," Sara moaned and vomited, splattering Charlie's legs and the seat in front of them. He didn't seem to notice although his grip tightened, and he rocked her faster.

"Please, I need her." Her crying escalated. "Please, please, please!"

Brenda began to cry harder. Mike patted her back awkwardly. *This is what you got when you let a woman fight. Hysterics when someone died.* He had lost friends in battle and knew the pain of it. This young girl couldn't handle it, that was clear. He wondered why they didn't sedate her.

As if reading his mind Rick said, "Maybe we should sedate them."

"I don't think we should go near them right now." Major Nelson eyed the blue mist swirling around them with a cold expression. "No one touches either of them. That's an order."

"God, Drew, I'm so sorry." Tears filled Rick's eyes as he glanced from Drew to his brother. "I'm calling my father. Maybe he can help them."

Major Nelson nodded, and Rick placed the call.

"I have some bad news, Dad," Rick said. "Joy has died." Rick winced as Drew made a small sound of distress. "No, everyone else is fine. Sara is losing it. She took four of us. No, I don't think it'll be permanent. We can talk about that later in person. You and Mom better come. They're pretty broken up about losing her. I love you too. Thanks, Dad." He hung up and rubbed his eyes.

"Is Joy her sister?" Mike whispered to Brenda.

"No, her daughter," Brenda answered absently, her gaze locked on the blue glow surrounding Charlie and Sara. Charlie and Sara clutched each other crying. Sara continued to beg louder and louder for Joy. Brenda thoughtfully fingered a small gun she took from her pack.

"Chief, should I tranquilizer her?" she called.

"Yes, she's on the verge of panic here. Her mental pain is intense." He turned to Sara. "Brenda is going to shoot you with a tranquilizer. Don't fight it, or us, please."

Sara continued to sob and beg for Joy. Charlie nodded at Brenda, who shot her. Sara collapsed in Charlie's arms. The blue cloud surrounding her shrank and condensed to a dark ball that careened around the cabin. A lighter blue cloud still surrounded Charlie. He held his hand out and the ball alighted and faded. In moments it had disappeared. Charlie cried quietly into Sara's hair.

Mike sat back in his chair. *Why did they have tranquilizer guns and why in the hell would they bring a baby along with them on a mission? Jesus, no wonder she was hysterical; she must be feeling guilty as hell.*

Brenda shrugged and shot Charlie. The blue disappeared sucked back into his skin as if vacuumed.

Major Nelson sighed in relief, and then glared at Brenda.

Brenda glared back. "Why was Joy there? Why weren't we told? She's going to kill you if you brought her there without telling them."

"Joy wanted to go. I didn't force her." Major Nelson glanced at Mike then away. "We'll talk about this later. I'm letting a lot slide here because I know you're all upset. I'm in command. I decide who goes where."

"You had no right to decide that for them." Brenda threw her hands in the air. "What's done is done and can't be undone, but you know she'll be beyond angry. They both will be."

Major Nelson nodded grimly. "Yes, which is why we'll say nothing until we've handled this." He gestured around him. His lips were so tightly compressed they were white.

Brenda leaned back in her chair and squeezed her eyes closed.

Mike patted her hand and she clutched it.

Damn, he didn't understand what was going on, why the major would bring a child along, but he understood better why they were so upset.

- 34 -

LET HER HAVE THEM

When they landed, they were loaded into the back of a large windowless van and driven somewhere for an hour. By the time they entered an underground facility Charlie was awake again. Sara was starting to stir.

They followed Major Nelson underground into a room with a large metal cylinder. Charlie's mouth tightened, and he stopped. "No, this isn't necessary. It'll kill her."

"We came here for the medical facility, not that." Major Nelson led them to a series of small rooms built into the rock of the mountain and sealed with a heavy door covered with warnings of radiation. Each room contained a hospital bed, and medical equipment lined the walls. "Liz is here now and will make sure everyone tests clear." Major Nelson opened a door and gestured for Mike to enter. Brenda gazed at him sadly and kissed his cheek before entering the room beside his.

"Have I been exposed to radiation?" Mike asked.

"You have, but we can fix it," Major Nelson assured him.

"I'm not putting Sara in one of these rooms. She'll completely freak out when she wakes." Charlie backed away from the doors, clutching Sara to his chest.

"There's a small conference room down the hall. Take her there. Liz wants to do some blood tests first on everyone. Let her do Sara first." Major Nelson pointed down the hallway.

Mike sat on the empty bed and debated his options. He wasn't going to settle for classified when he needed medical treatment.

Charlie carried Sara into the small conference room and took the empty blood vial from Liz to fill himself. He filled two vials with blood. Liz labeled them, and then hugged him before handing him two more for himself. He took his own blood and handed the vials to her.

"I'm so sorry," she murmured, and left them alone in the room.

Joy was dead, he thought and felt nothing except disbelief.

Charlie still felt woozy and disconnected and he wondered if it was from the shock or the tranquilizer. Whatever was causing it, he was grateful his magic was so much calmer now. It wasn't trying to push him or appear, and he slumped in the chair, resting his aching head in his hands.

Sara woke and grabbed Charlie, her magic instantly around her. "Oh god, Charlie, I need her!"

"I know. I feel your need. I'm so sorry, Sara." Charlie's eyes filled with tears for her emotional pain. She held him and cried, consumed with longing and pain. Suddenly she stiffened and screamed.

"What?" The sharp pain from Sara felt like a blow. No longer in only mental pain she was in physical pain now. "What?" he yelled again as she shrieked and recoiled. The echo of agony caused him to groan. Nothing could be seen but fire burned along her body.

Another shrill scream was followed by wild struggling in his arms as she attempted to get away from him.

Liz shone a bright yellow light over Mike.

"Stop, it hurts! Stop— stop!"

Screams echoed down the hallway. Mike bolted upright. "What's happening?"

"I don't know. Wait here, I'll be right back." Liz ran from the room and headed to Sara who was still screaming.

Charlie threw open the door to his room. "Stop dispelling them! It's hurting her!" Sara pushed past Charlie and grabbed him.

Mike didn't have time to be shocked, the lightning hit him again. In the closed space heat built up. The lightning flickered and pulsed as if it had a hard time manifesting.

He and Sara both screamed. He tried to push her off but couldn't make his limbs obey him.

"Stop dispelling them!" Charlie screamed. "You're going to kill her!"

Major Nelson into doorway.

Marcus peered over his shoulder.

Charlie said, "God, she's in agony, Marcus. Go to her, it's killing her!" He turned a furious face to Major Nelson. "Who else did you dispel?"

The major held his hands up and backed away. "Chief, you know we have to do this."

"If you do, it'll kill her! You have to stop! God it's hurting her so much. Marcus, go to her please! I'm begging you!"

Major Nelson grabbed Marcus's shoulder. Marcus shook him off and ran to Sara. Lightning engulfed him and her screaming stopped, and they slumped to the floor. Inside the small rock room, the lightning growled. Brilliant white light filled the space and heat flowed from the doorway. Thunder rattled everything in the room and glass exploded in tinkling shards.

Fire burned along Mike's skin and in his bones. He knew they were still yelling but pain had immobilized and deafened him, and he knew nothing else.

Hands on his hips, and lips in a furious line, Major Nelson faced Charlie. "Charlie, she can't have them all!"

"It's too damn late!" Charlie yelled. "If you try to take them from her, it'll kill her! If she dies, I'll kill you!"

Major Nelson lifted his hand and shot him. Charlie leapt for him and they both crashed into the wall. A struggle ensued for a brief moment before Charlie slumped to the floor. Major Nelson pushed himself to his feet as he casted a heal on himself using his white bracelet.

"You can't." Liz wiped her sweaty palms on her pants. "Let her have them. Give them time to figure this out. They planned to turn more eventually anyway. If you kill Sara, you have to kill all of them. You know that. The United States will have no magic. Let her have them. We can keep them safe."

Liz held out her shaking hands beseechingly as Major Nelson finger the forty-five strapped to his hip. "Think about this, please. Sara and Oz are more valuable than losing four soldiers. It's worth more to keep them safe somewhere while they study the magic than it is to kill them all now."

"The reason I'm not dead right now is Sara's shield, which I casted before coming in. Charlie would've killed me...." "He trailed off and turned away "You're right. Let her have them. If she can stop at these."

He turned back and took Liz by the hand. "Liz, don't lose sight of the threat she is. That is *not* a girl. That is an alien hiding in a girl's body." Major Nelson rubbed his eyes. "When he wakes, he's going to be furious. I better not be here. I'm sending for Captain Sanders."

Major Nelson glared at Charlie's crumpled form then left the hallway rubbing his throat. Liz let out a pent-up breath, ran into Marcus's room, closed the door, and called Oz.

"Is this call completely private?" she whispered when he answered. When he said it was, she told him what had happened. "The major almost killed Sara and Charlie. Take Stasia and Hawk and hide until I call again. They won't kill them if you're at large. I'm looking out for them here. And, Oz, don't tell Stasia about Rick, please. One crisis at a time."

Adrenaline still making her hands shake, she hung up and went to get her tranquilizer gun.

Sara woke screaming in pain and calling for Charlie. She began vomiting. Rick grabbed her and brought her to his brother.

"He's just sedated" he said, but doubted she heard him. She continued to cry and beg Charlie for help in increasingly piteous wails.

"We can't keep doing this. It's going to kill her," Rick said as he backed from the room and the magic swirling around her.

"We won't. We're letting her have you."

Rick snorted. "Oh, dear god, don't say that near Stasia."

"One problem at a time. We haven't told her yet."

Rick followed Liz into the room containing Marcus and Mike.

Brenda met them at the door. "They're fine. How's…" she shook her head and trailed off. It was clear to everyone Sara wasn't good.

Liz said, "We're letting her have you. Think really hard about not wanting Sara please."

Sara's wails had picked up in volume. She sounded angry now as she shouted for Charlie to wake and someone to bring her Joy.

Rick peered over his shoulder. "There must be something we can do."

Tears in her eyes, Liz glanced up from Marcus. "Go check them. I have sedatives here they can take that won't knock them out. Or sedatives that will. Ask her what she prefers."

Rick ran back into the room that held his brother. Sara cradled Charlie's head in her lap crying and rocking.

"Get me Joy, please!" she yelled when she saw him. "Please, Rick we need her, please!"

Rick knelt to feel his brother's pulse as he said, "She's dead, Sara. Please calm down. Charlie is fine. Everyone is fine. Calm down. Will you take a pill, please?"

"No! Joy— bring her to me! I know she's dead. Please, I need her. God. Charlie, please wake up. I need you too." Her magic swirled wildly. She tipped back her head and screamed, "Now, I need her now! Why won't anyone help me? Just get me Joy!" She put Charlie's head gently on the ground and ran for the door. Rick grabbed her but couldn't hold her. She still wore only a bra, the pain from touching her bare skin was too much. In less than a minute, he had to release her.

"Liz!" Rick yelled, "Bring the dart gun. Hurry, we have to stop her. Sara, she's dead. You have to calm down." He chased his sister-in-law as she ran, so panicked he could feel it in the thin skeins of magic trailing her.

Major Nelson stood beside the canister and opened it as Sara raced by.

She stopped dead and fell to her knees. A wail of utter despair burst from her. "No, I just need Joy, please!" She fell to her hands, then her face as her magic was ripped from her.

Major Nelson slammed the lid.

Rick shouted wordlessly and tackled the major. The two men rolled on the floor, both trying to grab the tranquilizer gun on the major's hip. Rick kicked the canister onto its side. The lights in the room flickered as the magic raced back out to Sara.

She didn't stir.

Rick wrested the gun from the major and the major reached for his forty-five. Liz screamed and both men glanced at her. Major Nelson hesitated, his hand dropping from his weapon. Rick used the tranquilizer gun on the major. Liz ran to Sara as the major hit the floor.

"Pulse is slow, but steady. Put Charlie beside her. Stay here with the gun and be prepared to tranq her again. Jesus, this is a disaster of epic proportions. Did you really just shoot the major?"

"What was I supposed to do? Let him kill my brother's wife?" Rick asked bitterly.

"No, you did the right thing. Let's get him inside one of the rooms, and I'll lock him in. Captain Sanders will be here soon. We need this under control before he arrives."

Liz got all her patients in their own beds hooked up and being monitored, except for Brenda who was with Mike explaining what was going on.

- 35 -

BAD NEWS

Mike calmly watched the recordings Brenda showed him. "I suspected something like this," he admitted. "Well, not this craziness, but something. I realized you could make yourselves invisible and do other things, but I thought it was some secret new tech." He paused in thought. "I understand what you're saying, but I don't understand what's happening now."

Brenda took a deep breath. "Sara can transform people, give them the magic. That's the lightning; it hurts her to do it."

"It's no picnic on the receiving end either," Mike said wryly.

Brenda gave him a grimacing smile.

"The lightning makes her sick and upsets her magic in unpredictable ways. Recently, she made Joy a rogue and formed a bond when she did it, a close bond. Joy was like her daughter. She and Charlie attacked anyone touching her instantly like an instinct, they couldn't help it. They learned not to, but they didn't want her put in danger."

Brenda sighed in exasperation. "I'm not explaining this right, let me go back. Charlie and Sara are in love, but more than that they have a magical bond. They can feel each other's emotions and need to share their magic when they're stressed. They have to touch to do so, the more skin the better. Are you following me so far?"

Mike nodded.

"They can only control that urge a little bit. If one or the other is afraid or hurt, it gets harder to control. If they ignore it, or try to deny the magic, it becomes an overwhelming compulsion for them to touch. They'll use all their abilities to get to each other. Sara has blown up buildings to reach him. Her magic takes control."

Mike nodded his understanding.

"Stasia is a rogue and in love with Rick who plays a warrior. Rick has no magic. Sara wants to change Rick for Stasia so they can share magic as well. Apparently, once you have it you want to share it. Before Sara would try to change Rick, she changed Joy." Brenda paused a moment in thought. "You have to understand the risk involved for them. They could've changed Joy and desired her physically. They might've needed to share her magic as well and been linked to her for the rest of their lives. That's why they did Joy and not Rick. Rick is a warrior like his brother.

Sara didn't want to take a chance she'd need him magically or want him sexually."

"So they made Joy a rogue first, a test subject," Mike said. "And they did bond with her."

"Yes, a protective bond and they were learning to deal with it. Joy had no bond to them at all. They were all still friends. If it had continued to go well, they would've tried to change Rick a few months from now." Brenda took a deep breath, "Rick will experience the change in four days; we all will."

Mike pulse thudded hard. "Me too?"

"Yes, I'm sorry, but yes. We did try to stop it, but you heard what it did to her. They'll let us change to save her. Mike, it's a hard, painful process and you likely won't have magic at the end of it. We'll show you the spells, but... We've all been practicing for years now."

"They'll sacrifice us for her? Why is she so special?"

"She can heal us all, any Marine. Heal anything, even lost limbs and raise the dead if she reaches them quickly enough. Besides the heal there's her amazing mind. She and Oz are inhumanly smart."

Awe rose goosebumps across Mike's skin. He examined Brenda but she seemed sincere. *Of course, that didn't make it true,* Mike mused. *She might believe in magic, but magic was impossible. It must be tech.*

Brenda ran her fingers over the white bracelet on her wrist. "I can heal with this bracelet, and she's working on making this available to everyone, not just the Marines. I would die for that, a heal for everyone. We all would, that's why we're here. That's why we agreed to let her change us if she ever needed to. She craves contact with warrior magic, she can't help it. Rick will be a warrior and it'll upset everyone if Sara wants him."

Mike watched the video again, his awe growing as he realized the United States was working with an alien. They called it magic, but they were aware it was an alien ability. Goosebumps shivered his skin again as he considered he'd be an alien host whether he wished to or not.

He had to admit the idea of being able to use magic intrigued him. The tradeoffs didn't seem that bad. Sara was a beautiful woman although not really his type. He preferred more outdoorsy types, women like Brenda, and if he had magic too, she'd likely stay with him, although he hated the idea of an alien entity choosing for him.

He snorted softly. It felt like all of his choices had slipped from his control. They weren't going to let him waltz out of here knowing what he now knew.

He rubbed his aching head.

"So, the magic spells come from UBM, depending on what character you play?"

"Yes," Brenda agreed. "We think about being the character during the transformation."

"Well, I have bad news for you all. I've played the game and I'm a warrior too."

"Oh, Jesus." Brenda rubbed her eyes with both hands and paced the room. "Charlie is going to freak. Try really hard not to need her."

"And us?" Mike asked softly.

Brenda shrugged lightly. "I'll be a moon priest. Priests like warrior magic. I don't know what that means for us. There's so much you still don't know. I have a serious case of lust for you, but we aren't in love." She grinned when he snorted. "Maybe it could be more someday; we hardly even know each other. Our raid is allowed to fraternize, so we can still, *um*, date if we want to."

"How come?" Mike rose an eyebrow and leaned back on the pillow.

"See, there's so much you don't know. I'll tell you the entire story from the beginning and give you my wristcomp to access our files. I'm sorry you didn't get a choice. We have about thirty hours before we're really sick." Brenda sat beside him on the bed and started from the beginning.

When Captain Sanders arrived, Sara and Charlie were still out. Charlie was sedated. Sara was unresponsive.

Liz nervously cleared her throat. "Major Nelson is sedated and I'm monitoring him." She explained what had happened. "Sara isn't responding at all. I don't know if permanent harm was done to her. Charlie should wake soon and might be able to tell us. Brenda is informing Sergeant Wallace on his new circumstances."

"Charlie's parents are coming here?"

"They should be here tonight."

"Let's get Sara and Charlie away from here."

"Doctor Gotlieb agrees. I need medicine for her. The last time they did this her hormones spiked, and this time she did it three times on four people. I'm really worried about this. I need access to her for medical care and I need to be here to monitor them."

"We can summon you back and forth as needed," Captain Sanders said. "We're stretched thin right now. Alpha Team is decimated. Beta is returning but won't be back for a few more hours. I have men setting up a campsite for Charlie and Sara. If you can handle this alone, I'll go there to summon them."

"The Scouts won't need medical attention for hours yet. Brenda can handle it for a while. I'll go with them for now." Liz took a deep breath. "Get Major Nelson out of here. They'll be furious on so many levels with him. The Scouts are already angry about Joy. They don't know about this yet." Liz gestured distastefully at the canister. "I predicted their response will be hostile."

"Damn, why didn't he just shoot her with a tranquilizer?" Captain Sanders asked plaintively.

"You'll have to ask him." Liz gave a small shrug.

"Yeah, I'll take him with me." Captain Sanders gave Liz a quick glance. "Maybe they don't need to know?"

"I won't say anything, but I can't promise for the other three."

"Damn, yeah they'll all know. He better have a good reason."

Liz helped wheel the major to the captain's car.

Charlie woke and remembered. Instantly enraged he jumped up and yelled his berserk attack.

His brother jerked upright, wincing as he dropped his hands from his head. Charlie realized he was in the conference room that had held Sara. He held his other hand out and attempted to summon a sword. None appeared. His sword was too far away. He slapped his wrist, engaging his white bracelet and used it on himself, then Sara. Rick grabbed him and shook him hard. He took Sara from him and laid her on the table while Charlie retched, gagged, and vomited, clutching his head. He sat back on his heels and again attempted to summon his sword.

"Get a grip, it's just us three."

Rick told him what had happened.

"Sara hasn't moved since, not even a twitch."

"I'm taking her away now."

"Where will you go?"

"Our boat."

"What?" Rick took off his shirt and tried to put it on Sara. "She's more painful than normal to touch. Like fingernails on a chalkboard under my skin when I touched her."

Charlie nodded and took over dressing her. "She feels like that to me too. It's the transformations. It helps if we touch. Never mind about that. I need her out of here. I got her a boat for Christmas. Don't tell anyone. I'll call Oz and have him take us off the grid. He'll know where we are. I can't trust them with her right now. She'll be safe at sea and unable to take anyone else. The magic needs time to calm down. This humming is awful." Charlie gave his brother a hard hug. "I wish I could be here for you, but she needs me."

"Go, I'll be fine. I love you guys. Stay safe." He handed his brother his white bracelet.

Charlie ran out the door, carrying Sara.

As soon as he was clear of the building, he called Oz. "You know what's going on?"

Outside of the building a narrow dirt road wound among tall pines. The road would be faster with less chance of getting lost, but in the woods it would be harder to spot them. Undecided, he continued down the road while he spoke with Oz.

"Liz called and warned us. As soon as this plane touches down, we're going into hiding."

"I need help. I'm out of the building, but Sara isn't responding. I want to get her on the boat and need help getting there and supplies."

"I'll meet you. I see where you are now. Get to the spot I marked on your map, and I'll pick you up. Stasia will bring the supplies." Oz placed a map on Charlie's HUD.

"Ask Liz to give her the medical supplies. I'll need stuff to counteract Sara's hormones, sedatives, and IV's."

"We'll get them. If not from Liz, we'll steal them. You're untraceable by wristcomp. We won't let them harm you. Stasia doesn't know about Rick yet."

"Good idea. I hate to lie to her, but Sara is completely defenseless."

Oz picked him up three hours later.

A flush on his cheeks, Charlie turned to Oz. "I need to stop at a convenience store for condoms. If her magic makes her desperate, I need to be ready. God, I wish she'd wake up, she hasn't twitched in hours."

"You're healing her?" Oz asked.

"Of course, every time my cooldown allows.

"Try Soothe instead," Oz suggested.

Oz drove him to the boat. Stasia and Hawk arrived moments later with the supplies.

Stasia said, "Liz said to call her. Oz can make sure you aren't monitored." Stasia placed the bags she carried on the deck.

Hawk ran a hand over Sara's hair, his eyes narrowing at the sight of her pale face and tear streaked cheeks. "Should I stay with you?"

"No, we need to be alone. I've never felt such intense pain in my life, and I was feeling it secondhand. She's going to totally freak when she wakes. I'm headed straight south. The sunnier and quieter, the better."

He started the engine and drove out of the dock with Sara lying at his feet. As soon as he was a safe distance out from shore, he put the IV in her arm and made her comfortable on a cushion by his feet. Crouched beside her, he shook her shoulder hard.

"Wake up!"

Nothing he did had any effect. Not begging yelling or Soothe. One sail raised, he headed south. At nightfall, he stopped. Moonlight shimmered across the water. The peaceful scene seemed to mock him. He carried her into the cabin and undressed her completely, then himself. Sara's cool body clutched to his chest, he dozed off. When he woke, she still hadn't moved. He tried shaking her and yelling, begging, and kissing. His magic rushed around the cabin in agitation and settled over them in a dense cloud.

He called Liz. "She's in a coma or something. I can't wake her. What do I do?"

"Wait, keep the IV in, and put her in the sun. If she doesn't wake in a few days, she'll need a feeding tube. What are you doing about bodily waste? Do you want me to come show you how to put a catheter in?"

"No, I'm just cleaning her. It isn't a problem."

"You only have enough IV for three days."

"She better wake before that. This is killing me. My magic needs her. I hate him for killing Joy. I'll kill him if she doesn't wake."

"She will. Everyone here is progressing normally. I'll text you updates. Take care of her, Charlie. I love her."

"Thanks, Liz, I will. You should still see our vital signs. If you notice anything I need to know, call me." Charlie hung up and changed her IV. All day he held her in the weak winter sunlight. He wished he'd bought her the tanning bed. Despite himself, he smiled when he thought of her being drunk on sunlight. He cried when he thought of her never being drunk on sunlight again.

It was a long day. Oz called and reported the Scouts were furious and concerned. Major Nelson said he'd meant to just trap enough of her magic to ease her. Charlie didn't know whether to believe that or not and decided he didn't care. If Sara didn't wake, he'd kill him.

- 36 -

HELP ME

Charlie was truly desperate. It'd been twenty-four hours since Sara had last moved. He spent all day holding her in the sunshine and slept curled around her at night. Another three days passed the same way. His magic surrounded him constantly his desperation was so great. When she finally opened her eyes, he sobbed with relief.

Clumsily, she tried to sit. He helped her sit up, his hands shaking. Her skin absorbed his magic, every spec disappeared, and her movements strengthened. With fixed persistence, she struggled to stand, and he knew it wasn't her in control. He held her down with both hands, using his body weight to stop her from struggling.

"There's nowhere to go! We're on a boat! Stop it!" he yelled, furious with the magic.

Both her hands held in one of his to stop the useless scrabbling against the deck, he yelled her name. She went completely limp and he cautiously sat. She remained limp and unresponsive to him. He rose and began to straighten out the IV, which had gotten removed in the struggle. Without opening her eyes or speaking, she rolled over and tried to crawl away.

This time when he grabbed her, she clawed and bit and fought him as hard as she could. The entire time he felt nothing from her as if he held a stranger. Again, he fell across her using his weight to hold her to the deck, panting in anger and fear. He held her wrists with one hand and called Oz and Liz.

"I don't know what to do, the magic has her, and I can't get her back!"

"It's trying to move her?" Oz asked.

"Yes, god yes! I can't stop her. She's trying to get away. What do I do, Oz?"

"Where is she trying to go?" Liz asked.

"There's nowhere *to* go. I'm at sea." He panted a second as he struggled with Sara, trying not her hurt her as she fought him. "Stop, please stop, Sara. I don't want to hurt you. Joy is dead. You can't have her. I'm so sorry, but please stop."

Liz said, "Bring her back, Charlie. Let her see Joy's body. I have her here. Doctor Elliot did an autopsy, and she'll be cremated tomorrow."

"Harrison will come get you. We can trust him," Oz said. "Stasia, Hawk, and I will remain hidden. If they try anything, we'll come for you, and they'll be very sorry."

"No one will do anything," Liz assured him. "Let her see Joy one last time."

"Send Harrison."

Charlie hung up and cautiously sat and she tried to crawl away. She'd stopped fighting him, which relieved him, he'd worried she'd begin to cast on him, but she kept trying to crawl away every time he let her go.

His head throbbed with the worst stress headache of his life by the time Harrison arrived in a helicopter with Tony and Sam. They pulled Sara aboard while she struggled, kicking and thrashing in an uncoordinated attempt to get free.

Charlie climbed up the rope to the helicopter, and Tony and Sam jumped down to the boat.

"We'll bring it back," Tony said.

Charlie didn't care a whit. "Stop it!" He yelled as Sara continued to struggle wildly. "We're going to Joy now!"

Nothing he said lessened her struggles. Angry with her magic, he shook her hard. "Stop right now!" She halted mid-motion and collapsed unresponsive.

She remained unmoving in his arms. When they arrived, Charlie jumped from the hovering helicopter and waved Harrison off. A tap on his wristcomp activated his combat HUD. Another tap opened a link to Team Valor. Anything that happened inside the building they would see and hear. Inside, the building was quiet. Liz stood beside the doorway with both hands in sight and empty.

"Joy's' down here." She led him to a small, but fully equipped morgue. An open drawer held a sheet-covered body.

Charlie sobbed, one sharp cry of despair. She was white with the greenish tinge of death. Black stiches ran across Joy's skull. A sheet covered her body, but an edge of black stiches showed on the top of her chest. Both of her arms were wrapped in gauze and strapped to her sides.

Sara tried frantically to get free.

Charlie let her go.

She fell over Joy's body and the lightning came. Liz screamed and ran from the room. Outside the doorway, she glanced back.

Sara pushed herself off Joy. Panicked eyes stared at Charlie and she reached a hand to him and spoke in a voice that cracked. "Help!"

"Oh, God, Sara, how? How do I help you?" Charlie grasped her hand.

"It wants Joy," Sara said. "I can't... she trailed off, then screamed and fell across Joy's chest. A yellow glow surrounded Joy. Sara was trying to resurrect her. As soon as Charlie touched her, his magic left him in a rush. The glow became brighter.

"It's not enough, Sara. We don't have enough magic. I'm sorry, she's really dead!" Charlie yelled.

Sara screamed in frustration and pain.

Liz called Oz. "They're trying to rez her and need more magic." She ran from the room and returned in moments with a box of spell-bracelets.

Hawk appeared and took Sara's other hand. The yellow glow grew brighter and Sara screamed again. Hawk moaned and sagged against the metal table.

"You have to stop, Sara! You'll kill yourself!" Charlie yelled.

Stasia and Oz appeared. "We're so screwed," Oz said as he grabbed Charlie's hand. "We have no protection now. They can kill us all."

Charlie knew it too, but he couldn't stop. Sara's desperate need kept him beside her. The magic had her and she was terrified and struggling to break free, but the magic fought her hard. Joy was its child and it would kill them all to save her.

"We're here," Manny said from the doorway. We'll protect all of you. Do what you need to." Manny stood behind Harrison, his rifle across his shoulder. At six feet five inches and three hundred pounds of muscle his cold stare made Charlie feel safer. Manny was as big as him and the only raid member who fought as eagerly as Charlie. Manny spent his time on Beta team because he loved the missions. He wouldn't hesitate, no matter who approached. They exchanged grim nods and Manny ran from the room.

Stasia grabbed Oz's other hand. Sara yanked their magic out and the glow became blinding. Sara screamed again.

"Oh god, stop, Sara," Charlie begged. The echo of her pain was excrutiang. Magic burned in his veins, leaving fiery trails of pain behind.

"I can't, it won't let me. I can't stop. Help me!" Sara turned to him, her eyes begging for help and it hurt his soul that he had no help to give her. She tried to say something else, the words emerging mangled beyond recognition and she began to scream.

Charlie bit back his own scream. It felt like he burned from the inside out. His arms throbbed with his heartbeat. The magic was going to kill them all. Human bodies were too frail to be conduits for this much power.

Stasia and Oz fell over. Hawk crumpled in slow motion. Charlie yelled Sara's name and fell into her, trying to knock her away from Joy. Sara fell away from Joy and the burning sensation in his arms dimmed. The magic felt relief, but he'd barely registered it before darkness claimed him.

- 37 -

THE PRICE

The yellow glow on Joy's body slowly faded. When it was totally gone, Liz cautiously approached and felt for a pulse on Stasia.

"Help!" She called and hit her open raid channel. "I need help in here right now. I know you're out there guarding. They're all going to die if I don't get some help." She engaged her white bracelet and threw a heal and nothing happened. Sara had used all the magic. Drew ran into the room.

"Pick one. They all need help." Liz sobbed and kept doing CPR on Stasia. Drew engaged his bracelet and casted a chain heal. He cast a heal-over-time on everyone, and then healed each of them individually until he ran out of magic. Harrison ran into the room right behind him; Lee followed.

Hawk sat up on his own, crawled to his sister and pulled her into his lap. Charlie moaned and tried to stand. Lee engaged her bracelet and cast a chain heal, and then went to check Sara.

"Oh my god, Joy's alive!" Lee gasped in disbelief. "Who has a heal left?" Lee took both of Joy's hands in hers and glanced around the room. Manny pushed into the room and healed Joy then Sara with his bracelet, then left the room at a run, his gun clutched in his hand.

Charlie sat up on his own.

Oz moaned while Stasia gagged and coughed.

Liz knelt beside Sara. "She's alive. They're both alive." She turned to Charlie. "How can we help you?"

"I don't know," Charlie shuddered. "That was.... Can we heal them again, please? I've never felt anything that bad. Harrison, can you take Sara back to the boat? I don't think I can pick her up."

Drew offered him a hand to stand.

He took it gratefully.

Lee put her arm around him, offering a shoulder to lean on.

"Are you guys going to be okay?" Charlie asked his friends.

Hawk nodded dully, stroking his sister's hair.

Oz said, "Yes," and waved him away. "Go, take her away. I only felt an echo of that. Poor Sara. We'll be fine. Take care of her."

"I'm so sorry, guys," Charlie said.

Hawk laughed dully. "It's not your fault, or hers either. Go."

Charlie leaned down and kissed Stasia's head. Lee helped him stand again. The room wavered, and he gripped Lee's shoulder hard to balance.

"Sorry," he said, and she patted his hand.

"It isn't hurting to touch you."

He nodded and plodded forward. The lack of magic left him feeling weak and confused. His bones still throbbed, and he worried he'd permanently injured himself. More than anything he wanted to sleep but it wasn't safe to sleep here. He needed to be away. Lee supported him, half carrying him to the helicopter, and helped him board. Harrison put Sara in his lap and he gratefully closed his eyes. Lee sat beside him and helped steady her while Harrison flew them back to the boat.

Lee jumped down, holding Sara.

Charlie tried to cast Waylay but didn't have enough magic and the attempt made him his head swim with pain.

Sam engaged his white bracelet and pulled him down. "Put Sara in the cabin," Sam said. "We're staying aboard until you recover enough to take care of yourself."

Charlie didn't answer, he followed Lee and collapsed on his bed, lacking the energy to remove his shoes or undress although he longed to feel Sara breathe against him.

"I got it," Lee said as he haltingly fumbled with his buttons. With cool competence, she helped him undress down to his boxers and placed Sara in his arms.

"We need to be alone. Thanks, Lee."

"You're welcome. Rest. No one will get by us. Your Scouts are guarding." Lee left the room, closing the door behind her.

Sprawled across his chest, Sara's lank hair clutched in one hand, he fell asleep.

Drew ran a gentle hand over Joy's head. Soft black hair just starting to grow back shadowed her skull. The patchy skin had faded and now not one injury remained.

"Drew... she's likely brain dead. I'm so sorry, but she's been dead for over four days." Liz leaned over Joy and removed the last black stich from her forehead. The small wound closed with magical speed.

"I know— it's still a miracle. Look what they did to her. She's perfect, not a scratch on her." Slow tears leaked from his eyes. "If we'd listened and given her Joy like she'd asked us to, maybe none of this would've happened."

"This is a tragedy, but we can recover. We know better now. That's cold comfort, I know. I'm so sorry, Drew."

"Is the government hunting them?" Drew asked as he stroked Joy's hair.

"I don't know. They know I helped them, I'm sure of that. They won't tell me. Are they hiding again?"

"Hawk is. Stasia is in with Rick. I thought you knew?"

"Yes, I did. I thought she might've gone though. I've been so busy."

Drew laughed a sharp bark of laughter. "I can imagine. Three warriors, another priest, and a rogue raised from the dead. Is Brenda able to heal them and dispel the radiation?"

Liz smiled. "She's smiting the hell out of the walls to heal them. Everyone is fine, and I expect her to show up here any second to throw a heal-over-time on Joy."

Huddled on the floor by the door of Rick's room Stasia watched Brenda do her best to heal him. The bright yellow orange of her smites crashed into the back wall, making a hollow of the rock and filling the room with a hot vapor. Rick thanked her and sat. "Go to Marcus or Mike. Thanks, Brenda. I'm good."

Rick ran a hand over his bald scalp and scratched the flaky skin on his arm as he slipped from the bed and steadied himself against it.

Too weak to go to him, Stasia leaned against the wall. "How do you feel?"

"Recovered but weak. You look like hell. What happened?"

"Too long a story to go into now, but we need to leave." Stasia called his father. "You need to come and get Rick. I'm too weak to protect him."

"Protect him from what?" John asked, sounding confused and alarmed.

"It's a long story. I'll tell you on the way, but please hurry. Don't bring Mrs. H, and come armed. God, she better go hide too. I'm so tired I'm not thinking straight. Get my mother too and hide them both."

"Okay, sweetheart, I'm coming to you now. Calm down and tell me what's happening?"

"They're going to kill us all, and they can use you to get to us; they know that."

"Who is?"

"Our government! They tried to kill Sara and Charlie already. I have no magic left and can't defend him. I don't know who else to call," Stasia wailed.

"Okay, I know what you're talking about now. Stasia, sweetheart, they won't hurt any of you. I promise."

"Didn't you hear me? They tried already and almost succeeded! Rick is in danger here!"

"I'm on my way, but there is no danger. I swear on my son's lives they're not trying to kill you."

"They are." She groaned in frustration.

"Stasia, sweetheart, what will it take to convince you?"

"Major Nelson dead at my feet." She started crying. "I'll get him out myself." She hung up and pushed herself up using the wall. She was so weak her hands trembled as she clutched Rick's arm and she had to use both arms to hold herself up.

"My father wouldn't lie to you. Please, Stasia, calm down. If he says it's safe, it is." Rick grabbed her in a hug. "I know you're scared, that you feel helpless without your magic, but we're safe."

Tear filled eyes met his as she pleaded with him. "If you love me, please come with me! Please, Rick!"

"I'll go. We don't need to though." Rick pulled her up.

Sobbing, she tugged him to the door.

"Where will we go?"

"To my brother."

"Where's Oz?"

"I don't know!" She wailed in frustration. "Please, let's just go!"

They left by the front door and found Major Nelson waiting, standing in front of his car with his hands raised. Stasia tried to use her invisible, then leap and didn't have enough magic to do either. She stepped in front of Rick and drew her knife.

Rick moved her to the side. "I have magic," he said calmly. "I'm weak, but not defenseless. I'm more than a match for one man." His hands glowed blue as he braced himself and raised them.

"I'm not here to harm either of you. I mean no harm to anyone here. I shot Charlie before he could attack me. It all happened very fast and I had no time to explain or ask permission. If my death will appease you, will reassure you that the government means you no harm, so be it."

"We know you have plans in place to kill us all, and we agree in theory." Rick pulled Stasia back to his side as she began to sidle away. "We're not a threat. Let us go peacefully and we won't attack."

"There's no need to escape *or* hide. I promise you're safe here."

"How can we trust you?" Stasia yelled.

"I made a mistake. I meant well, but hurt her, hurt you all. Tell me what you want me to do and I'll do it." Major Nelson held up his empty hands.

"Let us go," Rick said.

"The keys are still in my car." Major Nelson moved away from his car, keeping his hands in sight.

Stasia laughed bitterly. "Wouldn't that be easy for you; we get in and you blow it up."

"I'm so sorry, Stasia." Major Nelson gestured to the road with his open hands. "Go any way you wish."

Stasia reached for Rick's hand, not taking her eyes off the major. When his glowing hand touched her bare skin, she moaned and fell to her knees.

Rick leaned down and pulled her up, placing his other hand on her face. "*Ah*," he said in a whisper, making a soft sigh of amazement. He leaned down and kissed her then swung her into his arms and ran as far as he could. The road twisted and turned through the woods. Too weak to run for long, he headed into the shadowy trees and found a veiled spot to hide.

Oz and Hawk found them there beneath a cloud of blue magic.

- 38 -

WIN OR DIE

Sara woke and moaned, then gasped and cried, waking Charlie. His magic sought her, and she screamed shrilly. The scream redoubled when he healed her, so he stopped.

She was terrified and still in so much pain it left him breathless. He shot her with his tranquilizer gun and called Liz. "She woke in terrible pain, and my magic hurts her. What do I do?"

"I'll send morphine for her. I'm sorry, Charlie. I don't know what to do for her. It was too much what she did. If the morphine doesn't help her, knock her out again, give her body time to heal."

Charlie stole her heal and used it on himself. He felt depleted himself, still very weak and tired but the burning sensation had faded to mere soreness.

He visited the head before returning to heal Sara with her biggest heal. He stood over her while his Spell-Steal reset and casted her biggest heal six times before heading to the galley.

Three major heals should be able to cure anything. He hopped she'd wake in less physical pain.

"Liz is sending morphine for Sara. Let me know when we get it, please," he said to Sam as he took a can of soup from the cupboard.

Sam took the can from him. "I'll get this—sit. As soon as we get the medicine, I'll knock. It's very bad then?"

Tears came to Charlie's eyes. "It's so bad." He bit back a sob. "She's in so much pain. I shot her again. God, she just woke up, and I shot her again."

"I'm sure she was grateful." Sam handed him the cup of hot soup.

"Any word on the others?"

"Marcus Brenda and Mike are still with Liz recovering. All have magic but haven't been tested. Liz says everyone is healthy. Stasia and Rick ran away. Oz and Hawk left too. Harrison knows where they are."

Sam sat next to him. "Major Nelson—"

Charlie threw his cup at the wall, instantly enraged.

Sam sighed. "Sit. I'll make you more. Eat it this time." Sam set the soup on to heat and cleaned up the one that had hit the wall. "Your father believed him," he finally said as he handed him the new cup of soup.

Charlie held up his hand. "Tell me first."

Sam laughed and told him. "It could be true. Your father thinks it is. He told Rick and Stasia to stay.

"I can't risk Sara, I just can't. She's totally defenseless."

"Stay here. We'll take care of you." Sam handed him the soup.

"And Joy?" Charlie asked softly.

Sam shook his head.

"I hope it's satisfied now," Charlie said bitterly.

Sara woke screaming. Charlie ran into the room and gave her a shot of morphine, holding her while she cried until the drug took effect. She was in so much pain she couldn't speak. A hurt he shared as if his body burned. The heal he cast on her did nothing except make her scream shrilly. Soothe appeared to have no effect except to make her shake. He desisted; afraid the magic was hurting her.

"I can send for Marcus to share—"

She screamed and grasped him tighter. The idea of it terrified her anew or maybe it was his fear scaring her. He hid his teary eyes in her hair as she cried in his arms and slumped with relief when the drug kicked in.

Charlie came out of the cabin and showered quickly, ate the meal Lee handed him without interest, and leaned back in the seat with his eyes closed. Circles ringed his eyes and his cheeks were sunken. Stubble aged him ten years. "We can't take much more of this."

"We've already called Liz for stronger medicine."

Charlie put his head on his arms on the table and closed his eyes. Everyone's phones rang.

Charlie groaned. "Oh god, now what? Whatever it is, I can't do it." He answered the raid-wide call.

"Joy is awake." Emotion choked Drew's voice, making him nearly indecipherable. "She's awake and aware. Weak, but fine. Thank you, Sara, you don't know... thank you so much." He played his video over Joy who drank from a straw while sitting in a hospital bed.

"Joy," Charlie said and had to stop speaking or he'd burst into tears.

She smiled at Drew. "I don't remember anything, and I'm glad I don't. Thank you for bringing me back. Drew and I have so much we want to do together. They tell me Sara is recovering. I'm sorry I caused her to change so many at once."

Drew turned the video back on himself. "I don't know what to say... how to thank you." He glanced back at Joy. "Harrison is watching out for them. Major Nelson was here and made no attempt to harm or stop anyone. Marcus has left with Manny. And Mike is with Brenda here at the lab. We love you, stay safe." Drew ended his call.

Joy was well. Charlie wanted to touch her, to feel her pulse, to listen to her speak again. "God, did anyone record that for Sara?" he asked suddenly.

"I did," Sam said. I'm sending it to you now. Maybe it'll help her."

"Don't tell Joy about this." Charlie gestured aimlessly around the cabin.

"We won't. Get some sleep." Lee patted his shoulder.

Charlie returned to Sara, hugged her close, and fell asleep.

Liz's arrival woke him.

"I need to examine her, Charlie. I have a theory."

Charlie watched hopefully as Liz set out a tray of instruments.

"Please wait in the other room. I need to cut her and I'm not certain you can resist stopping me. This might take a while. I'll have to go slowly because of her defensive shocks."

Charlie bit his lip, then nodded. In the galley Manny and Harrison were setting up a microscope under Oz's direction.

"Got it, Liz," Oz said and flicked a glance at Charlie. He winced and turned his attention to the forest of screens surrounding him. No one glanced at the boxes beside Oz as if not looking would keep them unnoticed by Charlie.

Charlie turned away. He didn't need his magic that still gusted around to tell him they were uneasy. All of them gave him worried glances and moved slowly as if afraid he'd lose it and attack them any moment.

He retreated to the deck. Manny followed and put an arm around his shoulder.

"Liz will do her best," he said.

"I know." Charlie's voice broke and he cleared his throat.

"We'll make sure she's safe. Major Nelson has been back." Manny tightened his grip when Charlie tensed.

"Say the word and he's toast," Manny said.

Charlie relaxed and rubbed his forehead.

"I don't think he meant to hurt her. Why would he?"

"Fucker has it coming for Joy."

"He didn't mean to hurt her either."

"He had no right," Manny said angrily. "Sara needed her safe. We all knew that. It was stupid to risk her. It was even stupider to send a new rogue out alone."

Charlie's anger surged, and he needed a second to calm himself. The thought of Joy facing enemies alone made his pulse pound. His magic felt lonely and afraid when he thought of Joy, the anger was all his. Blue clouds twined around he and Manny. Manny's anger made him feel better.

"Thanks, Manny. We're lucky to have such a good friend."

Manny nodded, the magic assuring Charlie of his affection. Manny felt fiercely protective.

Charlie said, "Leave the major alone. I'll handle him."

Manny nodded again. Music suddenly blared from below them, and Charlie tensed.

"Stay up here," Manny said and drew him farther from the hatch. The soft drone of a bone saw could barely be heard beneath the music. Charlie clapped his hands to his ears and stared out to sea. They stood unspeaking until Liz joined them.

"As I suspected, Sara burnt out her m-nerve."

She placed her hand on Charlie's arm as he swayed.

"It's already regenerating. I assume it will take at least four days to repair itself, the same amount of time a transformation takes. Keep her sedated in a dark room. Heal her occasionally, but this isn't an injury exactly but a growth, and it'll take time. If she isn't better in a few days, I'll need to examine her again."

It's already been four days..." Charlie trailed off, his eyes narrowing. "How bad is the damage?"

Liz sniffed and cleared her throat, obviously debating what to say.

"Liz..."

Liz sighed heavily and rose her hands to cover her face a moment. When she dropped them, her eyes were red.

"Bad. The power of the magic scorched the bones themselves. Heals helped with that. We went through six entire bracelets, but the scorching disappeared, and the injured sections of her brain are now a nice healthy white. I think her pain will be much less now. Small barely visible filaments have begun regrowing where her m-nerve was. Exactly the same as happens in the first days of a transformation. I really believe they'll regrow completely but heals did nothing to speed that. I have no idea if sunlight will help or hurt her. I don't recommend a tanning bed. I recommend we treat this like a transformation and keep her somewhere quiet and dark."

"The bone damage delayed the transformation?"

Liz winced. "I think it was the brain damage. The magic had no place left to lodge. Repairs had begun on her brain but not her skeletal structure. We've never seen an injury of this sort in a magic user. The extra cranial nerves she fried took massive healing to fix. This wasn't simple cuts like Joy's autopsy but complete obliteration. The nerves had to reform from scratch. Your heals helped but the damage was severe. Healing her only appeared to hurt her because brain regeneration made her more aware."

Charlie gulped back his nausea. *She hadn't been able to speak because she couldn't.* The thought horrified him.

"Is it safe to give her drugs?"

"She doesn't need to be lucid to have the nerves regrow and sedation won't hurt her. We keep the newly infected as lucid as possible so they can concentrate on becoming the class they choose but Sara is already a sun priest."

"Will she remember?"

Liz sagged and rubbed her eyes again. "I have no idea. Joy remembers everything up to the moment of her death and her brain was dissected and m-nerves removed. In Joy's case, the pieces were put back and the actual damage to them was small. You said Sara clung to you, so she likely remembers you."

"Or my magic."

"I'm sorry I don't have better news. At least we could help with the pain…" Liz trailed off and took his hand.

They stared out to sea unspeaking.

- 39 -

REALIZATION

When Sara woke, he gave her the new medicine right away. She sighed in relief and drifted off to sleep. As soon as she stirred, he injected her again. He kept her drugged for four days. Lee and Sam helped clean her and the cabin as needed. Tony tried to help, but it upset him so badly to see her like that they left him on deck.

Sara was wasting away. She'd lost twenty pounds and her hair was lank and lifeless. Dark circles lined the dark pits under her eyes, her lips were chapped and her nails yellow and brittle.

On the fourth day, he let her wake; she moaned and thrashed until she was fully awake. To his relief, the pain was bearable.

"Charlie," she moaned and held a hand to her head.

His relief was so great he thought he might faint. The room swirled in dizzying circles.

"I'm okay," he said as her worry spiked.

She sagged against him exhausted and worried.

"You're okay too." He handed her two Tylenol and a glass of water.

"Thanks."

The normalness of her reply made him cry.

"Sorry," he mumbled as her anxiety bloomed into fear. "You scared me. But we're all okay. Rest, sweetheart."

"I'm so tired," she murmured as she snuggled against him. Her fear receded as he felt joy. She knew him. She loved him.

"Thank god," he whispered and kissed her temple.

Sam made her soup, which she ate slowly. She fell asleep afterward. A natural sleep with no drugs. Charlie slept beside her.

When she woke next, she asked him to help her shower. Her pain was lessening. She refused the pain medicine except for Tylenol. "Will I be addicted to it now?"

"I don't know. Worry about that later." Charlie kissed her brow. "Let's never do that again."

She nodded tiredly. "It wasn't my choice. I tried to stop it."

"I know. We can worry about that later as well."

She nodded unhappily, laid her face on his chest, and sighed with relief he shared. She placed a glowing blue hand on his bare chest and gave him her magic. His magic left him in a rush and went to her. She cried quietly as he held her. When she was calmer, he showed her Joy.

She said nothing, just touched Joy's picture with her fingertips. Her feelings were hard to decipher, fear, worry, pain, happiness more worry love, longing, more worry. They fell asleep together. The next day she wanted to sit outside, she was very unhappy. Anger and fear dominated her mind. "Can I sit here alone, please?"

He nodded reluctant agreement and left her. Her feelings were in turmoil. With dread, he recognized she was losing control to her magic, it was once again affecting her moods. She knew it too. He went and sat beside her, waiting for her to speak, the blood test and hormone injections in his hand.

"I love you and need you to trust me," Sara said, not looking at him. Her gaze remained on the sea. "We can't keep doing this. I can't do this again. I want you to leave, for everyone to leave."

"I can't do that," Charlie said, his voice even, his tone firm belaying his quivering insides. "You can't be left alone. You can barely stand." He swallowed heavily, knowing she wouldn't like what he would say next. "The magic can control you. It could kill you, make you fall from the boat or something."

"I know. I need to control it, but I can't do that with you here. It's trying right now. I want you desperately and it's trying its hardest to make me want you— to force me to go to you. Charlie, please, if you love me, if you really love me, you'll let me go. I need to be alone with it."

"Sara, I can't." Mouth dry, he took her cold hand in his. "I need you so much."

"I know. I need you too. Charlie, if I can't control this, I'll die anyway. Let me die fighting." She stared at him with clear eyes. Her beautiful blue eyes now dull and ringed with dark circles, her skin sallow and drawn. "My magic will take me and force me. I have to fight it. I *will* fight it, and I'll win, or I'll die. I won't let it take me again. Please, I know what I'm asking. Please take them and go. I have to be alone. Don't leave it anyone to take."

Charlie clutched her, his heart pounding in his chest. "We'll leave but give me some time to prepare. You'll need food and we need to move the boat somewhere safe for you with no one steering it." She kissed him, and he felt her desire growing. She pushed him roughly away. "Go, do whatever you have to do quickly. I can't hold back from you much longer." She spun away from him filled with fierce determination.

He went to tell Sam and Lee to make her food while he and Tony moved the boat.

"We can't just leave her here," Lee said in exasperation.

"We can, and we will." Charlie glared, a blue glitter in his eyes, and Lee nodded meekly. "Get another boat and make sure she's safe here. Don't come close, just make sure no one else does. If she needs us, she can summon us." He sat beside Sara until they were ready to go. When he kissed her goodbye, she moaned softly as he parted from her and she groaned in anger and swung away.

"Stop! I choose, not you!" Lips in a tight line, she pushed him away. "Go! I'll choose, not my magic. *I* will choose!"

"Summon us, Harrison," Charlie said. In three minutes, he'd accepted two summons and was back at the lab.

Hundreds of miles away from her, in a different zone, he felt her fury.

Oz and Hawk came in the room and sat beside him. "Did I do the right thing?" he asked, turning heartbroken eyes to his best friends.

"What else could you do, let the magic take her?" Oz shuddered. "God, I can't even imagine how scary that is for her to lose control of herself that badly— for something else to move you, to make you do things you don't want to."

"Sara's strong; she'll win." Hawk laid his hand on Charlie's arm. "She'll fight hard for you."

"She'll fight and win," Oz agreed.

"Or die," Charlie said and closed his eyes.

- 40 -

THE FIGHT FOR CONTROL

Sara fought; her magic wanted her to go him. She used it instead, placing magic in every pipe and pole on board ship. The magic filled her with desire for Charlie. Angry screams echoed over the ocean as she casted smite until she had no magic left.

She talked to herself trying to communicate with it, begging it to let her live in peace. It could have Charlie's magic, she told it, just his magic. It couldn't force her to make love to him. Her magic was quiet while she regenerated. Then she found herself wanting Rick, then Marcus, then Mike.

She screamed in rage, panting in fury. "I'll die first! I'll take every bit of magic from all of them and dispel it all and destroy you utterly!" Her magic burst from her, and she dispelled it while laughing hysterically.

The magic fled back into her, filling her with fear. Again, she stood at the rail and smote the water until her magic was gone. The days and nights blended. Huddled in her bed, she cried as she pleaded with the magic. On deck, she screamed until she was hoarse trying to communicate, offering it Charlie if it would leave her in peace. Hours at a time she dozed. More hours she sat in an exhausted stupor, casting heals, keeping the magic week. Slower and slower the magic regenerated and still it tried to force her to one of the warriors. Under the cold January sky, she lay shivering on deck.

* *

Charlie couldn't concentrate on anything. He was back at school, going through the motions, speaking to no one, eating almost nothing. His battalion leader sent him to the infirmary. Liz came and kissed his cheek. "You don't have to be here. Go to the lab, or the trailer or a hotel."

"I do have to be here. She's fighting and furious. I can't give this up. If I do, all of this was for nothing, and she'll blame herself," he said dully.

He returned to class and answered when spoken too. Polite and lifeless, he did what was required. A funk settled over the school, his aura effecting everyone. In his room, he lay in his bunk or sat unmoving at his desk. When Paul tried to speak to him, he ignored him.

437

Paul went to Hawk. "What's going on? he should be in a hospital or something. Look at him."

"Sara is very sick, and he's worried."

"How sick?" Paul laid a hand on Hawk's arm, wincing when Hawk's eyes filled with tears.

Hawk rubbed his eyes hard and looked away. He went to their room and sat on the floor beside Charlie on the floor.

"Damn," Paul said softly and left them alone. After class, he went to see Oz. All the guards at the lab were subdued. Oz taught his and Sara's classes in a lifeless manner. Stasia went to class, and then disappeared. He didn't know where she went, he never saw her in the lab anymore.

"Why isn't he with her?" Paul asked. "I'm sure he could get compassionate leave."

"She doesn't want him to see her like that," Oz said. "She's fighting, but he distracts her. All her energy is on the fight."

"How long?" Paul asked softly, and Oz inhaled sharply.

"God, I don't know. I don't know how much longer she can fight this." Oz hurriedly left the room.

Paul returned slowly to the dorm. Hawk still sat on the floor beside Charlie who sat in his desk chair, staring at nothing. None of them said a thing.

Stasia was with Rick inside the trailer. "This is my fault. I'm so sorry I said that to her. If you want each other, I can learn to share you." She cried in Rick's arms.

"It isn't your fault, honey. Sara doesn't want the magic to use her. She doesn't blame you, I'm sure of that. Charlie doesn't either. She'll fight it."

"How can she win? Rick, how can she beat it?"

"I don't know," he whispered into her hair. He absorbed the magic her distress produced and placed his own hands on her arms, letting her absorb his. The feeling was indescribably intimate, a sharing of himself he didn't have words for.

Her magic was wild; it energized him, made him feel powerful and alive, and he craved it. The only time he sensed her emotions was if their magic touched. He could spend hours just trading magic with her. Making love to her in a cloud of their magic was a feeling of closeness, of connectedness, like he never before experienced. Every touch was magnified. Every sigh or moan she made, he felt in his soul. His brother was right; he did pity people without that connection.

Lust would make their entire bodies turn blue. Oz had made a program for the wristcomps that gave the same effect. He'd had to do something to explain Stasia turning blue in public. She controlled it quickly, but it was seen. They said they were testing an experimental security device, and Oz programmed Amy's and Paul's wristcomps to randomly make them glow blue.

It worked. Everyone thought Stasia was blue from that. Every day she got a little better at controlling it.

"I'm so sorry I wasn't more understanding," Stasia mumbled. "This is hard. I always sort of thought she wanted you, maybe not consciously, but I thought in her heart she wanted you too." She punched Rick's arm lightly when he laughed. "You're so beautiful who wouldn't want you? I realize now she doesn't. She can't. Not if she feels half of what I feel for you for Charlie. There's no room left for anyone else, there's hardly any room for regular things."

Rick put his head on Stasia's and sighed deeply. His brother was suffering, he needed Sara's magic, he needed Sara. A shudder rippled his skin at the thought of never feeling Stasia again, never touching her magic. His grip on her tightened.

Sara was fighting for her life. The magic was desperate and so lonely it made her cry. She was desperate, angry, and afraid. Both were very weak. The magic pushed her to go to Charlie, and she spent it smiting the water. Every time she casted, it took the magic longer to regenerate. Hardly able to keep her eyes open, she got a stack of zip-ties and tied herself to the rail.

She debated calling Charlie to say goodbye, but that would be cruel. He would come to her, and she'd have to fight again. Tired and in pain, she laid down to die.

The magic would take her, she knew that, but it wouldn't be able to take her anywhere. They would both die. Out of the zone it couldn't reach any of them. Brenda could come and dispel her magic and burn her body. Her magic would be utterly destroyed. Too exhausted to cry herself to sleep, she fell into an uneasy doze full of nightmares.

Charlie knew she'd given up. He felt her sorrow, her despair, her fear and rage and deep loneliness. In the middle of class, he got up and walked out, headed to the Valor building. The Scouts watched him covertly. No-one approached him. In her office, he cried himself to sleep on her couch.

He knew when the magic took her. He ceased to feel her as if someone had flipped a switch. All day he sat in her office, praying it would release her. The sun was setting when he felt her pain and fear, but she didn't call him.

He closed his eyes and leaned his head back on her couch and ceased to feel her. He wasn't certain if she was even still alive. The suddenness of the separation gave him hope and he lifted trembling hands to his aching head. His magic was agitated, swirling around him and landing on his exposed skin with sharp shocks.

Hawk cringed from the magic but sat beside him. "She's dying?"

Charlie nodded and covered his face. "I want to go to her, but she doesn't want to be its slave. Oh god, Hawk, how can I let her die?" Hawk shook his head and hugged him.

Pain, fear, loneliness, smote Charlie on her return. With all his soul, he wanted her, and his need hurt her and terrified his magic, which careened around the room so forcefully it knocked over books and sent papers scattering.

Joy entered and sat beside them. Tears had left tracks across her face. Joy's pain hurt him more but his company helped her so he said nothing, taking her hand in his, offering her what comfort he could.

- 41 -

CONTROL

Sara woke and waited for the magic and it didn't come. All day she waited and cried herself to sleep, shivering on the deck. When she woke, a clear sky shone down on her. The stars were bright and close, illuminating the deck with a blue light. The magic fled from her, returned, and fled again. Gone for an hour it returned to her, surrounding her, but not absorbing.

"I'm in control!" She screamed and held her hand out. The magic settled onto her skin and slowly absorbed. "If this is a trick, I'll come back here and kill myself and you!" She called her magic out in a small amount and thought of Charlie with rising hope.

The magic remained quiescent, making no demands. Her hope surged.

Charlie jumped to his feet, calling Harrison as he ran. "Get the helicopter and pick me up. I'm going to her."

Sara knew he was coming. She pulled her magic back in. "I'm in control!"

The magic remained quiescent, making no demands but deeply afraid. Its fear gave her confidence that it would listen to her and she let herself think of Charlie with longing.

Charlie jumped onto the deck of his boat. He snapped the tie holding her to the rail and grabbed her as she tumbled free. Too weak to sit on her own, she leaned against him.

His magic swirled wildly around her. Everywhere their skin touched absorbed his magic. "I need yours, please," Charlie said.

A weak blue glow surrounded the hand she placed on his face, and he sighed in relief.

"I'm sorry I had to fight it, Charlie." Hoarse and weak she cried on his shoulder.

"And you won." Thankful and angry, he kissed her. The bones of her cheek stuck out in sharp relief. No extra flesh remained on her. Famine victims looked better than her. "You need medical care. This is beyond soup."

She nodded on his shoulder. "Liz will help me."

He stole her heal and used it on her.

She sighed with relief at his touch but remained tense in his arms. He knew she was waiting for her magic to strike, to reach out to force her to do its will. The magic remained passive. Her shoulders relaxed from their hunched position, and she lifted a glowing blue hand to Charlie's face, giving him more of her magic.

He called Sam. "Are you close? Can you come get us?"

Sam arrived in fifteen minutes. Charlie wrapped her in a blanket and handed her to him, then climbed into the motorboat. Lee kissed Sara's brow and grasped Charlie's shoulder before going aboard the sailboat. Sam drove them into the zone, the breeze of their passing making Sara shiver.

Liz summoned them to her and took over. She had Charlie place an IV while she handed Sara a nutrient drink.

"Drink it! If you can't keep it down, I'm putting in a feeding tube."

Sara drank it.

Liz had Charlie help her wash and put on a hospital gown, then put her in a tanning booth for ten minutes. "You can lie there, but no more sun for an hour. Ten minutes of sun every hour. Drink as much as you like, but no solids. Try to rest." She left them alone.

"Is the anger for me?" Sara asked in a small voice.

"A little. I know you had to do it. I'd do it myself if my magic took me over like that, but it was so hard being away from you, feeling you die."

Remembered fear made him shudder.

She said, "I'm sorry, I truly am. I wish I could just ask it to listen, to let me help it get what it wants, but it won't. It's listening now though."

Charlie traced her jutting collarbone with his fingertips. "Let's not talk about it. Rehashing how horrible that was for both of us won't help. Just like you had to fight I couldn't help being angry about it, but we can forgive each other and move on, knowing the hurt wasn't intentional. I just want to lie with you and feel you breathe."

The hum of the tanning bed ceased, and the room darkened. Charlie lifted her out and placed her across his chest, the slight weight of her body barely felt. On the floor of the room they both dozed off.

Liz found them asleep and covered them with a light blanket.

Harrison waited outside the door. "I sent everyone away. Stasia is pissed I made them leave, but relieved Sara is back. Joy is in their trailer. I wasn't sure if Sara would need to see her or not."

"She hasn't mentioned any of them. Let's not mention them either. She's weak as a kitten, malnourished and dehydrated. In fact, I've had kittens stronger than her. Let her rest. She'll ask to see them when she's ready."

When Charlie woke, his parents were there. He placed Sara in the tanning bed and turned it on for ten minutes; she didn't wake. He hugged his Mom and Dad quickly. His mother cried quietly. His father looked grim.

"She's going to be alright now?" John nodded toward the door where blue light from the tanning bed leaked into the hallway

Charlie shrugged, then sighed and rubbed his eyes. "God, I hope so. She hasn't met them yet. That could be a problem. She hasn't seen Joy either, and who knows what that'll do. I think she'll kill herself before letting it take her again."

"There's no other way to stop it?" His mother turned to him with tears in her eyes.

"None that we know of. What it did to her to bring Joy back, well... I understand why she wants to stop it so badly. She has more of them to worry about now. Major Harris has promised they'll never be put in harm's way without Sara's permission. I don't know that I believe that, but Oz is microchipping everyone. We'll know where they are at all times, like it or not."

"Your brother too?" His father asked. A deep scowl lined his brow.

"Especially him. Stasia has threatened to kill Sara over him. I can't afford to have her bump into him unexpectedly. It's too dangerous for all of us."

"God, this gets more complicated every day." His father ran both hands through his short hair.

Charlie laughed bitterly.

"What about school?" His mother gestured behind her. "If you're here with her..."

"To hell with school!" Charlie spun away, fighting his anger. "She almost died! I'm not leaving her now."

Charlie clenched his teeth on what he wanted to yell. They'd woken Sara.

She smiled at his parents, but he knew the smile was a lie. She was embarrassed and worried and growing frustrated.

He realized the frustration was for the lid of the tanning bed that she couldn't open, and she gave him a real smile when he opened it and set her in a chair.

"What happened?" she asked nervously.

He sat by her feet, placing an arm on her knees.

"Nothing, everything's okay now."

A worried frown on her face that didn't convey the sick guilt she felt, she turned to Mary. "I'm sorry. None of this was intentional. Are you angry about Rick?" Sara glanced anxiously from one to the other. "I'm sorry I did it like that instead of how we planned, but I wasn't in control. It wasn't my choice. I'm trying my hardest to make sure nothing like that will happen again."

"Maybe you shouldn't try quite so hard." Mary kissed Sara's cheek. "You look awful. There has to be a better way to handle this."

"I don't know what it is." Sara started to cry. "None of that was intentional. I just so badly want the magic to stop hurting me. I'm so sorry I hurt your sons."

Charlie glared at his mother, pulled Sara into his lap, and patted her back while murmuring reassurances into her ear.

"None of this is her fault." Blue sparked in his eyes as he glared. "She's doing the best she can. You have no idea how hard the magic is on her. If there were a better way, we would do it."

"Sara, sweetie I didn't mean to imply... well, I'm sorry. You both just look so sick and tired. I'm worried is all." Mary patted Charlie's hand.

Charlie nodded while he talked softly to his wife. "Don't cry. You're too dehydrated and giving yourself a headache, *shh*." He rubbed her back in small circles. "They aren't angry at you, just worried about us." She quieted and fell asleep as he whispered in her ear.

"Sara needs peace and rest, not recriminations. Her condition is my fault. I left her to fight alone, and it was the hardest thing I've ever done. I'm sick with worry about Rick. How can I not be? I wish to god she hadn't changed him like that, but she did, so we have to stay away from him while we sort this out.

"If you want to blame someone for this mess, blame Major Nelson for sending Joy in and hiding her presence from us."

Sara stirred, and he took a calming breath.

"No one is blaming either of you, son." John took Mary's hand and drew her toward the door. "Get some rest. We'll visit tomorrow."

"Our poor boy," Mary said sadly.

"This is a rough patch, but we'll all get through it." John leaned down to kiss her.

Charlie closed his eyes and stroked Sara's hair. He'd never imagined it could be so difficult to let her fight her own battles.

"You'll never fight another without me," he vowed.

- 42 -

PLANNING FOR THE FUTURE

Rick went to speak with Stasia's mother. "Mrs. Morales—"

"Camila," she interrupted.

"Camila, I've come to speak with you about Stasia. I love your daughter and she loves me. I want to marry her, and I hope we can have your blessing."

"You haven't asked her yet?"

"No, I wanted to speak with you first, then my father."

"I don't dislike you, Rick, but I'm aware of the magic— Sara's magic and what it does. Are you sure you can be a true and faithful husband to my daughter?"

Rick peered unhappily at Camila. "I can't guarantee Sara's magic won't take me. I *can* guarantee that I'll always love Stasia. She has my heart; I wouldn't willingly hurt her in any way."

"I believe you." Mrs. Morales rubbed her eyes tiredly. "She's my child and I have a responsibility to make good choices for her. I love her and want her to have everything she wants. I know she loves you. If I turn you away, she'd never forgive that." She patted his hand. "You have my blessing. Please, if Sara's magic changes your affection, be as kind as you can be."

"I will." He kissed Camila's cheek. "Thank you. I know you wish I was someone else, someone normal. I understand giving your daughter into my care is hard for you. But I promise I'll protect her to the best of my ability from everything, including myself."

"Rick, you're a good man. I'd be a hypocrite to turn you away because of the magic when the reason you have it is for my daughter. My prayers are with you, that you can resist Sara, and she can resist you."

Rick kissed her cheek.

The door closed quietly behind him.

Rick went to see his father. "I'm going to ask Stasia to marry me," he said without preamble.

His father settled farther back into his seat, tenting his fingers, smiling softly. "Have you spoken with her mother?"

"I have, and she's given her blessing. She's worried about Sara. Hell, we're all worried, but I'm not going to let the magic stop me from living the life I want with Stasia."

His father hugged him. "Stasia is a dear girl. Your mother and I love her, and I have no doubt she loves you too. You have my blessing as well. When will you ask her?"

"Her birthday. We'll marry whenever she wants." He showed his father the ring he'd bought her. "I've had this for four months now, burning a hole in my pocket."

"I'm glad you bought it before all this." His father gestured vaguely.

"I want *her*, Dad, not her magic. I admit that's amazing, but I wanted her first."

His father slapped his back lightly and went to tell his mother.

Charlie gently ran his fingers through his wife's hair as she slept and tried not to think of the three warriors and priest she'd made. *If she'd been trying she could hardly have picked a worse bunch to transform.*

Rogues were passionate creatures full of life an energy. But passion had a price. They were also quick to anger, and their magic made them able to act on that anger. Nothing and no one could Stasia— except herself. He hoped Stasia's love for Rick and Sara's love for Stasia would continue to be stronger than Sara's need for another warrior.

Their magic would shape them to be as their natures bade. He felt the need to protect them more very day and he knew it hurt his wife's healer soul to cause them pain. But their human halves were also powerful. Sara and Stasia had triumphed over their magic, their human love winning over the magic's needs and he was beyond glad that Joy was returned to them.

Joy had been named perfectly; he truly felt joy when he thought of her alive and well. The price Sara had paid to get her back was high. The price they might still have to pay was higher yet.

His Sara was strong and had fought bravely for them. Her love for him was so bright it lit her soul. He'd never tested his strength against his magic. But he was a warrior and would fight fiercely for them and be as strong as his healer wife. When they went to meet the others she'd made— his strength would be her shield.

THE END

Upcoming Book

Valor 6

HIDDEN NATURE

Charlie wants to find the man who's kidnapped his sun priest and mage. He assumes whoever has taken them knows about the magic. He prays casting Call-for-Help will save them.

Rage is empowering his aura but with no enemy to fight, his rage is holding him back from the search. He's causing a panic wherever he goes.

When Oz doesn't portal away from his captors, Charlie assumes his mage has been killed. He prays his wife is alive. He trusts that every effort is being made to find her.

But assumptions can be deadly—
Prayers are often unanswered—
And trust is sometimes misplaced...